NEVER LET YOU FALL

KATE SMITH

For Colleen & Trevor

Chapter 1

Alexis

THE FAINT LIGHT OF DAWN crept through the curtains as the baby's cries echoed down the hallway. Silence fell, but my eyes were wide open. Kellan never cried for long and he wasn't my concern, being blessed with a doting Mommy and Daddy, but my maternal instinct kicked in the moment he uttered an unhappy sound.

Soft footsteps sounded on the wood floor outside my room followed by the familiar creak of the third step from the top as Aiden headed to the kitchen. Soon the deep rich fragrance of dark-roast coffee would waft through the air, combining with the fresh sea breeze fluttering my curtains.

I crawled from between the cozy sheets and tiptoed into the room next door. Daniel's deep and even breathing was broken only by the occasional slurp as he sucked the thumb he'd crammed into his mouth.

Tears sprang to my eyes as I brushed my fingers over his soft brown hair. He reminded me of his daddy with his hazel eyes and long thick lashes. I sighed and pressed a hand to my aching chest, gazing at Daniel's sweet face, so peaceful in his slumber.

"Alex," Aiden whispered from behind me. "Everything okay?"

I brushed at my eyes before facing him. "It's fine."

Aiden frowned. "Give me a minute to deliver this," he said as he held up a glass of water, "and we can go for a walk. We'll be back long before Daniel's up."

I nodded. "I'll dress."

As he disappeared into the master bedroom, I retraced my steps to the guest room and hauled on my linen shorts and a fresh t-shirt. After a quick run of the brush through my tangled hair, I scooped it into a ponytail and examined the dark circles under my puffy red-rimmed eyes. I sighed. Not much to do about those.

I paused at the top of the stairs, closing my eyes and inhaling the expected tones of fresh-brewed coffee before trudging downstairs. "I could drink a gallon of that," I said as leaned against the kitchen counter, fixated by the wisps of steam rising from the two travel mugs.

"Then you're in luck." Aiden added a touch of cream and sugar to each and handed one to me.

I gulped a mouthful, my eagerness for caffeine rewarded with a stinging tongue. "Ouch." I pressed my fingers to my lips.

"Careful." He rubbed my arm. "It's hot."

"Yeah, you'd think I'd have figured that out." I trailed out the door after him and we ambled down the beach in the opposite direction from our house. My house? I wasn't sure anymore. Not about anything. "Emily doesn't mind me stealing you away?"

"She's feeding Kellan, and there's nothing I can do to help. I'd planned to lounge on the deck with my morning coffee, but this is better. It'll give us a chance to talk without interruptions." He gave me a knowing look. "Talk to me, Lex."

I sucked in a breath and concentrated on the cool sand squishing between my bare toes. One foot in front of the other. Keep moving forward was all I could do.

"Having trouble sleeping? Is Kellan keeping you up?"

"I can't shut it off. How can I stop thinking about Joel, and how our marriage is crumbling?" I shuffled a few paces closer to the water, allowing the freezing waves to lick at my toes. I loved this beach, but this morning even the soothing rush and dawn calls of the gulls did nothing to relieve the all-consuming ache in my heart.

"I understand." He heaved a sigh. "This should've been one of those amazing summers. Our group is together again, and I'd hoped we'd start new traditions and put the past behind us. But here we are, me sidelined and you in limbo."

"Limbo." I considered his comment. "Yeah, that feels about right. Whenever I want to talk to Joel, he clams up or disappears out the door. I can't stand to even look at him. And what he did to you. How will you ever forgive him?" I sniffled. "He almost took you from us, and I'm not sure I can forgive him for that, either."

"I wish I had answers." Aiden swept a hand through his hair before reaching for mine. "He put the three of us in danger that day. The past few weeks he's been a ghost and barely acknowledges my existence. There's only one thing I'm sure of—he needs help. The catch is he has to want it and right now, he doesn't."

"Is there any way to force him?"

"Only if he becomes a danger to himself or other people."

"He was dangerous to you. His stupidity nearly cost you your life. No one wants to acknowledge it out loud, but we all know it. Emily watches you like you might fade away. Isn't what he did to you enough?"

"It's not. He's not purposely inflicting damage on other people, or himself." Silence fell for several steps. "At least, I hope he didn't do it on purpose. It was a careless, stupid, drunken move."

There it was, the thing I'd feared asking. Aiden doubted Joel's motives. "Joel's carelessness and idiotic behavior nearly killed you. Vanna said you warned him to sit still and touch nothing because you knew he was tanked."

"Yeah, I knew." Aiden stopped to pick up a rock, sending it skipping across the waves. "He rambled on about things earlier. I should never have turned my back. That's my mistake."

I clamped my teeth onto my lip, fighting the cascade of tears trickling down my cheeks. "I couldn't bear losing you. You're my brother, the one who I can always talk to, the one who's always been there. Every breakup, every crappy date, and even when my mom died, you were there. Until I married Joel, and we drifted. I have you back but almost lost you. Forever."

"But you didn't." Aiden rested a hand on my arm before he pulled me into a hug. "I'm here, Lex. Don't worry, you'll get through this." He wiped away my tears and placed a gentle kiss on my forehead.

The words stuck in my throat as a shiver ran down my spine. Every time I pictured Aiden struggling for survival in that freezing water, at the agony and hopelessness he must have felt, at how he'd almost been lost to us …

"Cold?"

"A little."

Aiden peeled off his sweatshirt and tugged the soft fabric over my head, reaching back to free my ponytail as I tucked my arms into the long sleeves.

The lingering body heat and earthy beach house scent comforted me. "Thanks."

We wandered along, finally arriving at our favorite spot. This twisted branch of Quansoo Oak had beached itself during a summer storm years ago, and many times we'd sat here and shared both our joys and our troubles.

"How can I help?" He slid an arm around me, and I leaned against his firm chest. "I hate to see you two at odds."

"You've let me cry on your shoulder, and you've been amazing with Daniel at a time he's missing his daddy. You and Tom have both stepped up, and I appreciate it more than words can express." I half-shrugged. "I should have bet on a different horse."

"Well, everyone knows men are animals." He squeezed my shoulder. "And Joel has been an enormous horse's ass."

"Ha ha." I forced a smile. "You've got that right."

The sun appeared on the horizon, creating a bright path across the ocean. The water glinted and sparkled as the first golden rays warmed my face. I lifted my chin and closed my eyes, inhaling the fresh salty air. A multitude of vivid memories surfaced in my mind. We'd spent many summers here both as teenagers and as adults, and most of them had been amazing. This year nothing felt right.

I gathered my courage. "What's up with you and Tiffany?"

"Ahh, I wondered when you'd ask." He rubbed the back of his neck. "She asked to see Vanna."

"After all this time?" I tilted my head. "How does that make you feel?"

"Not great, but I talked to Vanna and placed the decision in her hands. Tiffany's her mother, and at one time Savannah wanted nothing more than to know her. Tiffany called the other night."

"Hmm, I figured. You get that look when it's her, like you'd rather be anywhere else." I rubbed his arm. "She's put you in a tough spot. There are days when I wish we could transport back in time and fix it. Rewind that spring and summer we turned fifteen."

Aiden stared at the water with a thoughtful look on his face. "This may sound strange, but I'm not sure I'd make different choices. If someone appeared right now and gave me the option?" He shook his head. "I'd never wish Savannah out of existence. Despite everything we've gone through, I've learned and experienced so much, and I have my daughter, here and now."

His heartfelt words made me reconsider my wish. What would I do if given the opportunity to rewrite my past? I couldn't imagine my life without Daniel. Even though Tiffany had broken Aiden's heart, his precious daughter had become his saving grace. "Change even the smallest thing and the effects ripple out."

Aiden nodded. "I've accepted that the pain and turmoil in my life led me to this moment. It's meant to be this way."

"What did Savannah choose?"

"She said no." Aiden bowed his head and shuffled his feet in the sand. "Telling Tiffany was awful. She melted down."

"As in she—"

"Sobbed and ranted and screamed at me. But you know what's strange? Even after everything Tiffany's said and done, I felt sorry for her. She may never know our daughter." He dragged in a long breath and turned his head away. "She blames me for Vanna's refusal to see her. What if she's right?"

"She's not. You gave her the chance, and she refused it," I said. "But I am sorry. This summer will go down as one of the worst in history."

My heart ached for him. Aiden's life had never been easy, and now he struggled with even more heartbreak. His continuous support amazed me. He'd ensured my survival during my latest tragedy, even as he battled his own demons and cared for his newborn son. I took his hand between mine and wished I could ease the incessant pain—for both of us.

"It'll work out." The words sounded hollow, and I wasn't sure if I meant them for Aiden, or myself.

"You're right, it will." He scrubbed his hands over his face. "We should head home. Emily might need help with the baby."

We remained silent for the walk back. Aiden seemed lost in his own thoughts, and I let him be.

"There you are." Emily smiled as we entered the kitchen, swaying on her feet, Kellan cradled in his baby wrap. She tipped her chin to accept Aiden's kiss. "We planned to go into town today, Alex. Care to join us?"

The perfect couple. They looked so damn happy whenever they were together. Had Joel and I ever looked this content after Daniel had been born? I blinked hard against the burn behind my eyes. "Thanks, but I'll stay here."

"How about we take Daniel with us, and you get some sleep?" Emily raised her brows.

"No …"

She kept her gaze trained on me, one eyebrow rising higher as she studied me. "It wouldn't be a problem."

I glanced at Aiden, who gave the briefest of nods. "Okay, thank you. I'll get him ready."

"I've got him." Vanna appeared in the doorway with a fully dressed Daniel on her hip. "I'll feed him breakfast."

A lump formed in my throat, and after giving my son a good morning kiss, I returned to my room. I hated to admit it, but I craved the break. I loved my boy, but my Daniel had become an untiring live-wire from the moment he'd learned to keep his balance. Over the summer he'd graduated from halting wobbly steps to an all-out run. Without Joel's help, every day was a marathon.

Chapter 2

Joel

W̲HERE WAS I? I BOLTED upright, immediately collapsing against my pillow as pain sliced through my temples. My head thudded to its own beat. I fought the rising sour taste, my mouth watering as I curled into a ball, clutching at my hair. I sucked for breath, a cold sweat beading my skin, my heart thundering at the high-pitched scream ringing in my ears. The memories of a pale tear-streaked face, tangled blonde hair, and fists pounding against my chest. Help me.

Would I ever forget? My stomach turned, lurching and dipping as it had that day on the sailboat, and I hauled myself to the edge of the mattress, fumbling for the small trash can. Even as I hung over it and heaved, I prayed to hit the target, sure the stench would never leave Alex's prized area rug if I didn't.

Alex. I dragged the back of my hand across my mouth and closed my eyes, digging my nails into sweaty, shaking palms, barely able to move. The unfilled space in our bed taunted me. My wife had surely holed up at Aiden's house. Again. Curls of anger twisted my gut. She twitched her little finger and the man rescued her. He always had and always would.

Be grateful. That little voice growled in the background. That our friend had survived the dunk in the frigid waters was a true miracle. If it had been me in the drink that afternoon, I'd be drifting around the bottom of the ocean, nothing but food for the fishes.

I drifted in a twilight haze and perhaps even slept, but a distant buzzing clawed at my consciousness. It stopped, then started again, digging at me like an annoying gnat. *Stop. Start. Stop. Start. Buzz. Buzz. Buzz.*

"Fuck off." I buried my head further into my pillow and clapped a hand over my exposed ear, but finally opened my eyes. Only one person would dare text me at this forsaken hour. Or maybe she was the only one still talking to me. Which meant I'd better respond.

I sat, massaging my temples before crawling to the end of the bed and retrieving my shirt, thankful my phone was in the pocket. Eight missed calls. And one solitary text.

How are you doing this morning? Or is it afternoon?

I imagined her accompanying snicker as I replied to her message.

Fabulous.

Awake. A good sign. Is she home??

Nope. Still holed up down the beach.

Guess you haven't talked to her. Meet for brunch??

Yup. One, usual spot.

Taking that as my cue to haul my ass out of bed, I dragged myself into the bathroom, avoiding even the briefest glance in the mirror. No point in examining the mess I'd become. I cranked the water on full blast and tipped back my head, allowing the heat to sink into my weary soul. I chased my steamy shower with two extra-strength pain tablets and a reheated cup of coffee.

At five minutes before one, I sidled into the café.

Crystal occupied our usual booth by the window. "About time." She tapped her manicured nails on the table before waving down the waitress to fill my cup.

"It's not one yet. Anyway, I had to shower. I was only half alive." I swallowed a mouthful of coffee. "Ahhh, better."

"I bet. How'd you even get home last night?"

"Um, cab. I didn't have my car."

"Good thing, though I suppose you'd have passed out before you left the parking lot." She stared out the window, still drumming her fingers against the wooden table.

"Expecting someone?"

"Gwen's joining us." She beamed.

"Why'd you invite her?"

"There she is." Crystal waved at her friend as she muttered, "Be nice."

Before I could protest, Gwen slid into the booth, sandwiching me between them.

"Joel Nichols. Didn't know you were joining us … Again." She performed a slow perusal. "You've looked better."

"Felt better too." I opened the menu, throwing a "why-did-you-have-to-invite-her" look at Crystal. Pain lanced through my temple as Gwen replayed last night's adventure in her cheerful, but grating, high-pitched voice.

The waitress interrupted with an offer of more coffee, and we placed our orders. I tuned out the nattering until our meals arrived and then picked at my food as I half-listened to Gwen drone on about nonsensical crap. I hated the inane small talk, but I couldn't say much of substance in front of Gwen. The woman was a notorious rumormonger.

"Look." Gwen tugged at my arm. "Isn't that Tiffany? Who's she with?"

I did a double take before sinking lower in my seat. Damn.

Emily rocked and patted her son's back as he snuggled against her chest in the baby sling. The slim young woman beside her tossed unmistakable honey-blonde waves over her shoulder and pointed at something on the menu board.

I understood why they assumed she was Tiffany. Hell, the first day I met Savannah, it struck me that she was a mirror image of her mother, except for those deep brown eyes. Those were one-hundred percent Aiden. It hadn't taken more than a second for me to add up the pieces and figure out why Aiden had welcomed the orphaned teenage girl into his life.

Gwen slid from the booth and sashayed across the floor before I could open my mouth to protest. I covered my eyes, peering through my fingers as she rested her manicured claw on Savannah's shoulder.

"Tiffany?" Her shrill tone carried through the air.

Both Savannah and Emily turned, the older woman studying Gwen with serious green eyes.

Emily slipped an arm around Savannah's shoulders. "Sorry, you have the wrong person."

"Oh. I'm sorry." Gwen stepped back. "You remind me of a friend of mine." She glanced at us, widening her eyes.

I hunched down, wishing to be absorbed into the faux leather, but Emily's gaze followed Gwen's. Her eyes narrowed. Pinned in place, I hung my head, not daring to meet her inquisitive stare.

Gwen crossed the floor and sat beside me. "Wow, that girl is—"

Aiden picked that moment to stroll through the door with Daniel in his arms.

My son clung to my friend's neck with his head resting on Aiden's shoulder. The ache spread as Aiden rubbed Daniel's back, and Emily lifted her chin to accept a kiss.

Savannah leaned in and whispered in his ear, and Aiden to turn and stare in our direction.

Crystal dug her elbow into my side. "Is that her? His wife?" she muttered. "Wow."

A massive understatement. The dark-haired woman cuddled against Aiden was gorgeous and sexy. Her sweet nature and genuine smile made her even more attractive, and only weeks after giving birth, she looked amazing. Her full figure and post-baby curves suited her, her hair shone, and she glowed as she leaned toward Savannah, tilting her head as the teenager relayed some bit of information.

"She's not so great." Gwen smirked. "Look at that ass. She's rather tubby."

"Don't even pretend she's anything but stunning." Crystal rolled her eyes at the other woman. "You're envious because she married Aiden."

"Ha! She can have him." Gwen waved her hand. "Who's the girl?" She ogled the group. "Until she turned, I could have sworn it was Tiffany. There's something different about her, yet so familiar."

The fear that Alex would appear kept me riveted on the group as they waited for the hostess to seat them. If my wife found me there with Gwen and Crystal, I was done for. Not that the Hamilton clan discovering our brunch meeting was much better, but none of them would fly at me shrieking like a banshee. To my relief, the group settled in a booth on the opposite side of the restaurant.

I blocked out Gwen's critical assessment of Emily and stared out the window. "Ouch." The sharp jab into my ribs from Crystal's elbow brought my attention back to the present and the silence that loomed over us. "What was that for?" I forced my gaze upward.

"Aiden." Gwen twirled her hair and batted her hazel eyes.

"Hi … Gwen. Crystal." He focused on me. "I don't mean to break up the party, but someone wants to see you." Aiden angled his body so Daniel faced me.

My son regarded me with sleepy eyes. I wasn't convinced that Daniel wanted me. He looked content resting against Aiden's chest, but I yearned to hold him. This opportunity was irresistible.

"Let me out." I propelled Gwen out of my way and rose from the booth. Aiden transferred my son into my outstretched arms, and I rocked Daniel against me. I kissed his soft hair and closed my eyes, inhaling that sweet little boy smell.

"Do you want to sit with us, or should I have his meal delivered to your table?"

"You'll let me have him?"

"For a couple of hours, but I'll take him home with us."

"Can I take him for the afternoon?"

"I don't know." He tilted his head. "Do you plan to stay sober and spend quality time with him? Or pawn him off?"

"You don't trust me with my own son?"

"Should I?" He pulled me aside and lowered his voice. "You look like crap, Joel. You're hung-over, and you've been drinking excessively. Your judgment is questionable. I want you to see Daniel, but if you put his life in jeopardy because you're letting Crystal lead you around by the balls, you know what'll be coming your way."

"Let me have him this afternoon, and I'll bring him home safe and sound. I'll take him to the park."

"Look me in the eye and swear you'll give him your undivided attention and have him home no later than five. And stop hanging around the likes of Crystal and Gwen. You're married, Joel." He scrutinized me. "You'd better be keeping it in your pants, or you are so done."

The hardest thing at that moment was to look him in the eye, but I did it. "I'm not sleeping with Crystal, I swear." I wanted to shout fuck off, none of your business, but I couldn't lie or evade the question, especially when my words would filter back to Alex.

His searching look burned into me, but I refused to blink or avoid it. Finally, he nodded. "Keep it that way. It's bad enough you're spending your time with her instead of Alex."

I squared my shoulders. "I need to see my son, Aiden."

"Then where have you been while your wife has been managing on her own?" He scoffed.

The bravado drained from me, but I fought the urge to curl into myself. "You don't know what it's like."

"Oh, don't I?" He quirked one brow as his lips twisted, his eyes darkening. "You'd better make the effort soon, or your marriage will be toast. Is that what you want?" His voice dropped but the edge sliced into my heart. "Is it?"

"I don't know how."

"Bullshit. Stop hanging out with Crystal McKenzie and her sidekick while they shit-talk women they don't even know. Quit drinking, get your ass home, and keep it there. Pay attention to your wife." Aiden's tone remained flat, but the undercurrent and warning translated loud and clear. "Do you have a car seat for Daniel?"

I nodded. "I promise he'll be safe. Does Alex know I'm taking him?"

"I'll tell her." Aiden ruffled Daniel's hair. "See you at five. Bye, Daniel. Be good for Daddy." He narrowed his eyes, his gaze directed at our table, one lip curling. No question Aiden noticed the two silent women craning in our direction, ears straining.

Gwen's gaze tracked Aiden as he returned to his table, her eyes bright with interest. "Damn. Did he hear us discussing his wife?" Her cheeks flushed.

I sat and bounced Daniel on my knee. "Oh yeah, he heard."

Crystal wrinkled her nose. "Now you have your kid all afternoon? Kind of puts a damper on the plans."

"I haven't had much time with him, and I promised Aiden I'd have him back by five."

"What business is it of his?" Crystal smirked. "You're a total pussy, letting the guy boss you around with your own kid."

I forced a smile as the waitress placed a kid's meal in front of me. "I'll take a pass on tonight."

"Fine." She huffed, but then gave me a look. "So. If I didn't see Aiden with my own eyes, I'd never have believed he'd gone through with the marriage deal. I thought he was terminally single."

"How married is he?" Gwen winked. "You could invite him out with us tomorrow night."

I snorted, and Daniel jerked his head up, his eyes wide and shiny with imminent tears. As I brushed a soothing hand over his hair and resumed the bouncing, I fought back my laughter. "You know why you never got a second date, don't you?"

Gwen shrugged. "He fell for Tiffany."

"Keep telling yourself that." I smirked. "Anyway, he's as married as it gets. Does it look like he's interested in shopping around? Look at them together."

We turned our heads on cue. Aiden cradled Kellan in his left arm while Emily snuggled against his right side. The adoring looks exchanged between them made it clear. The pure unadulterated love they shared emanated across the room.

"Besides, I didn't realize there were various levels of married."

Crystal snickered. "Well, there are. You're on your own level at the moment, or hadn't you noticed?"

"Ha, well …" I scooped mashed potato into Daniel's mouth.

Gwen's eyes lit up. "You're at the why-the-hell-did-I-marry-that-woman level."

I narrowed my eyes. "How would you know?"

Crystal's spoon clanked against the porcelain cup as she avoided my gaze.

What had she told her friend? I shifted my focus from Crystal to Gwen. "Right. Your husband dumped your ass."

Gwen's lips twisted as she clenched her fingers around her cup.

Damned if I'd explain or justify anything to this nosy harpy. Alex and I had hit a rough spot, but I didn't appreciate this mere acquaintance making assumptions when she knew squat about my relationship with my wife.

Maybe there were levels, such as *unofficially separated*, or *my wife is too pissed to talk to me married*. Or possibly even *I can't visit her because I can barely look Aiden in the eye* type of married, but it didn't give Gwen the right to comment.

A smirk crept onto my face. I'd take advantage of the fact that Aiden—one of Gwen's favorite subjects—sat across the room. "Aiden's son is two months old. The teenager's name is Savannah, and she's Aiden's daughter."

"What? How can he ..." Gwen's eyes widened. "How old is she?"

I sipped my coffee, sneaking a glance out of the corner of my eye. "Sixteen."

"He would have been fifteen? Wasn't he dating ...?" Gwen squinted.

"Holy crap." Crystal stared at me. "That girl is Tiffany and Aiden's sixteen-year-old daughter?"

"Best kept secret in town, but it's one-hundred percent true. Tiffany junior."

Daniel grabbed my hand, and I fed him another bite.

Gwen and Crystal both focused on Savannah, neither woman even blinking as they studied the girl.

"Don't stare. You're being obvious." I kept my attention on Gwen. "Savannah lives with Aiden in Boston, and he denied Mama Bear visitation rights. Aiden told her to bugger off." A part of me enjoyed the reaction and their ever-changing expressions as they added it up. Not that it was much of a secret, but a part of me felt like an ass laying out my friend's private business to the exes. It took the heat off me.

"Humph. Well, they're a disgustingly happy little family. I wonder how long it'll last." Gwen glowered at the couple across the restaurant.

Savannah lifted her chin and squinted as she caught Gwen gawking at them.

"Quit staring," I muttered.

Crystal rolled her eyes. "I don't get how Aiden and Tiffany never shared that they'd had a kid. Secretive." She dropped cash on the table. "Time to bail and leave you to your rug rat." She curled her lip, giving Daniel a sideways glance. "Bye. Call if you change your mind about tonight."

CHAPTER 3

Alexis

AFTER A FITFUL SLEEP, I wandered through the master bedroom and onto the massive private deck overlooking the ocean. I loved this house with its happy teenage memories. I curled up on the wicker couch, tipping my face and soaking in the rays of sun before opening the novel Emily left on the seat.

The words swam before my eyes. After several pages, I couldn't recall a single detail. I closed it and tossed it onto the table before stalking downstairs, pausing to stare through the wall of glass. The golden expanse of beach and sunshine enticed me through the French door onto the hot sand. I savored it squishing between my bare toes, the fresh sea breeze sweeping my hair, and the afternoon sun beating down. After a deep breath to clear my head, I strolled to the water's edge and let the surf wash across my feet.

My phone rang. "Everything okay, Aiden?"

"Everyone's good." His deep, warm voice carried down the line. "We had lunch, and now we're hanging out at the beach."

"I hear a but in there."

"Joel was at the café."

My lips twisted. "Alone?"

"Sorry, Lex," he said. "He took Daniel for the afternoon."

I ran a hand through my hair, scrunching my eyes shut. "You allowed him to …?" With *her* there?

"I can track him down if you'd rather he didn't—"

"No, no. It's fine. I'm ... surprised? Amazed? Joel hasn't shown the slightest interest in weeks."

"He'll bring Daniel home around five."

"You're a miracle worker. You and Tom have been incredible, but—"

"Neither of us is his dad," Aiden said. "He needs Joel. I'm happy to do what I can, but the man needs to step up, and I told him so."

I sighed as I drew a circle in the sand with my toe. Aiden protected me always and I loved him for it, but Joel was a grown-ass man. That his friends needed to clue him was disappointing. "Thank you. You get back to your own family, and I'll see you later. Maybe I'll text Joel and meet him at our house. It's time I get out of your way and deal with my errant husband."

"Call if you need me. Don't be scared to come back to our house. I meant it, Lex. Stay as long as you like."

"Thanks, honey." I dropped to my knees in the sand and stared at the glittering ocean. It made zero sense that my husband took orders from Aiden, but my every effort and request went ignored. My opinions and feelings no longer mattered. Tears flooded my eyes as sobs wracked my body.

My world had caved in, and there was nothing I could do about it. I'd been so happy, but now I couldn't recall the last time I'd genuinely laughed or smiled. I couldn't truly let loose, especially with Joel in the room. I'd pretended for my friends and struggled to contain my feelings. I'd pasted on a brave face and tucked my sadness around me while I'd donned my armor. What was left? Was love enough anymore?

It burned deep inside, the flames licking at the roots of my soul. He had time for her, but not for me. Disappointing, but I was getting used to the feeling.

I tapped a message into my phone.

Heard you took Daniel. Drop him at our house by 5.

I sifted sand through my fingers, watching it fan in the wind as I waited for his reply.

I'll be there. We're having fun at the beach. Glad you're not mad I took him.

Ha! As if I'd be angry that he'd actually bothered to see his son?

Course not mad.

Idiot.

Can we talk tonight?

The surge of anger rolled through me as I stared at my phone, the furious flow of thoughts like a never-ending tsunami. The first onslaught hit me. *Now he's willing to talk?*

"Asshole," I muttered and bounced to my feet, pacing up and down the sand as the next wave hit with a vengeance. *He wants to make nice after abandoning us? After hanging around with his notoriously loose ex-girlfriend?*

As I stomped back and forth, an enormous weight descended onto my chest, crushing me and leaving me breathless. My hopes, dreams, and aspirations were but floating driftwood on their way out to sea, along with the slowly receding, murky runoff of our formerly wedded bliss.

I clutched my hair in tight fists and shrieked, the wind carrying away my frustrations. If I had anything to throw, to break, to destroy, it would be reduced to shards like our marriage and our future.

Despair tore through me and I huddled on the sand, wrapping my arms around myself, rocking as the scalding river flowed down my cheeks. Nothing remained except a shaking, sobbing, wasteland of devastation.

My eyes stung, my cheeks red and raw from the wind whipping across my damp skin. Exhaustion crept over me. Despite the bright sun, I shivered as a chill seeped into my pores.

An endless string of colorful curse words flew from my lips before I regained control and typed out a reply, almost dropping my phone in the sand my fingers were shaking so hard.

Yes. We need to talk.

My feet propelled me to Aiden's house, in through the French doors, and across the cool tiled floor. A reflection of my windswept bird's nest of hair, bloodshot glassy eyes, puffy eyelids and red and blotchy face greeted me. The dark circles under those red-rimmed orbs gave away the lack of consistent and restful sleep. My entire body trembled.

A walking disaster. Someone I no longer recognized. A thought niggled at the corner of my mind. It was time to get it together before I met Joel at the house. Letting him see me like this wasn't an option. I refused to grant him the power of knowing he'd razed me to the ground.

I dragged myself up the stairs, my legs leaden, and my feet almost too heavy to lift. My eyelids drooped shut the moment I collapsed onto the bed. Now that I'd let it all out, I could only curl into a ball and allow darkness to descend.

⌒≼

"Alex." The voice echoed down that long, dark tunnel and dug into my subconscious. "Wake up."

Gentle hands shook me. I clutched the fuzzy, cozy blanket enveloping me, attempting to burrow deeper into the mattress, loathing the idea of leaving the comfort and warmth of sleep.

More shaking. "Alex?" Aiden sat on the edge of the bed gazing at me with visible concern.

"What?" I rubbed my sleep-filled eyes.

"It's after six. Joel's been texting like crazy, worried you hadn't shown up."

"Oh no." I swept trembling fingers through the knotted, wild mess of my hair.

"Relax." His warm fingers grasped mine, calming me. "I told him you were sleeping and to chill. He'll feed and bathe Daniel. They had a busy afternoon." He rubbed my arm. "Why don't you have a hot bath or a shower? I'll make you coffee and something to eat."

Everything blurred around the edges, taking its sweet time to come into focus. I combed my fingers through my hair, hoping to smooth the strands into some semblance of order. I must be quite the sight.

"I couldn't keep my eyes open. Having the afternoon to myself was great." I forced a cheerful note into my words.

It wasn't a total lie. I hadn't been so completely and entirely alone in forever. Sure, our friends had done what they could to give me breaks, but it never seemed to be enough. Every time I tried to sleep, I'd fume over my absent husband. The continuous stress had left me drained. And then Daniel would need my attention, or I had housework to do, or the million other things involved in life consumed me.

"I'm glad you slept." The look he gave me combined with the tone of his voice told me I hadn't convinced him. "Sorry for waking you." He appraised me, perhaps assessing my state of mind. "I'll bring Daniel back here. He can spend the night with us so you and Joel can deal with this."

"He told you?"

"Mmmhmm, but I doubt it'll be a simple conversation." He placed his hands on my shoulders as that tell-tale furrow appeared in his brow. "Daniel shouldn't be there."

How well Aiden knew us both. The brewing storm built, the swirling dark clouds rolling in. It would get heated.

No. Why lie, even to myself? The volcano inside me would erupt, and when it did, an eternity might pass before the ashes settled. My beach breakdown served as an omen of what was yet to come.

My head bobbed. "Maybe you should leave the light on."

"I'll keep my phone nearby."

I sniffled and peeked at him. I didn't have to explain it further. Not to him. "I'll shower now."

He pulled me in for a hug. "Whatever happens, I'm here, Alex. You're not alone."

I leaned into him, taking comfort from his embrace, but dreading what came next.

⌒≼

I stood on the beach and stared at the house as my heart pounded against my ribs, sending tremors through my entire body. Whatever happened, it wouldn't be pretty, and knowing Aiden had taken my son out of the line of fire was a relief.

After several long breaths, I gathered my courage and marched through the door. "Joel?"

"Hey." He appeared with his hands shoved deep into his pockets and his head hung low. "How are you?"

"Fine, I guess." I crossed my arms. "You?"

"Okay. Well." He shrugged and peered at me. "Daniel and I had fun at the beach today."

I wished my day at the beach had been enjoyable, but at least he'd spent time with our son. I bit back the scathing words dying to escape my lips. "Good."

He shuffled his feet and then motioned to the living room. "Should we sit?"

"I suppose." I preceded him into the beautiful, airy room with its floor to ceiling wall of glass and frosted French doors leading to the flagstone patio.

"So." He scrubbed a hand through his hair and rubbed the back of his neck. "I don't know what to say except I've missed you and Daniel. I want to come home. I want you to come home. To move back in here. With me."

I remained silent, waiting for him to expand on this, to apologize, to … something.

He sidled across the room and kneeled at my feet. "Will you," he said as he grasped my hands and blinked, "come home?"

"That's all you have to say after months of this-this … bullshit? Come on home?" I pushed him backward and jumped to my feet. My stomach twisted and clenched as I paced back and forth.

"Alex." He extended his hands toward me. "We've both made mistakes, and I want us to fix this."

"We've made mistakes? I wasn't the one hanging around with my ex. You've spent far more time with Crystal than with me or with your son. You have balls to stand there and say that. Don't be such an ass." My voice rose with each word. "Maybe I haven't been perfect, but I've been there."

"I want us to be together. Can't you give us another chance?"

"Did you fuck her?" I squinted, monitoring his expression.

His eyes widened and his lips parted, leaving me with the aching desire to slap his smug-assed face.

I clenched my fists, forcing my arms into stillness. "Did you screw Crystal, or anyone else while we've been apart?"

"I … I … No." He tipped his chin downward, shaking his head. "Never."

"Never?" I shuffled backward. "Look me in the eye."

He sucked in breath, rubbing his palms against his jeans as he finally looked at me. "Never, Alex. I told Aiden that."

"What. The. Hell."

"I love you," he whispered.

"A non-answer." A shudder shook me. "How do you propose we fix anything when you've been off doing … her?"

"I did not do that. I have never cheated. Ever." He scrubbed at his face with open palms. "Crystal is … easy to talk to. I can confide in her."

"What?" A cold spot grew in my stomach, spreading through me as my heart pattered and skipped. "Confided? About us?"

"So what?" He hunched his shoulders. "You bitch and moan to Jenna and Emily. And Aiden. You talk to him all the time. I have never made a deal about how you run to him every time you're the least bit upset."

"I don't sneak around texting him or meeting him without you or Emily knowing. He's not my ex-boyfriend. He's a friend. Our friend. Not some guy I dated way back and have reconnected with on the sly. Big difference."

"Because you say so? You tell him stuff about us."

"Not everything. How much have you told that woman? About our marriage? About our sex life?"

Joel snorted. "What sex life?"

I narrowed my eyes, concentrating on shooting daggers at him.

He dropped his head and fixated on his shoes. "Sorry."

"Don't blame that on me. You don't find me attractive now I've given birth to your child. These last months have been horrible"—I blinked against the burn of tears—"and you're making stupid-ass jokes."

"You're always busy with Daniel. You never have time for me. I needed someone to talk to, and Crystal is so damn easy to be with."

I smothered a snort. *Easy.* "Tom, Aiden, and Jenna, and hell, even Emily would listen, or-or … Ryan." Not that seeking advice from the resident playboy was a real solution, but no matter. Ryan hearing our shit was loads better than my dumb-ass husband spilling marital secrets to Crystal. "Why? Why would you go behind my back?"

"They're on your side."

"Or maybe they think you're a stupid asshole."

He eyed me like I was a mad woman about to stage a sudden and brutal attack.

"Have you even apologized to Aiden?"

Joel looked away.

"You don't even give a damn. You put Savannah in danger too. She's a kid and you—" My throat closed around the words and I threw my hands in the air.

"I regret my actions every single day." Joel turned away and covered his face. "I can't. Don't you get it?"

I shook my head. "How will you prove you want to be here? To be in this marriage. To be part of this family."

"I'll do anything."

"Counseling? Quit drinking? Make amends with your friends?"

He lifted his gaze and nodded. "Yes to all of that. I love you. I did not cheat. I never had sex with her. I swear it."

How I wanted to believe him.

Joel edged toward me, stretching out his arms. "Whatever it takes." He advanced another few slow and steady steps. "I've missed you."

Tears brimmed my eyes, but I remained frozen, lost in the acute longing of hearing these words, the longing to have him hold me and soothe my fears and pain. When he reached me and his arms encircled my body, I couldn't help myself. I leaned in and inhaled his masculine scent, that wonderful mixture of sun and salt with a touch of baby shampoo—the small reminder he'd cared for our son.

The warmth of his breath against my hair and tickling my neck weakened my knees and my resolve. This was my Joel, the wonderful, loving man I'd married. I hoped he'd come back for good.

"Ally." His voice trickled over me like warm honey, touching my heart. "I've missed you so. Say you'll come home."

A shiver raced down my spine as his lips caressed my neck, and he tangled his hand into my hair. I longed for the battle to be over. I craved his presence in my life. I loved him.

When our mouths met, our tongues exploring and entwining, the wall I struggled to maintain broke loose, crumbling under the onslaught of pure, raw emotions.

Joel scooped me into his arms and carried me upstairs as if I weighed no more than a feather, laying me out on the bed.

"I love you," he whispered as he plied tender kisses to my face.

I pulled back and peered into his eyes, craving the closeness, my will melting under his intense gaze. My lips met his.

Joel responded without hesitation, the kisses between us escalating and deepening as heat traveled through me. He ran his hand under my top, working the cotton t-shirt over my head before fumbling with the button on my shorts. He tossed them over the side before stripping off his own.

The desire and passion ruled my mind, and I gave myself over to it. Our bodies entwined, and for the first time in forever, it felt like I was where I belonged. I felt loved.

CHAPTER 4

Joel

WAKING UP WITH ALLY IN my arms made this morning an entirely different experience than the emptiness of yesterday. I planted a kiss on her shoulder, her neck, and then traveled to her lips.

Her sleepy blue eyes opened, and after a moment of confusion, they cleared, and the most wonderful smile teased those luscious lips.

"Morning, beautiful," I murmured, dropping more kisses across her face.

"Joel?" she whispered, her voice warm, but still fuzzy with sleep.

"Who were you expecting?"

She frowned. "What are you implying?"

"Nothing, never mind." I cupped her face, stroking her soft skin with my thumb. "I'm happy you're here. I've missed you, Ally." Sleeping in this massive king-sized bed alone had been horrible, and the thought that Alex may leave forever preyed on my mind.

Her fingers glided across my shoulder before she twined them through my hair, fixing an intense gaze on me.

It seemed forever since we'd been so close and intimate, so I captured her lips and proceeded to make love to her all over again. I lost myself in her soft scent, her warm skin, and the way she wrapped herself around me.

I dragged in a long breath to calm my breathing and flopped against the cool pillow. If only we could stay in bed all day.

Could we? Aiden and Emily were aware of our marital issues. Maybe they'd agree to keep our boy for another day. Coercing Alex into making the request would take some effort, but Aiden would never ignore Alex. Me? He might never answer. I'd plummeted to rock bottom in his eyes, a difficult circumstance to accept.

"What are you thinking?" Her soft voice drew me from my musings.

"Ahhh, where to start?" I turned my head toward her. "I can't even tell you how much I love and miss you and Daniel." This next part would be harder. "Do you think we could have the day, just you and me? We need time to figure things out. Will he keep Daniel for the day?"

"I'm sure *he* would." Her brows rose. "Why don't you ask?"

The challenge in her eyes told me she'd accept nothing less than me, down on my knees, begging forgiveness. Requisite groveling. An unfortunate bug meeting a windshield. There'd be a few scattered remains to scrape up, but not much else. "Maybe you could?" I nuzzled against her neck.

Ally pulled back and cupped my cheeks in her palms, staring into my eyes. "What are you planning to do? Summer will end, and we'll move to Boston. Then the three of you will open the doors of Hamilton, Grayson & Nichols."

"I get it, Alex." My gut twisted. This woman had occult powers in mind reading.

"Do you?" She propped herself on one elbow. "You owe him more than we can repay. If you screw him over with the partnership guarantees, I'll never forgive you."

"I won't, okay?" I tossed back the covers. Spending the day in bed didn't seem like an awesome idea after all. Not if Alex planned to be on my case the entire time. Yes, Aiden had come through with financial assistance for my partner buy-in, but I didn't need it rubbed in my face.

"See that you don't."

My soft, sweet Alex a nasty bite to her this morning, even after the physical and emotional connection of last night. *You're delusional.* I stalked into the bathroom and flattened my palms on the counter. *Damn, I craved those sweet tones of oak, followed by the burn as it trickled down my throat ...* My red-rimmed eyes taunted me. *Yeah, that'll make everything so much better, dumb-ass. Go drown yourself in a bottle.*

The cold water I splashed on my face brought some color to my sallow skin. Who was this man staring back at me? *You look like hell.*

I'd banished all thoughts of our impending return to Boston, but now the inevitable and unavoidable truths consumed me. Time to paste a smile on my face, get to work, and earn my keep. Repaying all the money Aiden had guaranteed would take commitment. What if he took it back and left me on the street like a sad, jobless hobo? He had all the power. I'd lose the apartment. *No. I'd lose everything.*

I snorted. No way would Aiden be responsible for Alex and Daniel being homeless. If she dumped my ass, it would be lonely me begging for change in the subway, never her.

"Get it together, you idiot. You're a talented lawyer. You'll find something," I muttered. Yet being canned by my former best friends wouldn't amount to much of a recommendation. Double the strikes when their last names happened to be Hamilton or Grayson.

Alex rapped on the door. "Are you planning to hide in there all day?"

"Nope." After splashing more cold water on my face, I inched open the door.

She sat cross-legged on the bed, tapping on her phone. "We can collect Daniel tomorrow morning." Alex muttered something under her breath.

"What?" The tone of those missed words didn't sound flattering from where I stood.

"You're such a pussy. You can't even say his name, let alone have a civil conversation. It's done, but don't ask me to carry your weight, ever again." She wagged a finger. "Stop acting like a petulant child."

"Why are you so …?" I swallowed hard as the words stuck in my throat.

"Don't say it, asshole."

That look could turn a man to stone. "What?"

"Who were you talking to in the bathroom?" Her eyes narrowed.

"Nobody?" Fear lanced me. Had my thoughts slipped out?

She scoffed and eyed me, her lips thinning.

"What's the problem?"

"Tone down your shitty attitude. One roll in the hay doesn't make it all better." The bravado in her tone evaporated. "This year has been hard." She tugged at a loose thread on the duvet. "Do you even want to be here?"

"Ally." My heart ached as I lifted her chin, drowning in those shimmery, sorrowful blue pools. "Don't cry." I swept away her tears with my thumbs and rested my forehead against hers. "I love you."

Her whole body trembled, salty tracks appearing on her reddened cheeks. "Do you, Joel? Do you love me? You can say it, but they're empty meaningless words. Where were you when I needed you?"

My gut twisted. This wouldn't be as simple as Alex coming home. "I'm sorry. I don't know where to start or how to fix this."

"Start by being here. You can't run away and leave me to handle everything." Her eyes blazed. "Make amends."

Aiden. She'd circled around to him. What could I say or do at this point?

"Can't we have today for us? Then we can move forward." I cradled her face. "Then I'll make all the amends you'd like."

Her unwavering eyes searched mine as one hand crept up to grasp my fingers.

"They may only be words, but I mean them with all my heart. I love you, Ally. Until the day I die."

She bowed her head.

The silence lingered forever, my heart pounding as I shifted and finally dropped my hands to my knees. My Ally, or the woman she'd been before everything fell to pieces, would have said those three little words back without hesitation. This time she hadn't, and maybe she never would. What came next?

A sick feeling grew in my stomach as my phone chimed. That woman had the worst timing. No way would I allow Alex to see her text messages. Crystal tended to be informal with me, and that wouldn't add any weight to my heartfelt pleas for my wife to come home. We were on a precipice. The smallest thing would push us over the edge.

"Aren't you going to answer?" Her eyes narrowed.

"Um, yeah." I pushed off the bed and dug my phone from the jacket I'd slung over the back of the chair.

Hey, you coming for breakfast or what?

I glanced at Alex. She pretended not to be watching my every move, but I wasn't fooled. My fingers trembled as I typed a response.

Nope. Can't.

Alex hadn't moved, but even from behind the curtain of dark hair obscuring her face my wife prepared for the kill. She'd become a bird of prey with its beady eyes focused, its only intent to murder that poor little mouse as it scrambled for safety. Her intended victim scampering in a desperate attempt to find cover.

The ole ball n' chain there? Or ya too hung over to get out of bed?

Before I could answer, or even protest, a hand darted out and snatched my phone. "Ally, don't—"

She sucked in a breath. "Wow. You're an asshole. I'm such a horrible burden?"

"Those were her words, not mine."

With a glower in my direction, she tapped in a reply. A moment later it buzzed again. Alex scowled before she shoved the phone at me and stomped from the room.

"Ally." *Did I run after her or see what had been said between the two women on my text?* I spun and pounded down the stairs. The patio door hung ajar. "Ally."

My heart twinged at the sight of the forlorn figure hunched on the sand only a few feet down the beach. An endless stream of sobs issued from her, her shoulders quivering as she curled into herself, hugging her legs tight to her chest.

I dropped to my knees and rubbed her back. "Sweetie."

"Don't." She jerked away. "Why don't you run to your skanky little girlfriend?"

"She's not—"

"Don't lie." She sniffled. "Did you see what she said?"

I gritted my teeth and peered at my screen.

Stop texting. He's married. Go find your own man.

Ha. Funny. Get your butt down here. We have some drinking to do. Don't be a lazy ass. Miss you baby. Hurry up and dump that sad little cow and join us.

My vision blurred at the line of stupid cartoonish cow emojis combined with a string of yellow crying faces.

My phone buzzed again.

The cow thing was Gwen, but ... why do you stay? She doesn't appreciate you.

Alex pushed to her feet. "Whatever. Go if that's where you'd rather be. Just don't ever come back." She stumbled toward the house with her head bowed.

"Wait." I jogged after her and grasped her shoulder. "I'm not dumping you, and I wouldn't rather be there. Please, please, give us a chance."

Alex snuffled, raising her puffy eyes toward me. "Prove it."

I scrubbed a hand through my hair, contemplating her commandment. Call me clueless, but how? What did she want?

Her hands curled into fists, and she gritted her teeth. "No more Crystal. No texting. No phoning. No sneaky diner visits. Nothing." She glowered. "Choose. Me? Or her?"

I closed my eyes and nodded, then hit my speed dial.

Crystal picked up after the second ring. "You meeting us for breakfast?"

"No." I peeked at Alex. She'd presented me with her back, but I didn't miss the furtive swipe of her hand across her face. "Stop texting. I can't see you anymore."

"That's crazy. We're only friends." Her voice dropped to a low pitch. "Is Alex laying down the law? Or Aiden? I know he demanded you stop seeing me. Either way, those two are handing you your balls."

If it hadn't been situation critical, I might have laughed out loud. It struck me as odd that Aiden said similar words about Crystal. Why did everyone assume I had no will or mind of my own? "Don't, okay? It's time I work on my marriage."

She snorted. "You're not allowed friends?"

"I'm serious. I need to spend my time with Alex and my son. I'm sorry, but we have to stop."

"What a sad little whipped puppy. Fine, Joel, you know where to find me."

"Goodbye." I ended the call. "I'm sorry, Alex. I want to make this right."

She hitched in a breath and shuffled toward the house without so much as a glance at me.

"Great." I trailed her, unsure of what to do next.

I wished for the rest of the day to be magical, that we'd spend it making love and reconnecting. But it wasn't to be. The day I dreamed of vanished with the arrival of those devastating text messages. Being in Alex's presence felt strange and awkward, but I stayed, refraining from uttering a single word lest her wrath rain down on me.

Finally, I dared rest a hand on her shoulder. "I should shower."

Alex shrugged it off and looked away.

As the hot water beat down on me, I pondered my next move. This game of "guess what I'm thinking" would wear me down to nothing. Clueless Joel had no idea what to do next.

By the time I emerged, dressed and ready for the day, she'd retired to the patio with a large glass of iced tea. She barely glanced my way as I lowered myself onto the edge of the lounger beside hers.

"Are we going to talk about this?"

"I ..." She shook her head, adjusting her sunglasses with one hand. "I have no idea where to start."

I rubbed back of my aching neck. "I don't know, Ally." Sadness overtook me. This beautiful and amazing woman with whom I'd shared so much sat before me, and I hadn't a single thing to say. "Would you be mad if I went to see Aiden?"

She lowered her sunglasses, her red-rimmed eyes narrowing. "Is that really where you plan to go?"

"Yeah. You want me to make amends and apologize, so I'll go. Then you can get off my case."

"Don't pretend this is about me." She straightened. "You're acting like you don't give a shit. Do you want your best friend back or not? Are you that clueless?" She folded her arms over her chest. "You know what? Do it or don't. Whatever."

Before I could even form a coherent thought, she rose from the lounger and dashed inside. Moments later, the sound of a slamming door echoed across the patio.

I longed to follow, to scream at her, to tell her she was the delusional one. How did one make amends for what I'd done? I didn't have the slightest clue of what to say, or how to begin repairing the damage. *I'm sorry* would sound damn inadequate.

Hey, Aiden, sorry I got tanked and couldn't sit still. I'm sorry I didn't listen and knocked you off your own sailboat. I'm sorry for acting like a complete ass. Sorry for yelling at Savannah and scaring the living crap out of her. I'm sorry you'll be off work for months and might need surgery.

The damage to his shoulder had been severe, sidelining him at work until he was able to lift substantial weight. Just add *fucked up Aiden's medical career* to my list of accomplishments.

You go, Joel.

When messing up someone's life, I did a proper damn job of it. None of that halfway bullshit. What had I forgotten? Oh, right. Sorry you almost died, man. Really. I'm very sorry.

See what I mean? Sorry was such a lame ass word.

CHAPTER 5

Alexis

M Y FACE BURNED AS I sobbed into my pillow, struggling to untangle my thoughts. Did Joel care so little about everything that mattered? Was he that clueless?

The right words came from his mouth, but were they simply what he thought I wanted to hear, rather than words straight from his heart?

When my tears dried, I tucked a pillow behind my head and contemplated life. Had I made a mistake falling so easily into Joel's arms? Should I have held out and demanded more? The questions zipped through my brain, making me dizzy.

Silence loomed, which did little to calm my fears. I tiptoed through the French doors onto our private deck and peeked over the railing at the deserted patio. Maybe he'd kept his promise and was heading down the beach to make an honest effort at reconciliation, but I lacked the energy reserves to chase after him.

Or maybe he'd taken what he wanted and gone back to her. But a woman has needs, and it had been too long since my man had held me like that.

No matter. It was great while it lasted.

I clutched his pillow, soothed by the remnants of his aftershave and his particular spicy masculine scent, and escaped into sleep.

When I opened my eyes hours later, the spot beside me remained cold and empty and the house remained steeped in silence. Where had he gone? Had he messed it up? Or was he sitting on Aiden's patio drinking beer?

After a long hot shower, I wandered downstairs, checking each room as I went, but still, no Joel. Nothing. No note or even a lousy text. Maybe he reserved that for her.

Damned if I'd be the first to break the silence. Instead of texting Joel, I tapped out a message to Emily.

How did it go?

It took a few moments, but soon I stared at the reply.

With what?

Aiden and Joel?

I anxiously watched those tiny dots roll across the screen.

Aiden is here. I haven't seen Joel since yesterday at the diner. What's going on? Isn't he there?

No.

Seconds later, my phone rang.

"How are you, Alex?" Emily's soft voice carried down the line. "What's going on? Is Joel supposed to be here?"

I sniffled. "I don't know. Joel said he planned to visit Aiden."

"Aiden received a cryptic text earlier, but nothing since then. Do you want me to come over? He could watch the kids for a while, or I could send him."

"Bad idea," I said, as I yanked on my sandals, desperate to vacate before Joel reappeared. "I'll come there. Are the kids up?"

"We're settling them for nap time, and Vanna's out with some of the local teenagers. Come whenever you like."

"Thanks." I hurried through the patio doors and set off down the beach. At the sight of a misshapen sandcastle with lopsided turrets, I slowed my pace, allowing it to pour light into my soul. This had to be Daniel's work left on proud display. Aiden had such patience with my son, spending hours with him while balancing the needs of his own family.

Emily lounged on the patio. A large frosty carafe of lemonade and glasses sat on the table, along with a plate of snacks.

My tummy rumbled at the sight. When had I last eaten? I managed about three bites of dinner before I'd given up, and I hadn't even thought about breakfast this morning.

She jumped up from her chair as soon as she spotted me and pulled me in for a warm hug. "How are you holding up?"

"Okay." The tears pricked my eyes as I sank into her embrace. How lucky was I to have these wonderful friends to lean on?

"Oh, honey, it's tough." She rubbed my back as she led me toward a chair. "Aiden will be down soon. Daniel roped him into reading *Green Eggs and Ham* for the millionth time."

"That's Daniel's all-time favorite." I sank into the chair, leaning my head against the back and closing my eyes. Silently I thanked her for not spouting meaningless platitudes about how everything would be okay. For now, I'd take each event as it came at me. I had little fight left to do much else.

"Hey." Aiden appeared and squeezed my shoulder. Without asking, he poured me an icy cold glass of lemonade and set it on the small table beside me. "What's happening?" He perched on the edge of a nearby chair.

My face grew hot as I remembered the previous night, and how I'd let Joel sweet-talk me into bed. "I feel so stupid." I glanced around, noting Emily had evaporated. The clever woman had left us, clearly sensing I'd be more forthcoming if allowed to talk with Aiden alone.

"Why?" His eyes widened. "Lex?"

I wrung my hands. "I believed him and called to beg you to watch our son so we could spend some time figuring things out together, but we ended up fighting. Now he's disappeared. I thought he'd come here, but he's been gone for hours, and Emily said neither of you have seen him."

"Watching Daniel is no problem, you never have to beg for that. But nope, no sign of Joel. Did you text him?"

I shook my head, biting my tongue in hopes of quelling the water works threatening to stream down my cheeks.

"Don't panic, and don't assume the worst. Give it some time."

"What if he ran back to her?"

"Her? As in Crystal?"

I bobbed my head. "What if he decided our marriage isn't worth it and he left me?" I leaned on my hands as heat crept up my neck. "Last night, I tried to hold out and punish him, but he won." I sneaked a look at Aiden, who frowned. "I slept with Joel," I whispered, ducking lower in my chair.

Aiden crouched in front of me and grasped my hands. "Don't be embarrassed, Lex. There's no shame in a little make-up sex."

His expression remained serious. There wasn't an ounce of judgment or discomfort in the look he leveled at me.

"I wasn't too easy?"

"Nope." He shook his head. "Maybe you're thinking withholding sex is a good way to punish him, but it's not."

"What?" I stared at him in shock. That was such a man thing to say and totally unexpected coming from Aiden. "You think it's okay?"

"I assume you were willing." He waited for my chagrined nod. "So it's something you both needed to feel closer to each other, and there's nothing wrong with it."

"What if he slept with someone else? What if he thinks it's okay and I've forgiven him. But it's not, and I haven't."

He sighed. "He assured me he hadn't slept with Crystal. Anyway, you can't beat yourself up for accepting physical comfort from Joel. It makes you human, not stupid."

"That's all you have to say?"

"I can't judge. Everyone knows what happened with Emily and me, so ..." He lifted one shoulder. "Yeah, anyway. Withholding sex is passive-aggressive behavior. If you're doing it as punishment, it's not healthy from a mental perspective. If you both wanted it to happen, then it was better for both of you to follow through." He gave me a hug before sitting back on his heels. "This is where you slap me, right?"

"I'd never—"

His eyebrows rose. Aiden could be a typical man at times, though overall, he was a good guy with his heart in the right place, but he'd definitely been slapped a time or two.

"Not today." I patted his cheek. "You'd have me believe it was healthy?"

"Sometimes you need a good fight." He winked. "It spices things up in the bedroom."

"Okay, now that's TMI. I already know far too much about your sex life." Despite myself, I laughed, though I couldn't discount the truth of his words. I'd been longing for my husband, and I'd acted on it. Would I feel better today if I'd refused Joel?

I also agreed he was in no position to pass judgment. Aiden didn't have a stellar track record with relationships. Nor did Emily. Those two had retreated into their bubble of hurt and denial, or whatever the hell else was going through their messed-up, lovesick brains. Hopefully, Joel and I weren't at the point where we'd torture each other for weeks afterward like they had.

"I've been there more than once. You helped scrape me off the floor after Emily left."

"We fished you out of the bottle." Somehow, this conversation made me feel loads better. Not because Aiden had been hurt multiple times. It pained me to see the emotional destruction caused by thoughtless women eating at his soul. I ached right along with him, worried he'd never come out of it the same man, fearing he'd lose his ability to connect and love. That he'd shut himself off.

The tiniest glimmer of hope flickered in the distance. Here Aiden was, still whole and able to love his wife, heart and soul. He'd forgiven, though maybe not forgotten. But they'd moved on, together, with a strengthened and committed relationship. Maybe I could do the same with Joel. Reclaim the magic we'd once had.

"I owe you, Alex, I do. I value you, and your friendship. And now I'm here for you."

"I did it because I love you. You're the brother I always wished I'd had. Emily knows, right? I'm flipping out about Crystal and Joel, but she understands it's never been like that with us, right?"

"I don't tell her details or anything, but she gets it."

"Good, because I don't want to be an issue in your marriage." I held his hand. "We're quite the pair, aren't we?"

"We are indeed. But remember, Joel has been there for a lot of things too. How he is now is not who he is, Alex. There's so much good in him. The trick is reaching him and bringing him back to you. If I thought he was a lost cause, I'd tell you."

Aiden had advised me to dump asshole boyfriends in the past. Joel was somewhat different, being his friend too, but if there weren't something decent about the man, Aiden wouldn't hang around him, ever. He didn't have time for phoney two-faced people, and he cut out toxic connections when needed.

He'd proven it with Tiffany. He'd loved my friend so hard, and she'd almost destroyed him. Long before the rest of us realized how she'd changed, he'd cut her off.

Not that I didn't feel bad. Tiffany had been a friend for a long time, but her actions over the past few years had been selfish and downright cruel at times. I'd taken a page from Aiden's playbook and spent less and less time with her. I missed her, but in order to keep my own sanity, I'd done what I had to do.

The fact that he hadn't written Joel off reassured me. I trusted this man's judgment. It gave me the courage to at least try to repair what had been torn asunder. I vowed not to panic and to give Joel an opportunity to explain his mysterious disappearance today. I'd give it my all.

This was our marriage and family we were talking about. If that wasn't worth fighting for, what the hell was?

Chapter 6

Joel

After hours of aimless wandering in the scorching August sun, I arrived at Tom's house, my head hung low as I rapped on the front door.

Maybe he would tell me to fuck off. It wouldn't be out of the question. What had I done these past weeks and months to deserve a warm welcome in his home?

"Can I come in?"

"Sure." He stepped aside and motioned me inside. "Let's head out back. Jenna's upstairs putting Adrianna down for a nap. She'll be a while."

I trailed along, wiping at my sweaty brow, grateful to be out of the sun. Maybe I'd copped out, but tackling Tom and asking his forgiveness would be a whole lot easier than facing Aiden.

Yes, I'd ducked the inevitable confrontation, stalling on the beach, unable to force my legs to carry me to Aiden's door before slinking off.

"How about a soda?" Tom raised a brow as he scanned my heated face.

"That would be great." Of course, the preferred ice-cold beer wasn't on the menu. Who could blame him? The past few times he'd seen me I'd been rather inebriated and perhaps a little out of control. After the fateful summer day Savannah and I brought in the sailboat with a worse-for-wear Aiden on board, I suspected none of my friends would rush to offer me an alcoholic beverage.

We stopped in the kitchen, and he fished soda from the fridge. The ice tinkled as he poured two tall frosty glasses. Every few seconds, he threw a glance my way, and a deep frown formed a crease in his forehead.

"What brings you here?" he asked as we settled on the shaded patio.

The ice clinked against the side and small fizzy bubbles rose to the surface as I swirled my glass. I shrugged, taking a long drink to soothe my parched throat and loosen the lump residing there.

"Hmm." He studied me.

Yes, Mr. Prosecutor, do a full assessment of my guilt level. The problem with both Tom and Aiden was that their professions demanded they become skilled at reading human behavior. We'd all taken loads of psychology courses while obtaining our respective degrees. You could run, but you damn sure couldn't hide much from either of them.

"You can talk to me." His words were gentle and his voice low. "It's no secret things have been tough for you and Alex."

"Yeah, I imagine there's no hiding it."

"Why do you feel the need to hide? You've hit a rough spot, and there are people around you who want to help. No one can force you to accept it. You have to want it. We're here when you're ready to crawl out of that pit you've dug for yourself."

I popped my head up at his words. I expected anger and contempt, but I only saw Tom, my long-time friend, with concern written across his face.

"I've truly messed up. With my wife, with my son, and with my friends. How can I dig out from under it all?" I sighed. Admitting it out loud was painful. Welcome to the complete failure that used to be part of this group. "The pit's too deep."

"You can still save yourself, and perhaps your marriage. There's certainly time to rescue your relationship with your son before he gets any older."

"Everything I do or say sets Alex off. I can't wipe my nose without her losing her shit."

"Did you really expect you'd say sorry and it would all be perfect? It takes consistent effort to have a good marriage."

I stared into my glass, shaking my head.

"You can't be hanging around with women like Gwen and Crystal. Put yourself in Alex's place. What if she texted some ex-boyfriend and hung out with him daily, discussing your marital woes? How happy would you be?"

Damn, the guy had a point. "She does text and hangs around that Aiden guy a lot, though." I forced a touch of levity into my words.

"Oh, for fuck's sake. That's like me losing it because Jenna gives him a hug and kiss whenever she sees him. He's like our brother. Aiden would never do that to either of us."

I sipped my soda and swallowed hard to clear the lump in my throat. Damn. It wouldn't go away.

"Besides, he's not Alex's ex-boyfriend. They've never had that kind of relationship. Ever." Tom rolled his eyes. "So get off it."

"I'm off." I held up a hand. "She's been a saint, and I've been the sinner. Whatever."

"Now you sound like a passive-aggressive dickhead." Tom's humorless laugh echoed across the patio. "If you're planning on digging out of that pit, start by being honest with yourself. You need to atone, and to stop hanging with the crowd you've fallen in with. They're all single or divorced, with no children, and they live to drink, party, and sleep around. Remember the rule of toxic connection."

I concentrated on catching the bead of condensation trickling down my glass with a fingertip.

"Annnnd on the topic of Aiden. When did you last speak to him?"

Would he ever let this go? I avoided his gaze, clenching my fist around my drink.

"That long, huh?"

"I talked to him yesterday." Well, not exactly, but did Tom know that? I'd at least half-listened to Aiden's lecture. So, close enough.

"You sat down and had a man to man discussion about all the stupid shit you've pulled?"

I shook my head.

"Yeah, that's what I thought," he said. "I know they saw you in town … with Crystal."

"What did he say?"

"Not much, but you know Aiden."

That meant the next play in this game would be mine. I inhaled a ragged breath and closed my eyes. "How can I fix what's beyond repair?"

"Is it?" His voice dropped. "Have you asked him? Gone to see him? Asked him how he's doing? Anything?"

The heat of shame rose and I was sure my face flamed red.

"About time you did, don't you think?"

"I tried today, but I couldn't. How do I even begin to apologize for what I've done? What I've cost him? Facing Emily will be even worse."

"Do you have a choice? You can get off your ass and talk to him, or avoid him and lose his friendship. Time's ticking, and the longer you wait, the harder it'll get." He leaned back and propped one ankle over his knee, taking leisurely sips of his soda.

Ahhh. This tactic. Soon it would be impossible for me to remain silent. The need to fill the space, to make conversation, would become overwhelming. I'd used this technique myself with clients to get information out of them essential to their defense and to vet witnesses. But still, I broke first. "Yes, Tom. I get it."

"I'll propose an exchange. Jenna will pack up Adrianna and head to Hamilton house, and the ladies can hang out. I'll invite Aiden here, and we can have a guys' night. Shoot a little pool—no beer—but lots of chicken wings and stuff. You can grovel and clear the air, and we can move on like actual grown men. What do you say?"

"Yeah, I'm in." I wanted to roll my eyes but that would have been unwise. Tom would call me on any bad behavior, and he was on point. If I'd visited Aiden right away to apologize, I wouldn't feel like such a low-life now. "I have to check with Alex. I disappeared on her."

He shook his head and shot a stern look in my direction. "Yeah, you'd better get her on board."

Tom rose and disappeared into the house, while I stared at my phone, gathering the courage to call Alex. My disappearing act was sure to have ticked her off.

My fingers had a mind of their own, and before I thought better of it, I hit send.

How mad are you?

I pushed up from the chair and paced to the edge of the patio, shading my eyes against the sun glinting off the water. White sails dotted the horizon, and I began counting. One little boat … All the amazing times we'd had here. Two little boats … I'd never be invited again. Three … Who saw this coming? Four … Where are you, Ally? Five … I kept adding, my phone clutched in my sweaty palm, until I reached sixty distant sailboats.

Nothing. Damn. I sank onto the edge of the chair, tapping my phone against my forehead in a steady beat. Finally, I dialed.

"Coward," Alex said.

"You're pissed."

"Genius observation."

"Sorry, but I'm at Tom's. I …"

"Jenna called," she said. "I hear you're spending the evening with Tom and Aiden? You'll get this nonsense sorted?"

Right now she was rubbing her hands together, an evil gleam in her eyes as she pictured me on my knees, groveling and begging for forgiveness. "Yes."

"We'll talk later." The line went dead.

I pinched the bridge of my nose. "Can't wait."

By the time I wandered into the kitchen, Tom was already busy preparing snacks.

"Can you grab the baking trays?" Tom pointed to the cupboard before returning to chopping veggies. "Jenna's changing, and Aiden will be here soon. No issues with Alex?"

I shrugged and pulled out the trays.

Jenna appeared seconds later, saving me from answering. "Nice to see you, Joel." She brushed a hand down my arm before hugging me.

Tom was a lucky man. This sweet, caring woman had a way of brightening a room, and this little show of support calmed my nerves. "Thanks, Jenn." I kissed her cheek.

A smile lit her face as she patted my cheek. "You boys be good. See you later." She stopped to kiss Tom, one of those long, lingering embraces that joyful newlyweds always seem to share, before she snuggled Adrianna in her wrap.

My stomach twisted. I wasn't sure that Ally and I would ever regain that intimacy in our marriage. And I sure missed it.

⌒⤚

The moment Aiden appeared, Tom wiped his hands on a kitchen towel and bestowed one of those brotherly man-hugs they'd perfected over the years. "How was the appointment?"

"I'll start physio when I get back to Boston." He rubbed his shoulder. "Em has been massaging it nightly."

Time to man up and make my amends. There was nowhere to run or hide in any case. "Hey."

"Joel." Aiden gave me a look I couldn't quite decipher, but I received my own brief, but decidedly awkward, man-hug.

"How are you?" I patted his shoulder, careful not to be too rough. Last time I'd seen him wearing the arm brace, I'd been too drunk to focus on much of anything aside from my own anger, and now I had no clue as to which arm was injured.

"Some good days, some bad."

An awkward silence fell, punctuated only by the sound of Tom's knife on the cutting board and the meaningful looks launched my way.

"I don't know quite how to say this," I mumbled, focusing on the tile flooring. "I've been an idiot, and I'm sorry, you know? For everything." A glimpse of the expression on Tom's face told me it wasn't close to enough.

I held up a hand, palm toward Aiden and forced my gaze upward. "This feels like too little and too late. Apologies are inadequate, but I don't know what else to do. I'm sorry, I felt like such an asshole, and I couldn't face you after doing what I did. Maybe someday you'll forgive me, and ..." I shrugged, at a loss for further words.

Fortunately, Aiden took pity on my bumbling, stumbling self and he nodded. "I agree, you've truly been an asshole, but here's the thing. You've always been there when I needed you. You're family, a brother, and I can't give up on you quite yet. It's not okay that you made numerous dumb-ass moves. Dangerous dumb-ass moves. But we're both adults, so I'm sure we'll figure it out."

I stared at him. Why the hell was I so worried about this? Perhaps because I could never have been as gracious or accepting of the situation or the apology. Maybe that was the lesson. The bigger picture. Aiden would always be the better man.

"Thank you." This time I hugged him like the brother he was to me. He'd been best man at my wedding and was an amazing uncle to my son. My friend had stood by me through countless nasty break-ups, and now he'd be there as I pieced my life and marriage back together.

"Family sticks together." He patted my back.

Tom grinned. "Who's hungry?"

For the first time in days, I had an appetite. The crushing pressure lifted, at least partway. I'd still have to face my wife, but maybe she'd allow some leeway now I'd taken the crucial first step with Aiden. I didn't kid myself. It was only the first tiny step of many enormous ones.

CHAPTER 7

Alexis

NOT LONG AFTER AIDEN LEFT the house, Jenna appeared and joined us on the flagstone patio.

Jenna settled into a chair with Adrianna draped over her shoulder. "You had a good chat with Aiden?"

"Always. I thought I'd been too soft on Joel, but Aiden made some valid points. I hate how right he is, like all of the time."

Emily laughed. "It's annoying, isn't it? He's so damn reasonable."

"You two never fight?"

"Don't kid yourself." Her mouth formed a rueful smile. "We've gone several rounds, but we learned early on how to communicate, and we pay attention to the dynamics."

"What do you mean?" I asked.

"It's easy to get caught up with work, the kids, and everything else in life. No matter what, we spend at least ten minutes daily giving each other undivided attention, and we schedule regular date nights."

"Tom and I are doing that. I'm sure Aiden gave him the idea." Jenna nodded. "It makes a huge difference, especially considering the demands of a baby. It's a fact. The first years of marriage are a challenge. Adding a child, who commands your attention, can tear down even the strongest of relationships."

I sighed. "It sure has taken its toll on us. Now it's impossible to get Joel's notice for even five seconds. Though last night ..."

Emily's brows went up. "Last night?"

"I managed to get Joel's undivided attention." Heat rose in my cheeks. "Aiden didn't think it was an issue, but what's your opinion? Did I give in too easily?" I looked at Emily.

"Don't ask me. Aiden and I were barely speaking and we still landed in bed multiple times." Emily lifted a shoulder but didn't show an ounce of embarrassment at the admission. "That's no secret. But"—she held up a hand—"I craved the physical connection, and it led us here, so I don't regret it. I do regret allowing stubbornness and pride to interfere in our relationship."

I turned toward Jenna.

"I don't know." Jenna sighed. "It's hard to express an opinion when it's not my marriage, and I'm not privy to all the details. All I know is you can't back down on the counseling." She frowned. "If you love Joel as much as I love Tom, then give it your full attention."

"Aiden gave you names," Emily said. "Insist on counseling as a couple and individually. Even if you've been assured that he didn't sleep with her, it's still an affair."

"What?"

Emily edged her chair closer. "I'm not sure what you talked about with Aiden."

"Aiden's convinced Joel never slept with Crystal, and Joel swore he didn't. Still, it hurts that he ran to her, and he did spill private details about our marital troubles." I could tell she had thoughts brewing. "What are you thinking?"

She twisted a lock of hair between her fingers and shifted in her seat.

"Please? You're concerned about something." I leaned forward to grasp her hand.

"I don't want to cause issues when things might be resolving." She squeezed my fingers.

"Whatever it is, I need to hear it. I'm so confused. Another woman's perspective would be appreciated."

"The sneaking around bothers me," she said. "Have you heard of emotional affairs?"

I clamped my lips shut and shook my head. *Affair.* That word lanced my heart.

"If Aiden sneaked around to see an ex-girlfriend and confided our personal issues, he'd be a dead man walking. It's a major violation of trust. If you and Joel hope to fix your marriage, he needs to understand his actions were wrong and hurtful. There has to be consequences for his behavior, and he needs to promise to never do it again."

"He promised he wouldn't see her."

She closed her eyes for a moment. "It's a start, but Joel had, or is still having, an emotional affair. It happens far more often than people realize, and it's as damaging, or sometimes even more difficult to deal with than a physical affair."

My stomach rolled, but her words resonated. "You don't think I'm overreacting by demanding he cut Crystal from his life?" Delving deeper into this subject frightened me, but I suspected she was right. She'd seen many situations in her professional life and hadn't enjoyed smooth sailing in any of her own relationships.

"No." Emily shook her head. "Even Aiden advised Joel to stop seeing Crystal. We've both seen where those connections lead, and there are signs."

I peered up at her. "Signs?"

"Sneaking around to see an ex-girlfriend?"

I nodded.

"Hiding texts?" She lifted her brow. "Secret phone calls? Neglecting you and Daniel? Confiding personal matters to an ex-girlfriend?"

Damn. I blinked back tears as Emily passed me a tissue.

"I'm sorry, but those are huge red flags."

"You're right," I whispered, dabbing at my face. "You said it's common?"

"I've told guys off on occasion and made sure they knew it wasn't kosher to be so damn secretive," Jenna said.

Emily shot a look at Jenna. "I appreciated it." She turned to me. "You have to admit it's not quite the same, but still …"

"I don't understand," I said.

"Aiden contacted Tiffany before Christmas last year, but he didn't tell me until afterward. He wasn't confiding our private business or looking for her advice, but the secrecy bothered me. With a small push from Jenna, he came clean. And it only happened one time."

"Tiffany ratted him out," Jenna said. "I believe she wanted to stir up trouble."

"It's not the first time. She sent those airport pictures to Aiden," I said. Tiffany clearly harbored serious regrets about their separation and divorce. Rumor had it she'd propositioned him at Jenna's wedding, even though she'd been engaged at the time. "She's not that sweet shy girl I knew at boarding school, that's for damn sure."

"She's not, but enough about that. Let's deal with you and Joel. I don't want to see you two break up." Jenna blinked several times as her eyes grew shiny. "I wish you'd been more open about this earlier. I thought Aiden claimed the title of king of secrets, but you're a close second."

"I'm sorry." I held up my hand. "Aiden lectured me already. You're right. I've been stupid. I let it go too far and refused to admit what's been happening." I stole a look at Emily. "I criticized you for ducking Aiden when my own marriage needed first aid."

"Until you're ready, you can't admit it out loud. It makes it too real." Her vibrant green eyes took me in. "I lived in my own land of denial for months before I pulled myself together. Allowing Aiden to leave Chicago without me was ludicrous. As was … everything else I did to torture the poor guy."

I couldn't argue. Many of her actions seemed selfish, but how could I condemn her? Telling a man you couldn't live without him delivered absolute power over your heart. Despite numerous reservations, I was on the verge of serving myself up to Joel.

For strong and independent women who'd had nothing but cheating assholes in their lives, the rules of self-preservation dictated they avoid forming serious attachments to men, no matter the cost.

What was a woman to do? You never knew what you might give up. If you took a guy like Aiden at surface value without knowing him or his real worth, most women would, and often had, labeled him without any qualms. Rich spoiled playboy.

"Joel isn't the first guy who's hurt me. I've had countless awful experiences with lying bastards." I blinked back the tears, exhausted by the constant crying and emotional ups and downs over the past few days. "Joel was supposed to be the one, the man I'd be with forever. I still hope …"

"He is, honey." Jenna reached across to rub my shoulder. "Anyone can see you love him. And you have Daniel, so it's worth every attempt at saving your marriage."

The first step was accepting I wasn't ready to give up or give in. My Joel hid in there somewhere. Or I sure hoped so.

Emily stretched her arms over her head, and I glanced at my watch, my eyes widening. The sun had set and darkness had descended. Jenna had gone home hours ago, the poor woman fighting to keep her eyes open.

"Sorry. It's so late."

"Don't worry about it. I don't mind having you here." Emily smiled as we gathered the last of the dishes and carried them into the kitchen. "You should stay overnight."

"No, I'll go home. I'll get Daniel."

"You could leave him. Why risk waking him?"

"Are you sure?"

Emily waved a hand. "It's fine. Aiden will be home soon, and he can get up if Daniel needs anything." She grinned.

I smiled back as I gathered my things and stepped into the balmy summer night. Halfway home, I flopped onto my back in the sand, pillowing my head on my arms. I loved nights on this deserted beach, staring up at the Milky Way while listening to the soothing shush of the waves hitting the shore.

What a joy it would be to return to those happy times we had as kids. Running wild with no responsibilities. Embracing glorious summer days filled with endless possibilities.

Then my own words echoed back at me. Change even the smallest thing and the effects ripple out." Aiden had asserted he wouldn't change a thing. Where would we be now if we'd made even one alternative choice? The unanswerable question. One could never know.

With a deep sigh, I rose to my feet and brushed the sand from my shorts before wandering home. A dark, silent house greeted me, so I filled the tub with steaming water and fragrant mineral salts and soaked my weary body. After a long and luxurious bath, I donned a soft sleep shirt and crawled between the crisp sheets.

When I heard footsteps on the stairs an hour later, I focused my attention onto the TV screen, pretending to watch a movie. My brain refused to stop analyzing the conversation I'd had with Emily.

He sidled into the room, watching me through lowered lashes. "Daniel's in bed?"

"At Aiden's he is. He fell asleep, and I didn't have the heart to wake him."

"They should adopt him already." Joel rolled his eyes. "I'm starting to wonder whose kid he is."

"Hilarious." I set my lips in a flat line. "I'll get him in the morning." I twirled my hair as he started his nightly bedtime routine. "How did it go?"

"Fine. I begged and groveled if that makes you happy."

"None of this makes me happy." *Idiot.* "So you and Aiden are good?"

"As good as we can be. He took his pound of flesh and made sure I admitted what a stupid ass I'd been. It's a start." He perched on the side of the bed. "Am I allowed to sleep in here? Or am I banished to the guest room?"

"Hmmm." I tilted my head and considered if, after last night, it would be advisable. If I said no, it wouldn't help either. I bobbed my head.

A small rush of air left him, like he'd been waiting with bated breath as I mulled things over. He climbed under the sheet and wiggled close, curling against my back. "I've missed this, Ally. I hope we can get past all of it, and you'll forgive me." His breath tickled my skin. "I'm trying."

"I know." I patted his hand while striving to ease the tension in my body and fully relax in his embrace.

He massaged my shoulders and dropped little kisses onto my back, brushing my hair out of the way. "I love you, baby." He buried his face into the crook of my neck. "You're tense. What's the matter?"

I bit my lip. I didn't want to say it out loud or repeat the words Emily had uttered. *Emotional affair.* What an unsavory concept.

Joel holding and kissing me made everything seem normal. I wanted the world to go away and for our troubles to disappear, even if for only one night. I rolled, pressing my lips to his and inviting him in.

His embrace tightened as his kisses became deeper and more passionate.

Perhaps I'd be allowed to forget everything, and we could be us for a few precious hours. I could pretend I'd never heard Emily utter those awful and damaging words. There would be plenty of time tomorrow. Tonight was our momentary reprieve before the battle continued.

CHAPTER 8

Joel

I TUCKED THE LAST ITEM INTO my bag and slung it over my shoulder. "Are you sure you don't mind?" The enticing scent of her lotion tickled my nostrils as I looped an arm around her waist.

"Why would I? You need time with your friends, and it's the last sail of the summer."

"Thanks, baby." After a quick kiss, I bounded down the stairs, tipping my face toward the sun as I strolled down the sunny beach toward the dock. Life felt good, or at least better than it had. Something still lurked under Alex's calm exterior, but I'd leave that alone. Maybe it would blow over and end up being nothing.

"You made it." Tom glanced up from his task.

"Alex gave me time off for good behavior. How are you doing, Aiden?"

He shrugged and moved toward the bumpers.

"Sit. Don't strain your shoulder." Tom pointed toward the bench.

"I'm—" Aiden halted as Tom narrowed his eyes. He held up both hands in surrender and sat on the bench. Everyone knew it was useless to argue with Tom.

"I'll get the lines." With an effortless movement, I flipped the bumpers and helped get the boat underway.

Aiden fidgeted, riveted on the churning waves.

"Are you okay, man?" Tom patted Aiden's shoulder.

"I'm fine." Aiden waved a hand before turning his attention to the shoreline.

"Testy," I muttered under my breath to Tom. "He should relax and feel lucky he doesn't have to lift a finger."

Tom frowned as he tied off a line. "I doubt he sees it that way."

Being unable to sail his own boat must irk him, and the occasional disgruntled look he threw my way confirmed whom he blamed.

A light salty breeze swept across us as the bright sun beat down. We picked up speed, and the sailboat skimmed over the water. I inhaled deeply, loving every moment. Freedom. Flying across the waves. Fresh salty air. I closed my eyes, savoring it. Too soon it would be confinement in an office. "I've missed this."

"Yeah."

Something about the tone of Tom's voice pulled me from my reverie.

Tom nodded toward Aiden. "Maybe we should head back."

"We've been out less than an hour."

Tom shook his head and scowled.

"What?"

"You're clueless." He rolled his eyes and steadied the wheel.

I opened my mouth, and then snapped it shut again. What could I say? I took another long look at Aiden.

Our friend appeared ill at ease and immersed in his thoughts, which struck me as odd. Aiden loved being on the water, being a life-long sailor, but today he appeared pale and drawn and unhappy.

"Is he okay?" I mumbled at Tom.

"Does he look in top form?" His brows rose, then he turned his back to me.

"No," I said, more to myself than to Tom. The urge to find out why overtook me. I dropped onto the seat beside Aiden and offered a water bottle. "Where's Savannah?"

"Thanks. She decided to stay home and help with Kellan."

"Ahh." I nodded.

Aiden twisted the top off the water, his hands shaking as he drank.

"What's up with you? You're twitchy."

"Nothing," he muttered before closing his eyes and reclining on the bench with his arms folded across his chest. Given the way Aiden retreated, it seemed like our great guys' night had never happened.

I crossed the few feet to join Tom and jerked my head toward Aiden. "Is it me? Should I have stayed home?"

"Have patience, Joel." Tom clapped me on the back. "He hasn't been sailing since that day. I'll check on him, but first, help me bring her around. We'll sail her to the marina."

Once we'd changed course, I took the wheel, keeping my eyes averted as Tom joined Aiden on the bench. They spoke in low tones, the rush of wind obscuring their conversation as we skimmed over the water.

When we reached the dock, Aiden stepped off the boat before we'd even tied up. He stopped several paces away, leaning on one of the pillars as he raked a hand through his hair.

"Is he—"

"Leave it alone." Tom barely looked up from his task of tying off lines.

After a moment, Aiden continued his journey down the dock, flagging down one of the workers from the storage yard.

"Why isn't he docking at his place. He has boat storage."

"Maintenance. I offered, but he said no."

"Why …" *I'm an idiot.* Aiden had all the equipment to maintain his craft, but he couldn't manage the task this year. That was my fault. I grabbed my bag and one of the crates, following Tom to the SUV. "You planned ahead," I said as he stowed the gear in the back.

"Yup. Once we're done with the boat, I planned to buy Aiden lunch." Tom closed the hatch. "Interested?"

I glanced at Aiden, who supervised the crew hoisting his sailboat from the water. "I'll catch a rain check."

After a brief hug for Tom and a wave at Aiden, I headed downtown, intending to take a taxi home. However, my feet carried me to the pub. Alex had mentioned hanging out with Emily and Jenna. It would be hours before I'd be expected home.

After stepping into the dark interior, I surveyed the scene and spotted the familiar dark-haired woman seated at a booth. *No, I couldn't.* Instead, I planted myself on a stool at the bar and requested a dark ale and a plate of nachos.

The bartender filled a frosty pint and set it on the counter in front of me.

The baseball game being shown on the big screen captured my attention, and I sipped beer and munched my chips.

"I thought you'd be home with the little wifey," Crystal said as she slid onto the seat next to me. "Things not so rosy these days?" She smirked.

"It's all fine," I said with a sideways glance. "Just stopped for a drink." The action on the television caught my eye, and I groaned as the referee ruled the runner as out.

"Ah." She pointed to her glass as the bartender passed by. One of those mock cutesy pouts formed on her face. "You're not talking to me? I thought we were friends."

"I can't hang out, Crystal. Alex threw a fit over your stupid texts." Annoyance crept into my voice. "That cow emoji thing …"

"That was Gwen. Besides, you're here, not there." She tapped her scarlet nails against her glass. "What's eating you?"

"Huh?"

"You're in a mood. Tell me, what's up?"

I sent a dark look her way. "Leave me alone."

She remained rooted to the seat. Her inquisitive glances broke my resolve.

"It's the usual crap." I forced out a breath. "That whole thing with Aiden."

"Which particular thing?" She raised a perfect brow, her eyes glittering. "What doesn't annoy you about that man?"

I shifted in my seat and stared at the images flashing across the big screen.

She placed a hand on my arm. "We're friends, and you're in a funk, so spill it."

"He's pissed at me. Today we went sailing, but he acted like I wasn't there. Talk about grouchy." I snorted. "I've got nothing on him."

"Why's he so bent out of shape?"

The bartender placed a second pint on the bar in front of me, and I swallowed a mouthful before clamping my mouth shut.

The thing was, I enjoyed hanging out with Crystal because she listened without judging my choices. "Everyone, but Aiden in particular, seems to be holding a grudge ..."

"Well," she said once I finished my long ramble, "I guess he has a right be angry, but he said he forgave you, so I don't know why he's acting like a jerk." Crystal rubbed my back and waved for another round of ale.

"Yeah, right?" *Finally.* Someone who understood and supported my side of the issue. Even in the short time since our last brunch, I'd missed this woman.

Crystal motioned toward an empty pool table. "Let's play."

I eyed her before taking another gulp of ale.

"It's a game, in a public place. Does she have your balls tied so tight that you're incapable of making the simplest decision?" She poked my ribs.

"Stop."

Crystal captured my hand. "Look, I get it. You want to stay married, but if you're here, and she's not, it says a whole lot about how things are at home. She's probably on the phone complaining to Aiden right now."

I drew my brows together. No arguing that point. "Those two confide in each other all the time."

Even after most of our friends had learned about Savannah's existence, he'd outright refused to discuss it with me. When his daughter moved in with him, I was the last to know.

"Why are you sweating about hanging with me for a while? Come on, Joel. One round?"

"Fine, rack them up. Just one," I said, holding up my index finger, "then I should go."

"Perfect." She wrapped her fingers around mine and pulled me from my stool. "I won't keep you long."

"How did it go yesterday on the boat?" Alex zipped her suitcase. "Must have been a great night out with the guys since you came home so late."

"Umm … Not so wonderful." I shrugged it off. "We barely left the dock, and we had to come back."

"What happened?"

"Not much." I ducked my head and busied myself with stacking my shirts in the open suitcase on the bed.

"It must have been something." She crossed her arms. "You're acting funny. What did you guys do afterwards?"

"No, I'm just sick of constantly explaining myself." After snapping the lock closed on the French doors that led onto the deck, I set my suitcase by the door. "You have everything? We should hit the road."

"If you weren't out sailing, where were you?"

"I had a beer. Then I came home."

"No need to get so snippy. And what's wrong with Aiden?" Her brows rose. "What did you do?"

"Why is it my fault? Blame Aiden's crappy mood. Maybe he had a fight with Emily. Or maybe the baby kept him up all night. Didn't she beg off of the girls' thing?"

"You went drinking? Alone? Until two in the morning?"

"You were out, so why should I sit around the house? Let it go."

A dark and stormy look shot my way, but she snatched up her bag. "Fine. I'll get Daniel." She marched from the room, her footsteps resounding on the floorboards as she stomped down the hall, muttering something indistinguishable.

Loading the car became an awkward and silent dance around each other as we finished loading the car. Every time I opened my mouth, she sent me a scathing look, and the moment we pulled out of the driveway, Alex cranked the music. Even the short time on the ferry was tense.

The traffic and the silence between us grew heavier the closer we got to our destination.

I tapped my fingers on the steering wheel, finally stabbing at the controls to lower the music's volume. "The silent treatment, huh? Real mature."

She glowered as she spun the knob on the dash, the rising bass joining the headache pounding in my temples.

"Alex!" I turned it down.

"Quit yelling." She glared. "You'll wake Daniel."

"He sleeps through everything." I rolled my eyes. "What's your problem, anyway? Nothing I do is enough, is it?"

"If you'd quit sneaking around, that would help." She curled her lip and shifted toward the window. "Whatever. I don't want to talk, or hasn't that sunk into your thick skull?" Alex adjusted the current song a few notches and resumed her position while I focused on the gridlock of cars.

With a deep sigh, I resigned myself to what awaited me at home. The evil-eye-cold-shoulder treatment, combined with the expectations of my new position at the law firm, added to the dread building within me. Settling into a routine of our day-to-day lives wouldn't be easy.

The move to Boston had taken its toll, stealthily breaking our lives somewhere along the way.

⁓≼

With the opening of the firm, there wasn't much time to dwell on our home issues, but the heightened tension remained. Meetings and interviews dominated the work hours that grew longer while the nights at home grew shorter.

After the first two weeks, when things started to take shape in the office, I faced the bigger issue.

I didn't want to go home.

Especially tonight. As a reminder of the tense and crappy morning with my grouchy wife, a notification appeared on my phone.

Between the irate tapping of her finger on the chart in the kitchen as I ate my bagel, the mid-morning reminder text, and the final mention of our pending appointment as I dashed out the door, I felt like a chastised school boy about to miss a dentist's appointment.

After dismissing the reminder, I wandered into the break room, finding Savannah loading the dishwasher.

"Surprised you're still here." I poured a cup of coffee and eyed the girl. "You know that's not part of your internship. Sarah will do it."

She shrugged as she wiped the counter.

"Would have thought you'd have a big date."

"No." Savannah pushed the start button and headed for the door. She brushed past Tom, muttering a string of unintelligible words.

"What's up with Vanna?" Tom cast a glance over his shoulder at the retreating teenager.

"Umm …" My brain spun as I struggled to concoct a plausible explanation, even though we both knew she hated—and actively avoided—being in the same room as me. "Maybe she's late for her evening plans." I added cream to my cup.

Tom leaned against the counter. "She mentioned finding another job once we're up and running," he said, crossing his arms, "which would be a shame as this position is perfect for her. There's no stress, allowing her to concentrate on school, she gets to see how a law firm works, and we can trust her." His blue eyes bored into me. "Any idea why she feels uncomfortable working here?"

"Okay, I get it." I held up my hands in surrender. "It's me, right? She's jumpy all of the time."

Tom stared at me for a moment. "You haven't talked to Savannah about the sailing incident?"

"Not really." I turned to add another splash of cream.

"Don't you think you should?" Tom asked. "Between you and that damn woman, the girl has endured a whole pile of crap."

"Tiffany, you mean?" I frowned. "I thought she'd shoved off and married good ole Harrison." First I'd heard of a new Tiffany issue, but Aiden hadn't confided in me about anything. Not that I could contribute much in the way of advice. I had enough to deal with in my own messy, convoluted world.

"Nope, they're done. Tiffany asked to see Savannah. After all this time, she's stirring it all up. The woman always did have terrible timing." He squinted at me. "You know Aiden has Savannah in counseling again."

My eyes widened. Of course. Tom and Aiden were waiting me out, playing a game of cat and mouse. "Damn it, he knows?"

"He's not stupid, Joel." Tom's brows rose and he shot daggers at me with his eyes. "His daughter was severely traumatized. The only person who's ignoring that fact is you. Until you get your head out, talk to Vanna, and at least try to make up for how you treated her, you're not even close to making meaningful amends."

I shoved my hands into my pockets and stared at the floor. Of course.

"Joel." The firm, no nonsense tone in his voice forced me to look up. "That nobody died is miraculous. Clue in, man. You've hurt your wife, your son, your friend, and his daughter. They're family."

Tom's question about the apology was rhetorical.

My shoulders hunched as Alex's shrill voice echoed in my head, calling me a pussy, berating me for such cowardice.

"Have you started therapy or gone to marriage counseling yet? Aiden is giving you time to get it together, but he won't stay patient forever."

A mere waggle of my head was the only reply I could give. Anyway, who in their right mind would pay hundreds of dollars an hour to whine about feelings with a complete stranger? Not me. Ever.

Tom stared at me as if he could read the thoughts flying through my head. "It couldn't hurt to let out some of that anger."

"What anger?" I snorted. "Just because Dr. Hamilton loves therapy doesn't mean it's the only answer. Talking to some overpriced hack won't make it better."

"You, Joel Nichols, are a complete fucking moron." He spat out the words at me. "Your choice. Live in denial for the rest of your life, or deal with things like a man. Keep on this path and you'll lose everything." He threw his hand up before stalking from the room.

I scoffed and rolled my eyes upward. Whatever. He didn't know shit. Alex and I would be fine once everyone quit nagging about therapy. It wasn't like I'd meant for any of it to happen, but I'd learned my lesson. Why did we need to yap on about it at every opportunity?

Back in my office, I grabbed my coat, ignoring the buzz of my cell phone that was followed seconds later by the ping of a text notification. During the ride to the lobby I scanned the screen and then turned off my phone before heading into the brisk autumn air.

It would be a couple of hours before Alex would be done at that stupid appointment. I knew exactly where I wanted to be in the meantime.

⁓

"Honey. I'm home." With a bounce in my step, I progressed into the kitchen and wrapped Alex in my arms, planting a kiss on her luscious lips. "Smells deeeelicious."

"Yuck." She turned her head and dragged the back of her hand across her mouth. "You stink. Get off." Placing both hands flat against my chest, she shoved me away.

"Buzz kill."

"Why do you have a buzz for me to kill? Asshole." Alexis stepped backward as I advanced and spanned her waist with my hands. She wiggled free and wagged a finger in my face. "What about our session today? Where were you? Oh, wait." She jabbed her index finger into my chest. "You were at some pub drinking beer when you were supposed to be with me, working on our marriage."

"I told you I didn't want to go." I leaned against the counter and folded my arms across my chest. "We're doing fine without spending hundreds of dollars yakking about our feelings to some woman we don't even know. Besides, we're good, aren't we?"

"Yeah. Our marriage is fucking awesome." Her face became a blank mask as she mimicked me by crossing her own arms. "You agreed. No more drinking. You promised to work on us. Remember that, Joel? Was it all a lie?"

"I wasn't lying." I shook my head. "I love you."

Her face crumpled. "You sure don't act like it." She swiped at her cheeks with the back of her hand. "You were drinking. Next thing you'll tell me you were with the skank."

"Quit calling her that." I gritted my teeth. "She doesn't live in Boston, so how could I be with her?"

"Ha. You knew right away who I meant. It's not the first time she's gotten in the middle of our relationship."

"I didn't date her until after you and I broke up. That's not getting in the middle, Alexis. That's me moving on with my life after my girlfriend dumped my ass."

"Neither of you wasted any time, though. I left town and next thing I heard, you were with her. You didn't give us a chance, you just moved on." Her scorching look made me cringe. "Now we're married, yet she can't leave you alone. That makes her a skank."

"I haven't seen her since that day in the Vineyard." No point in arguing, I could spot a no-win situation. It would be fine as long as she didn't ask which day I referred to. "So take it down a notch or two."

"You had an affair with her, Joel. I have every right to be angry."

"An affair?" My blood ran cold as the words hit me. "I didn't have sex with her. You have to believe me." I raised my hands. "Who told you I had an affair?"

"If you'd gotten off your lazy ass and come to our session, then you'd know."

"Well, you'll have to inform me, since my lazy ass had to slave away at work to put food on our table. Anyway, I never said I'd come to the stupid session."

"You can never admit to anything, can you? Deny, deny, deny. Pretend everything's fine, that's you. But I'll tell you, Joel. I asked my therapist, and she agreed about the emotional affair. Emily was right."

I clenched my hands into fists. I'd been sold out. "Oh? Where did Emily get that ridiculous idea? Aiden?" My voice swelled and my entire body quivered. My so-called friends accused me of cheating? "What the fuck is an emotional affair? You're making shit up."

"An emotional affair is a real thing." A steely look appeared in her eyes. "Sneaking around, texting and confiding in an ex-girlfriend, and betraying my trust? Spending more time with her than your own wife and son? Sharing personal things about our relationship instead of talking to me and trying to resolve it? You've done all of those, and they equal an affair."

"I'm not having an affair. Anyone who says I am is dead wrong. I've never cheated on you. I'm allowed to have friends, though perhaps the people around me who I assumed were my friends aren't."

"Except they are. You want to pretend that running off and sharing our problems with Crystal is okay? It's not." She smacked her fist into the palm of her hand. "Grow up. Decide if you want to be in this with me or not. If not? Then you know where the damn door is." She fled from the room, sobbing.

Yet again, the echo of the slamming bedroom door carried through the apartment.

I slumped into a chair, my good mood evaporating. An affair. My wife had accused me of cheating. I buried my face in my hands, overwhelmed by my thoughts. I'd believed everything would improve, but instead, they'd become worse. Far, far, worse.

CHAPTER 9

I FLOPPED ONTO THE BED AND stared at the ceiling. So much for assurances. Joel's actions spoke volumes about his commitment—or lack of it, anyway. A wake-up call? Was that what he needed?

I crawled from the bed, brushing my fingers under my eyes. My tear ravaged face reflected back at me, and I splashed cold water on my cheeks, desperate to feel human. Time to learn some truths about my husband, even if I didn't truly want to know. I stared at the screen for a moment before dialing.

"What's up, Lex?"

"Can I ask you something?"

"Always."

"What happened between you and Joel that last day you went sailing?"

"Nothing."

"It had to be something."

"What did he say?"

"What time were you back?"

"Around eleven. Why?"

Thoughts whirled through my mind, the pieces fitting together as neatly as a jigsaw puzzle. Joel's words from that day in the Vineyard echoed in my ears.

"Lex? Are you okay?"

The numbness that crept over me was easier to bear than the burn of betrayal that was sure to follow. But no time to dwell as I was sure my son was now awake. "Daniel needs dinner."

I tapped the disconnect before taking several long breaths and wiping my eyes. Daniel's babbles carried through the air, but otherwise, the apartment remained quiet.

"Come on, little man. Let's eat," I said, lifting him from his bed and carrying him toward the kitchen.

Joel lay on the couch in the adjoining family room with his eyes closed and said nothing as I passed by. Dinner smelled overcooked to my sensitive nose, but that jackass ignored it. Maybe he'd passed out after his afternoon of swilling beer. I didn't know or even care at this point.

After fastening Daniel into his booster seat, I rescued the lasagna I'd slaved over this morning, examining the dark, crispy ring of almost-burnt cheese around the edge. Salvageable, at least.

Out of the corner of my eye, I spotted Joel leaning in the archway. Now he showed up? So damn typical of him these days, waiting until I had everything done. I yanked a knife from the butcher block and turned my back on him.

"Let me do that." He appeared at my side, removing the knife from my hand as if relieving me of a weapon fit to be driven straight through the blackest of hearts. Throwing a dark look my way, he served portions onto the plates I'd pulled from the cupboard.

Soon we were assembled at the table. Joel shoveled dinner into his mouth while I managed the occasional bite around feeding Daniel. I angled away from Joel and focused on our son. "More?"

Daniel nodded. "Noodos, Mommy." He pointed at his bowl and bounced in his highchair.

Joel grinned. "Did you hear that? He said noodles."

I glared. Daniel had first said noodles weeks ago.

An oppressive silence hung over us as I pushed the last few bites around my plate.

Joel rose as soon as he finished. "I'll bathe Daniel and get him ready for bed."

I set my lips in a flat line. It had been forever since he'd been home early enough to eat with us, let alone tuck his son into bed. All summer he'd been off in his own miserable little universe, and I'd been managing our son's needs while teetering on the edge of losing my sanity.

"You won't drown him?" I narrowed my eyes as I assessed his competency to take charge of our precious child.

"I'm not drunk." He exhaled a heavy sigh, combining it with an exaggerated eye roll. "I'd never do anything to hurt him."

As he spirited a babbling Daniel down the hallway toward the bathroom, I flicked on the sound system. Music always soothed my troubled soul, and I lost myself in the beat, hips swaying and head bobbing, becoming engrossed in the task of cleaning the kitchen. Raising my arms above my head, I swiveled around, my eyes closed and head thrown back.

"Nice dance moves."

I clutched my chest as my eyes popped open. "Quit sneaking around."

"I didn't sneak. You have the music cranked up so loud a bomb could drop and you wouldn't hear it. I tucked Daniel into bed and read him a story." He crossed his arms, leaning against the counter and smirking. "Are you relieved to hear he survived bath time?"

"I'll say good night." I slipped past, slapping away his outstretched hands.

Daniel had curled up with his arms wrapped around his favorite bear with his eyes closed. I kissed his temple, watching him for a moment before I turned off the light and tiptoed from his room, leaving the door open a crack.

By the time I returned to the kitchen, my upbeat music had changed to a sultry song I loved.

Joel appeared, wrapping me into his arms. Instead of pleading, he pulled me against his firm chest and swayed as the music drifted through the air.

My ultimate weakness. This song always made me melt, washing away my dark mood. Burying my head into his shoulder, I gave myself over to the soothing tones, enjoying being cradled in his strong arms, inhaling the sweet earthy tones of his aftershave.

He hummed against my hair, before crooning the lyrics into my ear in his sweet and mellow voice.

"Joel." My voice sounded husky. "You need to stop." Tears brimmed in my eyes as each word of the song sank into my aching heart.

"Why? Every single word is true. I'm sorry." He cupped my face between his palms, kissing me for so long, I lost the ability to breathe. "I love you, baby."

"Do you?" I dragged in a long breath, disentangling from his embrace and turning away. "You think every time we fight you can sweep me off my feet, take me to bed, and it'll be all better."

"I don't—"

"Yeah, you do. Don't deny it." A hot flush rushed into my cheeks. "You blew off our session and went drinking. How does that equal being sorry or loving me?" I bowed my head, focusing on the floor, avoiding the beautiful hazel eyes that would weaken me and make me come undone.

"I'm under pressure at work, and I needed to blow off steam."

"That's crap. Tom isn't cracking a whip over your head. You have to put in the hours to establish your practice in Boston, but not at the expense of your family. Remember when you sold me on this whole move?" I lifted my chin to stare him down.

He didn't blink those red-rimmed, bleary eyes trained in my direction.

"What about the promise that moving would allow us more family time? That joining Tom would give you more control over your hours. You said there'd be no more insane days or struggling to attain partnership."

"I don't work insane hours."

"So why are you never here? This summer we were supposed to reconnect, but you ignored us."

"Well, shit. Here we go again. Are you planning to nag and whine about it? I'd hoped we could put it all behind us."

"Fuck you, Joel. You spent our summer drinking and partying and leaving me to manage on my own. Am I to forget any of it happened? Give you a free pass?" I backed away as he advanced toward me, shaking my head. "Don't touch me."

"You know what? I bust my ass so you can stay home with our son. And then I get home, hoping for some peace and quiet, but the moment I walk in the door it's *Joel, do this. Joel, I need that.*" He smacked his flattened hand onto the counter, making me flinch. "You think I did all of this on my own? That our troubles are because I've been absent? Think again, baby cakes. You're just as guilty."

"Of what? Raising our son while wishing for my husband to spend time with us?"

"How about all those times when it was *not tonight, honey, I'm so exhausted* or *I don't want to go out because I don't want to leave Daniel.* You had time for the girls but nothing for me."

"Sorry for feeling less than sexy. I had a baby hanging off my chest most of the day, changed endless dirty diapers, not to mention the feedings at all hours. Then you'd come home all *hey, baby, let's get it on.*"

"Well, Jenna and Emily seem to manage fine. Tom and Aiden have sex lives with their wives. You cut me off." He sneered at me. "Their kids are three months old, and those guys both get lucky on a regular basis."

"You did not just say that." I cringed. "How dare you even compare. They both took time off and helped their wives, and Aiden takes care of Kellan full-time while Emily works."

"I bet that's a hardship. What? Did their hot Irish nanny quit on them? Boohoo." His lip curled. "Poor Aiden. He can't go back to work because of me."

"You're such an ass, but yeah, it's the truth. He can't. And Tom is home most nights for dinner, and they both get up and help with diaper changes and support their wives. You snored while I did everything for our son. Maybe if you had helped once in a while, you would've gotten lucky too."

"Yeah, right." He scoffed, rolling his eyes toward the ceiling. "And I did help."

"When I asked. Remember last summer when you were out on the deck with Daniel sitting in a nasty diaper? You didn't even notice. Who dealt with it? Aiden, that's who, and Daniel's not even his kid."

Joel mumbled something under his breath.

"If you want to make smart-ass comments, say them so I can hear them."

"It's always *Aiden this, Aiden that.* He's taken quite an interest in Daniel. Why is that, I wonder?"

"You're unbelievable." My whole body trembled as the hot flush crept up my neck. "The guest room is calling your name, asshole." The thought of sleeping beside him made my skin crawl. One more stupid comment out of his mouth, and I'd launch him off of the balcony.

"Huh. Fine." He performed the combined eye roll and head shake he'd perfected over the years.

How I longed to slap that smug look off of his face. I clenched my fists, willing myself not to move.

We glared at each other for the longest time before I spun and stalked into the bedroom, slamming the door behind me. I collapsed on the bed and dissolved into a weepy mess.

He'd given up on our marriage and me. He denied any wrongdoing and couldn't bother finding the will to try. I'd tried to fight and save us, but at this point, was there anything left worth fighting for?

CHAPTER 10

Joel

THE GRIM SET OF HER lips and narrowed eyes had me bracing for her to lunge across the room and wrap her hot little hands around my neck before squeezing until the life drained from my body. When the slamming door reverberated through the apartment my shoulders drooped, and I swept a hand across my face.

Maybe my comments went too far, but Aiden's position as golden boy irked me. The man did no wrong. Ever. *Oh, the irony.* Aiden had acquired a mountain of mistakes, but he'd barely cleared the age of thirty.

The man dished out advice yet his troubles with women were legendary, and him and Emily, well, those two had about killed each other. The woman left, not once, but how many times? Three? Four? I wouldn't have tolerated her shit, but Aiden refused to give up.

Emily had a softer side, a sweetness lacking in many of his previous ladies, but the aftermath in the Vineyard had sent a ripple of unease through our group. Tom's reaction to the news of Emily's departure and Aiden's temporary disappearance had been dramatic. The man bolted, staging an immediate rescue.

What happened with Tiffany all those years ago? I'd never been privy to that story. Maybe I never would be. Aiden hadn't trusted or confided in me as he had Tom, or even Alex. And no doubt Ryan knew.

Damn. I tipped my head back and groaned. Alex. I tiptoed down the hall, listening for the smallest sound from the master bedroom. Maybe she'd gone to sleep and it would be easy to retrieve my suit and tie for tomorrow. "Ally?" I tapped on the door before inching it inward.

"Get lost."

"I need—" The door shuddered as a heavy object thudded against it before clattering onto the hardwood floor.

In the morning, then.

Only one person understood my current troubles. One single person I wouldn't have to explain to, or justify to, or pretend with.

"Hey." She answered after two rings, her voice rising over the thump of club music in the background. "To what do I owe the pleasure of your call? Or maybe who?"

"What's up?" I managed to keep my tone casual. No point in crying into the phone like a pussy.

"Hanging out in the usual spot. Are you in town? Or still in Beantown?"

"Boston. Thought I might escape for the weekend and visit Ryan." Now the idea occurred to me, it seemed like a perfect plan. Get away from it all for a few days and give Alex a chance to chill out. "You'll be around?"

"Text me with your flight info, and we'll meet up."

"Perfect."

"You two fighting?"

"It's worse than usual. She banished me to the guest room."

"I'm sorry," she said. "Want to talk about it?"

"Not right now. I need sleep so I can slave away at work tomorrow. Talk later?"

"I'll text you. Night, honey."

I buried my head into my pillow, closing my eyes for a few moments before my phone buzzed.

Looking forward to this weekend.

It felt good to have someone say they wanted to see me, that they understood. Seconds later, another text appeared.

Hope we can get together Saturday night.

We will. See you soon.

A vague unease ran through me. Alex had no right to dictate who my friends were. Anyway, I wasn't doing anything wrong, and I needed someone to talk to. She'd be complaining about me to Aiden soon enough.

After sending a message to Ryan asking if I could stay with him, I closed my eyes. It took a while, but I managed to lose myself in sleep.

The next morning my luck held, and I managed to sneak in and out of the bedroom without disturbing the sleeping beast.

After a hot shower, and breakfast consisting of reheated coffee and a bagel, I tiptoed out the door. The longer I waited to straighten things out with Alex, the angrier she'd get, but I couldn't face her yet. Nope, I still had to break the news I'd be in Chicago for the weekend.

Ryan had responded and agreed to pick me up at the airport, and I'd booked my flights. I'd been to Chicago other weekends without Alex, so it wasn't unusual. Besides, she'd be thrilled to have me out of the way.

I dug into the pile on my desk, working straight through until noon before checking my phone. Nothing from my wife, but no surprise there. Crystal was a different story.

Can't wait to see you this weekend. How are you holding up?

Okay. Haven't talked to her since our fight. She's really pissed.

What did you do?

What didn't I do? She loses it over the smallest thing, and it's annoying the crap out of me.

We messaged back and forth for the next hour while I sorted paperwork, and by the end, I felt somewhat better. I still had to see Alex, my anger was dissipating.

After my afternoon client meetings, I cleaned off my desk and prepared to head home.

Tom stuck his head in the door. "I haven't seen you all day."

"I cleaned up a bunch of files before the weekend. Anything big for tomorrow afternoon?" I leaned against the wall and folded my arms across my chest, forcing the tension from my shoulders.

"Nope, I have court in the morning, and I promised Jenna we'd take Adrianna out for the afternoon."

"If I take off early, it's not a problem?"

"We've put in a ton of hours. Go home and spend some time with your family. Spoil your wife, she deserves it."

"Sweet." I snagged my briefcase and headed for the door.

As I let myself into the apartment, I heard music and voices as she talked to Daniel, and he answered in his high-pitched *I'm too excited to sit still* voice. During the waking hours, my little boy had only one speed—fast forward.

I plugged in my cell phone and laid it on the desk in the kitchen before entering the family room.

"Daaaddddeeeee." Daniel launched himself at my legs, wrapping his arms around me.

After a skillful dodge to avoid a painful collision, I scooped him up and tossed him into the air. Despite how little time I'd had with him over the summer, I loved this boy more than anything or anyone in the entire world. "Hey, champ. Did you have fun with Mommy today?"

"Yup." His head bobbed like it was on a string. "Went pak."

"Oh, that does sound fun. I need to change, be right back."

Alex hadn't said a word, but had her expression softened a teeny tiny bit?

When I returned, Daniel grinned and pushed his toy truck, making sputtering sounds. He squatted on his heels, inspecting the tower of blocks in the middle of the room.

"Should we load those blocks in the truck?" I dropped to my knees beside him, pointing at the pile.

"Bocks?" He tilted his head and examined me before plopping onto his bum and beginning the transfer. The moment that was done, he bounded across the room to play with his action figures.

Daniel barely finished one task before he raced off to another. He'd turned from a baby into an active little boy, and I made a mental note to buy him a soccer ball to kick around in the park before the weather turned cold and snowy.

Alex disappeared, the occasional rattle of pots and the savory smell of tomato alerting me she'd started on dinner.

Daniel tugged on my hand. "Play, Daddy."

I scooped him up and tossed him over my shoulder, grinning at his delighted squeal. We spent the next hour roughhousing, finally collapsing onto the couch. When I heard her footsteps, I looked up with a smile, eager to share my current state of bliss. I wished I hadn't.

Alex glowered, her eyes shimmering with tears. "Unbelievable. I thought maybe you'd changed, but you haven't. Pack your crap and get the hell out."

"Wha—"

"Shut up, shut up!"

Daniel whimpered, followed by a shriek and a cascade of tears as he bee-lined for Alex. She hugged him close before spinning and stalking toward the foyer.

The sound of the door and murmur of voices alerted me, but by the time I arrived the elevator had closed and returned to the lobby.

"Who was that? Where's Daniel?"

She crossed her arms. "Aiden picked him up."

"Why?"

"I asked him, that's why."

"Alex." I held up my hands and inched toward her, but she backed away.

"Don't touch me. Pack your bags and go. I'm done. I've tried, but you keep breaking your promises."

"I don't understand."

"You can look me in the eye and pretend you have no idea?" She waggled a cell phone in the air. "She can have you." Alex hurled it at me.

"Damn it." I fumbled as it rebounded off my chest and slipped through my fingers, tumbling to the tile with an unhealthy crunch.

"When were you planning to mention you're leaving me?" Tears streamed down her cheeks.

"Where'd you get that crazy idea?"

She uttered another choked sob as she hurried away. The bathroom door crashed shut.

I needed to assess the damage, but I was terrified to look. What had she seen on my phone that turned her hostile? Oh, holy shit. A new text. I was done for.

Can't wait to see you, baby. What time is your flight tomorrow? I'll pick you up.

My intention wasn't to cheat on Alex and I never had either. I wasn't the cheating kind of guy, even if the row of undeleted texts complete with a nauseating row of those damn little kissy and heart emojis running down the cracked screen made it seem otherwise. That's why Aiden picked up Daniel. He'd removed our son from the line of fire.

It didn't bode well. Alex had time to get extra riled, her imagination rampaging with scenarios and possibilities that led to this. I was screwed.

"Alex." I tapped on the door of the bathroom. "Sweetie? Please talk to me. It's not what you think."

The door ripped open. "How come she knew your plans when I didn't? Ever think to ask me? No. Course not." She shoved past, stomping toward the living room.

"I wanted to see my folks and get out of your way for a few days. You're angry. I figured you wanted space."

"You promised you wouldn't see her or talk to her or text her. So why do you have missed calls and little kissy face messages? Quit lying. I want you gone." She pointed toward the door. "Get out."

I shook my head even though I couldn't argue about promises made and broken. Last night I'd given in to my weakness, only wanting to talk to someone on my side. At least Alex hadn't figured out I'd seen Crystal that night in the Vineyard. If she had, she'd plunge a knife straight through my heart. "I'm sorry, I won't go. I didn't do anything with her."

"I don't care. Do whatever the hell you want." She folded her arms across her chest, her voice settling into an eerie calmness. "You've failed to take any of this seriously. You've broken every single promise. And you accused me of—of … sleeping with Aiden?"

"I didn't say that."

"Your sneaky little insinuations were enough. No wonder you neglect Daniel. You're such an asshole. I can't believe I ever loved you."

"Alex—" I stepped toward her, my hands outstretched, wanting to hold her and soothe her pain.

"No. You're out of chances." The façade of calm shattered as the flood of tears broke free. "Take your lying, cheating, promise-breaking ass, and get out of my sight."

Her whole body trembled, and she collapsed into the chair, flopping forward and dropping her head in her hands. Her shoulders shook as her dragging breaths rasped through the air.

"Alex." I froze with my hand only inches from her hair. I couldn't bring myself to touch her only to have her slap me away. Instead, I settled onto the couch opposite, bowing my own head.

That was it, then? All there was? There I sat, holding my head in my own hands, wondering where it all went wrong. I loved this woman with all my heart, yet now, there was only anger, resentment, and recriminations.

Getting married and welcoming our son into the world should have been the start of many years of happiness. Yet it had all come apart, fallen like the silent leaves that tumbled to the ground outside our windows. The question was—could we save our marriage? Ourselves? Was there anything left to save? How could two people who'd been so in love, now be so miserable?

My knees shook as I rose and hoped my legs would hold me up. I didn't have the strength to argue with her any longer. This time alone would be painful. Time to regret. Time to wonder if it was far too late.

CHAPTER 11

To SAY LIFE HAD BEEN hard these past months would be an understatement. As the leaves drifted from the trees, the vibrant autumn colors adorning the ground in a swath of bright oranges, reds, and golden yellows, I maintained a vigil, a powerless observer as my life and marriage crumbled to the ground. Endless tears had been shed in the name of love.

My body refused to obey the simplest command, so I balled up on the chair. Finding those awful messages on Joel's phone had doused the final flickering hope that we'd survive as a couple. Those hurtful, malicious texts laid out in clear and devastating terms how he felt about me and our faltering marriage. My husband had shared our private troubles … with her.

He'd broken every promise. I'd added up his caginess and refusal to talk about his whereabouts after the early return to port from the sailing trip with Tom and Aiden. Why else would he lie to me? It gave me zero joy to be right when I so wished to be wrong. Now I had solid, irrefutable facts to support my suspicions. He'd used lawyer speak to state a fact while still avoiding the bald truth.

He spoke in a rough and shaky voice. "I'll pack a bag and stay at a hotel for a few days."

"You can gather the rest of your crap next week. Text me, and I'll make sure we're out so you can do it without interference."

"You want me to … move out?"

"The sooner, the better." The last pieces of my heart shattered. Did he not get it? It no longer mattered if he'd had sex with the woman or not. Our marriage had collapsed because he refused to put in the effort to make it better.

"Please don't do this." He dropped in front of me, grasping my knees. "You can't mean it."

I curled up tighter, shoving his hands away. "But I do mean it. You can deny, and pretend, and justify all you like. You're damn good at selling a story, being a lawyer and all, but I'm not buying. We're done talking. Get out."

"I'm sorry, but I can't deal with the silence, and the anger, and—"

"You know what I can't deal with? The lying, the cheating, and the secrets. I won't put up with it. You want to be with her? Go. I don't want or need you."

"What about Daniel?"

"Like you care?" After his accusations and neglect how could I back down? "Don't concern yourself. We've managed for months without you."

Dead silence fell as his jaw dropped, and he swallowed hard. "I love you and Daniel, so much. I didn't mean it. It was a stupid thing to say."

"It doesn't matter. Even without your dumb-ass comments, we're done."

"Ally," he whispered. "I'm so sorry."

I couldn't answer. His actions had spoken so words were nothing but a waste of air. I buried my head in my arms to hide my tears, thankful my baby boy hadn't witnessed my meltdown.

A long deep sigh issued from Joel's chest, and he rose, his footsteps retreating. After forever, I sensed his presence in the room again. "I've packed enough for the weekend, and I'll let you know where I'm staying." He cleared his throat. "I'd never cheat, Ally. I love you."

"You love me? You *love me*?" All the pain of the summer surged through me. How could he be so blind? "If you gave a damn about me or your son, you wouldn't be making plans with another woman. You're texts made it pretty damn clear how you feel about me."

"It's not like that—"

"Isn't it? You might want to tell her that. She'll be thrilled. She got what she wanted."

"Which is?" He scrubbed a hand through his hair before he dropped it to his side.

"How can you be so naive and clueless? She helped destroy our marriage." I sniffled and peered up at him. "She can have you."

His eyes widened. Maybe the denial he'd been living in had worn thin, and the shell had begun to crack.

Perhaps I'd let it slide too long, but I'd been taught to never give up on those you love and to make a solid effort in everything. Now I had no choice but to call time of death on our relationship. If the other party refused to participate and make an equal effort, then what was the point?

Something Aiden said stuck out in my mind. *You can't help someone who doesn't want to be helped.* Maybe I could add my own observation. You can't love someone who doesn't want to be loved. Joel didn't want to be loved. At least not by me.

"This is really happening," he whispered. "You've given up on us. You don't love me anymore?"

"How can I ever trust you again?" I gazed at him, meeting those hazel eyes, refusing to allow them to hold any power over my heart. "Don't you understand? Your lies and half-truths and deceptions have caught up with you."

"This isn't …" A ragged exhale tore from his chest, followed by the rustle of his overnight bag as he draped the strap over his slumped shoulder. "If that's what you want." His brows drew together and he stared at me for an interminable time before he headed toward the foyer with slow measured steps.

The sound of the closing door created an odd sense of relief, tempered with deep disappointment. Even though I knew I'd made the right decision, the apartment felt massive and empty, the silence oppressive and heavy. My new reality sank in, and I closed my eyes.

⌒≼

My phone buzzed, rousing me from a deep, dreamless sleep.

"Hi," I mumbled through the despair that clung to me.

"Are you all right?" Emily asked.

"No, but not much I can do about it." I rubbed at my tired, gritty eyes.

"Do you want to talk about it?" Emily's soft voice reassured me.

"Not yet. Can you keep Daniel until tomorrow?" I assumed from her question they didn't know I'd booted Joel out of our apartment. It made total sense. Why would Joel call Aiden?

"Of course, anything we can do to help. Call if you need anything," she said. "Or you could stay overnight if you need to get out of the house."

"I'm alone," I whispered. "Joel's gone. I kicked him out."

"What happened?"

I burst into tears, no longer able to hold back the rising tide. "He's a ch-cheater and a liar. He texted that woman again, and said awful things. It's over."

"For good?" She sighed. "You shouldn't be alone. Do you want me to stay with you?"

"No." I didn't have the energy for anything and gathering myself to make the trip to their house felt impossible, as did the thought of making any sort of conversation.

"I'll send Aiden."

"No. I'll call tomorrow." I sank lower into the sofa and pulled a throw from the back, hauling it over me. My hands shook so hard I fumbled with my phone, tightening my grip on the tiny device. "Kiss Daniel for me."

"Don't worry, I will."

I hung up and tossed my phone onto the table, curling into a ball. Alone. That's what I was, yet again. The satisfaction of booting my husband's ass out of our house wasn't much of a consolation. How could it be? He was about to leave me anyway.

The ugly truth invaded my thoughts. The man I loved no longer loved me. The inevitable had come to pass. My marriage had ended.

CHAPTER 12

Joel

THE MOMENT THE PLANE TOUCHED down in Chicago, I turned on my phone. It vibrated and several text messages arrived in succession. I scrolled through, but they were all from people I'd been ignoring. Only one person mattered right now, and her final text made my stomach clench into a knot.

I want a divorce.

I stared at her words, unable to delete them even while refusing to believe them.

My arms felt heavy as I dragged my carry-on bag from the overhead bin, my footsteps leaden as I escaped the stifling confines of the airplane. I stumbled into the nearest men's bathroom, flattening my palms against the damp counter, sucking for air.

A divorce. My eyes burned and I clenched them shut, bowing my head. It couldn't end like this, could it?

At the sound of rushing water sloshing into the sink beside me, I opened my eyes, averting my gaze from the concerned looks of my fellow traveler. Time to pull it together. Shake it off. I straightened and turned on the tap, the cold water soothing against my skin as I pressed my hands to my face.

I forced my legs into motion, dodging through the concourse to the designated meeting area for my flight.

"Hey, Joel." Ryan's voice rang out from behind me.

"You're here. Thought I'd be cabbing it." I pasted on a smile and hugged my friend.

"Nah, I didn't forget." He clapped me on the back. "Surprised you wanted to stay with me. I thought you'd bring Alex and the rug rat and stay with your folks."

My noncommittal shrug was met with a raised brow, but he only beckoned me to follow him to his SUV and stowed my bag in the back.

"What gives?" After a glance at me, he pulled onto the main road. "You're too damn quiet."

By now we should be catching up, joking, and laughing, but I didn't have the energy. Instead, I sunk lower in my seat and closed my gritty eyes. Last night, a never-ending replay of Alex's words had run through my mind as I tossed and turned in a hotel bed.

Ryan tapped his fingers on the steering wheel, flicking the controls to change the music streaming from the stereo. "This should be a fun visit. I'll just talk to myself."

"Alex kicked me out." I peered at him.

"Huh?" As he glanced my way, his eyebrows rose. "Did you just say …?"

The city streets flashed by, blurring together. Saying it out loud made it far too real.

"Dude. You left Alex? That's why you're here and she's not?"

The lump lodged in my throat prevented me from uttering a single word.

A frown formed on Ryan's face, and moments later he pulled into the lot of the neighborhood pub our gang frequented before we moved to Boston. He motioned toward the bar. "I bet you need a drink. We'll grab dinner, play pool, and you can tell me what the fuck is happening. Let you guys out of my sight and all hell breaks loose."

"Yeah," I muttered, yanking on the door handle. I appreciated that Ryan wasn't as close to Alex as the rest of my friends, so maybe he'd spare me the lecture and hear my side of the story. Being a confirmed bachelor, he had a unique viewpoint compared to my married family-man type friends.

The pub bustled with office workers who'd escaped for the weekend, but we managed to claim one of the last vacant booths near the back. Ryan ordered us a round, and we sipped our ice-cold beer.

Ryan tapped his fingers and threw looks at me from across the table. He heaved out a long sigh. "What'd you do?"

"Why do you think it was me? Maybe Alex did something."

"She kicked you out. Ergo, it was you." He jabbed a finger in my direction. "Spill, buddy. I've been way out of the loop since you asses ran off to Boston."

"Blame Aiden. He started it." I flipped the menu open, burying my nose in it to avoid Ryan's gaze.

"Don't bullshit me." He squinted.

"I don't know? She's up in arms about everything these days. I love her, but how do I deal with the constant nagging? Be home more, spend more time with Daniel, work harder to afford the move to Boston. But don't expect any affection. Not to mention the constant refrain of *why can't you be more like Aiden and Tom?* So damn annoying."

"Oh." Ryan rolled his eyes. "I get it. You're mad because you're not getting any, and you're being compared to the Dream Team."

"Funny guy." I threw him the darkest look I could muster in my miserable state. It wasn't too hard, my soul felt jet-black, and even the thought of Alex shot pain through my heart. "We were on the road to recovery, but now she's on about counseling. After this summer and the whole Aiden overboard crap …" I shrugged.

"I heard about the adventure on the high seas. Bet you won't be invited sailing anytime soon. But I don't get why you're bent out of shape about those guys. They're like her big brothers. You should know that by now. Besides, they're both married to gorgeous ladies. Not that Alex isn't, but—"

I slammed my bottle on the table. "I don't want to talk about it anymore." The last thing I needed to hear was how wonderful those guys' lives and wives were. I clenched my drink and pasted on a smile. "What's new with you?"

"I met someone." A sappy grin appeared. "Her name's Kaari, and we've been dating for six months. I asked her to move in with me."

"Not you too. I thought you'd be single forever. The incorrigible bachelor." I snickered at the expression on his face.

"Fuck off, mate."

"Joel." A feminine voice purred next to me.

"Oh, hey … Crystal." I cursed that I'd forgotten she hung out here.

I had no choice but to slide over and allow the woman to sit.

A frown settled over Ryan's features and he widened his eyes.

"Ryan." Gwen appeared and pushed at Ryan with perfectly manicured fingertips.

These two women were like glue. One of them appeared and the other followed. Perhaps because they were both single.

Ryan didn't look the least bit happy at the intrusion. "What brings you here?"

"I heard Joel would be in town and thought I'd drop by to say hi." Crystal wiggled closer, her thigh pressed against mine. "Haven't seen him since the Vineyard."

The server picked that moment to come by, handing menus to the ladies.

Ryan's brows lowered, his lips thinning as he squinted at me. Our guys' night had been hijacked.

As soon as we'd ordered, Crystal dragged me to the nearest pool table and shoved a pool cue into my hands.

"You left the little wife at home, right?" She curled her fingers around the stick and chalked the tip as she eyed me.

"Alex is in Boston." I racked the balls.

"Good, it'll be more fun this way. Ladies first." She leaned over the table, wiggling her hips as she lined up to break.

The balls scattered across the surface, but none of them sank into a pocket.

Crystal smiled and motioned to the table. "You're up." She waved down the passing waitress to order another round as I set up my first shot.

Soon we were both laughing and joking, and I banished my domestic issues. Maybe the beer helped, but it felt great to not think about it, even for a little while. That's what always happened with Crystal. She enabled me to escape and pretend everything would be okay.

⌒≼

After our meal, we returned to the pool table, this time with Gwen and a reluctant Ryan in tow.

Ryan glanced at his watch and raised his brows at me.

"Hot date?" Gwen ran a fingertip down his arm.

He brushed her off and skirted around to stand beside me. "We should go, Joel."

I watched Crystal as she smacked the cue ball. "You can go if you want."

His gaze traveled over the two women who were now shimmying to the music and laughing. "And leave you alone with those two man-eaters?" He rolled his eyes. "Not a chance."

Crystal swayed over to join us and entwined her fingers with mine. "Dance with me." She tugged me onto the tiny crowded patch designated as the dance floor. One of her arms curled around my neck, her sweet breath wafting across my skin as she nibbled on my earlobe.

I closed my eyes and buried my head in the crook of her neck, losing myself in the music and savoring her closeness. Alcohol buzzed through my system, and a smile twitched my the corner of my mouth.

She pressed a kiss to my temple, maneuvering to capture my lips, the sweet taste of liquor on her tongue, her lithe body against mine, and a heady sense of intoxication swept through me. Her hands roved and caressed my body as her floral perfume swirled around me.

Her soft curves felt amazing under my fingertips, and I pictured how it would feel to be with her, with her silky limbs wrapped around me...

"Why don't we get out of here?" The soft purr of her voice against my ear sent a shiver down my spine. One of her hands slid down, rubbing me through my pants.

I froze as Crystal's face morphed into another woman's in my mind. Alex. The way she'd looked into my eyes with such tenderness that last time we'd made love, followed by her tears, her voice changing from sweet to harsh tones as she accused me of being a lying, cheating bastard. Was I? Allowing this woman, the cause of those angry words, to touch me, to kiss her in return, and to fantasize about her naked flesh against mine…

I pushed her back. "Stop. I can't …"

She leaned into me. "You know you want to. You aren't getting the loving you deserve. She doesn't even want you anymore." A coquettish smile formed as she trailed a fingertip down my chest. "Remember what it's like to be with a woman who wants it? You'll enjoy it, baby."

A hand grasped my arm, and Ryan propelled me toward our table, his eyes blazing. He shoved my coat at me and hauled me through the exit, shoving me toward his SUV. "Get in. What the fuck are you doing?" Ryan slid behind the wheel and yanked his door closed. "No wonder she kicked your ass to the curb. I never expected that from you. Idiot."

"I didn't do anything." The cool leather enveloped me as I leaned back against the seat, my words slurring out through numb lips. "Jus' a kiss…"

"Tell that to Crystal. Next, she would've dragged you into the bathroom for a quickie. Hell, she might have stripped you naked on the damn dance floor."

His incensed words poured over me as I exhaled a deep sigh. My eyelids were too heavy, and darkness descended.

Chapter 13

Alexis

$\mathcal{M}$Y EYELIDS FLUTTERED AS THE odd sensation of floating crept over me. A pair of strong, muscular arms cradled me, and I wiggled, intent on breaking free. "Lemme go." I pummeled at the firm chest.

"Relax. It's me." The familiar deep voice soothed me. "I'm putting you in bed. That couch isn't the best place to sleep." A soft mattress greeted me as he laid me on the bed and tucked the duvet around me.

"Is Daniel okay?"

"He's fine. Emily and Jenna are keeping him entertained. Get some rest." He smoothed back my hair and kissed my forehead.

The tears welled up, and I clutched his arm. "Don't leave me." Even the idea of being alone for another long and miserable night was unbearable. Talking to Aiden always made me feel better. "Lie down with me, please?"

"I'll call Em and tell her you're okay. We were all worried about you."

He stepped into the hall, the low tone of his voice carrying back to me.

I struggled to sit and plucked at my top. I fought my way out of my tight jeans and fluffy sweater. Where were my favorite sleep pants? "They have to be here," I said under my breath as I crawled across the bed in my bra and panties.

"Alex? What're you doing?" Aiden leaned in the doorway, watching me with a frown.

"Pajamas?" I peeked at him, pushing my hair back before patting at the duvet.

"Alex?"

"My blue ones." I collapsed in the middle of the bed, sobbing.

"Here." He strode to my dresser and dug into the drawer, coming up with the pair I'd wanted. "Can I get you something? Maybe water or tea?"

I nodded, and he exited the bedroom.

While he was gone, I divested myself of my bra, yanked on the pajamas, and crawled under the covers. Goosebumps rose on my flesh as I drew the duvet up to my chin.

He reappeared, offering a glass of ice-cold water and setting a cup of steaming tea on the nightstand. "Better?"

"Uh-huh." I sipped the water, tapping the bed beside me. He obliged and allowed me to wriggle over to rest against his chest as he wrapped an arm around me.

"What am I going to do? He didn't even fight it. Did you know he planned to go to Chicago?"

"No. It's not like he confides in me these days." He kissed my temple and stroked my hair. "I'm sorry. It sucks seeing you two fall apart, and I wish I could do more to help."

"He's such an asshole." More tears fell, but I didn't bother to hold them back for Aiden's benefit. "Stupid jerk made a ridiculous comment about Daniel. He acts like he's not even his son."

"What?" Aiden narrowed his gaze. "Just whose kid does Joel think he is?"

I wiped at my cheeks, keeping my head down.

"What aren't you telling me?"

Now I had no choice but to spill it. "He insinuated that … you and I … you know?"

"So … he implied that Daniel's mine?" Aiden let out a long exasperated sigh. "How long have he and I been friends? I'd love to beat some sense into him."

"Do you plan to chase after him?" I cuddled closer to Aiden. "I've told him that you're my brother." The lump in my throat choked me up. "He's one to talk."

"Don't stress over her. Ryan called, and Joel is staying with him over the weekend. He's not with Crystal."

"For now."

"Don't fret, sweetie." He handed me my tea, propping me against him while I sipped the soothing hot liquid. "You can count on Ryan to keep him in line."

"This is embarrassing." I buried my head. "Everyone knows he's cheating. And you've done so much for us, I don't know what I'll do. We're up to our eyeballs in debt, I have no job, and this apartment …" Thought after thought rambled through my overwrought mind. Aiden could lose every dime of the money he'd lent Joel if my soon-to-be-ex-husband imploded.

"You need to calm down. I'd never let you or Daniel end up on the street. We're family, and we'll never let you fall."

I set my empty cup aside and squirmed around to get comfortable, allowing Aiden's steady heartbeat to lull me into a half-awake state. It seemed like forever since anyone had held me like this, with no expectations, with only complete love and tenderness. The comfort I drew from his presence helped me shut down the swirling thoughts.

I woke up with a start about the time the room brightened with natural light. My eyes snapped open.

"Oh. You scared me." I sat and rubbed at my eyes.

Emily seemed frozen in the doorway, a frown on her face. "Sorry."

"What's happening?" I mumbled, taking in her expression and narrowed eyes. I turned my head and realized Aiden slept beside me.

He'd sprawled face down on top of the duvet. Sometime during the night, he'd divested himself of his shirt and jeans, leaving him in only a pair of boxer-briefs.

"Oh, this isn't …" I half expected to find Emily behind me with claws extended, ready to gouge out my eyes.

"Relax." She waved her hand, and her frown disappeared. "He told me he'd stay over. How are you?"

"Better now that I had some sleep." I shrugged, not knowing how to answer. What do you say to the woman whose arguably hot husband was almost naked on your bed? It would have been funny if I didn't feel numb from shock.

I'd kicked my husband out of our home, and he'd left without a fight. Flown away to Chicago to do who knows what with another woman without a backward glance, instead of begging for forgiveness and saying he couldn't live without me.

"Can I get you something? Maybe a hot bath and some breakfast?"

"I'm not hungry, but a bath sounds marvelous. How's my little man?"

"Great. Jenna and Vanna are watching the kids. I thought maybe you'd like to get out of the house. We could take the kids to the park. It's sunny and warm today. Or …" She sashayed around the end of the bed and smacked Aiden on that fine, well-toned ass. "We could leave Aiden and Tom with the kids, and us ladies could enjoy some pampering at the spa. Up, sleepyhead." She brushed her hand over his broad, tanned back.

"Hey, trying to sleep here." He rolled and grabbed Emily, pulling her in for a kiss. "Morning."

"Good morning, honey." She caressed his cheek with her fingertips. "What do you think? Can you manage the kids for a few hours?"

"Sounds like fun. I'd bet Tom and I could survive the rug-rats. Leave me bottles for Kellan." He stretched and sat on the edge of the bed, and then pulled on the jeans Emily dumped into his lap. "I need coffee and a shower."

"Getting out would be good. After a hot shower, coffee, I'll be ready." If Joel was out having fun, I'd do the same. Damned if that man would keep me down.

"Sounds like a plan. I'll call Jenna and fill her in while you to get dressed." Emily pointed to a bag by the bedroom door. "Aiden, I brought some clothes if you want to shower and change."

"Thanks, Em." He paused to kiss her before he headed toward the door.

I noted how Emily's gaze followed as her husband disappeared into the hallway.

"Sorry for keeping Aiden all night."

"He's not shy, is he? I'm still not used to that."

"What the hell does the man have to be bashful about?" I grinned.

"Ha, true."

"I promise it won't happen again. I'm all pissed about Joel and Crystal, and then Aiden stays here with me. It couldn't have been thrilling to find your husband half-naked on my bed."

"It's not the same, Alex. Put it out of your mind."

"Thanks." I hugged her, relieved that I hadn't caused issues for Aiden and Emily.

Aiden's presence had helped. Last night had been the longest I'd slept in at least a week, and the security of knowing I'd never be on my own even if Joel and I split had helped. My own family had formed right here in Boston, and it consisted of these close friends. We'd bonded, becoming our own tight-knit and loving unit. Hope rose within me. I could survive this. Life would go on while I raised my beautiful baby boy—with a little help from my friends.

CHAPTER 14

Joel

MY FACE SMACKED INTO THE mattress. "Ouch." I peeled open my bleary eyes and massaged my nose.

Ryan loomed over me. "Surprised you can feel anything." He tossed my pillow aside, showing no concern for my pounding head. "You're not lying around in bed all day because you can't control your drinking, dumb-ass."

My tongue seemed unwilling to obey my basic command to form words. "Whadda ya want?" I mumbled through a dry, cottony mouth and over parched lips.

"For you to get your ass out of bed."

This grouchy, bossy Ryan wasn't real. We were drinking buddies. We'd shared many hangover following a Friday night at the bar. We'd sit around and watch sports, eat pizza, drink more beer …

I looked at his stormy face. "I'm sick."

"You mean hung-over." Ryan tipped the mattress.

I hit the hardwood with a thump. "Ouch. Fuck, man. What's your problem?"

His lip curled as he wrinkled his nose. "You reek." He stalked out, leaving me curled up on the cold floor, clutching my pounding head.

So much for being an ally and brother-in-arms.

I dragged myself from the floor and into the bathroom, sniffing each armpit. A rank, nauseating mixture of vomit, stale beer, and sweat permeated my nostrils, and I recalled hugging the porcelain bowl during the night. *Yuck.* I even disgusted myself.

The blasting hot shower provided some relief, and I leaned back against the tile, little flashes of the night before taunting me. *I didn't kiss her, did I?* My chest tightened, and I hauled in a labored breath as the emotions poured over me. Why? I should've walked—no, run—from her. Engaging in kissing and intimate touching with Crystal had been insane. No question, my impaired judgment and loss of control would bite me in the ass.

Worse, Ryan witnessed the entire sordid affair, and he'd never let me live it down. But I consoled myself with the knowledge that he wouldn't call Alex ... would he?

After yanking on a pair of jeans and a soft sweater, I headed into the kitchen. A fresh pot of coffee and oversized mug beckoned me.

Ryan paced back and forth in front of the French doors, his phone pressed to his ear. "I hear you." He glared and turned his back. "Sure, no problem." My friend stepped onto the deck, the door clicking shut behind him.

Who was he talking to in those hushed tones? Maybe it was his new woman, that Kaari chick. Somehow, I doubted it. An ominous feeling crept over me at the continuous glances flying in my direction.

I slumped onto the couch, slurping at the hot brew, allowing it to soothe my raw throat. As the caffeine coursed through my system, the shake of my hands subsided.

"You found the shower and the coffee. Good man." Ryan sat across from me, stroking his jaw. "What gives?"

"What do you mean?"

"Don't play dumb. Why would you waste your time with an easy woman like that? I have no plausible explanation for your stupidity. You have a beautiful and amazing wife, yet you let that ho crawl all over you?" He threw his hands upward, shaking his head.

I shrugged, pushing up from the couch to pour another cup of coffee.

He crossed his arms and narrowed his eyes. "Not good enough."

"Things aren't so wonderful with Alex, and Crystal listens to me. She's fun to be around. Alex is all serious about everything, and she bitches at me every moment of every day."

"That's why you have a guys' night, but it doesn't involve picking up a ho and cheating on your wife, dumb-ass."

"You been talking to Tom? Oh, let me guess ... Aiden?" I glowered. "You sound an awful lot like them. When did you get so damn boring?"

"Shit, man." Ryan scrubbed at his face. "You're fucking everything up, you know? You want to know why I always make those comments, calling you all whipped and stuff?"

"Because you love being single and think we're a bunch of pussies?"

"No, you moron. I'm envious. Damn, Aiden was as single as I was, and then he's announcing he has a daughter and saying, 'I do' to that super fox Emily. I thought he'd be the last of us to find the one and do all the daddy stuff after the Tiffany debacle. Tom took Jenna off the market, and you claimed our sweet little Alex. I'd give anything to have a woman look at me that way, to have someone vow they wanted to be with me forever. You had that, Joel, and you blew it." His lip curled. "Even worse, fucking it up over the likes of Crystal. What the hell are you thinking, man."

"You …" I could only stare. My mind wouldn't absorb his words. "You're jealous?"

"If I had a Jenna, Alex, or Emily waiting at home, that's where I'd be. I don't love the single life, but it's not easy to find a special woman. Believe me, I've tried."

I swirled my coffee before taking a large gulp. Ryan always seemed so carefree and content with his bachelor lifestyle.

"Don't even get me started on your pathetic attempt at drowning one of our best friends, or your idiocy in putting Vanna in danger. I don't think anyone's gotten over that."

"Aiden's fine." I waved a hand.

"Fucking fine?"

"Owww." My ear stung from the force of the slap Ryan dealt upside my head. "Take it easy, man."

"He almost died, you stupid …" He lunged off of the couch, turning to place his flattened palms on the counter before bowing his head. "You're unbelievable," he muttered. "He's not fine. He's skilled at hiding his true feelings. You're delusional."

"What do you mean?" I frowned, striving to clear my muddled brain.

"You haven't even bothered to ask." Ryan shook his head.

"I did ask. We've been out a couple times, and I apologized."

Ryan narrowed his eyes, anger simmering within them. "Apologized?"

"What? I did."

"Never mind." He scrubbed his hands over his face and turned away, moving with forceful steps into the kitchen, huffing as he rinsed the pot and added fresh coffee grounds and water. His shoulders hunched as he slammed a frying pan on top of the gas range.

"What aren't you telling me?"

He glowered in my direction.

"Ryan." Pain shot through my temples, and I massaged them with my fingers. "He's my friend. I have the right to know what's going on."

"Oh, do you." His brows shot upward. "You've been a shit friend. Only an insignificant little man-child abandons their wife and son."

In a few strides, he'd covered the space between us, and he slapped my cheek hard, then again.

I rubbed my cheek to ease the sting. "Hey. If I wanted abuse, I could've stayed in Boston."

"Good idea. Get your stupid ass back to Boston. I'm sick of looking at you."

"Huh. Some friend you are."

"Count yourself lucky I dragged your sorry butt out of that bar before you did something you'd regret. Crystal doesn't give a damn about your troubles. Take your pathetic ass home before it's too late."

His words struck me as hard as his slaps, and I bowed my head. "What's the difference? She's done with me." My eyes burned. "Alex wants a divorce." I buried my face in my hands. How could I let Ryan, of all people, see my tears?

"Damn, Joel. Why didn't you tell me it had gotten that bad?" The couch sank under his weight. "When did this happen?"

"Yesterday. By text. It's too late."

"Except it's not. We've all made mistakes and begged for forgiveness. Are you ready to pull your shit together? Get your wife back, watch that adorable little man of yours grow up, and make me jealous of your sickening happiness?"

My shoulders shook, and I couldn't hold it back any longer. I pinched the bridge of my nose, struggling to hold it in, but something tore loose, a rivulet of tears trickling down my cheeks. I wept for everything I'd lost, every mistake, every angry word.

"Hey." Ryan squeezed my shoulder. "You love her, right?"

My throat tightened, making it impossible to force out even a single, solitary word. I bobbed my head.

"Then fix it. Go home to your wife and son. Don't let it end this way. You'll regret it. Forever."

Chapter 15

Alexis

Pattering footsteps echoed from the hallway before Daniel bounded through the doorway and lunged onto the bed.

"Mama."

"Morning, lovely boy." I grabbed him and squeezed, dropping kisses on his sweet face. His adorable giggles made me smile as I nibbled at his neck. "Ready for breakfast?"

"Yup." He nodded. "Egg n' toes."

"Eggs and toast it is." I balanced him on my hip and shuffled down the hall to the kitchen, tucking him into his booster chair with a toddler cup of water.

He babbled as I scrambled the eggs and sliced fruit, thumping on the tray with his spoon.

"Here you go. Breakfast." I placed the small plate in front of him.

"Stawbear?" He inspected the bright red berry before biting into the sweet fruit.

A dribble of strawberry juice ran down his chin and I dabbed at it, smiling. It felt peaceful here with my son as we enjoyed our simple breakfast. Daniel seemed content, no thanks to Joel. I gave credit where it was due. Tom and Aiden filled the empty space left by Daniel's daddy and I owed them my eternal gratitude and my son's happiness.

Yesterday's mud wrap, long massage, manicure, and pedicure, followed by a long overdue haircut, had refreshed me. The camaraderie of Emily, Jenna, and Savannah cheered me immensely.

After our afternoon of indulgence, we'd returned to Emily and Aiden's where the savory smells of a fantastic gourmet meal greeted us. Daniel had been fed and bathed, and Vanna had taken over his care after we all shared a leisurely dinner.

After last night's deep and dreamless sleep, I felt prepared to make plans for my future. The dark clouds had hung overhead for far too long, and I couldn't live with them any longer. The all-consuming gloom and doom attitude needed to be banished while I took the necessary steps to be happy.

The mild fall weather enticed me to dress Daniel and head outdoors. It wouldn't be long before the days became shorter and colder, and we'd be confined indoors as winter descended. We started down the street but didn't get far.

"Pak. Pak, Mommy, pak." Daniel bounced in the stroller and kicked his legs.

"You want to play in the park?"

"Yup." His gap-toothed grin made it impossible to say no. Daniel charged toward the play structure the moment I freed him.

I spent the next blissful hour chasing him around the playground. How should I be so lucky to have this beautiful boy with such a sweet and sunny disposition? But then Joel's mother always commented how adorable and loving her son had been as a child.

The smile faded from my lips, and my good mood evaporated. This wonderful boy might be the only child I ever had. When Joel and I married, I'd imagined at least three children, but my dream dissolved as our marriage fell apart.

I pushed the dangerous thoughts of Joel away. Why torture myself and picture what he might be doing in Chicago? It wasn't my concern. Not anymore. He'd made his choice, so I'd made mine.

Perhaps it was time for me to return to the working world. I'd trained in interior design, but I had given it up to stay home when Daniel was born. Now I drifted, the events of the past months a reminder I'd become far too dependent on Joel for everything. If I could find even a part-time position, I'd utilize my expensive education and regain some independence.

I longed to be more than someone's wife or mother. I wanted to be me again. A real person with their own hopes and dreams, not a wife who'd given up everything to support the husband who'd betrayed her.

~⤬

We arrived at the apartment in the mid-afternoon, Daniel whining and kicking as I wiggled the shoes from his feet. He rubbed at his eyes, his lids drooping.

"Nap?" I carried him down the hall and tucked him into his bed, hoping he wasn't overtired. Those afternoons were always the worst. "Have a good sleep, sweetheart." I kissed his temple before shutting his door.

I tiptoed down the hallway with fingers crossed. My luck held, silence reigning as I reached the living room, and I breathed out a long sigh.

"Alex."

"Joel." I clutched my chest. "What are you doing here?" I crossed my arms. "You were supposed to call before you came to pack your things."

"I'm sorry, I didn't mean to scare you." He hung his head. "Can we talk?"

"What's left to say? How you've crawled home after visiting your little trash bag in Chicago? No thanks. I'm not interested in her leftovers. Please leave, and call before you come to clear your clothes from the closet."

"I didn't sleep with Crystal. I stayed with Ryan, and he made me realize something."

"Oh? What's the big epiphany?" *Asshole.*

"I've been an idiot. I can't bear to lose you or Daniel, and," Joel said as he took several steps toward me, "please let me come home." He sank to his knees. "I'm ready to do the work, go to counseling, anything you desire. Please?"

His arms sneaked around me, and he clung to my legs with his head pressed against my belly.

Doubts crowded my mind as my heart tore in two. What if I said yes, and he did it all again? It seemed we'd been in this exact spot before, with him promising me the world yet indulging himself with further bad behavior.

But what if I said no? What if he walked out that door forever, and I regretted it? Daniel needed his father, and Joel wasn't a bad person. I'd known him forever and loved him since we were teenagers. Maybe he'd simply lost his way.

"I don't know if I can." The words released from my throat along with all of my fears. "You've said it all before, you vowed you'd try, and you didn't, and then you made plans with her. Are you being honest? You didn't see her in Chicago?"

"Alex." He took my hands in his. "I promise, I've never slept with her."

Alarm bells rang. "You saw her?"

"I'm sorry. I didn't plan it. She showed up at the pub while I was there with Ryan." He took a long ragged breath, his voice quivering. "She kissed me, but I stopped her, and then Ryan and I left, and I haven't seen her or talked to her or texted her. It's you I love, and I couldn't do it. You made me leave, and the whole idea of divorce is devastating, and"—his body shook as he buried his head against me—"I love you."

Devastating? That word echoed in my ears as I yanked away, turning and sucking for air. Ironic. That's what my swirling thoughts fought to grasp and make sense of—the complete and utter devastation as it swept through me. My stomach twisted and bile rose as the horrible picture of my husband kissing that woman flashed before my eyes. My legs folded, and I crumpled to the floor, dissolving into tears, surrendering to the awful empty numbness pervading every corner of my being. How could I ever trust him again?

"Ally, sweetie, please."

The cold seeped through my quaking body as I curled up on the tile, my soul tearing into pieces. The damned man had done it again, coming at me with his promises, sweet talk, and those meaningless words. *I love you* flowed too easily from those treacherous lying lips. I cradled my head and clapped my hands over my ears to block everything out.

"Ally?" He pulled my stiff and unwilling body onto his lap, rocking me as his own sobs reached my ears. "Forgive me. I promise nothing happened. I never kissed her before. I've never cheated. I promise. I can't go on without you."

I shook my head, struggling to catch my breath. "Oh, Joel, why'd you do that to me? You kissed her? You say you've never cheated, yet you kissed her. For months, you've put that woman above me. Above Daniel. Above your friends." I pushed at his arms, wiggling to free myself. "How can I—"

"Please listen."

"—you say Daniel's not your son."

"Alex, stop."

Confusion clouded my thoughts and I blinked hard.

"Listen, please?" He reached for me.

I shoved his hands away and crawled across the floor, desperate to escape not only his touch but also the torment in my heart. "You've broken us. There's no way back. Once a cheater, always a cheater."

"Don't say that. I'll never speak to her again, I swear." His shaky words pursued me. "The Daniel comment was stupid. I admit it. I'm jealous, okay? Aiden breezes through life, while I can't—"

"What?" My mind grasped at his words. *Jealous? Of Aiden?* That ridiculous notion made no sense. How could Joel ever say it, let alone think it?

"Breezes? After what he's endured?" *The sweet man pretended and covered, but underneath unexpressed pain lurked* ... How after all these years was Joel so damn clueless? "This isn't about him. It's about you, and me, and broken promises. I hate this part of you. I don't know if I can forget or forgive," I said, jabbing a finger at his chest, "any of it."

"How do I make it up to you? I'll do anything if you'll give me one last chance. Anything. Please, Ally."

My eyes blurred with tears and I stared at the trembling mess of Joel, the arms wrapped around his knees, the shiny red eyes. My inhaled breath sounded rough, and I rubbed at my sore, puffy eyes, failing to stem the cascade of salty drops dripping from my chin and splashing onto the floor. I shook my head and dropped my forehead into my hands, sobbing as my heart broke.

"I love you." He curled his arms around me, holding me close, his breath warm against my hair. "I'm sorry. Please, don't let this be over," he whispered, burying his head against my neck.

We sat there forever. Holding each other. Crying. I wished I knew what to do next.

Chapter 16

To my surprise, Alex allowed me to hold her, which I took to be a step in the right direction. "I'm sorry, Ally. I love you. I've been stupid. Don't let it be over. I need you." My gut clenched.

Maybe Alex wouldn't believe me, and I understood her hesitation. Denying I'd broken promises was pointless, but maybe the truth would reach her. I loved her more than life itself along with my little boy. If I had to give him up, I'd die.

She looked at me, her red, puffy eyes scanning my face as I cupped her cheeks in my hands.

"Joel," she whispered in a faint and lost voice. Her hands encircled my wrists as she held tight to me.

Give her time. But I couldn't. Even with her face ravaged with grief and tears, her beauty struck me. I needed and wanted her. It felt like centuries had passed since I'd last made love to my wife.

She gazed up at me with those stunning blue eyes as I scooped her up and carried her to our room, her lips parting as I laid her across the snow-white duvet. Her heavy gasps as I kissed her neck, her cheeks, and her eyelids ignited me, and I devoured her mouth. Those wonderful warm hands slid into my hair, twining through the strands, bringing me ever closer as her arms wrapped around me.

Then we were stripping off our clothing, her yanking at my shirt and peeling it impatiently over my head. Her soft breath, and the little moan she emitted as her satiny bra tipped off the edge of the bed egged me on.

"Ally, oh my sweet, sweet Ally," I murmured against her hot skin, unable to wait another second to possess her, body and soul.

I cuddled Alex's warm body in my arms, lost in the most wonderful dream, luxuriating in holding my precious wife, never wanting to let her go. "I love you."

Her sweet sun-drenched scent surrounded me as I dropped kisses on her neck, her cheeks, and her forehead. It transported me to the long days spent at the beach and the hours upon hours on the sailboat during our carefree teenage years. "Can I come home?" I wound my hands through her silky hair. "Please?"

She patted my cheek. "It's too early for promises. Let's start couples counseling first." Her voice took on a firm, no-nonsense tone as she gazed into my eyes. "We've been here before."

"Book us an appointment as soon as possible." The thought stressed me out, but if I flinched at counseling, my ass would be out the door.

"Really?" Her eyebrows rose.

"Whatever we need to do to work this out, Ally. I won't lose you." I tucked a stray wisp of hair behind her ear. "You want some water?"

"Please." She smiled, brushing back her hair, looking so sweet and lovely.

My foot landed on one of the many articles of clothing scattered across our bedroom floor. I bent and retrieved the shirt from the floor, laughing as I remembered how we'd ripped the clothes off of each other. I dangled it from my index finger and waved it at her. But this familiar blue shirt wasn't mine.

"What the …?"

Alex opened her eyes, a frown settling over her features.

"Wow. I beg like a dog for you to take me back, and what do I find? Another man's shirt on my bedroom floor." I glowered.

"No, Joel." Her eyes widened. "It's not what you think."

"Aiden's fucking shirt on my damn floor isn't what I think? It wasn't there when I left for Chicago." I bounded from the bed, yanking on my jeans and shirt before snatching up the offending piece of clothing, shoving it toward her and waving it in her face. "You heartless, lying, faithless little bitch. How could you? All that whining about me and Crystal, and the minute I turn my back, you're screwing my so-called best friend. Classic."

"No, Joel, I didn't. We didn't. It's not like that. It's never been like that. You have to believe me." She clutched at my arm, tugging as she trailed me toward the front door. "Joel, no."

"Get off." My eyes narrowed as I peeled away her fingers. "Forget it. Forget it all. We're done." I stabbed the elevator button and left her standing there with tears streaming down her face.

The doorman waved as I stalked across the marble foyer, battling my growing rage. I pressed my key fob against the panel and punched the button marked PH. Damn convenient that we'd shared apartment keys. No way would he turn me away.

I clenched his shirt in my fist, willing myself not to shred it, saving my energy to show him what I thought of him and his so-called friendship.

The elevator swished open and I stepped in, glancing around to get my bearings.

Aiden appeared a few feet away, a frown on his face. "Joel, what—"

"Fuck you." I lunged across the floor and flung the shirt in his face, following it with my fist. Smashing that pretty little face of his felt incredible, the blood streaming down his chin gratifying as he raised his arm to block my next swing.

I tackled him, propelling us into the hall table. It tipped and shattered with a satisfying crash as I hauled him to the marble tile amongst the shards of glass and pottery. Pinning one of his arms to the floor, I swung hard, delivering several quick and dirty shots to his head. My fist drove into his face as his connected with my jaw.

My eyes watered as he slammed his palm into my nose and wound a leg around mine, flipping me. He followed up with a solid left hook to my face.

Aiden wasn't a lightweight. We'd been on the same side of one or two altercations in the past, and he knew how to brawl. He'd taken down guys much bigger than me.

"What is …?" Emily's voice echoed through the hall. "Tom! Holy crap. Tom! Get in here. Aiden. Joel. Stop it."

My head connected with the tile floor and spots danced before my eyes. I braced my flattened hand against Aiden's chest and twisted his other arm as I threw my body weight against him. I gained the upper hand, getting in two more solid punches.

"Joel! Stop!"

Someone wrapped an arm around my neck from behind, crushing my windpipe as they grasped my wrist. I raised my hands to my throat, attempting to break free, gasping for air as my lungs burned in protest. Unintelligible words buzzed in my ears before the chokehold on my throat released. Arms squeezed my chest like a vice and yanked me to my feet.

"Have you lost your fucking mind?" Tom muttered in my ear as he propelled me backward. "Calm down."

"Asshole." I lunged forward, half-blind from the hot, sticky fluid trickling into my eye.

Emily crouched over Aiden who lay amidst the pile of glass, his chest heaving.

Savannah pushed past us. "Daddy?"

It all blurred together. Savannah's stricken look. The tears rushing down her cheeks. The sick feeling in my gut as she let out a choked sob and shrank against the wall.

Tom spun me away from the scene. "What the fuck, Joel? Are you trying to finish him off?"

"Should have left him in the drink." My rage died, and my entire body shook, a metallic taste lingering on my tongue.

"Will you behave? Can I let you go now?"

"Yeah, I'm done." I shrugged off his hands and wiped the back of my hand over my face. Sinking onto a stool, I accepted some tissues from Tom, pressing them against my split lip as I fought to catch my breath. I rubbed at my burning neck. "Fuck, you didn't have to choke me, Tom."

"That was Emily." He shoved another wad of tissue into my trembling hands.

"What?" *That tiny woman?*

"How's Aiden?" Tom positioned himself between me and the flurry of activity, one hand pressed flat against my chest.

"He's alive. Don't even think about getting up, Aiden. Stay down." Emily dashed down the hall, coming back moments later with a medical kit. She gave me a perfunctory glance. "Does idiot boy have any other injuries?"

"A few cuts, a split lip, and maybe a black eye. Perhaps a broken nose. His hand is scraped and swelling. Don't you move." Tom went into the kitchen and retrieved ice from the freezer, wrapping it and putting it on my knuckles. "His neck is bruising where you tried to strangle him."

Emily threw a scathing look in my direction before turning her attention to Aiden again. "He deserved it," she muttered as she pulled out a small light and flicked it over his eyes. "You've got a huge lump on your head. Anything else hurt?"

He muttered an indistinguishable reply, but if the blood smeared across the tile were any indication, the answer was a solid yes.

Savannah sniffled and wrapped her arms around herself, sneaking glances my way.

"It's okay, Vanna. Aiden will be fine." Emily sat him up and cupped his face with her palms as she peered into Aiden's eyes. She swiped at her cheeks with the back of one hand.

"Yeah, you wouldn't be babying him and showing so much damned sympathy if you knew the truth. Just wait, you'll punch him too."

"What are you talking about?" Tom turned to glare at me. "You come flying in here, go nuts, and attack him. The explanation better be damn good, Joel."

"I found his shirt on my bedroom floor, and I've been out of town. Clear enough for you?"

Savannah sniffled, appearing rooted to the floor.

Tom followed my gaze and gave me a warning look before he crossed the floor and wrapped his arm around the girl. "It's all right, honey."

"My shirt?" Aiden held a compress on his head as Emily brushed glass out of his hair and dabbed at the blood on his face.

"You were at my house while I was out of town."

"So what?"

"Tom, give me a hand," Emily said.

Between Emily and Tom, they lifted Aiden from the floor and helped him to a chair.

Emily cracked two ice packs and pressed one to his shoulder, and the other to the back of his head. "Okay?"

Aiden grimaced. "No, it fucking hurts."

"I'll give you something for the pain, but we should take you both to the ER." Emily poured a glass of water and rooted in the cupboard, coming up with a prescription bottle. She shook out some tablets and gave them to Aiden. She cradled his pale, blood-streaked face between her hands. "Aiden?"

"Call Will." He closed his eyes.

❧

The ride to the hospital was short and quiet.

I stared in the rearview mirror, noting how Emily's mouth had settled in a grim line.

She cast continuous worried looks at Aiden who had his head tipped back against the headrest. Emily pulled into a spot marked *reserved-physicians only* before rounding the car to open the passenger door. "Aiden." She stroked his cheek. "Can you walk?"

"Yeah." He'd climbed out, groaning and leaning on one hand against the hood of the SUV.

Tom shot a look at me. "Out."

We were only part way to the door when Will Kavanagh appeared and assisted Aiden into a wheelchair. Tom and I trailed behind as Will wheeled him into the elevator and hit the button for the third floor.

"We'll avoid the ER. You don't need the gossip." Will pushed him out of the elevator and past the nurses' station.

"Thanks, Will." Emily accepted the tablet the doctor offered her and consulted it before pointing me into one of the rooms. She followed me and handed me a gown. "Change, and the orderly will take you to radiology. Will lined it up."

"Thanks," I muttered, rubbing at my aching jaw.

"You're in pain?" Emily peered into my eyes with a small light, and then pressed gloved fingertips over my nose and jaw line and ran her hands over my head. "Pain meds and an IV, please. I'll input the order now." She nodded at the nurse as she tapped on the tablet. "You have a huge lump on the back of your head."

Emily stepped into the hall while I changed into a gown.

"I'll put your clothes in here." The nurse tucked everything into a bag and started the IV. "In." She motioned to the wheelchair and beckoned to the orderly.

Soon I was on a table being poked, prodded, and x-rayed. I sank into a twilight haze as the medication took effect, for which I was grateful. My entire body hurt. For someone who didn't have full function of his shoulder, the guy packed incredible force into those punches.

Once the tests were finished, the orderly returned me to my room and helped me into bed. My mind wandered as I stared at the ceiling. *Aiden.* That guy always managed to wiggle out of every situation and played the sympathy card magnificently with his wife. Mine, on the other hand, forgave me nothing.

Chapter 17

Alexis

I'D SPENT MY TIME SINCE Joel had stormed out pacing back and forth, checking my phone. The text messages I'd sent to both Emily and Aiden after the altercation had gone unanswered. As had the calls to Tom and Jenna. Joel hadn't responded to the many texts or calls either, but if he was off licking his wounds, he'd ignore me.

At long last, a text popped up on my phone.

On my way up.

"Jenna." I greeted her at the door, taking in her concerned expression.

"You're okay?" She hugged me then grasped my shoulders.

"I'm fine. What happened?" I asked. "Joel blazed out of here. He had a total fit—"

"Aiden and Joel are in the ER."

"What?" My stomach lurched, and I fought the urge to throw up. "Is everyone okay?"

"They're both injured, but nothing life threatening. Joel showed up at their apartment and attacked Aiden."

"He didn't." My eyes burned. "That asshole. He didn't even wait to hear what I had to say, and he went after Aiden?" I sank into Jenna's embrace and burst into tears.

"They'll recover, sweetie. Joel needs insurance information. I can take it to the ER, or I'll stay with Daniel while you go." Jenna rubbed my back.

"I'll go. I should visit Aiden, and Joel and I have some matters to clear up."

Not long afterward, I stared up at the gray structure. What would I say to either of them? Prolonging the agony wouldn't help, so I squared my shoulders and entered through the sliding doors.

I approached the admission desk, glancing around the ER intake area but I didn't recognize anyone. "Joel Nichols was brought in. I'm supposed to find Dr. Kavanagh? I'm Alexis Nichols, Joel's wife."

The receptionist tapped on her keyboard. "Check in at the nursing station on the third floor, and they can locate Dr. Kavanagh for you."

I proceeded through the sliding doors to the elevators and rode to the designated floor. "Joel Nichols' room? And is Dr. Kavanagh here?"

"321." The nurse smiled and pointed down the hall. "Go in, and I'll page Dr. Kavanagh."

I steeled my nerves, inhaling and flexing my fingers before stepping gingerly down the hallway. The antiseptic smell turned my stomach, and my whole body trembled. Even that unavoidable squeak from my sneakers on the polished floor struck a note of fear in my heart. Memories tumbled through my mind from the night my mother died, but I pushed them away. I hated hospitals, but I couldn't avoid them.

I stepped through the doorway. Joel lay on his side with his eyes closed, snuffling. That I attributed to his swollen nose. A dark bruise ringed his eye, and his hand was wrapped in gauze and elevated on a pillow.

"Joel?" I whispered. "Are you awake?"

One eye opened a crack. "Alex."

"I brought your insurance papers." I dropped them on the bedside table and crossed my arms, glaring at him. "How could you be such an idiot? You went after Aiden? I can't believe you."

"Sorry," he mumbled through his puffy lips before closing his eye.

"Alex?"

The familiar voice made me turn. "Will. How are you?" I wrapped my arms around him.

"Better than him." He motioned toward the bed. "Joel has been medicated for the pain and been in for scans on his hand and his face. Good news on his nose. There's swelling but that should go down soon, soft tissue damage only there. He wasn't so lucky with his hand. He has two fractures, which I've realigned and a resident is on the way to cast it. He had a good bump to the head, but no signs of a concussion."

I glance at Joel who'd opened one eye again. "How's Aiden?"

"I can't disclose anything about his condition." His gaze rolled toward Joel. "Patient confidentiality. But he's in room 323, if Emily will allow you to visit."

"Thanks. I left the insurance papers there." I pointed and squeezed Will's arm before I left him to attend to Joel. That idiot didn't deserve any pampering or sympathy. If Aiden hadn't done such a sound job of thumping him, I would've finished up with a solid punch to his stupid face.

I hesitated in the doorway of 323 before shuffling toward his bed. "How's Aiden?"

"We're waiting for results on his shoulder, and he has a mild concussion. Will wants to keep him overnight." Emily ran a hand through her dark hair as she rose from the chair. "The pain meds knocked him out, so I have to wake him regularly."

"I'm so sorry he got dragged into the middle of this crap between me and Joel." I gazed at his bruised face and noted his wrapped and elevated hand. "He broke it?"

"It's scraped and swollen, but not broken." She patted my arm. "None of this is your fault."

"Can I stay for a while? If you need to check on Kellan, I'll hang around and wake Aiden. Just tell me what time."

"Thanks, Alex. Kellan will need to be fed, and I didn't have time to prepare anything." She lowered her voice. "I'd like to check on Vanna. The poor girl freaked out, and she needs some extra reassurance that Aiden's okay."

"No doubt. This is the second time he's been to an ER because of Joel. Take your time." I hugged her before she pressed a kiss to Aiden's temple and disappeared out of the door.

⌐◝

"Aiden." I patted his cheek, waking him right on schedule.

"Whadda ya wan'? I'm tryin' to sleep."

"Wake up, honey. Doctor's orders." My heart ached. No matter what Emily said, I blamed myself for this fiasco. "Open your eyes and look at me." I stroked his hair.

"Water?" He blinked, his voice thick and sleepy.

"Here." I adjusted the head of his bed and held the cup and straw so he could take a sip. "Better?"

"My head hurts."

"I bet it does. You smacked it on the marble tile." I rose, meaning to find a nurse, but at that moment, the door opened and one peeked in.

"You're awake. Good, let me check your vitals." She smiled as she performed a quick and efficient exam. "Headache?"

"A splitting one." Aiden rubbed at his temple.

The nurse nodded and handed him a small plastic cup containing two tablets. "Try to rest."

"Where's Emily?" Aiden asked after the nurse made notes on his chart and left the room.

"She went home to feed Kellan. She'll be back soon." I held his good hand and perched on the edge of the bed. "Joel lost it when he found your shirt on the bedroom floor. I tried to call and warn you, but you didn't answer your phone."

"It's not your fault." He squeezed my hand.

"It feels like it. Joel went nuts. Maybe I should stay away for a while. I cause nothing but trouble."

"No. Joel needs to get himself sorted. Don't isolate yourself because of his actions."

It pained me to see the sadness on Aiden's face. It seemed impossible that he and Joel could ever repair the chasm in their friendship. Aiden and I had our moments, but we'd always resolved our issues by talking. Joel had headed in the opposite direction, unable to come to terms with anything, and him earning forgiveness from Aiden would be a miracle.

Maybe Joel's staunch belief that men and women couldn't be platonic friends had fueled his irrational behavior. I didn't like to consider that scenario. If it were true, then it followed he and Crystal weren't platonic despite his insistence they were only friends. Whatever. He'd played me for the fool for the last time.

"You're sweet, but it is my fault. You've been a wonderful and supportive friend, but look at you."

"I'd do it again. You're family, Lex. If he doesn't like it, well too bad for him. Please don't let his stupidity come between us."

"Oh, Aiden." Tears burned my eyes and I bowed my head, blinking hard. I loved this man who never let me down. "I wish there was more I could do for you."

He drew me down to rest against his good shoulder and stroked my hair. "Don't cry, sweetheart. I've had worse beatings than that. Joel fights like a girl."

Despite myself, I laughed. "Nothing ever gets you down." My cheeks flushed at my ludicrous words. "Sorry. Tell me, Aiden. When? And who?"

"When and who what?"

I lifted my head and peered into his eyes. "Who did worse than Joel?"

"That a was a joke." He closed his eyes, but not before I caught a glimpse of that tell-tale shadow. That swift, fleeting pain crinkling his brow and dragging the corners of his mouth downward, even if only for a split second.

"I bet you won't tell, so I'll save my breath."

"There's nothing to tell."

"It's okay. You can confess your deep dark secrets when you're ready." I kissed his cheek. "Get some rest. I'll sit with you until Emily returns."

"Thanks, Alex," he said. "Is Vanna okay?"

"Emily's with her now." I smiled. "Quit worrying and rest."

Moments later, he closed his eyes and drifted to sleep.

It pained me to see him like this, but we were family, and I would do anything to help him recover.

CHAPTER 18

THE ROOM CAME INTO FOCUS as I blinked and cleared the blur swimming before my eyes. I wanted to rub them, but my hand was too heavy.

Memories flitted through my murky mind. The last thing I remembered was Alex's voice, but now I had no clue what she'd said. I searched for her words, but maybe they didn't matter. Instead of keeping watch at my bedside, she'd run off to check on Aiden.

I stared at my right hand encased in white plaster while I'd been unconscious. The cast ran from my aching fingertips up to my elbow.

Wiggling out of bed, I stumbled to the bathroom and peered into the mirror through my bleary and swollen eyes.

If I looked this bad, what did Aiden looked like? As the haze of sleep lifted and my mind cleared, I remembered. I'd gotten in some solid shots. I felt bad for attacking him, but the rage had risen hard and fast. I'd lost control.

Then he played innocent, like my anger about finding his shirt on my floor was ridiculous. Why in the hell would he undress in my bedroom if nothing happened with my wife? Why would she be more worried about him than me? She professed to love me so much, and she'd been less than understanding about my relationship with Crystal, yet she let Aiden strip down in our bedroom?

Peeking into the hallway, I noted the dimmed lights. All seemed quiet, and the clock over the desk at the nurses' station read 3:17.

Room 323. That was his room number. My fuzzy mind had at least registered that much when Alex had the conversation with Kavanagh.

With slow steps, I moved down the hall, scanning the numbers on the doors. 323 happened to be only two rooms away from mine. The muted sounds of a late-night TV show greeted me as I inched open the heavy door.

Aiden was propped up with pillows. His eyes were closed even though the screen flickered in the low light.

He turned his head and stared at me for a moment. "Coming to finish me off? Get in your final shots while you can?"

"Surprised you're awake." I cringed at the damage I'd inflicted. One eye had puffed up, he sported a fair-sized bruise across his cheek, his shoulder had been strapped into an immobilizer, and his hand was elevated and wrapped in gauze, though the lucky bastard had avoided a cast. He looked far worse than I did.

"I've given up on sleep." He sighed and closed his eyes again. "What do you want?"

I hesitated, but then lowered myself into a nearby chair. "Why'd you do it?"

"Do what?"

"Why were you there? In my bedroom?"

"Oh, that. It's nothing. Alex was upset after you walked out."

"So you consoled her, right?"

"She's like my sister, Joel. How many times do I have to tell you that?"

Maybe once more. At least. "And your wife has no comment and is fine about you sleeping with my wife?"

"What?" He rolled his head toward me again and fixed his good eye on me. "You're being stupid. Why don't you go back to your room?"

"I don't—"

"Shut up and get out. I can't deal with you right now." Aiden's voice sounded monotone.

"I—"

"Get. The. Fuck. Out." He turned his head toward the window. "Stay away from me and my family. You're a walking disaster."

"Now I know there's more to the story, or you'd tell me."

"Joel." A hand landed on my shoulder. "You shouldn't be in here." Will helped me to my feet and angled me toward the door. His gentle but firm grip allowed no argument as he steered me down the hallway.

"Stay in bed, and leave Aiden alone." Will made some notes on the tablet he held. "I mean it. You both should be resting." After a stern look in my direction, he was gone.

I rolled onto my side, propping my throbbing hand on the extra pillows.

A nurse peeked in the door. "Can't sleep, Mr. Nichols?" She approached the bed and performed her routine checks. "How's the pain?"

"My hand aches."

"I'll give you something for that, and then perhaps you should rest."

After she left, I turned on my TV and flipped through the channels, finding nothing that could hold my attention. My hand no longer hurt, but my mind wouldn't stop spinning.

He'd dismissed my concerns. Didn't he understand how I felt? Would he be so accepting if it were the other way around, and he found my shirt on his bedroom floor?

The anger rose again, but I couldn't do anything about it. Not with Will Kavanagh, Aiden's personal watchdog, on duty. No doubt Will had alerted the nurses to prevent me from wandering.

In time, exhaustion won out and forced my eyes closed. I welcomed the escape from conscious thought and the hollow ache in my chest that accompanied the ominous feeling that this time, I'd lost her forever.

CHAPTER 19

Alexis

THE SILENCE OF THE APARTMENT surrounded me as I brewed a large pot of coffee and rubbed at my gritty eyes. By the time Emily had returned to the hospital last night with Kellan snuggled in his wrap, Daniel had been tucked into bed at Jenna's house.

For that, I was grateful. I'd mentally prepared an enormous list of tasks for today. What else does one fill the hours of silent vigil while contemplating the untold damage your mistakes caused to a man's life? Daniel would be well taken care of until I picked him up this afternoon, and I'd make the most of this meager time to sort myself out.

At the top of my list was packing Joel's things. Maybe I should leave that chore for him, but I needed to burn off the nervous energy that continued to build. Action provided a sense of accomplishment. Gave me a purpose to not dissolve into a useless puddle of overwrought emotions.

Empty his clothing from the closet? *Check.* Toss the lying bastard's socks and underwear haphazardly into a box? *Check.*

Limiting the time he spent here would make it easier for everyone.

My phone buzzed.

How are you?

Trust Jenna to worry. Not that the others weren't concerned, but they had their own problems. Emily's day would be consumed in preparing her home for her incapacitated husband along with caring for their baby boy and a distraught teenage girl. Tom had volunteered to drive Aiden home from the hospital. Ryan was on the other side of the country.

Managing. How's my sweet boy?

Wonderful. I hear Joel's being released this afternoon. Come for coffee?

I'll see you in an hour.

I sighed and lugged the last box to the vestibule by the elevator, pausing to survey the results. The neat stack of boxes spelled our untidy end. What would happen to all of it? Not that it mattered, just like it didn't matter where my errant husband would land. Anywhere I didn't have to deal with him worked for me.

No time to wallow. I ripped the sheets off of the bed and tossed them into the machine.

Erase all sign and scent of him. *Check.*

As I worked my way into the living room seeking Joel's belongings, I contemplated the frames littering the mantle. My throat burned and closed up as I brushed at my damp cheek. How had we gotten here?

I straightened and exhaled a long stream of air. Better to know now than later. I'd been too close to allowing him back into my life, but his harsh words and loss of control had cured me of that notion. This heartless, lying, faithless little bitch refused to excuse his hypocritical behavior. Enough was enough.

My vision blurred as my gaze fell upon the joyful faces preserved for eternity in full color, contained in the intricate silver frame. That dark debonair tuxedo looked amazing on Joel, creating a flawless duet with my expensive ivory princess-style wedding dress.

How many hours had I spent dreaming, planning, and creating that perfect day? For what?

In seconds, I had the elegant photo clutched between my fingertips, the glossy paper shredding as the jagged tear appeared between us, separating us forever.

⁓

Daniel charged toward me the minute I set foot inside the door.

"There's my boy." I scooped him into a hug and kissed his cheek.

"Mama." He laid his head on my shoulder as he wrapped his arms around my neck.

"How are you?" Jenna slipped an arm around my waist.

"As good as I can be. Thanks for watching him." I planted another kiss on Daniel's cheek before releasing him to play. "I finished packing Joel's things, though I have no idea where he'll stay or how he'll move any of it."

"Tom suggested he use the partner suite for a week or so." Jenna shrugged. "We can't have him here, and he damn sure won't be bunking at Aiden's."

"I forgot they had that."

"It's not big, but I doubt Joel needs much space, and it's only for a short time until he finds something permanent." Jenna motioned for me to sit. "I'm not sure what will happen. Apparently, Joel visited Aiden at about three this morning."

My eyes widened. "What happened?"

"Nothing besides an exchange of words. Will removed Joel from the room before any physical altercation occurred. Not that either of them is capable of fighting at the moment."

My chin sank to my chest. "I suppose not, but at least Joel didn't cause further damage."

"Tom drove Aiden home. Emily mentioned they won't be up for visitors for a few days."

"Right, because I bring them nothing but trouble."

"That's not what I meant." Jenna wagged a finger at me. "Let Aiden settle in at home and rest, and then go see him."

"When I visited Aiden in the hospital last night, he looked awful." I rubbed my hands over my face.

"He'll recover." Jenna patted my knee. "Be patient and let things calm down."

"I'm responsible for this mess. I wouldn't blame Emily for hating me. She's had enough interference in her marriage already."

"She doesn't hate you, but she's overwhelmed. Give her some time and space. In the meantime, what can I do to help you?"

I shrugged and picked at a fluff stuck to my sweater.

"Alex." Jenna sat beside me. "Don't avoid this. I'm here to talk whenever you need."

"Thanks," I whispered. "I should head home."

"Do you want company for when Joel arrives?"

"It's best if I do this alone."

"I'm only a call away."

I nodded and gathered Daniel and his belongings. Nothing about this was easy, but knowing my friends were there helped.

The thought our empty apartment was depressing, so Daniel and I stopped at the park for some outdoor playtime. His joyful giggles soothed the hurt lingering inside. This adorable, sweet, and loving little person was the single best gift from our faltering relationship.

After a solid hour of chasing him around the play structure, Daniel plopped onto the ground, rubbing his eyes. "Ready to go, bud?" At his nod, I cradled him to my chest and headed toward home. Except my feet carried me in another direction.

"Mrs. Nichols."

"Afternoon." I waved at the doorman as I crossed the foyer and touched the fob against the panel. The light stayed red so I tapped it again. The elevator door refused to open.

The doorman approached. "I'm sorry, I'm required to announce all visitors." He shuffled his feet and pointed to the fob. "I need that."

Tears sprang to my eyes. I set Daniel on his feet and worked the small device from my key chain, handing it over as heat crept into my cheeks.

"I'll call for you."

I bowed my head. "Please."

Moments later, we were in the elevator as it rose upward. The doors opened revealing the foyer. A deep gash in the wall to my left caught my attention. The beautiful heirloom table gifted by Aiden's grandmother was missing, leaving a blank space. I pressed my hand to my mouth.

"Alex." Emily lips tugged downward. "I didn't know you were coming by."

"I wanted to check on Aiden." I set down my squirming son, and he dashed toward the playroom.

She beckoned me to follow her to the kitchen. "Can I get you something?"

"How's Aiden?"

"As good as can be expected." She pulled a carafe from the fridge and poured two glasses of lemonade, setting one on the counter in front of me.

"Thanks." I swallowed a mouthful, the icy liquid soothing my burning throat. "How is he really?"

"Physically, he's a mess." She crossed her arms and lifted her chin. "He's starting his recovery over again. Will only discharged him because I'm here to monitor his concussion."

"I'm so sorry about Joel." I bowed my head, ashamed that my husband had taken out our problems on hers.

"Neither of us blame you. Joel is a grown man and should be responsible for his own actions and decisions."

My stomach rolled. "You disabled my key fob."

"That's not directed at you. In the confusion, I forgot to get Joel's key."

"Oh, I'm sorry. What a mess."

"I hate it." Emily pushed her hair back and emitted a deep sigh. "Nobody gets open access until things settle down. Having someone we know walk into our home and attack my husband was frightening." She leveled her gaze at me. "We should feel safe here, so I made the decision to reset our security and reprogram the door codes."

"Does Aiden know?" I raised a brow.

"Not yet, but he isn't in any condition to discuss it. I doubt he'll argue with my decision. It's not meant as a punishment. I'm sorry it's come to this." She flattened her hands on the counter. "Vanna woke up screaming in the middle of the night. She had a horrible nightmare and a huge panic attack."

"Is she okay?" My heart ached for the sweet girl and the pain my family had caused her. It had been months of struggle to get her panic under control, and now she was back to where she started.

"The knowledge that I'm controlling who has access to the apartment helped."

"Good. I'll go so you can rest." I fought to control my tears as I located Daniel in the playroom. "Come on, sweetie, time to go home."

Emily trailed me as I headed toward the front doors. "Alex? Please give it some time. Call me if you need to talk."

"Okay," I mumbled, keeping my head bowed. The elevator swished shut and a wave of regret swept over me. I longed to be home burrowed under my covers, the world passing by without me. No matter what anyone said, this was all my fault.

CHAPTER 20

Joel

DREADED WAKEFULNESS. CONSCIOUSNESS MEANT THINKING about the complete disaster of my life. Being at odds. In limbo. Today could bring nothing good.

"How are you feeling this afternoon?" Will's voice cut into my reverie.

"Everything hurts." I pressed my face into my pillow.

"We'll switch you to over-the-counter pain medication and an anti-inflammatory." He pulled a small light from the pocket of his pristine white lab coat and shone it into my eyes before examining the bridge of my nose. "This looks as good as can be expected. We'll discharge you this afternoon. You should call someone to pick you up."

"Great." Who'd drop anything to rescue me after what I'd done?

"I'll start the paperwork." Will turned to leave.

"Wait. How's Aiden?"

Will paused in the doorway. "I'm not at liberty to discuss another patient's medical conditions, Mr. Nichols. You know that." He raised a brow.

"Can I see him?"

"I'm afraid not. The nurse will be in with your care instructions shortly. Any other questions on your condition or injuries?"

I shook my head, and he left. *That went well.* After hauling myself from the bed, I wobbled into the bathroom and stared longingly at the shower. What were the odds that Alex would take pity on me and help me bathe, or shave, or feed myself for the next several weeks? *Slim to none, dumb-ass. Not after you attacked her golden boy.*

I splashed icy water on my face and combed my fingers through the overgrown mop of hair sticking up at all angles. The sight of my scruffy, swollen face made me grimace.

A nurse bustled into the room and pulled my bag of clothing from under the bed. "Let's go over Dr. Kavanagh's orders, shall we?" She covered the long list of instructions on caring for my stitches and cast, and then handed me the printout. "Sign here." She pointed to the bottom with the tip of the pen.

I scrawled my name on the indicated line.

"Do you need any assistance?" The nurse motioned to the clothing on the bed.

I shook my head.

Her eyebrows rose, but she shrugged and left the room.

That decision proved rash. It took several agonizing minutes to work my tight black t-shirt over my cast, and even longer to tug on my jeans. I held up a sock and sighed before shoving my bare feet into my shoes.

Time to make the dreaded call, but my phone screen remained black when I pressed the button. I closed my eyes and tapped the device against my forehead. A dead phone battery on top of everything else didn't bode well for the rest of the day.

At the nurses' station, I leaned on the desk. "Any chance I can use a phone? My mobile died."

"There's one in the patient lounge." The nurse pointed.

"Thanks." I slunk to the lounge and sank into a chair. Even that short walk, on top of dressing myself, had exhausted me.

In keeping with the trend, Alex didn't answer either the house phone or her mobile. Whatever. The few blocks home wouldn't take long, and if Emily had managed it daily while pregnant, I could do it even in my current condition.

I rode the elevator to the main floor and exited into the bright sunshine. At least one thing was going my way. It wasn't pouring rain.

━━⋞

I leaned against the side of the elevator and closed my eyes, rubbing my forehead to ease the pounding ache in my temples. Walking home hadn't been an inspired choice. The bright sunlight had seared my unshaded eyeballs and become a curse, my bones ached, and my pasty tongue was glued to the roof of my mouth.

The doors slid open, and I stepped into the foyer. A pile of boxes and two suitcases sat against the wall. The sight didn't fill me with optimism for the future.

I skirted around them. "Anyone home?"

Alex appeared, halting three feet away and crossing her arms. "Keep it down. Daniel's napping." She scanned me from head to toe. "You're a mess."

What could I say? I focused on the gray floor tile and nodded.

"We have to talk," she said.

"You packed my things."

"It's for the best," she said softly. "Your actions and how you spoke to me were unacceptable." She sniffled and brushed at her eyes. "I can't have you here. You don't trust me, and I sure don't trust you."

"I'm sorry, Alex, that wasn't me. I lost it."

"I wish I could believe that." Alex scuffed at the floor with her toes. "After your long string of poor choices …" She shrugged.

"I'm sorry. Truly." My throat closed up. Mentally, I kicked myself for the stupidity. We'd been so close to moving forward and repairing the rift.

No question I'd handled the situation badly. There might be no recovering from this mistake. My wife as fed up, as was every single person I'd considered a friend. Tom and Ryan would be ready to kick me to the curb for hurting their boy.

"I'm not sure where to go." I kept my head down, desperate to hide the building tears.

"The partner suite is open. The movers are on their way for your boxes."

The words knocked the wind out of me. Everyone had conspired to remove me from my home, but how could I argue. It made perfect sense for me to go. Leave Alex to provide for Daniel. Our son would be better off with her than with me.

"Fine." With a heavy heart, I turned toward the entrance.

"Joel?"

A flicker of hope leaped within me. Pathetic, yes, but I didn't want to walk out that door. The minute I left, I'd be admitting defeat.

"Leave your keys," she said in a flat voice.

"My keys?"

"You don't live here anymore."

CHAPTER 21

Alexis

$\mathcal{D}$AY FIVE OF MY POST-JOEL life had begun, and everything looked bleak. His dresser stood empty, his clothes were absent from our closet, and all of his personal items vacated from our bathroom. The boxes and suitcases had been transferred to Joel's temporary residence. The other side of the bed might remain cold and empty for a long time.

I'd grown accustomed to Joel's absence, so this shouldn't be much different from his rare appearance over the summer. Yet I sensed the monumental change. I doubted he'd ever come home.

"Mama." Daniel's sweet voice echoed down the hallway along with the pounding of his tiny feet. He launched himself onto the bed and landed on top of me.

"Oof." I wrapped my arms around him and blew kisses onto his face and neck. "Morning, sweet prince."

My darling boy laughed. "Mama, stop." He curled up, protecting his belly from my tickles, his grin and sparkling hazel eyes blowing the dark clouds away.

"Shall we have breakfast?" I lifted him from the bed and hugged him close as I made my way to the kitchen, humming as I prepared fruit and yogurt.

My phone rang right after we'd begun eating.

"Aiden. How are you, honey?" I hadn't spoken to anyone in our group all week, though both Jenna and Emily had left me messages.

"Hi, Alex."

"Oh, I thought …"

"You haven't called back, so I borrowed Aiden's phone. Sorry."

"How is he?"

"Better. He'd like to see you," Emily said. "I don't want you to think I was intentionally shutting you out that day. We were all exhausted and in shock. It had been a rough twenty-four hours, and I reacted in the only way I knew how."

"I don't blame you. Can I come this morning?"

"Text when you're on your way and bring Daniel."

At nine, I bundled Daniel into his coat and we strolled up the street. The crisp fresh air touched my cheeks, invigorating me. The last of the lovely deep orange and red leaves drifted around us, tumbling across the sidewalk.

Daniel's short legs propelled him across the grass as he pursued a leaf fluttering in the breeze. He waved his tiny hands in a futile attempt to catch it, tilting his head as it finally settled on the ground. He crouched on his heels, leaning close and prodding it with a finger before he picked it up. "Leave." He clutched his prize in his fist.

"It's beautiful, sweetie." I smiled even as my heart broke for him.

Joel hadn't called one single time since he'd handed over his keys and slunk away. Our son wasn't even a year and a half old, and he'd lose the precious connection to his father all too fast. I feared it had already happened.

"Let's go." I grasped his hand and led him to the front doors.

"Ain?" Daniel hopped up and down. "Unca Ain."

Though grateful that my son had Aiden in his life, it saddened me that he never showed this much excitement when Joel arrived. I shook off the thought as we crossed the lobby.

The doorman smiled and waved. "Go on up, Mrs. Nichols."

Emily met me at the door with a warm hug and a sweet smile. "Good to see you, Alex. How are you holding up?" She cradled Daniel and kissed his cheek. "Sweet boy."

"What can I say? I tossed my husband out and haven't heard from him since." I attempted a light tone while blinking back hot tears.

"Oh, honey. That's rough." She balanced Daniel on her hip and squeezed me with one arm. "Aiden's in the living room."

"Unca Ain." Daniel kicked his feet and squirmed.

Emily rubbed his back. "You be gentle, okay?" She peered into Daniel's eyes. "Uncle Aiden isn't feeling well."

"Yup." He nodded.

She carried him through to the living room and let Daniel say hello while I hovered in the doorway. After a minute, she took Daniel's hand, stopping to pat my arm. "I'll entertain Daniel."

"Hey, stranger." I leaned in to kiss and hug Aiden, taking care to avoid both his injured arm and Kellan, who slept cuddled securely against his dad's chest.

"Hey, yourself. How are you?" He lifted his gaze to mine.

My breath caught in my chest at the ugly purplish-black bruise that encircled his bloodshot eye and spread across his cheekbone and over the bridge of his nose. I brushed a hand over his scruffy cheek. "Oh, Aiden, I'm so sorry." A tear dribbled down my face. "You must hate me."

"None of this is your fault, Lex. Joel is a grown man, and how he reacted is his issue."

"Has he been by to apologize?"

"He wouldn't be allowed inside. Emily would call security or worse, the police. I have nothing further to say. He came to see me in the hospital that night." He exhaled a long slow breath. "I've tried to be his friend and help with whatever is happening with him, but I'm exhausted."

"Still, I've drawn you into the middle of our marriage troubles. That's not fair to you. Joel is carrying around this load of resentment, and I'm not quite sure where it's coming from." I glanced up as Emily appeared.

"Vanna is playing with Daniel in the toy room. Let me take Kellan." She eased the baby from Aiden's arms, settling in the rocker nearby. "Sorry, I didn't mean to eavesdrop, and I'm the newcomer to the group in so many ways. I don't have the history, I wasn't there when you were kids ..." Emily brushed a hand over Kellan's head.

"But?" I turned toward her.

"You come to Aiden with your troubles, and I've noticed it happening more often over the past few months."

"Oh." I glanced at Aiden, who'd closed his eyes. "Are you concerned that something's going on between us?"

"No, well ..." She studied Kellan's tiny fingers.

"Well, what?"

"I don't want this to come across the wrong way because you're my friend. The last thing I want is to wreck what we have as a group. The closeness you all have is something I love, but it's a touch overwhelming at times."

"So you want me to keep my distance?"

"That's not what I'm saying." She peered toward Aiden. "Maybe this isn't the time for this."

"You started it, so tell me. What's the problem? Aiden and I have been friends since we were twelve, and we've always talked about everything. There's nothing going on with us."

"No, and I trust you and Aiden, but look at it from an outsider's perspective. Take the issue of Joel finding Aiden's shirt in your room. If I'd found another woman's clothing in our bedroom, I'd be livid. Even walking in that morning, I didn't want to make it into a big deal, but it made me uncomfortable."

"Nothing happened."

"Fine, but if any other woman had walked in on her half-naked husband sleeping in your bed, she wouldn't have been nearly as understanding. Your group has an unusual comfort level with each other, and it's weird for me. I get that you spent countless summers together and seeing each other in various states of undress isn't a thing for you, but it is for other people. You're not teenagers or single. You're married. And not to each other."

"It's no different from seeing each other on the beach in swimwear."

"Except it is. Practically naked in your bedroom is completely opposite to a bikini on the beach. Sure, Joel could have handled this better, told you he didn't like it, and asked you what happened. Instead, he lit up like a Roman Candle, as would many men." Her gentle and level voice took some of the sting from her words. "You turn to Aiden for everything. Are you even speaking to Joel? Do you tell him when he's pissing you off?"

Joel and I rarely spoke these days. We'd shouted, we'd raged, and we'd fought, but there had been limited discussion or honest communication. It usually ended with one of us storming out.

"Aiden?" I pleaded with my eyes for him to rise to my defense.

He scrubbed a hand over his weary-looking face. "She's right, Alex. I love you like my sister, except you're not my sister. I'm used to being single. The majority of women in my past never gave a damn what I did or about my close relationship with you and Jenna."

I frowned, but couldn't speak.

"I will always be there and be your friend, but we need to find some balance. Maybe I've let you lean on me too often."

"Meaning what?" My shoulders slumped as the overwhelming urge to burst into tears and run swept over me.

"I want to support you through this, and I love you, but even you've recognized I've gotten in between you and Joel. I have to turn it around and look at it from the other side. If Emily ran to another man to discuss our marital issues, I'd be pretty damn upset about it. I'd worry and be insanely jealous."

Scalding tears burned my cheeks as I wrapped my arms around myself.

"Hey." Aiden wrapped an arm around me, cradling me against his shoulder. "I'm still here, but me being in the middle is only making it worse for everyone."

"I can't go through this alone."

"You don't have to, Alex. I'm not cutting off our friendship, but I need to create some space so you can work this out with Joel."

I glanced at the rocking chair and noted that Emily had left. "I'm creating problems in your marriage?" I whispered. "She's angry?"

"Don't worry about my relationship with Emily. The entire reason this discussion is happening is that we communicate. This situation is a wake-up call for everyone. We're not teenagers anymore. We can't act like we used to, out of respect for both Emily and Joel. If we'd talked earlier, maybe we wouldn't be here. You know I'm right, Alex. The minute Joel got those ideas in his head, everything changed, and we can't pretend that it hasn't."

"I need you. You're my best friend."

"Oh, sweetheart." He dropped a kiss on my head. "I'm here, and I'm still your friend. I love you, always."

CHAPTER 22

Joel

THE WEEK FOLLOWING THE INCIDENT, I spent most days locked in my office, avoiding the curious looks at my battered face.

Tom agreed to manage all the incoming cases with the assistance of the new intern he'd found at Harvard. Savannah had taken a leave of absence. I could only assume she didn't want to encounter me in the workplace. Who could blame her?

Nights were endless dark hours. Holed up in the small but adequate partner suite, I tossed and turned and fumed over the recent turn of events. Anger rose, but then a deep sense of longing would take over, and I'd mourn my losses.

All those hours I'd poured into my career now seemed crazy. That, and my wasted summer. I missed Daniel's sweet smiling face and Alex's lovely one. I'd always believed they would be there waiting for me. Now they weren't.

I'd love to see Daniel, but I worried I'd scare him to death. Every time I looked in the mirror, I cringed. As for my wife, shame prevented me from facing her and whatever came next in sorting out this mess. My own stupidity had ruined everything, yet I remained frozen in place, unable to do the many things that urgently screamed my name.

A sharp rap on the door broke my reverie. I spun my chair and opened a file. "Come in."

Tom slipped through the door, pushing it closed behind him. "Getting much done?" He wandered over and set a coffee onto the desk in front of me with a clunk.

"Oh, tons." I trailed the tip of my pen under a line of the legal brief, keeping my head bowed. "How's the new intern?"

"Fine." He tapped the casted arm I'd propped up on my desk. "You could've taken a few days off."

"Why? So I can loaf around my claustrophobic room all alone and catch up on daytime television? No way. It's better I earn my keep or my ass is out of here. Aiden will evict me."

Tom heaved a sigh. "Don't be melodramatic."

"I'm not. Aiden implied everyone would be happier if I went away. He doesn't want me anywhere near him or his family. Even Savannah can't stand my sorry face."

"Well, you deserve the wrath of Aiden. It was moronic of you to visit him that night. He was amped up, pissed off, and in a major world of hurt. Caused by you, I might add."

"Yeah, whatever. The guy hates my guts, and my wife booted me out of our apartment. What does that say?"

"That you need help. Stop feeling sorry for yourself and do something to fix it." He pushed the cup of coffee closer to me. "Have some caffeine and take it down ten notches."

"Like Alex will ever take me back? Yeah, that'll happen." I obediently took a sip from the cup.

"Have you tried?" He waved a hand as I opened my mouth to protest. "Don't give me that look. I'm talking about actually trying, Joel." A flash of white caught my eye before he slapped a card onto the desk and slid it toward me. "Commit. Take action."

"What's this?" My eyes rolled upward at the name in fine print. "A therapist? Kill me now."

"Keep up that attitude and I'll grant your wish, asshole." He leaned back, crossing his arms. "Aiden could press charges."

"Shit." My heart rate skyrocketed, and I broke into a cold sweat. "Should I hide under my desk? Are you here to serve me legal papers?"

"I said he could, not that he will." His brows rose as his gaze cut to the card. "He could be talked out of it."

"You have got to be fucking kidding."

Tom shrugged. "Your wife could also use the incident to gain sole custody of Daniel in the event she files for divorce."

My stomach twisted as the word sank in. "She's filing?"

"You know all of this, Joel." He rubbed at his jaw as he examined me. "What you did could not only end your career, but also what's left of your marriage."

"It would serve me right. That's what you're thinking. And Aiden, well, I bet he's thrilled now he can take revenge."

"There you go assuming the worst of him. Seems to be a common theme lately."

"What?"

"Aiden doesn't want to ruin your life. Not that you need assistance. You've done a fine job of messing it up all on your lonesome."

"Huh, right. You're implying he had nothing to do with it?"

"It's easy to point fingers and assign blame, but grow a pair and own it. You know what you've done. We don't have to go over it all again." Tom pointed at the card. "Talk to her."

"I can't."

"Why the hell not? Are you telling me that you refuse to talk to someone?"

I cleared my throat and sank back in my chair. "This is embarrassing."

"Lots of people talk to therapists. So what?"

"I'm in so much debt it makes me sick. I haven't built a clientele here, and right now, I can't do much legal work. Can you see me appearing in court like this?" I hooked my thumb toward my yellow-tinged face. "Let alone procuring clients. Sure, I'm earning a decent salary, but this move killed us financially."

Tom leaned toward me, nodding his head.

"The first payment is due on my financing. If I default, they'll go after Aiden."

He lifted his chin, peering at me through half-closed eyes. "I'll discuss it with Aiden. You have coverage through the firm for medical expenses, so most of that'll be paid."

"Still, I can't—"

"Therapy isn't optional," he said in a flat voice.

We stared at each other for several seconds before I dropped my head to rest on my arm. "Everything has built and built and built, and I can't get out from under it. Alex is in the apartment, and I have to find a place to live. My time is about up in the partner suite. I'm drowning with the mortgage payments and partnership loans, and I just ... can't."

"Let me help," Tom said in a low voice. "You've never been this person. Stay in the suite for now. Deal with your other issues, and then we'll find you somewhere to live."

"Why are you doing this?"

"You're my friend. If you're ready to get to work and mend a few bridges, then I'll support you all the way."

"What about Aiden?"

"What about him?"

"He'll be angry you're on my side."

"Don't be ridiculous. There are no sides here." Tom wagged his index finger. "If you think he'll be upset about me helping you, then you don't know the man. Aiden will understand."

"Will he?" I lifted my head. "It's gone too far. How can I ever make it right? I can't face Alex, and I'm scared to even attempt a visit to Aiden." My throat tightened, and I massaged the tender spot left by Emily's strangle hold.

"Keeping your distance from Aiden is a good idea for now. He has enough issues of his own. Get your act together. Take care of yourself and your family."

"I'm a mess." I sighed and rested my forehead on my desk to hide my eyes. Even thinking about this exhausted me, and I wanted to break down and weep. "I'll never recover."

"Yeah, you will. I've seen worse."

"I doubt it. Aiden won't forgive me, ever. He doesn't get it."

"The real problem is that he understands far too well."

"How's that?" I looked up.

"Never mind. Just make the call. Deal?"

That left me out of options. Follow the plan or be taken out of the game. "Deal."

CHAPTER 23

Alexis

As I settled into the oversized chair in my therapist's office, I clasped my hands and took a deep breath.

"How are things, Alex? You look tense."

I pasted on a faint smile. "That obvious, huh?"

Cynthia, my all-knowing therapist, bobbed her head. "You missed your last appointment."

"Sorry." I peered at her. "Things haven't been great at home. Joel's moved out."

She nodded, shifting in the chair.

"He lost control, and it scared me. Worse, he hurt someone dear to me, and …" My throat closed up and I swallowed hard. "It's my fault."

Cynthia offered me the box of tissues from the table beside her. "Why do you think that?"

"I relied on this person, and it's interfered in his friendship with Joel." The sordid story flowed from my mouth. Once I started, I had to get it out, and at the end, I took a breath and reached for the tumbler of ice water.

Her concerned frown seemed answer enough, but she said nothing, only nodding as her pen scratched across her notebook.

"Am I leaning on this man excessively?" I fidgeted, and then sipped my water. As eager as I was to hear her answer, fear enveloped me.

"You already know that answer." Cynthia's eyebrows lifted.

"Perhaps …" I twisted the tissue in my hand. "I am, right?"

"There's no easy answer, but your friend has asked you to redefine the relationship. How do you feel about that?"

"Hurt." The word slid out with little thought. "But I understand it. His wife said I'm too close, that I'm over the line."

"Then take his wife's feelings seriously. From everything you've said, you've had this close, bordering on intimate, relationship with this man for years. There don't seem to be any boundaries. Even not having the freedom to simply walk into his home unannounced bothers you."

Heat rose in my cheeks. "We've have never been intimate."

"There's only a small degree of separation in your case. You can't deny you're far closer to this man than to your husband at this moment. Sex is sex, you can do that with anyone. The emotional connection is what makes or breaks the relationship for any couple."

"Do you think I'm too close and need to step away? Joel has always maintained that a man and woman can't be best friends. He can't fathom why I'm not romantically involved with Aiden." I froze. *Damn. Why did I say his name?*

Cynthia's expression didn't even flicker.

"You knew?" My eyes widened. "Savannah?"

She nodded. "I've spoken with both Aiden and Emily, and we discussed the issues. They agreed if you brought it up, and if it would help in your sessions, I could share."

"You talked to Emily about me?" I frowned. "Why?"

"They had a joint session."

"Couples counseling? So I am causing issues. Aiden told me not to worry about him and Emily. The big fat liar," I muttered.

A smile appeared. "No, he's right," she said. "Those two have learned to communicate. If every married couple talked to each other with such openness and honesty, I'd be out of business. The session was more about Savannah, but a few interesting things surfaced."

"Like?"

"Aiden recognizes that Joel harbors insecurities about the relationship, and Emily is uncomfortable with status quo. Their marriage depends on his ability to respect her feelings and act appropriately. As does your relationship with your husband."

"Then I should be more careful of my interactions."

"Aiden's asked you, as a friend, to respect certain boundaries. He's struggling to get out of the way so you and Joel can deal with your issues without interference. Aiden talked to you, didn't he?"

"Now it all makes sense."

"Aiden is a part of the friend group that includes Joel, but perhaps you've claimed ownership. You knew him long before Joel did, but does that make him more your friend than your husband's?"

"Oh, umm …" My eyes widened. Is that what I'd been doing?

"It's something for you to consider." Cynthia waved a hand. "Now, on to Joel."

I sighed. We'd been down this road before. "He hasn't called or taken out Daniel, so there's not much to say." A shiver ran down my spine. "Should I be worried about our son?"

"From your own admission, it would be unlike Joel to hurt a child, but his actions are cause for concern. Has he ever been aggressive with you?"

I shook my head but my lips twisted.

"What's the look about?" Cynthia folded her hands under her chin, her head tipping downward as she regarded me.

"I've never pictured my life without Joel. Until this last year, he's always been a warm and loving man, and somehow he's morphed into this …" I slumped in the overstuffed chair and hugged a pillow against my body. "I worry about Daniel and how this will affect him." My eyes misted, and I swiped them with the back of my hand.

"Has he always been so disconnected from your son?"

Getting a read on his feelings about Daniel seemed impossible. "It goes in cycles. One minute he's warm and loving, and then our relationship seems hollow and distant." My lip curled. "He's implied more than once, to both me and to Aiden …" Tears trickled down, leaving raw tracks on my cheeks.

"Alex?" Cynthia asked in a low and even tone. "What has he implied?"

"He insinuated that Aiden is Daniel's father." I sniffled, avoiding her gaze along with the inevitable judgment.

She cleared her throat. "Is he?"

"No way. I've never cheated on Joel, ever."

"People don't always tell the entire truth," Cynthia said. "Sharing the private details of your life isn't easy, and people fear judgment. Sometimes they don't even admit their failings to themselves. If you had an affair with Aiden, could you ever tell anyone?"

I crossed my arms. "Well, we haven't, so it's not something I've worried about."

"It makes it easier if you haven't, but your husband's suspicions explain the rage directed at Aiden. Given this new information, a level of caution with your son is warranted. If there is any question in his mind about his biological connection to Daniel, it's something we have to resolve."

A mixture of fear and anger rose within me. "Daniel is his son, and I'd like Joel to trust me enough to believe it."

"I understand." Cynthia drummed her fingers against her notebook. "Joel called and asked for counseling with me."

"What? Why would he call you?"

"He was referred by one of your friends."

"Who would do that?" I narrowed my eyes.

"Someone who understands the importance of couples counseling. It's not an attack on you, Alex."

"Tell him to find someone else."

"Let's take a step back before we decide. Married couples have a better chance of resolving their differences if they attend counseling together."

"We're never getting back together."

"Even for separate sessions, it's more productive to be attending the same office." She held up a hand. "It may seem darkest now, but what if I said there's a chance of saving your marriage? What if this small sacrifice could ease the way to peaceful co-parenting of your son if you decide on a permanent separation?"

"He never wanted to before."

"Things change. There are few downsides to this. It may feel like too little and too late, but you have a child who needs his father. You have to find a way to smooth that path, no matter if you're married to Joel or not."

"Maybe he doesn't deserve it." I crossed my arms and gritted my teeth. "He hasn't bothered to see his son since he left. Perhaps I should let him walk away, file for divorce, and be done with it."

Cynthia's brows drew together. "This isn't about you. This is about Daniel. He deserves to have his father, and simply dictating and letting that bond break … you'd come to regret it. Joel has to do his part in creating a relationship with his child, but you have to clear the way. Try a few sessions. If it doesn't work, we can stop."

Heat flooded my face and I bowed my head. I couldn't deny the facts. If we managed to resolve our differences, allowing Daniel the opportunity to build a relationship with his father, could I refuse?

I'd watched Aiden and Savannah struggle with the issue of Tiffany and the rejection of her daughter. Did I want to be facing needless emotional battles with my own child? Parental neglect caused lifelong damage.

"Joel can see you, and if he's willing, we'll schedule couple's sessions. I don't know if I can ever forgive him, but I won't hurt my son that way."

"You won't regret trying." Cynthia produced a faint smile. "Offering therapy to couples puts me in the middle like a mediator. I have to act in the best interests of both the husband and wife."

"What does that mean, exactly?"

"It's hard to keep secrets. Ethically, I can't hold back information from either party that would affect their ability to heal. You both have to agree to speak the truth in our sessions, and there will be a certain amount of sharing. What I propose is I have an individual session with Joel, then we move into joint therapy. Agreed?"

I squirmed, goosebumps rising on my arms. "Fine." Facing my husband might be uncomfortable and create more stress, but the sooner we resolved this, the better. Limbo was not a great place to be.

CHAPTER 24

Joel

$\mathcal{I}$ SHIFTED IN THE OVER-STUFFED CHAIR, fixing a blank stare on the woman across from me. How to even begin?

"Let me start." Cynthia smiled. "Alex agreed with our plan, so today I'd like to get to know you and answer questions. Next session, we'll include your wife. You can talk to me about anything, but this isn't about unloading your secrets on me and keeping them from her. We'll be building a strong communication loop. To make this worthwhile, you need to learn to share with Alexis."

"I understand."

Cynthia had warned me during our initial phone conversation that by entering into this, we were providing our permission to share. It didn't make me feel any better, but no other viable options existed. Time to man up and face the mess I'd created or the next visit would be to a divorce lawyer. Or worse, if Aiden changed his mind.

"Tell me what brought you here? Why did you agree to counseling?"

"Things have fallen apart, and I can't seem to do the right thing."

"Let's explore that."

Explore it? My mind scrambled to decipher her request. I had no idea what to say. Not a great start to this sharing thing.

"It'll get easier." Cynthia folded her hands in her lap. "Tell me what you're thinking."

"We'd reconnected, but it all went wrong. I don't know what came over me, or how to fix it."

"It seems you're both willing to try. That's an excellent start."

"I want my wife and son back. What do you want me to do? Tell me how to fix this."

"Have patience." Cynthia eyed me. "There are no quick and easy answers. This is a serious commitment, and I commend you for taking the first step."

I rolled my eyes. "She's planning to make this as damn difficult as possible, right?"

"Why do you think she'd purposely make it harder?"

"Alexis is stubborn and pigheaded, and she thinks this is all my fault." I pushed out of the chair and paced back and forth.

Cynthia pursed her lips. "Do you resent being here?"

I halted and crossed my arms. "Airing my marital issues to a complete stranger isn't the highlight of my day."

"No, but will you give it a chance? Why are you here, Joel?"

"I have no choice. If I don't, then I lose everything." I slumped into the chair.

"I hope you'll be open to this process. Can you give one hundred percent commitment?"

I shrugged. "Again, I have no choice."

"You do have a choice. If you don't want to be here, you're free to walk out that door anytime."

I contemplated this woman, pondering her angle. If I walked out that door and didn't come back, what then? I stood and reached for my coat.

"I hope you change your mind, Mr. Nichols. You have obvious anger issues that concern me. And I'm not the only one who worries."

"About what? I'm fine."

"Your wife doesn't think so." Cynthia leaned back in her chair and folded her hands. "Neither do your friends."

"Huh. Right. She has them all on her side."

"There are no sides to be taken in this office. Are you aware that Alex has serious concerns about your interactions with your son? That your outburst frightened not only her but others among your friends?"

I eyed her. Who had she been talking to?

"Who asked you to come here? Why did you call me?"

"My friend Tom suggested ..." I bowed my head, gripping the armrest, digging my nails into the fabric. "No. Aiden. He's the instigator here. If I get help, he won't pursue charges against me. Or so Tom led me to believe. Such an asshole."

"Or a good friend who wants you to deal with your problems." Her brows rose. "His intentions aren't malicious."

"How do you know that?"

"Aiden attended some family sessions with Savannah."

"Great. So you've not only talked to my wife but him too? You already know everything?"

She nodded.

I sank into the chair. "And Alex is worried about Daniel? She thinks I'd do what?"

"You lost your temper. You hurt someone, and both of you ended up in the hospital. No matter the cause, it's a concern."

"Okay. I get it." I held up my good hand, surrendering. "Let's set up the first couples session."

"Good." She smiled. "It's the right decision."

As I entered the coffee shop, I spotted Alex ensconced in a corner booth and slid in across from her. "Thanks for coming."

"How have you been?"

"Alright." My mind rebelled at my falsehood. "That's a lie. This has been the worst time of my life. I miss you and Daniel." I reached for her hand. "Let me come home."

She reared back in her seat, her brows rising. "What?"

"I miss you," I whispered. "I've made so many mistakes. I love you, and I need to fix this. Please, please let me see him." I refused to flinch or look away, aware this mess could cost me my career and custody of my son. Courts liked to have parental involvement with children, but given my outburst, I couldn't be sure of anything

"You want to see him? What about the whole ...?" She looked away.

"What?"

Alex fidgeted, clenching a hand around her ceramic tea cup. "Why haven't you called?"

"I thought you'd refuse, or I might scare him. My face looked horrendous for a while. Aiden got in some solid shots."

"Good." Alex straightened and crossed her arms. "You deserved it."

"I took my jealousy out on him."

"You messed up his life."

"I'll deal with that, but now is not the time. I'm staying clear until Aiden's ready." Tom had been adamant that if I went anywhere near Aiden, he would pummel me into the ground. "How is he?"

"Not great." She lifted a shoulder. "This set him back, and he may be off work for a year if he needs surgery."

"Damn. How do I fix that?" My stomach plummeted. "Or us?"

"Maybe there's nothing left to fix."

"Then why are we doing this stupid rigmarole? You've already written us off. You don't even want me to see Daniel."

"Why should I let you see him? How can I trust you?"

"You think I'd damage our son? It hurts that you don't believe in me."

"That's rich coming from you. Your whole innocent *you don't believe in me* whine fest after your nasty insinuations about my behavior. Worse, you act like I've deceived you about Daniel." She scowled as she slapped an envelope onto the table and shoved it at me. "Here."

"What's this?" My breath caught in my chest as I spotted the return address. *A genetics lab?* "Alex?"

"Let me know when you're free, and I'll bring Daniel in so you can watch them take the samples."

"We don't need to—"

"Yeah, we do." She stood. "You're living in some fantasy world where I'm the guilty party. That's not okay. Make up your mind if you want Daniel or not. If you do, set up the appointment. If you don't, then say so."

"How can you believe that?" I grabbed her as she turned to leave. "Why wouldn't I want him?"

Alex froze, staring at the hand I'd wrapped around her wrist. "Let me go," she whispered. Her whole body trembled.

"I'm sorry." I released her and scrubbed the rough stubble on my jaw. "Please, stay and talk to me."

She shook her head. "There's nothing to say."

"What?" I examined her stormy face. "I made us an appointment. I'm doing this counseling for you, Alex."

"Do it for yourself or not at all. Don't think I'll come running back to you just because you're seeing Cynthia. It doesn't work that way."

"Then why bother?" I muttered as I turned the envelope in my hand.

Alex heaved a sigh. "No reason at all. Do what you want. Text and let me know your decision." She stalked toward the door, exiting without a backward glance.

"Can I get you anything else?"

I peered at the waitress. "No, thanks." Both my optimism and hopes had been dashed.

Text me your decision? Right. Like I had one to make. If I didn't go back to this therapist, I might as well drown myself into the harbor. My life would be over.

Chapter 25

I LEFT THE CAFÉ FIGHTING BACK the tears. *Why bother?* The thoughtless response and lack of effort after one lousy session told me how little I meant. And to assume I'd take him back? He'd had it easy all these months. I hunched my shoulders against the chill wind. What was it with men?

Calling Aiden and crying on his shoulder was tempting, but I'd promised to do that less. The potential damage to my friend's hard-won marriage wasn't worth the risk. Besides, Emily had a valid point. If I'd found Joel in bed with another woman, no matter what the circumstances, I'd have lost it.

Aiden's wife had shown great restraint. She'd chosen to discuss her fears with her husband and given her calm and perpetually collected demeanour, I'd bet she expressed them rationally. If Joel and I had learned to communicate like that we wouldn't be facing our current troubles.

The doorman buzzed me into Tom and Jenna's apartment.

I stepped out of the elevator and glanced around. "How's my boy?"

"Great. He's with Tom and Adrianna in the playroom. I'm sure he'll sleep well tonight. We took them to the park and he only napped for half an hour." Jenna hugged me tightly. "Come on in. Did you want to stay for dinner?"

"That would be lovely, thank you," I said as Jenna poured me water.

"So?" She widened her eyes. "How did it go?"

"Lousy." I clutched the icy glass and wandered to the windows, over to the mantle to inspect some pictures, then back to the windows. My mind wouldn't stop, my thoughts consuming me.

"Calm down."

"What?" I halted and stared at my friend.

"You can't stop moving. What's bothering you?"

"I'm scared," I whispered.

"Of what?"

"Everything. What if it's over? What then? I love Daniel, but my whole life has become about taking care of my child and waiting for my jackass husband to come home. I need more." I twirled a finger through my hair. "Does that sound selfish?"

"Not at all. When Adrianna is bigger, I'll find part-time work or volunteer. Living for only one thing isn't healthy."

"I've thought about finding a position in interior design, and working a few hours a week to get out of the house."

"Excellent idea." She nodded. "Having something for yourself couldn't hurt."

"Except I may spend as much on babysitting as I earn. Everyone knows we took on huge partnership loans to swing this."

"Joel took on huge partnership loans." Jenna crossed her arms. "You didn't sign, did you?"

"No, but my name is on the apartment." A small frisson of hope grew the dampened. "Aiden guaranteed those loans."

"Don't worry. The law firm is a solid investment. As for the childcare, maybe we can work something out. I don't have a nanny, but I could help some days. Emily and Aiden hired a full-time nanny as Aiden is restricted from lifting, and he can't manage Kellan alone."

"Are you suggesting I share their nanny?"

"It wouldn't hurt to ask. Aiden will recover over the next few weeks, but he can't go back to work. I bet he'd love to have Daniel around."

"Joel might not like it."

"Joel needs to get over it. Don't let his attitude prevent you from moving forward."

"There's a lot he has to get over. I gave him the DNA test information." I dropped onto a stool. "He threw a hissy fit about me not trusting him, if you can believe it."

"Ironic, huh?"

"Moronic, you mean." I rolled my eyes and picked a red pepper from the veggie plate on the counter.

"You need a drink." Jenna dug into the cupboards. "Hmm. Too cold for Margaritas."

"Bite your tongue. It's never too cold for Margaritas."

Jenna giggled and rustled around in the cupboard, producing two glasses and several bottles. "I'd call Emily to join us, but she won't leave Aiden." After adding a splash of liquor from each bottle, along with a liberal dose of pineapple juice and ice, she topped the shaker.

"I'm sure she doesn't want to be around me. She confiscated my key fobs, and I've been informed to back off of her husband. What does she really think of my relationship with Aiden?"

Jenna paused before pouring the drinks and dribbling in a touch of grenadine. "Emily felt threatened, and she went with her gut reaction and blocked access to their home. It's not about you, Alex. Joel royally screwed up, and it's caused a backlash. That's on him."

"Good luck to him. I'll let Joel fight that battle on his own."

"Ahh. Making him work for it, are we?"

"Damn right. I've struggled through all of this, why should he get a free ride? If he wants it fixed, then he can get off his lazy ass and fix it."

"I hear you." Jenna pushed my drink across the counter. "It's not a Margarita, but it'll take the edge off."

I sipped the refreshing juice, savoring the tang and bite of the alcohol as it hit my palate. "I don't know if he's even grasped reality, and he seems to believe a couple of visits to Cynthia means he's back, but he's belligerent about the entire thing. I guess Daniel and I aren't worth it."

Jenna slid onto the seat next to me. "He'll come around. It's not like he has a choice about any of this. Tom told him to deal with his issues, or he'll be facing worse than counseling."

"Oh?" I shifted to face her. "How's that?"

"Aiden could take him to court for assault. That's a professional issue."

"Aiden would never—" My eyes widened. "He didn't."

"Yeah, he did. Some back room deals are happening. I thought you should know."

"Damn, Aiden. I'm not happy with Joel, but blackmail?"

Jenna rested a hand on my arm. "Don't be pissed at Aiden. He found a way to force Joel into counseling, and he took it. The ends justify the means in this case."

"It won't help the relationship between Joel and Aiden. That grudge will last forever." I dropped my head onto my forearms and closed my eyes. No wonder Joel had been so grouchy.

"We hope that Joel will realize Aiden considered all the angles before he acted. Perhaps you can see it too."

Where would this mess end? That Joel had been coerced into therapy didn't make me feel better, but at least someone had shared the machinations happening behind the scenes.

My phone vibrated, and I peered at the screen.

The session is for Friday at 10 am. Can you be there?

"Well, something worked. We have an appointment on Friday." I gulped the last of my cocktail and pushed the empty glass toward Jenna.

She raised an eyebrow but retrieved the shaker to concoct another round. "Are you going?"

"I don't know." I shrugged. "His enthusiasm is underwhelming. He even had the balls to ask what the point was. Well, now I know how to answer him. If he attends sessions, he saves his own ass."

"True." Jenna passed me my refilled glass. "What are the reasons you should go?"

"For Daniel."

"Bingo. Do what's right for you and your son. Let Joel take care of himself."

I sighed and tapped in my answer, hitting send before I reconsidered. I'd now committed to couples sessions with someone I had no plans of being a couple with, ever again.

⌒≼

I stepped into the small waiting room at Cynthia's office, half expecting it to be empty. To my surprise, Joel sat fidgeting with a large coffee cup, another on the table in front of him.

"Hi." I eyed him, taking in the yellowish tinge spread across his clean-shaven cheek and the dark circles under his hazel eyes.

Dressed in jeans and a sweater, he reminded me of the man who had stolen my heart. Except that recent events had proven he wasn't. No matter how much this person appeared to be Joel, he wasn't that same sweet guy.

He extended the second cup. "It's extra hot."

"Thanks." I perched on the edge of the chair across from him.

An uneasy silence fell over us, and I stared at the chai, letting random thoughts flow through my mind.

"It's not poisoned."

"Hmm?" My attention snapped back to the present. I opened my mouth to answer, but at that moment, the office door opened and Cynthia beckoned.

We shuffled in, taking seats on opposite ends of the overstuffed couch.

"Let's get started, shall we?" Cynthia folded her hands. Her gaze traveled to me, then to Joel, her eyebrows rising as neither of us uttered a word. "Joel? Why don't we start with you?"

He hunched his shoulders. "I don't know what to say."

"Tell Alex how you feel about being here."

His knuckles whitened as he clutched his cup, then he shrugged and turned his head away.

"Great," I muttered. "You know what? If you don't want to be here, then leave. It's what you do best."

"No, you kicked me out. There's a difference."

"Is there?" I hugged a pillow to my chest. "You've done nothing to make up for being a jackass all summer, and then you lied and cheated, not to mention the unprovoked attack on one of our best friends over a ridiculous fantasy you've concocted in your head." I stood and tossed the pillow onto the couch. "You had it right. What's the point?"

"You dragged me into this, and now you don't want to do it?"

"Alex. Please sit." Cynthia motioned toward the couch.

I eyed her for a moment and then slumped onto the far end of the couch again. "Don't you get it? I asked you over and over to do this, and you didn't care. You're here to save your own ass, not because you give a damn about us."

"That's not true. You're the one who doesn't get it. Everything I do is wrong, according to you." Joel's eyes blazed, but then he rubbed his hands through his hair and exhaled a long slow breath. "You know what? Your boyfriend wanted me in counseling, and as usual, he got what he wanted. I'm here."

I curled my fists around the pillow, fighting the urge to deck him.

"You believe Alex has been unfaithful?" Cynthia turned her attention to Joel. "Who is this boyfriend?"

"She knows." He curled his lip.

"Huh. That's hypocritical, coming from the guy with another woman on the side."

"I don't have her, Alex. She's a friend, that's all."

Cynthia raised her brows at me.

"See? He expects me to trust him. Yet he refuses to trust his wife or his best friend."

"You have to earn it," Joel said.

"Ha. I couldn't have said it better."

"I want to take Daniel. I haven't seen him in over a week."

I frowned. "Why would you want to see him?"

"Back to this again?"

"Yup. You can't see him until we visit the lab and get the results."

"I'd never hurt Daniel."

"You know what you need to do, Joel." I crossed my arms and narrowed my eyes.

"It's all about what you want these days. Don't I get a say?"

"No. You don't. Maybe once you have solid proof, and you lay your stupid fantasies to rest, things will change." Maybe I was being harsh, but I needed Joel to see the hurt he'd caused. His lack of trust cut me deep, and nothing could ever be the same.

CHAPTER 26

Joel

ALEX DIDN'T TRUST ME WITH our son. That sad reality consumed me. Our failed session with Cynthia was over with, and I couldn't wait to get out of there.

Alex scurried toward the elevator like she couldn't stand my presence.

"Hey." I reached for her shoulder. "Do you truly believe I'd put the life of an innocent child in danger? He's been a part of my life ever since he was born, and regardless of who—"

She spun toward me, the cold glare she leveled my way causing me to snap my mouth shut. "You'd better not finish that sentence." Alex crossed her arms. "If you want to see him, then you know what you have to do."

"I don't want or need testing."

"Well, I do. Let me know when you can go, and we'll get it done. If you won't, then Aiden will."

"What? Why would he do that?"

"Because he has nothing to hide. There's no possible way he could be Daniel's father." She narrowed her eyes. "Unlike you, he trusts me."

"Fine." I threw my hands into the air. "I'll call and make the appointment. Then maybe you'll let me see Daniel. I'm the only father he's ever known." I stabbed at the elevator call button.

She scoffed as her gaze became icy and she muttered something under her breath.

"Say it out loud, Alex."

The doors slid open and we both stepped inside.

"Bullshit. A real father would be there." Alex turned and lifted her chin. "Tom and Aiden have both stepped in and become substitute fathers for your son. Neither have any moral or legal responsibility for Daniel, yet they make an effort to spend time with him."

The rush of emotions flashed through me. Anger topped the list. "Quit punishing me for my mistakes."

"I'm not doing this to punish you. But you aren't acting"—Alex shrugged— "rational."

"It feels like punishment. Aiden and Tom have ganged up to force my hand. You're holding Daniel hostage until I submit to testing. Even Ryan gave me a lecture. Why can't we keep this between us?"

"I tried that. I pretended for months, kept it from our friends, and put up with your nonsense. If you want to blame someone, then look in the damn mirror. Besides, how dare you get on my case when you admitted you shared our problems with *her*." The moment the doors opened on the ground floor, Alex barreled toward the front doors.

I let her go. What was the point in chasing after her? I loved Alex, but I didn't hold out much hope for us. We'd never repair our relationship or get past our differences if we couldn't even have a civil conversation.

Daniel's arms wrapped around my neck, and I held him close. Alex looked on, her mouth set in a grim line.

"You be good for Mommy." I kissed his soft cheek and gave him a last squeeze before setting him on his feet. "Alex, please ..."

She shook her head and took Daniel's hand. "We have to go, and you need to get back to work. Say bye-bye, Daniel."

My son fluttered his little fingers and gazed up at me with those trusting hazel eyes. "Bye-bye, Daddy."

My throat closed up, so I waved in return, remaining frozen as Alex led Daniel down the sidewalk. Seeing my family walk away tore my heart to shreds, and a sense of hopelessness crept over me.

It seemed that nothing could make this better or make Alex happy. My attempts at conversation had been discouraged. A stony silence had loomed over us as the technician had swabbed our cheeks, hovering over us like a harbinger of doom, broken only by our few harsh words.

After they disappeared around the corner, I hunched my shoulders and buttoned up my collar to fend off the chill wind before I shuffled down the street toward our office building.

Alex had made her views clear, so I'd consider the next steps. I had no intention of putting Daniel through an emotional tug-of-war. The children of separated and divorced parents often suffered the consequences, but I refused to give up my son. There had to be a way to get through to Alex and make her see Daniel needed me as much as I needed him.

Memories flitted through my mind, pictures of those long ago days when I'd walk in the door and Alex would launch herself into my arms and cover me with kisses. An intense longing to rewind our lives and relive our young and carefree days enveloped me. I missed that magical time before the weight of the world rested on our shoulders, and the dreaded R word took front and center.

Responsibility. We all had to grow up, but when did it become so dreary? A daily slog, where you dragged yourself from your bed, worked hard for hours, and then shuffled home, caught on a wheel like a sad little hamster. When did that awful word become the keystone to our entire lives?

As I reached my office, my phone buzzed, breaking me out of my daydream. I grimaced at the name on the call display. She'd called several times in the past two weeks, and I'd ignored her messages, but at some point, I'd have to deal with her. She had impressive persistence, but it needed to end. We lived in different states. It couldn't be that difficult to avoid each other.

"Crystal."

"Hi, honey. You've fallen off the planet, and I miss you."

That purring tone used to seem cute and playful, but now it plain annoyed me. "I'm not your honey, and you have to stop calling and leaving me messages. I can't see or talk to you."

"That's what you said during the summer but you still came to me when you needed someone. Quit letting Alex tell you who you can or cannot have as a friend."

"It's not a simple friendship. You're my ex-girlfriend. Alex is my wife, and she has to come first." I sank into my chair. "It's no secret my marriage is in trouble, and I have to make a choice."

"And if it doesn't work out with Alex?"

"I won't be jumping into another relationship, and it wouldn't be with you. Move on, and find someone else."

"That's harsh, considering how many times you cried on my shoulder this summer."

Cried? Not exactly soothing to the ole ego, but Crystal had always been good at playing the game. "No, it's realistic and honest. Besides, I have Daniel to consider, and we both know you don't have a maternal bone in your body."

She snorted. "No, I don't want to play mommy to someone else's kid, and you don't want to play daddy, either."

Damn alcohol had loosened my tongue. I rued the moment I'd opened my mouth and voiced my concerns regarding Aiden and Alex. That I'd ever mentioned my suspicions about Daniel's parentage was one of my biggest regrets about this summer.

"Please, no more calls or texts. Let me fix things with my wife."

"But—"

"I'm sorry, but this is the way it has to be. Take care of yourself. Goodbye, and don't call or text again."

Relief came over me as I tapped the red disconnect icon. One more step in reclaiming my life. I made a mental note to block her on my social media accounts.

The summer had been fun, and I'd enjoyed hanging out, but Crystal and I weren't on the same path. She wanted to party. I longed for my family. My life with Alex hadn't been perfect, but it had been close enough.

That old saying about not knowing what you have until it's gone taunted me. Some people you needed to hold close, while others needed to be removed from your life. If I had any hope left for my marriage, I had only one choice. Cut Crystal and allow no further contact.

Our next session occurred three days later. Alex hadn't bothered to phone or text to confirm she'd attend. What if she'd given up on me, and didn't come?

The constriction in my chest eased when I opened the door to Cynthia's reception room and found Alex perched on the edge of a chair, flipping through a magazine.

I exhaled a long slow breath as I shut the door, and set her coffee onto the table before sitting opposite to her. "How's everything?"

"Fine." She shrugged. "I got a job."

"What? Why?"

"I want to use my interior design skills." She crossed her arms, a frown settling on her face. "Do you even listen during our sessions?"

"I wasn't expecting it so soon, is all. I assumed you meant you'd work part-time when Daniel got older. I thought we'd ..."

"We'd what?" She examined me.

I shook my head and bit my tongue. I expected we'd be planning our second child by now, but mentioning it would open an intense and controversial subject. One where Alex would roll her eyes and remind me of how I'd been absent for Daniel's first months.

Then I'd have to hear about how perfect Tom and Aiden were as fathers. How they'd been so involved. Resentment oozed from my pores when my wife got onto that track.

"Humph." She snorted. "Things won't get better until you're honest, Joel. I need to do this, and it would be great if you could be happy for me."

"I am, Alex. If it's what you want, then do it." I pasted on a smile, but I could tell she wasn't convinced.

More tears, more disappointment, and even more sadness flashed across her face until I felt I'd drown in it. I slumped in my chair and wished for that one single thing I could say or do right.

Chapter 27

THE SMILING DOORMAN RELEASED THE elevator when he saw me, which relieved the sting of no longer having a key. Not that I blamed Emily. The safety and happiness of her family depended on solid decision making, and so much rested on her shoulders with Aiden still recuperating

I slung my coat onto the rack and walked through to the kitchen. "Hi, Vanna."

"Oh." She spun to face me, her eyes wide. "Aunt Alex. I didn't know you were there."

"Sorry to startle you." I eyed her pale face and stepped forward to wrap my arms around her trembling shoulders. "How are you? I thought you'd be in school."

"I don't feel well today." Savannah bowed her head. "Everything has been so weird."

"How so?"

"Every time I walk into a room, conversation stops." She brushed at her eyes.

"What? Tell me, Vanna."

"They'll be mad if I do."

"Who'll be mad?"

"Dad and Emily."

Her emotional reaction concerned me. I knew Aiden had her in therapy again. The whole incident with Joel had brought back her intense nightmares, and even my showing up in the apartment had scared her.

"I don't want them to get a divorce," she whispered. "Once they got married I figured we'd be a happy normal family, but we're not."

"Honey." I tucked an arm around her waist. "Life is like that. And what is normal anyway? That whole deal is bogus marketing and encourages people to buy into false ideals of perfection. We're all individuals, doing the best we can in less than ideal circumstances."

Savannah frowned. "I've never had a typical family. Even with my Mom and Dad in Portland, people knew I was adopted, and they treated me different."

"People don't always understand, but don't worry about Aiden and Emily. Their relationship has strength. If anyone can make it through the tough times, they can."

"I hope so." She clutched at the sparkling heart pendant around her neck. "I love them both, and I can't stand to see them so sad."

"That's my fault. They're not unhappy with each other, it's the circumstances. You know that Joel and I have hit a rough patch and your dad's been dragged into the middle of our mess. It'll all work out, but I do owe you an apology, Savannah. This is your home, and my troubles with Joel have invaded. I'm so sorry."

She studied me with those deep brown eyes, still rubbing at the pendant. "Joel thinks ..." She tucked her chin to her chest, her breathing becoming raspy.

"Vanna." I grasped her shoulders. "There is no basis to what Joel thinks. Your dad and I have been good friends for a long time, but there is nothing romantic between us. There never has been. Please believe me, I would never, ever be involved with Aiden like that."

Savannah lifted her head. "Why does Joel think you would?"

"Because we're so close, and I confide in Aiden a lot." I guided her onto a stool. "Tiffany loved your dad, and she was like a sister."

"She doesn't love him anymore." A tear trickled down her cheek. "She doesn't love me either."

"I don't think that's true." I suspected it wasn't at all the case, but Savannah didn't need to hear the gritty details of her mother's behavior at Jenna's wedding. "Your dad is like a brother to me. Our friends are family, and we've all known each other for over twenty years. Neither of us would do anything to ruin it."

"Why does Joel think it's more?"

"I don't know, sweetie, but it isn't. That old code comes into play; thou shalt not sleep with your best friend's man."

"Ick." A tiny smile twitched the corners of her mouth. "Please don't say stuff like that about my dad."

"Deal. As long as you remember your dad is an innocent party. He did nothing but be my friend, and he's never betrayed Emily, or Joel, or anyone else in our group. Emily understands that, and they're working through the issues."

"Hey." Aiden appeared in the doorway. "I thought I heard voices. Everything good?" His eyes seemed drawn to Savannah's weepy face. He moved across the room and drew her into a hug, dropping a kiss on the top of her head. "What's the matter, sweetie?"

"Nothing," she murmured as she buried her head against his chest.

"It's not nothing."

"I still don't feel good. I'm going to my room." She stretched and kissed Aiden on the cheek before she shuffled off.

A frown appeared as he watched her go.

"You look done in. Why don't we sit?" I rubbed his arm.

We settled in the living room and Aiden leaned back, pale-faced and exhausted.

"Still bad?"

"Some days are better than others. What did Vanna say?"

"I scared her when I came in. She worries about you and Emily."

"We're talking about it in the sessions. She's struggling, Alex. She seems to level out, and then something else happens and cancels every bit of her progress. I don't know what to do."

"You're doing it, honey. Be there for her, listen, and let her know you love her. Maybe showing your affection for Emily in front of her wouldn't hurt, either. She needs to know you two are solid. She didn't say much, but she did express concern that you two are in danger of divorcing."

"Damn, really?" He leaned back and closed his eyes. "I'll talk to Em about that." He opened his eyes again. "How are you doing?"

"I got the job."

"Congratulations?" A small frown creased his brow. "Why don't you seem happier?"

"Two guesses and the first doesn't count."

"Oh. I'm sorry, Lex." Aiden sighed and rolled his eyes. "How's counseling?"

"We're both going, but it isn't doing much for our relationship. And we went through with the DNA test."

"That's some sort of progress."

"Yeah, I had to force him, but maybe he can let go of his ridiculous fantasies."

"And Daniel? How is he?"

"Confused. I can see it in his eyes, but what can I do? I have to protect him. What do you think? Am I wrong to deny visitation to Joel?"

"There's never an easy answer with kids." He raised his brows. "Given my involvement in this mess, I'd prefer not to express an opinion."

"I'm sorry." I nibbled on my lip. "You're right, I have no right to ask it of you."

"No worries, Lex. What does Cynthia say?"

"Exercise caution. That's what confuses me." I tipped my head back against the couch. "Joel is so up and down, but in my heart, I refuse to believe he'd hurt a child."

"You've known the man forever, so go with your gut on this one." He patted my knee. "I miss Daniel, you should bring him by for a visit. I'm off work for a while, so if you ever need someone to watch him, let me know."

"Are you up for it?"

"I'll manage, and we have Iona coming in to help with Kellan when Emily's not home. Unless it will interfere with Joel."

"I don't give a damn what he thinks. The man acts like a big baby, and my patience is worn out." I narrowed my eyes. "Jenna talked to you about watching Daniel, didn't she?"

"Busted." He smiled. "I asked Iona, and she'd be fine watching Daniel for a few hours now and then, and I'll be better soon. If you need childcare while you work, Jenn and I can alternate until you settle things with Joel."

"You two." Tears burned my eyes. My friends were the best in the entire world. "You asked your nanny?"

"Sure. She adores Daniel, and Kellan is an easy baby. She'd love an extra little boy to chase around the park."

I hopped up to hug him. "Thank you, honey. You're more supportive about my work than my own husband."

"He'll come around, but in the meantime, send your work schedule, and we can sort out the days."

"Aiden?" I glanced toward the doorway and lowered my voice. "I said the *t* word to Savannah. I hope it didn't upset her too much, but she had questions. She knows what's going on and why. You're aware of that, right?"

"The *t* word?" His eyebrows rose.

"Tiffany. It fit into explaining our relationship, and the assurances that we've never been involved romantically."

"Don't worry about it. Vanna and I talk about Tiffany." He waved a hand at me. "I'm curious. How did it explain you and me?"

"You know … the rule about not moving in on your best friend's love interest?"

"I know it well." He smiled ruefully.

I'd meant it to be rhetorical, but it highlighted the dangers of being too comfortable with members of the opposite sex who were not your brother. Nobody could deny Aiden's appeal to women, but … "Funny I've never thought of you that way." I sighed. "It seems like forever since Tiffany and I were friends."

"You could still be her friend. I appreciate the solidarity, but I never wanted anyone to take sides."

"Is that why you waited so long to confess that she cheated on you?"

He bowed his head and lifted a shoulder.

"Aiden." I curled an arm around his shoulders. "What?"

"It feels like you've given up on your marriage, and it's hard to watch."

"He gave up first."

"Wow. You sound like me in every relationship I've ever had. That's bad. Don't be like me."

"You're with Emily, so how can you say that?"

"It doesn't mean I didn't say those exact words to her when things got rough. It's impossible for you to see past the pain right now."

"What about Joel's cheating? You went through that with Tiffany, and you never forgave her."

"But I am trying, Lex. At the time, part of me wanted to make her suffer for what she did, while the other part could barely function and crumbled into pieces. I'm not blameless, but I never wanted to confess what I did."

I frowned. "What did you do?"

"I exacted my revenge, and I made sure she knew it. Then I buried it because I didn't want to be reminded or to hear the I told you so crap. Not that it mattered, my family ensured I'd never forget."

I bit my lip. The meaning of his words was pretty clear in my mind. "You cheated on her?"

"She'd already cheated on me, and I'd left her. Is it still considered being unfaithful?"

"That's a good question." One I wasn't sure I could answer.

"I'm not proud of my actions, but you do stupid things after someone rips your heart out. I fell apart, and the moment I thought I'd survived, it got worse."

"How?"

"She showed up a few weeks later to announce her pregnancy."

My mouth went dry. "You two had another baby?"

"No," he said softly. "She miscarried early on, and that's when Michelle swooped in and moved Tiffany back to Chicago."

"Was the baby—" I snapped my mouth closed. How could I even ask that?

Aiden shrugged. "We'll never know," he said. "I've always wondered what would have happened if I'd tried harder and forgiven her sooner."

"Why do think you should have forgiven her? She slept with someone else."

"She'd been having a hard time with living in Philly. I'd missed our anniversary because I had to study for a major exam. If I'd paid more attention to her …" He cleared his throat. "It became a huge mess. Everything we had or dreamed of having disappeared."

"That had to have been hard." And even harder to share with me. I rubbed his back. "Sadly, I can relate to that sentiment."

"It doesn't have to be that way. Can you do something for me?"

"Anything."

"Don't give up yet. One of my biggest regrets is not making more of an effort and giving up too soon. Look how our ending affected everyone and everything for years."

"Joel is so angry and resentful, I don't think we'll ever get past it. I made a note to ask Tom for some names of divorce lawyers. I can't take it anymore."

"I've been in that place filled with overwhelming anger and animosity, and look where we are now. Savannah suffers because neither of us can hold a civil conversation."

"You think I'm being too hasty?"

"Maybe I'm wrong, but I think you two are meant to be together. You can tell me to get lost, but I worry you'll end up like we did. The day we signed the divorce papers was the worst ever, complete with a horrible blowout in the damn elevator. Now we can't even be in the same state, let alone the same room."

"I understand your anger. She betrayed you."

"Yeah, she ripped out my heart, and it took me ten years to gather enough courage to love another woman. When you love someone, any betrayal is devastating. They steal a piece of you, and maybe you never get it back."

"I know."

"Yes, but do you love him?"

I blinked and searched for the words. The answer should be simple, but it wasn't. *Yes* burned on the tip of my tongue, but I couldn't say it. I loved Joel, but I hated him too.

"Maybe there's a way back. Don't let what you have devolve into the mess that became my first marriage. Try to work through the anger before you file for divorce."

"He cheated. I don't know if I can forgive that." I choked out the words. "Even if it wasn't physical, it really hurts. How do I forgive him for turning to … her."

"The fallout from any affair is painful, and it won't be easy, but he's your family." He squeezed my hand. "It's your life, but I don't want you to look back and experience the same regrets. And please, don't stop being friends with Tiffany on my account. This mess is bad enough without everyone joining the fray."

"Thanks, honey. I'll try." I leaned against his shoulder and closed my eyes. This conversation had been exhausting, but worth it. If he'd forgiven Tiffany, perhaps I too could find forgiveness in my heart.

CHAPTER 28

Joel

After another long and useless session, I headed to work and walked straight into Tom's office. "Mail come in yet?"

He looked up from the pile on his desk. "I'm sorting it now." He beckoned me into the room. "How did it go?"

"The usual." I dropped into a chair.

"Hmm." Tom eyed me before he went back to the mail. "What do you mean by the usual?"

It had become a habit to censor everything I said, so I took a moment to gather my thoughts.

Tom frowned and then pushed an envelope across his desk. "I don't even want to ask."

"It's not what you think."

"Huh. The last time a friend of mine handed me an envelope like that, he announced he had a fifteen-year-old daughter."

"You didn't know?"

"About Savannah?" He shook his head.

"That Alex forced me to do DNA testing with Daniel." I folded my arms across my chest. "She won't let me see him until she's proven her point."

"Nope. I hadn't heard, but I'm not surprised. You went ballistic. You've been making sneaky little comments for months and convinced yourself it's true. Open it, and lay it to rest."

I tapped the envelope on my hand. "Aiden told you?"

"It's hard to keep secrets, and I wanted to know why you'd pull a dumb-ass move like you did on the boat. He didn't want to tell me, but I pried it out of him."

I rolled my eyes. "He tells you everything."

"No, he doesn't. That man is a vault, I swear. I can tell you this, though. The lack of trust you've shown toward both him and Alex has damaged your relationships. Maybe you don't care and it's time to walk away from both of them."

"Why would you think I don't care?"

"Your crap attitude is written all over your face every time you mention therapy or this situation with Aiden. So decide whether this is worth it or not."

"Aiden blackmailed me into it. He doesn't give a damn about me."

"Have you even thought about why he did that?" Tom huffed out a breath. "I need to get back to work." He waved toward the door.

"Yeah, I have stuff to do."

I wandered back to my office and dropped into my chair, spinning it so I viewed the city. *Why did Aiden give me an out?* I stared at the envelope clutched between my fingers, itching to rip it open, but … what if I did? Alex seemed so certain of the results. If I looked, would she leave me anyway because I hadn't trusted her? If I left it sealed, could I lay my suspicions to rest?

A part of me rationalized that I'd never questioned Daniel being mine until … *until when?* That crucial moment remained elusive in my mind. Even the why had become fuzzy.

I set the envelope aside, turning my attention to the files on my desk though I found it impossible to focus. My mind and my gaze kept wandering to the envelope as I debated the issue. Open it, or not?

When five o'clock hit, I rushed to lock up my files, scooped the offending envelope off of my desk, and retreated to my tiny suite. After pacing for several minutes, I yanked open my top drawer and stuffed it underneath my socks.

And then I made the call. Regardless of how we arrived at this place, I loved Daniel, and I loved my wife. Tom's words may have been harsh, but they had made me question everything I considered to be true.

⌒≺

I squared my shoulders and gazed up at the building. I'd almost begged Tom to come with me, but his response had been straightforward and unapologetic. *Man up and face this head on. It won't impress anyone if you need someone to hold your hand.*

As always, Tom had been on point, and I acknowledged the man knew our friend better than anyone. He'd said go it alone, so I would.

My biggest fear had been getting past Emily, who'd assumed the role of gatekeeper. I'd expected her to outright refuse my visit without Tom's presence, but she'd surprised me and agreed.

I rubbed the back of my neck, remembering my impromptu lesson about dealing with Emily. Despite her petite stature, she had mad skills in handling badass behavior. I suspected if Tom hadn't been there to peel her off, she would have laid me out cold. It had taken a week for the bruises ringing my throat to fade.

The doors rolled open, and I peered into the foyer. The gaping space where the table had sat, along with the gash in the wall, stood as constant reminders.

"How are you?" Emily halted several feet away as she eyed me.

"I've been better." No point in the usual *I'm fine* lame-ass response. Why deny anything?

"Me too." The dark circles and red-rimmed eyes relayed Emily's exhaustion. Even her usual glowing complexion appeared paler than usual, and she appeared to have lost weight. "Aiden is in the media room." She motioned for me to go in. "Can I get you anything?"

"Water. Or coffee if you have some made."

"I just brewed some for Aiden. I'll bring in a cup for you."

Aiden had his feet propped on the ottoman with his arm supported on a pillow. He turned toward me, his face pale, and his eyes dull and lacking their usual sparkle.

I hadn't visited him those first few weeks after the sailing incident, and seeing him now made me further understand the devastation I'd caused. Even after one of those rough party nights we'd been fond of in our early twenties, he'd never looked quite as bad as he did now.

"Hey." I paused in the doorway, uncertain of what to say. I'd sound like a complete moron if I asked how he felt or how he was doing. Anyone could see the answers to either question would be *not fucking great, asshole.*

"You plan to sit or just lurk?" He shifted on the couch, rearranging the sea of pillows surrounding him.

I shuffled in and dropped into the chair across from him.

Emily appeared and placed a steaming cup of coffee onto a coaster in front of me. "Here you go."

She handed Aiden a glass of ice water and transferred two tablets into his hand. "Need anything?" Her hand brushed his hair.

"I'm good for now. Thanks, Em."

She nodded and retreated.

I sipped my coffee to relieve my dry throat and set it on the coaster. "I'll lead with I'm sorry, even if it's inadequate given the damage I've done. I don't know what else to say because nothing I can do will ever make up for it."

"What are you doing to fix things with Alex?"

"We've started counseling. I thought she'd have told you that already, after all—" I bit back the next words. They might get me thrown out on my ass.

"Mmmhmm." He narrowed his eyes. "Get over it, Joel. She and I will always be friends."

"I get it. Nothing happened. It's been drilled into my brain. But tell me how you'd feel if you found some guy's shirt on your bedroom floor? Wouldn't you be upset?"

"Sure, but I'd have given my wife a chance to explain. You invaded my home in full attack mode. After all these years, I thought you'd know me better."

"Fair. I should have talked to you. But ..." I rubbed my damp palms across my jean-clad thighs. "It upset me. Alex runs to you for everything instead of me. I love how close you are with Daniel, but I'm his father, not you or Tom." Saying it out loud felt good and a tiny portion of the anger dissipated.

"Agreed, Daniel needs you. I've never argued that point, but you've been absent. He's my nephew, and little boys need male influence as much as they need their mother's. You were slinking off to see Crystal or wherever the hell else you were hiding. That made it impossible for them to count on you."

"You'll back off?"

"I've never tried to replace you with either Alex or Daniel. All you ever needed to do was step up. I told you that months ago, but you didn't want to hear it."

Fuzzy memories overtook me. Everything Aiden had said in the pub that night made perfect sense now.

"Not like I have a choice. It's Cynthia or lose my son and go to jail for assault."

"Don't ever pretend you don't have choices."

"We're going now."

"So I hear." He contemplated me through weary eyes. "Don't forget that I've been in that dark place where it seems like nothing will ever be right again. I lost everything, and I regret not trying harder."

I clasped my sweaty hands in my lap. Where was this headed?

"I'm happy with Emily and my family, but it took a long time to get here. You have something irreplaceable with Alex. Make it right."

"Ally doesn't want to hear it."

"Except she does. She needs you to walk into that office like there's no place you'd rather be. Alex needs you to be committed, and she wants you to trust her."

"Huh." I narrowed my eyes. "Case in point. She told you instead of me."

"Don't start." He glowered. "Offload the resentment and hear what she's telling you."

"She's closed off and doesn't speak to me."

Aiden rolled his eyes. "Since when do women tell you exactly what they're thinking?"

"Touché." I closed my eyes, concentrating hard and picturing Alex in our last session. Everything about her screamed—back off. Why though? Was he right? Was she still committed to our marriage? I opened my eyes. "Do you think I have a prayer with Alex?"

"You might if you change that crap attitude of yours. Fight for her."

"I am."

"You're not. Quit whining and making excuses like a spoiled man-child, and someone might believe it. You're angry, we get it already. Get over it."

"That's harsh from someone who can barely keep a relationship together."

"You're not doing so hot yourself, idiot. At least my wife still talks to me."

I narrowed my eyes. "That's a miracle after all the shit you've pulled."

"It is, and I'm thankful every day." A sad look crept across his face. "I don't know how I'd survive without Emily. If I lost her, I'd never recover."

I lifted my chin and met his gaze. Did he believe I'd never survive without Alex?

"I don't wish bad things for you, even if it's been forever since you even gave a damn about anything."

The flush rose in my face as his words hit home.

"You wonder why I didn't come to you when Savannah showed up? Why I walked away that day you ambushed me with the whole damn Tiffany thing at the beach house? You stopped caring or listening. When Kellan was born, you didn't bother to show up. You acted like you were doing a big favor by sailing with me, and you almost drowned me. Then it took you weeks to manage a half-assed apology."

My throat locked up, and I dragged in a breath as his words sunk in.

"When you did manage, you barely looked at me. We come home, and you act as if you haven't learned a damn thing. You haven't been man enough to straighten things out with Savannah, and now this? You've been out of control for months." He hung his head and scrubbed a hand over his face.

His words shook me to the core. A cold sweat crept over me, and my chest tightened. This man had been my friend for years, but I couldn't recall when we'd last laughed together. Every conversation in recent memory had been filled with anger or animosity or ... shame.

As much as I resented his closeness with Alex and my son, I'd done my part in hurting Aiden. Not just physically, but on a much deeper level. It had started long before my marriage troubles with Alex.

"So how do I fix it?"

"Do you even want to?"

I nodded. "Can I see Vanna to apologize?"

"That would be up to Savannah. I'll ask, but no promises. As for the rest, we'll see. I'm not up for much right now, and I need some time."

Given his drawn and pasty complexion, I figured I'd taken as much of his time as I should. Tom warned me not to push too hard, and now I knew why. Aiden was struggling with his recovery.

Had it been this bad last time, or had I been too oblivious and wrapped up in my own miserable world to notice?

"I should go. Is there anything I can do for you?"

It seemed to take massive effort for Aiden to shake his head. "No, nothing."

"Will you call me about seeing Savannah? I need to set that right. And again, I'm sorry, and I hope we can find a way to get past it."

"I'll discuss it with her. That's all I can promise."

I rose and took an awkward step toward him, wanting to do something, anything, to show him I did care.

"Ready for a rest?"

I spun, almost knocking my coffee cup from the table.

Emily stood in the doorway. "I'll walk you out, Joel." She motioned toward the foyer.

"Thanks." I glanced at Aiden. "Hope you feel better soon." I followed his wife toward the elevator. "He's in rough shape."

"This round has been tough. The pain keeps him awake."

"I'm sorry," I said for the hundredth time as I stepped into the elevator. The doors slid shut and I leaned against the side, tipping my head back.

Facing the consequences of my actions would be much harder than I expected. The fallout and damages were far beyond the devastation of my marriage and family life. It had affected everyone in our circle of friends.

Maybe we'd find our way through. Maybe we wouldn't.

I had to try.

⌒⤞

Tom tapped on my office door and peeked inside.

"That doesn't look like a legal file." He smirked as he caught sight of the glossy magazine on my desk. "Redecorating?"

"Sort of. What do you think of this one?" I pointed at the table.

"You're still in the suite, so why are you shopping for furniture?" He dropped into a chair and crossed his arms.

"I hate to ask, but I need an advance on my salary."

"Why? So you can buy a fancy table for the non-existent place you're renting?"

"It's not for me. It's not the best timing, but I thought I'd pay for the damages to Aiden's apartment. Maybe hire someone to fix the wall, repaint, and order them a new table for the hallway."

Tom lifted a brow. "Oh. Well, it's a good idea, but you should ask them what they'd like. Then offer to pay for the replacement table. Emily already scheduled the repairs with their usual contractor."

"Right." I deflated, but he made sense. Offering to fix the damages and to pay for the replacement table might be the smarter route. Sending a grand gift appealed, but visiting and doing it in person would be far better. It had been tough to face them. Having stuff delivered might seem to impersonal; the coward's version of what should be happening. "I saw Aiden."

"Did you." Tom remained expressionless. "How did that go?"

"Fine. Does my visiting him meet with your approval?"

Tom squinted. "Watch the sass. Your attitude is less than amusing at the moment."

"Sorry." I glanced at my watch. "I have another session today with Alex in half an hour."

"Go." Tom waved a hand as I collected up my coat and headed for the door.

CHAPTER 29

FROM THE MOMENT I SET foot in Cynthia's waiting room, the change in atmosphere was palpable. The scruffy disgruntled man had disappeared without a trace. Joel's hazel eyes seemed brighter, his smile more genuine and welcoming.

"Alex." He handed me my usual cup of coffee along with a small bag.

I inhaled the light scent of cinnamon and peered into the package. "Fresh muffins?"

"I thought you might need a snack."

"They smell divine." My mouth watered at the fragrant scent rising from the bag, so I broke off an edge and tucked it into my mouth. "Mmm. Blueberry."

Joel grinned and winked.

"What do you want?" I narrowed my eyes.

"Can't I bring my wife her favorite muffin?" His eyes widened, and his adorable dimples appeared.

"Oh, no you don't." I wagged a finger at him. "Stop that."

"But …" He held his left hand, palm facing me.

"Uh-uh." I shook my head. Then it hit me. "You got the test results. So now it's all roses and sunshine, right?"

"That's not why. I haven't …" His mouth formed a grim line.

"Haven't what? Did you or did you not get the results?"

"Yes, but—"

"Uh." I thrust a flattened palm toward him. "Don't even. Now you have proof, it's all okay?"

Joel raked shaking fingers through his hair. "I didn't say that."

"You didn't have to," I whispered, before clearing my throat.

"I guess that means you have no more excuses to keep Daniel from me." His brows knit together. "When can I take him?"

I studied him for a moment. How could I refuse when he'd kept his part of the deal? It made me sad his joy came from the solid evidence that Daniel belonged to him, but at least our son had his dad back.

"It's short notice, but can I take him this afternoon? I've missed him."

"If you can manage." I motioned to his casted arm.

"It'll be fine," he said. "You could come with us."

"No." I leveled my gaze at him. "Daniel needs one-on-one time with you, and after our session, our together time for today is over."

"Right." His hand wandered through his hair again. "Is this only about Daniel now? Will we ever get back together?"

"Please. Don't push."

"Sorry." He sighed. "I miss spending time with you." His shoulders slumped as he fiddled with his cup. "I messed up, but I love you, and I'll wait for as long it takes for you to forgive me."

I love you too. The words flitted through my mind, but something held me back. This one-eighty reversal of direction confused me. Could we return to where we'd once been? Did I even want to?

Sometimes love wasn't enough. Sometimes life got in the way. Without trust, relationships withered and died.

What about the equality of our love? Did I love him more than he loved me? Too often I'd made the effort and done the giving and him the taking. Forgiveness had been given on previous occasions, but this time he needed to prove his love and commitment.

Charmed words fell from Joel's tongue, but maybe that's all they'd ever been. Words. I craved that light-as-air feeling that took over when you knew, without a doubt, you were loved and treasured. I longed for us to regain our passion.

Joel cleared his throat and looked away. "So that's a big fat no."

"I want to believe we can fix things and that you mean it, but you hurt me. I need to process everything. Please, have patience." Tears sprang to my eyes.

"Don't cry," he whispered. "Please don't." He caught an escaping salty droplet and brushed it away with his thumb. "I understand, I do. I'm here, and I'm not ready to give up on us. You're worth waiting for." Joel pinched the bridge of his nose and muttered, "I hate it when he's right. Damn it. I'm an idiot for not listening."

"Who?" I stared at him.

"Aiden. He told me, and I should have …"

"Not that again!" I shoved his hand away.

"No, Ally. I meant that he's been there. He knows yet I didn't trust his advice. If I had, we wouldn't be in this mess. I wish I'd listened, and I wish …" He hung his head. "Can I take Daniel for the afternoon?"

"Yes." I hesitated for a second before taking his hand in mine. "Joel? You'll keep coming to our sessions, won't you?"

"Yeah. Of course."

It was a relief to hear it. I hoped he'd keep his word.

The first week at my new job gave me an unexpected sense of freedom. Being at home with Daniel for his first year and having the summer with him had been amazing. However, being a kept woman and relying on my husband wasn't an option. Besides, I loved working. I always had.

The elevator swished open, and I stepped into the apartment. The smell of fresh paint greeted my nose. The gash in the wall had been repaired.

"Alex." Aiden's voice carried from the other room. "Come on through."

"I love the new color in the foyer," I said as I rounded the corner and stepped into the family room.

"Thanks. Joel covered the cost to repair the wall and repaint, and our new table is on the way."

"Mama." Daniel squirmed from his seat on the couch beside Aiden and scampered toward me sporting a huge endearing grin.

"I missed you." I scooped him up, covering his tiny face in kisses and savoring his adorable giggle. "How did it go with my little man?"

"Wonderful. I took them to the park." He grinned as my eyes widened. "Don't worry, Iona came with us and did all the heavy lifting."

"Sorry, I trust you, but I worry you'll strain your shoulder." I smiled. "You hate sitting around."

"You know me well. I'm stir crazy from being cooped up."

"You look better."

The color had returned to his face, and he seemed more relaxed.

He rubbed his shoulder as he lifted his arm. "I have a long way to go, but it's not so bad. Will came by, and we put the finishing touches on my new program. The hospital board approved it."

"Congratulations. That's exciting."

"I'll be working from home, but the hospital wants me to run some of the intake seminars and information sessions for the new students and residents. Thank goodness. I'd go insane otherwise."

"That's great. I worried you'd get behind with your career plans."

"I have the supervisory and teaching experience to fall back on. Looks like I'll avoid surgery, so I can go back sooner than anticipated."

I loved seeing the smile on his face.

"How are you doing?" Aiden asked.

"It's hard with Joel, but he hasn't missed any appointments or made any excuses. It's helping, but we have a long way to go. I'm not ready for him to come home or anything like that, and having some space is what we need. Less stress at home without him there all the time."

"I can imagine." He studied me closely. "Has he been taking Daniel out?"

"He is now that we got the test results. It's working out so far, and he's taking it seriously."

"I noticed. Vanna agreed to sit down with him and Cynthia for a session." He motioned to his shoulder. "She took pity on me and agreed to a house call. That way I can step in if Vanna needs me."

"Great." I stared at my folded hands. "Do you think I should take him back?"

"Don't worry about making that decision yet. It's been less than a month. You can't expect to know all the answers."

"I still feel like I'm living in limbo, but at least he's making an effort with Daniel. For Daniel's sake though …" I peered at him.

"Daniel can have a relationship with his father even if you two aren't living together. It's like having another baby to keep a marriage together. Bad news."

"Nope, no babies for that reason. Having one child in this uncertain situation is plenty."

"True," he said. "Do you love him?"

"I love him a lot, but is it enough?"

"I understand your dilemma. There were times when I figured I'd deluded myself, and Emily didn't love me as much as she said she did. Insecurities might mess with your mind, and you'll doubt everything you thought you knew about your relationship. Try not to let those get in the way. Joel loves you."

"How do you know?"

"The same way you knew Emily loved me. How did you know we were right for each other?" He lifted a brow. "Why did you push me to commit?"

"Ah." I waggled my index finger at him. "I was right, though, and she's amazing."

"Yes, on both accounts. You didn't let me give up too soon, and neither will you. Stick it out. It may take months, but at least then you've given your marriage every opportunity to succeed. Don't shut down, no matter how much you wish you could."

His answer relayed a whole lot to me. Aiden had buried his feelings and convinced himself Emily couldn't love him enough. His doomed relationship with Tiffany, along with some of the others he'd dated, had created a deep mistrust of women and their motives. Maybe some of his suspicion and hesitation to take things at face value had rubbed off on me.

It would be a challenge, and I needed time. I resolved not to let Joel push too hard, but not to cut him off either. Aiden wouldn't lie to me, so Joel had to have said or done something to make him believe the love was real. For now, that would have to carry us, until we could rebuild our trust.

CHAPTER 30

Joel

ANOTHER LONG WEEK PASSED, AND I feared I'd be stuck in this tiny suite forever. Despite my efforts, things with Alex seemed at an impasse. Every session with Cynthia, I donned my best smile. *Fake it till you make it.* Isn't that what they said? Not that pretending excited me, but I wanted both my wife and my life back.

Aiden met me in the foyer of their apartment. The two weeks since I'd visited had been good to him. The bruises had faded, and the stiff and pained expression had vanished from his face.

All traces of our altercation were now gone. The new table gleamed in its spot against the freshly painted wall.

Aiden followed my gaze. "Thank you for ordering the table. It looks great."

"It does." I trailed him into the kitchen. "Least I could do, being the one who smashed it to bits."

This produced a faint smile. "They're in the office."

"You're not joining us?"

"Not yet. You don't need me hovering. Go on in."

I nodded and headed down the hall.

"Joel." Cynthia beckoned me inside.

"Hi." The collar of my shirt felt too tight, and I slid my fingers inside and tugged to loosen it. I lowered myself into a chair not far from where Savannah had curled up on the couch.

The girl gave me the once over. Otherwise, she remained still, with one leg tucked tight beneath her and a pillow clutched to her chest like a shield.

"Why don't we start with what you want to say to Savannah?" Cynthia turned my way.

"Okay." I cleared my throat and forced myself to look at Vanna. Hiding was of no use. I needed to meet this head on. "I've done some stupid things, and I never meant to hurt you or anyone else. I'm so sorry, and I know that seems inadequate. How can I make it up to you?"

"Why?" she whispered. "Why did you do it?"

How much did she know about the situation? What could I say that wouldn't make it worse? Or let her know the thoughts and resentments I'd been harboring about her dad? I opened my mouth, and then snapped it shut while I considered her question. "I don't know."

"You don't?" Her eyebrows rose. "You must have some idea why you hate my dad being friends with Alex. You think there's something going on between them. Admit it."

My breath caught. She knew far more than I'd anticipated. "Aiden told you?"

Savannah furrowed her brow. "I'm not a stupid child. Why do adults think teenagers are clueless idiots?"

"I don't—"

"Yeah, you do." She smacked the pillow and glared at me. "I saw how you looked at my dad that day on the boat. If I'd insisted we turn around right away, it wouldn't have happened. My dad almost died because I was too weak to stop you." Tears streamed down her face. "Then you barge into our home. You're creating problems for him with Emily. Do you want them to get divorced like you and Aunt Alex?"

"What?" The word divorce struck me like a hammer blow. "Who said we're getting divorced?"

"Nothing. No one," she mumbled before snatching a wad of tissues from the box on the table.

"It's something if you're this upset. Are Emily and Aiden fighting?" I asked.

Savannah refused to meet my gaze. "Don't pretend you don't get it." She clutched the ever-present pendant between her fingers.

"Calm down, Savannah," Cynthia said softly. "Let's take a few beats."

Savannah nodded, rubbing her fingers across the sparkling heart. After several long breaths, she turned to Cynthia. "I'm good."

Cynthia directed a reassuring smile at Savannah and then turned to me. "Savannah has picked up on the issues, so you need to be direct and honest with her."

Explaining my actions to Aiden or Alex was embarrassing, but humbling myself before Savannah represented humiliation on a whole new level. "I'm sorry if this causes problems for your dad and Emily. I didn't mean for that to happen."

She buried her face in the pillow, peering at me from over the top of it with shimmering eyes.

"If I could rewind and change it I would, but you can never blame yourself for what happened that day. I drank too much, and that's on me." There was nothing to lose by being honest. "Yes, I've resented the dynamics between Aiden and Alex. They're super close, but like family."

I stared at the sobbing girl on the couch before pushing out of the chair and heading for the door. I couldn't bear watching. I'd done this to her.

"That was quick." Aiden contemplated me, a frown settling on his face. "What happened?"

I wanted to run without looking back, but I froze. "Are you and Emily fighting?"

"What?"

"Has this caused problems between you two? And what the hell did you tell Savannah?"

"Don't worry about my relationship. Emily and I are dealing with things in our own way and in our own time. Concentrate on Alex and your own marriage issues."

"Savannah knows an awful lot about everything." I crossed my arms, staring him down.

He motioned me into the media room and closed the door. "Give her credit for having some intelligence. She lives with us, and it would have been impossible for her to miss after you barged into our home." He narrowed his eyes.

Exhaustion overwhelmed me. "I'm sorry." My shoulders slumped.

Aiden leaned back against the arm of the sofa. "Perhaps you are, but sorry fixes little. Savannah blames herself for not stopping you. I can't live with that. It's never been her fault, Joel."

"I know. It was all me. Jealousy got the best of me, but it seems like you've always had it so good. Women, money, travel … everything."

"Oh yeah, my life has been fucking awesome." He crossed his arms, the stormy look on his face speaking volumes. "Don't you get it?"

"Maybe I don't. I know your parents were never around, but you did have it pretty easy overall."

His brows rose. "Yeah, it's amazing when your parents dump you in boarding school and leave the state. Not to mention learning your girlfriend is pregnant, and having the whole world come down on you. You have no clue how hard those years were for me. None. Or how it's affected my entire life. You've never cared."

"I did care. You never bothered to tell me. How do you think I felt, being one of the last to know? You could have told us when we were teenagers."

"No, Joel, I couldn't. You don't understand, at all. We were threatened into silence. You can't even fathom the pressure we felt. We were scared kids, and blaming either of us for keeping it to ourselves is plain stupidity."

"Right. What could they do to you? Nothing."

"Nothing? Yeah, David's goons separating us and taking it out on me was nothing. Sending me away from my friends for my last years of school was nothing. Destroying my relationship with someone I loved, yeah more of that nothing. Forcing me to sign legal papers I didn't want to sign and stealing my kid—even more nothing." He pointed a finger at me. "Don't you *ever* tell me it was nothing. You didn't have to live it."

Did this flow both ways? Aiden considered me a clueless dumb-ass about the hardships he'd gone through, and maybe he was right. I'd never understood why they'd kept Savannah a secret.

"Tell me." Time to take this down a notch, and remove the harshness from of our exchange. "What do you mean, David's goons?"

"Never mind. What matters now is you're clinging to these hard feelings and become so immersed in your own misery, you've forgotten that the rest of us have our own problems. You have an amazing woman who loves you and friends who have tried to help, and you don't want any of it. It hurts that you've pushed us all away."

"You know what hurts? When my wife runs to another man to confide our marriage troubles and then finding his shirt on my bedroom floor. Take a good long hard look in the mirror, Aiden. You are half of our problem. I never meant to hurt Savannah, but she's been caught up in our mess. And I am so sorry about that, but it got the best of me."

"I stand by what I said before. Be accessible to Alex, so she can turn to you. You're not the only one who's suffered." Aiden gave me a long look. "I'm stuck in the middle, and it's not a comfortable place to be. She's my friend, she felt alone, and I did what I could to help her. I couldn't walk away."

"But you could have."

"No, I couldn't. You don't ..." He rubbed his hands over his face. "My friends stood by me when I needed them, and I couldn't abandon her. You forget, Joel, I've been through a divorce, and it took everything I had to get through it."

"You never shared that with me, either. Why?"

Aiden stared at the floor. "It wasn't easy to share. I fell apart, and then I didn't want to think about it anymore. Reliving it is still difficult, and ..."

"What?" I stepped toward him, grasping his shoulder. "What could be so bad?"

"This isn't about me. I never wanted to interfere in your marriage. I'll try to stay impartial so you two can resolve your issues, but please don't ask me to stop being friends with Alex," he whispered.

We stood there for the longest time, neither of us looking at the other. My mind spun. Whatever he had hidden was big, but until we could get past our differences over Alex, he'd refuse to confide in me.

"I care about her, and not being there would kill me," Aiden said. "But is that what you want and need me to do? We can buy back your portion of the partnership so you can walk, or Tom buys me out, and I'll walk."

"What? No, Aiden, I …" Confusion clouded my thoughts. "I miss how close we used to be, and I fear we'll never get back there. I'm ashamed I've caused everyone so much pain. I don't know what to do." The shaky breath shuddered into my chest, and I hung my head. "My marriage is a disaster, and it's impossible to do the right thing with Alex. My former friends hate me, and I've felt alone for a long time, and now you want to end our friendship?"

"No one hates you, and you're not alone. We've all made mistakes, but I feel trapped. I'm creating more issues for you and Alex. This runs deeper than I imagined, and I can't be responsible for ending your marriage. I don't want to walk away, Joel, but you can't handle me being around her."

The thought terrified me and wrenched my heart. "That's not an answer, and you know it. It would only make it worse. If I cost Alex your friendship, she'd never forgive me."

"Then what's the solution? We can't go on like this."

I lifted my chin and stared at him. Damn, he was good. "Huh, you missed your calling. You should be a damn lawyer."

His brows rose, and his eyes glimmered, though his expression hadn't otherwise changed.

"You sneaky bastard." I shook my head and crossed my arms. "Reverse psychology, right? You offer to step back and remove yourself, but you know I can't allow it. Alex would rip me a new one."

His face remained a blank mask.

"You win." I sighed. "And I get your point. These are my issues, and I need to deal with them. Alex accused me of not trusting her, although I demand that she trust me. She threw the whole Crystal thing at me."

"Well, you haven't been honest or fair."

"How do you mean? I didn't sleep with Crystal."

"It's still not acceptable behavior. Whether you had sex with Crystal or not, you betrayed your wife." He eyed me. "Alex asked about the day we went sailing. Remember, we came back early and you said you were heading home?"

I let out a long slow breath. "Busted."

"Yeah, you sure are. Where did you go that day?"

The heat rose to my face, and I avoided his gaze.

"Damn, Joel. You expect her to trust you, yet you pull a bonehead move like that? Cut that poisonous woman from your life."

"She's not that bad." I caught his disbelieving look before I ducked my head. "Anyway, she's gone for good now. Please don't tell Alex where I went that day."

"For a smart guy, you're a complete idiot." He snorted. "Why do you think she asked me about it?"

My heart sank. "She already figured it out," I muttered. Of course, Alex saw right through me and my pathetic attempt at deception. "I didn't deny where I'd been, though ..."

Aiden scoffed. "I call bullshit. Not telling her you spent that time with Crystal is the same damn thing as lying straight to her face."

I refused to look at him. The words were true, and I had no defense against them.

"Joel."

His tone forced me to raise my head. I expected more anger, laced with a heavy dose of hatred and disappointment, but not the regretful expression written across his face.

"Get your ass back to the office. Be honest with Vanna. I can handle whatever you have to say."

"Can you?"

"Yes. Don't run from this. It won't make it better."

He knew me too well and understood I had one foot out that door. If he let me run, it would be that much harder to come to terms with my mistakes. If I valued my friendship with this man and wanted to fix my marriage, I needed to finish this, and then make amends to Alex for my many lies of omission.

CHAPTER 31

Alexis

I SIPPED MY COFFEE AND MADE my to do list for the weekend, enjoying a few minutes of peace while Daniel played on the carpet. Our morning routine was comforting, and though I missed Joel, I also didn't miss him. Not having the constant weight of our fights and oppressive silences made the apartment seem brighter.

A text appeared from Joel. "Daddy's here." I forced a cheerful note into my voice.

Daniel rose from his task and scuttled toward me. "Fish?"

"Let's put your coat on." I maneuvered Daniel toward the foyer as the door opened.

"Daddy." Daniel bounded over to Joel, extending his arms.

Joel grinned and swung him into the air before planting a kiss on Daniel's cheek. "Hi." He balanced our boy on his hip and leaned in, brushing his lips against my cheek. "You look beautiful."

"You don't look so bad yourself." I smiled despite my reservations, enjoying the scent of his crisp aftershave. "The cast is off."

"And I'm thrilled. It felt like carrying a lead weight." He gazed at me with those beautiful hazel eyes. "What are your plans today?"

"I have a few errands to run." I narrowed my eyes. "Why?"

He raised his brows. "Would you like to come with us to the aquarium?"

"I don't know. This is your time with Daniel."

"Come on. When was the last time we did anything as a family? Remember when we used to have actual fun?" He grinned.

"I do remember." A smile touched my lips as I recalled better times. We were never home, always out with friends or sailing, hiking, or skiing. Life had never been mundane, and I suddenly longed to have those days back. "I guess I could."

"Perfect. Get your jacket."

While I gathered my things, Joel bundled Daniel into his coat and then we headed down the elevator with Daniel clutching his hand. Seeing the two of them together touched my heart, and a warm glow ignited as our eyes met.

Something about this man had always made my knees quiver. Staring into his eyes now, I felt a deep-rooted attraction that made me eager to rip his clothes off and feel his smooth hot skin against mine.

The ding of the elevator interrupted my reverie. I broke our locked gaze and flushed as I pretended to search for something in my bag. Did he know I'd lusted after him just now? "Let's get going."

"Yes, before someone gets overexcited." He caught my hand, bringing it to his lips before entwining our fingers.

A shiver ran down my spine and I glanced his way, trying to determine the meaning of his comment.

"Our son wants to see the fish." He raised a brow.

"Fishes." Daniel clung to the collar of Joel's coat, a smile lighting his precious face. "Go." He pointed toward the door.

"Patience, Daniel, we're going." Joel released my hand as he play wrestled with his son. "Ready, Ally?"

～≼

Daniel spent the morning zipping from exhibit to exhibit, pointing at the animals and sea creatures. After two hours of running at full speed, his energy flagged.

"Why don't we grab some lunch?" Joel kneeled to zip Daniel's coat. "Mitts, buddy, it's cold out there." He tucked a small wool cap onto his son's head.

"Sounds great. He wore me out, making me chase him all over the aquarium."

"There's an awesome little restaurant not far from here." He clasped Daniel's right hand, while I held the other.

"Weeeeeeeeeee." Daniel sang as we swung him off of his feet. He skipped for a few steps. "Again."

It felt like it should, how it always needed to be, here with Joel, our son giggling and laughing out loud as we made our way down the snowy streets of Boston.

"In here." Joel propped open the door so we could enter.

I stomped the snow from my boots and rubbed my hands together as the warmth of the cozy and homey interior enveloped me.

Joel busied himself removing Daniel's coat and mitts. "Can you order me a burger with fries? I'll take Daniel and wash his hands."

His attentiveness to his son surprised me. I followed them with my gaze as he led Daniel from the table. I'd noticed the same thing all morning. Joel had stayed engaged and focused on our son.

The waitress delivered steaming cups of hot chocolate as the two returned to our table.

"You read my mind." Joel strapped Daniel into the high chair and handed him a crayon. "The aquarium was fun."

"Yes," I twirled a strand of my hair around a finger before sipping my hot chocolate.

Joel grinned as he reached out to brush my upper lip with his thumb. "Whipped cream."

"Thanks." I dropped my gaze as butterflies, caused by his gentle touch, flitted in my stomach.

He smiled and turned back to Daniel, handing him another crayon and helping him color on the kid's menu until our food arrived.

I reached for the fork to help Daniel with his lunch.

Joel waved away my hand. "I've got it, Alex. Eat."

This was new. It felt odd to sit back and enjoy my food and let someone else manage Daniel's demands.

I pointed at the napkin. "Oh, you should—" At Joel's intense look, I snapped my mouth shut.

"We talked about this. You have to give up some control. I'm trying, but …" He dabbed a blob of ketchup onto Daniel's plate before tucking the napkin around him as a makeshift bib.

"I'm sorry, it's habit. I'll stop, I promise." I held up a hand in surrender and forced myself to sit back. "Joel?"

"I heard you." Rubbing his hand over his jaw, he contemplated me from across the table. "You realize it's part of the reason we're having issues, don't you?"

"I do now, but I didn't then, and I'm sorry. Those first few months were a blur, and it felt like I had to do it all. If I didn't, I'd be a failure as a mother." I pushed my salad around the bowl.

"I understand." His words were gentle. "I wanted to help, but I couldn't do anything to suit your high standards. He's my son, and I am capable of caring for him. Things still get done, even if not exactly the way you want. You worried about being a failure as a mother, but in the process, you made me feel inadequate as a father."

I twisted my napkin, finally forcing myself to look into his eyes. "I'm sorry. If I make you feel that way, you have to tell me. I'll try to relax my iron grip." I offered him a tentative smile. "Please, don't stop. I need you to be part of his life."

"And I want to be there, I always have, but I felt shut out. It led me to bad decisions, though that's on me. I wish we'd had this conversation months ago. Everything could be different."

"Maybe that's our lesson of the day."

"Maybe it is. Can we both promise that when something's bothering us, we talk it out right away? It seems ridiculous that we both hold it inside."

"Deal." I nodded and reached for his hand. It felt like the most honest conversation we'd had in a long time. Even with Cynthia in the middle like a referee, we'd held back.

"Alright, then." A smile appeared.

My heart did a little flip. That special bond we'd forged so many years ago had emerged from under the layers of hurt and denial, and it gave me hope.

⁓

By the time we finished lunch, Daniel's eyelids were drooping. Joel worked our boy's arms into his coat, then snuggled him against his shoulder for the walk home.

"I'll put him down, Ally."

I frowned at his use of my pet name, but removed Daniel's boots and Joel carried him to his room. At loose ends, I tidied up the forgotten toys scattered across the carpet and pulled out some chicken for dinner.

When I sensed his eyes on me, I glanced toward the archway, our gazes meeting. Another jolt trembled through me. I licked my lips as I set the bowl aside and rinsed my hands. "What plans do you have for the rest of the afternoon?"

"I thought I'd search the rental listings." He studied me for a moment before opening and closing his mouth, like he wanted to say something, but couldn't speak.

"What?"

"I'm sure you don't want to hear this, but I miss you both." He tilted his head. "Is there any chance for us?"

I leaned a hand against the counter and hung my head, letting my curtain of hair hide my confusion. A week ago, I would have answered with a vehement *no*. Today, I wasn't so sure. Something had shifted. The change wasn't even subtle. When he'd walked into Cynthia's office for our last session, he'd been a different man.

Perhaps the testing had been a good idea, though it irked me we'd had to go to those lengths. With his fears laid to rest, he could now look at Daniel and see his own flesh and blood.

"I should go," he muttered.

My focus returned to Joel. "Can we not do this right now? I can't make promises or plans for the future. I simply don't know."

He moved across the floor and stopped in front of me. "Ally, I love you. I meant what I said. I'll wait. No rush." Joel cupped my face between his palms before leaning down to brush his lips against mine.

I brought my hands up to grip his wrists, torn between the desire to kiss him fiercely and the need to shove him as far away as possible. Tears rose to my eyes. "Please don't. I'm so confused. You keep changing so fast, I can't keep up."

He let his hands fall to his sides and stepped back. "Okay."

Moments later I heard the elevator swish shut.

I leaned against the counter, not knowing what to do next. I had been so certain my marriage was over. That I could never forgive him. Now, I wasn't so sure.

CHAPTER 32

I RUBBED MY GRITTY TIRED EYES and stared at the ceiling of the cramped suite I now called home. It had taken superhuman effort to force myself back to this pitiful space after spending the day with my family. The night had been long, and I'd only dropped off to sleep in the early hours of the morning.

There had been an undeniable attraction between Alex and me yesterday. There were points when it had become almost overwhelming. That fleeting look in her eye that surfaced and then vanished, but had given me a glimmer of hope. Only days ago, she'd sworn we were over and done. Now it appeared doubts had crept into her mind.

If I'd stayed yesterday and pushed her harder, I suspected where we'd have ended up, but my mind screamed *too soon*.

So instead of holding my beautiful wife close, kissing away her pain, and loving her into the early hours of the morning, I'd restrained myself. It made sense to allow the anticipation to grow, to let ourselves heal, and to connect without it being about sex. She mistrusted me, and I had to rebuild before moving forward. Without patience on my part she'd have regrets, which always led to us being further apart than ever.

I crawled from the bed and wandered into the bathroom, turning the shower on low. The cool water beating down on me calmed my thoughts and doused the flames of desire I'd been reining under tight control.

I flexed my hand, enjoying the movement and lightness in the absence of the heavy cast. At least all signs of the altercation were disappearing from my body. We were healing, even if only on the surface.

The trill of my phone had me dashing into the bedroom.

"How are things?" Tom's deep voice greeted me.

"Fine, I guess." I sank onto the edge of the bed. "I saw Daniel yesterday."

"So I hear," he said. "The group is brunching today if you're interested. Ryan's in town with his new lady."

"I'm not sure that's a good idea. What about Alex?"

"She asked me to invite you. Are you in or out?"

"In. What time should I arrive at your place?"

"Umm." Tom fell silent for a moment. "It's Alex's turn to host."

"Huh?" I furrowed my brows. Turn? "When did we start the brunches again?"

"We never stopped," Tom said softly.

How had I'd missed this fact? This revelation meant they'd gone on without me, and I hadn't even known about the gathering. How many times had Alex hosted a party without me?

"You're coming, right?"

"Yeah, I guess."

"We're heading there now, so come over when you're ready."

I bit back a retort. Being invited to my own apartment aggravated me, but I had no choice but to accept that I wasn't indispensable.

We hung up, and I dressed with care, fuming the entire time. As I gathered my keys and wallet, I caught sight of my reflection. I looked different. Older? More mature? Whoever this man in the mirror was, he wasn't the old Joel Nichols. Whether good or bad, only time would tell.

❦

The chill early November air and light snow had me tightening my scarf. The fresh air cleared my head, giving me time to consider the situation during my trek from downtown to my home—*former home*—in Back Bay.

Mentally, I claimed ownership of our luxurious apartment, but those cruel words that had escaped from Alex's mouth that day rattled in my brain.

"You don't live here anymore."

It hurt to know how life had gone on without my presence, but could I be angry that my inclusion today felt like an afterthought?

I paused before entering our building and crossing the foyer. Heat flooded my face as I waved at the doorman and shuffled my feet as he summoned the elevator.

"Thanks," I mumbled as he ushered me inside and I pressed the button for my floor.

"Mr. Nichols." He tipped his head and turned back toward his station.

Had I detected a smirk on his bearded face? Probably. *Even this virtual stranger knew my darling wife had tossed me out on my ass.*

Tom gave me the once over as I stepped into the apartment before bringing me in for a hug. "Looking good, man. How are you holding up?"

"Not bad." I shrugged out of my coat and allowed him to hang it as if I was a guest. I shuffled into the main room, cringing. Each and every one of the people now staring my way had been disappointed or hurt by my actions. I no longer knew how to act around any of them.

My palms grew sweaty as I negotiated this minefield, and I paused to observe the body language. Today called for sharp attention to detail.

"Ryan." I stopped short. Last time I'd seen him, I'd behaved like a blubbering idiot, curled up on his couch sobbing like a baby. Since then, our conversations had been non-existent.

For sure this man would have a few choice words about what went down with Aiden. "Hey, Joel."

My mind whirled through the possible courses of action, and I planted my feet, ducking my head and hunching my shoulders in case Ryan took a swing at me. Maybe I deserved a swift punch upside the head, which would be a fair return for blindsiding Aiden.

"How are you?" Ryan hugged me and patted my shoulder. "I hear we've had some interesting times."

"I'm ..." My shoulders sagged as I exhaled and lifted my chin. "I'm getting by." I stared at him. "I'm sorry about my behavior on my last visit. It was a bad time, and I made some stupid choices, but I'm getting help now."

"So I hear. Let me know if there's anything I can do." He squeezed my shoulder. "I mean it, Joel, never again. You don't have the luxury, and you have a great family. Don't let that slip away."

"I won't. I promise." Before I could stop myself, I hugged him tightly, thankful for his supportive words. "I thought for sure you were planning to hit me." A nervous laugh snuck out.

"Nah. Aiden did a fine job beating your ass without my help." He smirked, but it soon faded. "No more fighting. That's not how our family works out our issues." He led me toward the living room. "Kaari, this is Joel."

The tall, willowy caramel-skinned beauty held out her hand. "Nice to meet you, Joel. I've heard so much about you."

"Ryan mentioned you, too." I pasted on a smile, wondering what Ryan had said. All of it true, I assumed, though surely unflattering.

We chatted for a few moments before I set my sights on the next hurdle. Aiden and Emily.

Emily studied me before gracing me with a hug. "You look better every time I see you." She rubbed my back.

"Hard to look worse than I did." I smiled and kissed her cheek.

Now we'd had it out, I found facing Aiden much easier. I had no doubt he'd withheld many secrets about the past, but over time, maybe he'd open up. The picture forming in my mind from the little he'd said caused a hard tangible fear to lodge in my stomach and reminded me about the dangers of making assumptions. It had been easy to convince myself that his lack of trust in our friendship and his attachment to Alex had caused his silence. Nothing could be further from the truth

"We good?" I murmured in a low voice.

"Yeah, we're fine." Aiden gave me a brotherly hug.

The dread lifted, and I could breathe. Now when I looked around the room, instead of disappointed adversaries, I saw an amazing and loyal group of friends. They were rare and precious, every single one. Not many would've allowed me a second chance or even the third or fourth I'd been granted. I'd been damn sure I'd never set foot inside any of their doors after the sins I'd committed.

I'd left a path of destruction in my wake, but now I'd returned to reality, found my way out of that deep dark pit in my mind, and I could be nothing but thankful.

They'd cared enough to try, over and over. They'd been there to care for my family while I wallowed in self-pity, to provide emotional support for my wife, and to love my child as much as their own. We'd bonded over the years, through the good and the bad, and we'd passed another hurdle.

Alex's intense stare caught my eye. She skirted the room and drew me into the privacy of the hallway. "Are you okay?"

"Never better." I slid an arm around her waist. "They're true friends, aren't they? They've forgiven me, even though I'm unworthy."

She cupped my face in her palms, a single tear trickling down her cheek. "But you are worthy. Underneath, you're a good man, and you've done the same for them. Think of everything we've been through, the ups and downs. Our friends have experienced them with us. We're family. That's what I've been telling you. Everyone in this room is part of our family, not competition."

"I see that now, Alex, and I am so sorry for thinking the worst, for treating you like I did, and for the stupid jealousy. I always thought you'd fallen in love with him, and when he moved overseas, that left me as the convenient backup."

"I do love him, but I've never been in love with him. There's a huge difference. For me, it's always been you. Trust in us and in what we have."

"I'm the one getting in our way, it's never been Aiden."

She nodded, smiling through the tears. "I never knew you felt that way, and I'm sorry."

I didn't trust myself to speak or even know if my voice would work. Where did we go from here? I didn't know, but I acknowledged my reality to be far better than what I'd imagined, and I could dismiss the deceitful illusions that taunted me and led me astray.

Her soft lips invited me in, and my heart pounded as her hand twined in my hair.

"I love you, Ally," I whispered, tipping my forehead against hers.

"And I love you. I always have."

Oh, those sweet words from her lips. The sign I'd been searching for, hoping for, pleading for. Alex's love meant everything. I couldn't be whole without it.

"Brunch is served." Jenna's voice carried even over the din of conversation, a fussing Adrianna, and the delighted squeals of Daniel.

Every sound became crystal clear, breaking me from our private little world.

"I'd better get in there," Alex murmured. "It's my party, and everyone else is doing the work." She dabbed at her eyes. "Come eat?" Her smile lit me up inside, heart and soul.

I followed, reveling in the buzz of voices and comfortable dance swirling around me. A smiling Aiden accepted Kellan from Emily and draped the tiny boy over his shoulder. Ryan scooped up Daniel, placing food on a plate as my son pointed out his selections with a chubby finger. Out of the corner of my eye, I spotted Tom snuggling Adrianna into a carrier as he waved Jenna toward the buffet set out on the large granite island.

A warm camaraderie surrounded me. These sounds of home and friends enveloped me along with a deep sense of longing for what I'd lost. I dragged in a breath, wishing to sink into it. To become part of it. My place here seemed uncertain, and I blamed myself.

"Are you planning to eat?" Aiden appeared beside me, swaying as he soothed Kellan with a gentle back rub.

"How about I take Kellan, and you can eat? I haven't …" *Ever held him.* My breath stuck in my throat.

My best friend's son, and I couldn't even remember his birthday.

"Really?"

I nodded. "I'd love to get to know my nephew."

Aiden transferred his son to my waiting arms, and I pointed toward the kitchen. With a smile, he made his way over, stopping to bestow a kiss on his wife before he loaded a plate.

Kellan stared at me with deep brown eyes, a small frown creasing his brow as he crammed his thumb into his mouth.

I rocked back and forth and he relaxed.

Alex's gaze took on an intensity, a watery smile crept over her face, and she gave a small nod.

Maybe I'd found the way back into her heart, after all.

CHAPTER 33

Alexis

WHEN I TALKED TO JENNA earlier in the day, I'd been a complete wreck. Yesterday's events had thrown me into a state of utter confusion, robbing me of precious sleep. Should I let Joel back into my life? Had I been wrong about it being over?

Watching Joel cuddle Kellan after our interlude in the hallway did nothing to calm the raging tide of emotions threatening to swamp me. I blinked back the tears, turning and almost colliding with Emily.

"What's wrong?" she asked as she steadied me with one hand.

"Nothing." I clamped my teeth onto my lower lip, gnawing at it as my friend studied me.

"Liar," she muttered under her breath before rolling her eyes toward Joel cradling her baby boy. "That's got you all wound up. Why?"

I grasped her arm and hauled her into a quiet corner. "I had it figured out, and I vowed to never take him back. And then he does that."

"Ahh." Emily nodded. "Damn men. Just when you have them pigeonholed, they get all sensitive and understanding. Annoying, isn't it?"

"So you get it." I whispered, still looking toward Joel, who'd now been joined by Tom, Aiden, and Ryan. "I want to hate him, but it's impossible. I love him too much. But if I take him back, he'll do it again." The final few words rushed out, almost obliterated by my choked sobs.

"You don't know that. From what I've seen, Joel is making an honest effort." Emily patted my shoulder. "Anyway, who says you need to decide tonight? Make him work for it. Let him see what he's been missing out on."

"Is that what you did with Aiden?"

"Ha, no." Emily shook her head. "I believe I was the Joel in our little melodrama. Aiden had no reason to take me back, but he did, and I'm thankful every day."

"No reason except he's madly in love with you."

"And I almost ruined it. There's only so much you can inflict on someone before they break. That's especially true for Aiden after what he's been through."

I closed my eyes. Somehow, once I'd tracked Aiden down in that little pub not so long ago, I'd convinced him to give Emily that crucial opportunity to set things right . Should I heed my own advice? I met Emily's serious gaze.

"I've never thanked you for what you did with Aiden. You gave him back to me when I thought I'd lost him forever. I didn't deserve him, and I'd taken him for granted, but he gave me another chance."

We stared at each other for a moment.

"Maybe Joel ..." Her brows rose.

"Perhaps," I murmured. "But Aiden didn't cheat, so it's different."

Emily fiddled with her fork and pushed the salad around her plate. "He kissed Jazlyn." Her eyes shimmered. "That was hard to take."

I placed a hand on her arm. "He didn't cheat, Emily."

She blinked hard and nodded. "Even if he'd had sex with her, I would have no right to be angry, because I left him with zero expectations. Maybe that's why I forgave him. After everything, he didn't." Emily dashed the back of her hand against her eyes and forced a smile. "Imagine him turning a woman like that down ... for me."

"Oh, Emily, she has nothing on you." I squeezed her arm.

Was that where I'd left Joel? Had I doused that last glimmer of hope he'd carried? Yet, he hadn't followed through, even when he'd had the opportunity. Crystal wasn't a super model, but still ...

"Thanks for your support. Reliving it can't be easy for you."

She grasped my hand. "You've become family, and I want you to be happy. Without him, you're not."

⌒≺

After the remnants of our meal had been cleared and the babies had been fed and put down for naps, the group gathered around the flickering fireplace.

"We should have a pool tournament." Ryan rubbed his hand together. "Ladies versus men."

I glanced toward the large windows, shivering at the flurry of icy snowflakes pattering against the glass. Definitely a wonderful night to spend indoors.

"Excellent plan." Tom rose from his chair. "I'm taking drink orders."

"I'm in." Aiden grabbed Emily's hand, lifting her from her seat. "What can I get you?"

My stomach clenched as I watched them together. Part of me filled with joy at their close and practically indestructible relationship, while the other mourned the special connection I'd lost and might never regain with my own husband. I peeked at Joel, who turned and disappeared through the doorway into the recreation room.

By the time the rest of the group had congregated in the room, he'd joined Tom at the bar to pour drinks.

When we'd moved to Boston, I'd given Joel a hard time at the extra expense and size of the pool table. Now I had to admit he'd been right; that pool table along with the large comfortable chairs made this room perfect for entertaining. Perfect for these gatherings with our closest friends.

"You're up." Ryan handed me a cue and steered me toward the table. "Break."

I lined up my shot and smacked the cue ball as hard as possible, rewarded as a solid sank into the side pocket.

Joel appeared at my side. "Excellent shot, hon—"

I stared at him and narrowed my eyes, my gaze drawn to the glass in his hand.

He took a step backward, a guilty look flickering across his features.

With a sigh, I turned my attention to the game, concentrating on the next shot, my fingers trembling. It went wide, and I extended the cue to Joel. "Here."

He handed over his glass, lining up and sinking three shots in short order, but he missed the fourth.

As he moved aside for Emily, I pushed the glass into his hands.

"That's yours," he murmured as he pressed it into my fingers.

"You're not …?"

He shook his head. "I promised."

Our eyes met, and a jolt ran through me.

"Alex, your turn," Aiden said.

I hid my confusion as I took another shot, missing yet again. Every time I thought I had Joel figured out, he surprised me.

⌁

The afternoon flew by, and at dinnertime, everyone pitched in to make the evening meal. Brunch days meant the morning straight through to evening with our family.

The bustle inside the kitchen died down as I retrieved the last platter from the counter.

"I'll take it, Alex." Joel took the heavy plate from my grasp and motioned for me to proceed him into the dining room. He set it in the middle of the table and sat in his place.

I took in the happy faces of our friends surrounding us in our home, replicating the idyllic vision I'd had for us, with our children growing up together, just as we had. Not for the first time today, the sense of longing rushed through me. I wanted our life back, along with the days of laughter and camaraderie, both with my old friends and my new ones.

A sidelong look down the table made me smile as Joel leaned in to listen to Ryan.

I stood and lifted my glass, and the buzz of conversation died down. "Thanks for being here today. I love you all. Cheers, everyone."

The tinkling of glasses and the smiling faces brought tears rushing to my eyes. The buzz of conversation rose again as I sat, and the dishes were passed.

I placed the last scoop of mashed potato onto my plate and the inevitable happened. The sound of tiny feet pounded down the hallway, and Daniel appeared, tears dribbling down his face.

Before I could react, Joel pushed back from the table and scooped Daniel into his arms. "What's the matter, buddy?" He cradled his son against his shoulder and rocked him. "Hungry?"

Emily widened her eyes at me, and I sank into my chair. Her gaze reminded me to relax and let Joel take care of his son. I had to release my usual choke hold of control over every detail concerning my little boy's care.

By ten, almost everyone had packed up, shared a round of warm hugs, and left for home.

Daniel had been running non-stop since dinnertime, and he clutched my leg, whining as Ryan and Kaari disappeared behind the elevator door.

"I'll get him ready for bed. You look exhausted." Joel appeared behind me. "Sit." He pried Daniel off of my leg and slung him over his shoulder. "I turned on the kettle if you want tea."

Daniel kicked and fussed as they disappeared down the hallway.

I wandered through the apartment, checking for anything out of place. Pristine and spotless. The soft sounds of the water swishing in the dishwasher greeted me in the gleaming kitchen. The cup Joel had prepared sat on the counter, and I poured in hot water. I left a second cup waiting as a subtle invitation for Joel to stay and chat with me.

The fragrant scent of cinnamon rooibos soothed me as I carried it through to the living room and sank onto the couch. Through the blur of exhaustion, I replayed the day.

"Can I join you?" Joel's voice broke my reverie, and I wondered if I had drifted to sleep.

"Sure." I beckoned him over.

"That was great." He settled onto the couch beside me with a cup in his hand. "Being here with everyone worried me, but it turned out to be a good day. I didn't realize how much I missed this."

"I don't know why you're surprised." I tucked my feet beneath me.

He slid closer and curled an arm around me, and I rested comfortably against his shoulder. My head spun from the wine I'd consumed, so I sipped my tea before closing my eyes.

The silence soothed me, and our closeness reminded me of better times before our world had fallen apart.

Joel pressed his lips to my hair, and then to my temple, then he nuzzled against my neck.

I sighed in contentment, enjoying the feel of his lips as they captured mine. The attraction and passion we shared had been rekindled, and he proved it as he took the cup from my hand and set it aside, soon twining his fingers into my hair.

My traitorous body responded, desire overruling the warning flag waving in the back of my mind. I trickled my fingers through his soft hair, inhaling his familiar scent. The tender kisses he placed on my overheated skin sent tiny shivers down my spine. Why resist?

Joel grasped the bottom of my shirt, and I lifted my arms, allowing him to peel it off.

The silence was punctuated only by our heavy breathing as we worked at freeing each other of clothing, my body begging for his touch.

I wrapped my arms around him, basking in the glory of his smooth, warm flesh under my fingertips. My desire overrode everything. I wanted him, needed him, and I let go, sinking into our mutual desire.

～

Soft kisses rained down on me, and I pried open my eyes. Staring up, my smile widened. "Good morning, my love. Sleep well?"

"Yeah, better than I have in months." He brushed my hair back, leaning down to capture my lips in a sweet kiss.

It felt wonderful to wake up in his arms.

"Last night. Mm-mm, baby. Amazing." He nibbled on my ear, and then a mock pout appeared. "Now I have to go to work. Are you home today?"

"No, today's a work day, and I have to drop Daniel with Jenna."

"Oh. I guess I'll see if I can find movers who can bring everything after work?" He kissed my nose.

I sat and combed my fingers through my hair. "Movers for what?" Even as I said it, a sinking feeling took hold.

"For my things. I can't wait to come home."

"Whoa." I held up a hand. "One night doesn't spell back together, or all is forgiven, or anything like it. We have a long way to go before our marriage is fixed."

"But"—he blew out a long breath—"wow. I assumed—"

"Yeah, you assumed. You always do that. You take one little thing and make it into whatever you want it to mean. Did you even consider discussing it first?"

"We've had such a great weekend."

"One weekend. Yes, it's been a great one, but we can't base our whole relationship on two good days in a row."

"Right, of course not. So last night meant nothing to you?" He swung his feet to the floor, scanning the room. "Damn, where are my pants?"

"Joel." I shoved my arms into my robe, trailing behind him as he stalked into the living room.

His shirt hung open as he hauled on his pants. "Whatever, Alex, I get it. I'm trying, and after last night …" He scrubbed his hands through his hair. "I thought we had more than one moment there, that we'd made real progress, but I guess I'm mistaken," he muttered. "Nothing I do will ever be enough for you."

"Hey." I sank down beside him and rubbed his back. "Last night was amazing, and we've made progress, but there's so much we need to figure out. We can't rush it, we need to keep working on us. It's nowhere near resolved."

"Isn't it?" He turned to face me. "I miss you, Ally. I want to come home."

"Oh, sweetie." I slid a hand to the back of his neck and pulled his head against my shoulder. "It took us years to break what we had, and it will take more than a couple of weeks and a few counseling sessions to repair it."

"Let me come home. Please? That place is depressing."

"When you come home, I want it to be forever, and I want it to be for the right reasons. Not because you miss our bed, or you don't like where you're living. Why can't we continue this way? We can go on dates and see each other more often. It'll be fun."

"Fun?" Joel raised a brow. "My wife refuses to let me move home, but I can call her for a damn date? We're way past that."

"That's how it is, Joel. It's too much pressure having you living here full-time. It doesn't mean I've given up, or that I don't appreciate your efforts. I want us to work at our relationship before we take that step. We've had two or three good days in a row before, but it didn't solve anything."

"If we take that step." Joel's tone went flat. "I can read between the lines. You think our marriage is over."

I sank into his embrace. "I want this to work, but we were in a horrible place two weeks ago, and I can't go back there, ever. This is serious, Joel. There's no quick or easy way to fix us."

"I suppose." Joel rose and buttoned his shirt. "I should go. Tom's expecting help on a new case, now that I don't look like I lost a bar brawl."

"Ah, you looked roguishly handsome." Patting his face, I leaned in for a hug. "Please, don't give up on us or the counseling."

"Alright, I hear you." Tipping up my chin, he kissed me, long and slow. "I won't lose you. I can promise you that."

CHAPTER 34

Joel

ISAPPOINTMENT FLOODED ME AT THE way Alex shut me down the moment I mentioned moving home. I tried to understand when she reminded me of where we'd been in our relationship not so long ago. Though I considered my communication skills to be excellent, they hadn't translated to my marriage, that remained clear.

Damn. I'd pushed too hard and taken it for granted that we were on track. Did my assumptions set us back? How far back? Weeks? Months?

I arrived at the office and poked my head around the corner. I harbored a faint hope I could sneak in unnoticed. No such luck. Our hard-working receptionist peered up at me as I slunk by.

"Good morning, Joel." A smirk twitched her lips as she gave my rumpled clothing the once over.

"Morning," I mumbled and hurried toward the suite.

Tom appeared from around the corner. "Looks like someone stayed out allllll night." He wiggled his brows, a huge grin spreading across his face. "Alex?"

I allowed a small grin of my own. "Who else?"

"Go change. Our meeting is in two hours, and you need to review the file." He patted my shoulder before striding toward his own office.

Once showered and dressed, I poured a large coffee and spent the next several minutes skimming through the details of the legal brief Tom had left on my desk.

"Ready to go?" Tom appeared twenty minutes later, his briefcase in hand.

"Yes. Interesting stuff." I motioned to the folder on my desk as I slid on my suit jacket and grabbed my own briefcase.

"It'll be a big case, so I need you as back up until Savannah is up to speed and has more direction on research."

"How's it going with her working here again?"

"Excellent. She takes after her dad. A mind that works at warp speed, and she's articulate and intelligent. With the right education, she'll be an amazing addition to this firm. Maybe we can keep Hamilton over the door even after Aiden bow's out."

"That'll be a while, for both." I mentally calculated my growing debt clock ticking away in the background. "Maybe she won't want to work here."

Tom shrugged. "It's her decision, but I want her here. Having a family run firm has always been my dream. At one time, I'd assumed it would be Aiden, but instead, I'm working with his daughter. Funny how things turn out."

"Yeah." I followed him down the hall. "If Vanna wants to be part of the firm, I support it. She'll be a top-notch lawyer if she chooses that path."

"It's great you patched things up with her and Aiden. It's a positive step in your recovery, and a bonus that things have improved with Alex."

"We're working on it. I suspect it'll be a long and bumpy road. Can I stay in the suite a while longer?"

"Sure, as long as you need to, Joel. You've pulled it together, and it's not disrupting our work."

That was a huge relief. Renting an apartment would make our separation feel permanent, and I couldn't get my head around it. That, and Alex seemed to be changing her mind on the *no way in hell are we ever getting back together* view she'd held previously.

I'd spotted a faint ray of hope, and I wasn't about to let that fade away.

⌒⚊⚼

Tom appeared in the doorway, his woolen overcoat buttoned. "I'm heading home unless you need anything?" He pulled on his gloves.

"Nope, I'm good. Get home to that lovely wife of yours."

"Goodnight." Tom waved and disappeared down the hall.

I spun my chair around to admire the city lights, wishing I had something more exciting to do than hide inside my tiny suite. Sitting in a pub lacked appeal, and my friends were home with their families.

My life had morphed into something unrecognizable. I closed my eyes, picturing what Alex might be doing now. Warmth overtook me as I envisioned her feeding Daniel dinner and imagined his sweet giggles and splashing as he played in the bathtub.

Regret consumed me, and I wished for it to be more than imaginary. I'd spent the summer avoiding the domestic scene, but these days I'd trade anything to rewind and be there for every moment. I needed to shake it off and vow to do better, no point in kicking myself yet again.

As much as I wanted to throw on my coat and charge to the apartment, I held back. That would be pushing. Nor could I sit here feeling sorry for myself.

I tapped the message into my phone before I thought better of it.

What are you up to? Interested in getting out of the house?

After a few moments, the little dots danced along my screen.

Can't go out. I have Kellan tonight.

Just my luck. I rested my mobile face down on my knee while debating on what to order for my solitary dinner. Chinese? Pizza? Burgers? I lived on the stuff now. My phone vibrated.

You could come here and watch the game. Feeding Kel, then making dinner if you're interested.

My heart lifted at the casual invitation.

Sounds great. Leaving the office now.

Warmth surrounded me as I entered the building, brushing flakes of snow from my wool overcoat. I didn't miss the commuting in Chicago. Winters in Boston could be cold, with tons of snow, but the office and our respective homes were all within walking distance. It had taken me less than half an hour, but then, I'd practically run the whole way.

It seemed sad that a home-cooked meal and sofa-surfing could hype me up, but if Aiden had managed to forgive me, then I'd take it.

The fragrant scents made my mouth water from the moment the elevator slid open. I hung my coat and wandered through to the kitchen.

Kellan bounced in his seat, kicking his legs while chewing on a toy. He squawked and screwed up his face like tears were imminent.

"Hey, drooly boy." I brushed my hand over his downy head. "Teething already?"

"I think so." Aiden glanced our way. "He's been a grouch all day."

"Where's Emily?" I unfastened the safety belt and draped Kellan over my shoulder, rubbing his back and bouncing.

"Work." He pulled out a pan. "You good with him while I finish here? I hoped he'd sleep, but he refuses."

"Take your time. We'll be fine. Right, buddy?" I picked up the cloth from over the back of Kellan's chair and wiped his face. Then I paced with him, keeping him soothed while Aiden put the final touches on dinner. Eventually he closed his eyes. "He's asleep," I whispered.

"Can you put him in his bed?" Aiden looked relieved.

I nodded and headed down the hallway, placing Kellan in his crib, stopping for a moment to peer at him. He rolled onto his side, looking so sweet and peaceful that my heart ached. How many times had I been home for Daniel at bedtime? How much of his life had I missed with my absences?

Aiden set the plates onto the counter as I returned to the kitchen.

"He's down," I said.

"Thank you. Nothing made him happy today."

"You're good with him though. How do you have the patience?"

"He's a baby. What else can you do?"

"Yet you still had time for this." I took the first savory bite. "Do you think I neglected Daniel?"

Aiden turned toward, frowning but remaining silent.

"You spend a lot of time with Kellan. Way more than I ever spent with Daniel." I cut into the chicken. "What if he hates me when he grows up because I wasn't there when he was a baby?"

"That won't happen." He squeezed my arm. "He's still young, and you have every opportunity to be a part of his life. Make the most of every moment."

"You sound like a fortune cookie."

"Maybe." He pushed his roasted potatoes around with his fork. "They stole that time from me with Savannah."

"You have a great relationship with her."

"One that almost didn't happen. She wanted to find her mother, not me. It's a miracle that she's here, and forming a bond with her wasn't easy. With Kellan, I get to be here for everything." He stabbed a piece of chicken.

Except he almost died because of me. He almost missed it. All of it. Would there ever be a time when I would look at Aiden and not be reminded of my failures? "I'm sorry," I muttered.

"Stop." He lifted his palm toward me. "Let's get past this part. I can't stand hearing it over and over. We've both been through too much crap in our lives and done things we wished we hadn't. This whole mea culpa thing is wearing me out."

"But—"

"No buts." His fork clanked against the plate as he set it down. "I've forgiven you, and I meant it. Quit looking back. The only way out of this is forward."

"How can you let it go so easily?"

"What's easy about this? That stupid word drives me insane." He propped his head on one hand, lifting the other to massage his neck. After a moment, he stood and picked up his plate and cutlery. "Let's watch the game."

"Sure." I gathered my own dinner and followed.

We settled onto the couch as Aiden flicked on the wall-mounted big screen and lit the fireplace. Soon we were engrossed in the game, and it began to feel like old times.

"Half-time. I'd better check on Kellan and tidy up the kitchen before Em gets home." Aiden stretched.

"Ha. Scared of Emily." I laughed out loud. "The house husband better get his act together."

"Yeah, you got me. Have to keep her satisfied." A smirked appeared. "She makes it worth my while." He headed toward the kitchen with our plates.

I followed with our empty glasses. "I haven't seen you this happy in a long time."

"Damn right, I'm happy." He glanced at me before returning to loading the dishwasher. "Are you planning to see your parents over Thanksgiving? We're flying to Chicago on Thursday afternoon if you want a lift. Or did Tom mention it already?"

I couldn't meet his eyes. "I don't know what I'm doing."

"Wait." His brows lifted. "You haven't told your parents that you're separated from Alex?"

"How did you …?" I couldn't fool Aiden about anything. "I'll never hear the end of the lecture. My mom will go ballistic when she finds out Alex booted my ass."

"No doubt she will."

"Is Alex going to Chicago?"

Aiden leaned against the counter and folded his arms. "Talk to your wife, Joel. It's not my place to share what her plans are. While you're at it, talk to her about Christmas."

My stomach lurched. I hadn't been able to ask about Christmas or make plans for any of the upcoming holidays. The will to act evaded me. "Christmas should be tons of fun."

"Maybe more fun than you think. I have two words for you," he said. "Fresh powder. Interested?"

"Hell, yeah." Despite my misery, a grin crept in but faded seconds later. "Damn. I wish. I can't afford it. You know that."

"Ah." He waved a hand. "We rented a huge chalet, and you seem to forget we own a corporate jet. There's plenty of room, so pitch in for groceries, and buy your lift ticket. Then you're all set."

"I don't know." I picked at a callous on my finger. "I should check with Alex. Maybe she'll let me see Daniel over the holidays."

"Alex the snow bunny? When has she ever said no to three feet of glorious fresh powder and unlimited runs down the slopes? Iona has agreed to travel with us and watch the kids while we ski." Aiden met my gaze.

"It's been eons since we took this sort of holiday trip." I tapped my fingers against the counter.

Aiden nodded.

"It would be good for Daniel to have both of us in the same house for Christmas."

He remained quiet but nodded again.

"Alex might not feel so pressured if it's a group in the house. No way will she let me stay in the apartment with her, and I can't bear spending the holidays with my mother and her certain disappointment."

"So you're in?"

I chuckled. This guy managed to get me to talk myself into the trip, and I appreciated it. "You want us to get back together. Why?"

"You love her," he said. "And she loves you. That's reason enough to give your marriage a fair chance at surviving."

"Thank you." I stared at him without blinking. "Your support means everything."

His look said it all; friends didn't leave when you needed them. I'd been granted an undeserved chance to make it right.

CHAPTER 35

Alexis

DARKNESS HAD DESCENDED BY THE time the plane touched down onto the runway in Chicago. I stared at the fluffy flakes striking the small porthole window as we taxied down the runway. A shiver ran down my spine at the thought of facing the icy cold, but we coasted to a halt inside one of the many hangars.

Everyone rose from their seats and stretched—not that it had been a long flight, or even crowded like an economy flight. Instead, we'd lounged in oversized seats and wandered to the galley kitchen for coffee and snacks.

Jenna squeezed my hand and glanced at Joel as he maneuvered Daniel's arms into his winter coat. "It'll be fine."

"Why did I agree to this again?" My whole body shook with nervous anticipation at the days ahead.

"Because you don't want to deal with his mother's nosy questions."

"Right." I giggled, and the nerves dissipated.

I loved Joel's family. They treated me like a daughter after I'd lost my mother, and now that my dad's mental faculties had deteriorated, I appreciated them even more. But, and this was a big one, telling his parents that their precious boy had done me wrong wouldn't be a pleasant experience.

Jenna pushed me toward the door, which Aiden had opened, and I followed the rest of the group down the short flight of steps.

The luggage had been transferred into the trunk of the waiting sedan, so I had nothing left to do but to wish everyone happy Thanksgiving and slide into the back while Joel buckled Daniel into his seat.

"Thanks for doing this, Alex." Joel peered at me over Daniel's head. "Things are so …" He shrugged.

"Yeah, they are." I nodded. How we would get through this weekend, I hadn't any clue.

The moment we arrived in the driveway, the front door flew open, and Joel's mother dashed down the steps. I'd barely managed to slide from my seat before she wrapped me into her warm embrace.

"I'm so glad you decided to join us for the weekend." She ushered me toward the house, while Joel trailed with Daniel. The moment we were inside, Sarah turned and scooped Daniel from Joel's arms. "Let me see my precious grandson." She smothered his face with kisses.

Daniel giggled and pushed at her face with one hand. "Nana."

"Oh, sweet boy." She rested him on her hip as she leaned in to kiss and squeeze Joel's cheek. "And here is my other sweet boy. It's been too long."

"Sorry, Mom." Joel slung an arm around her waist. "It's been crazy."

"Let me help with the bags so you all can get settled." Joel's dad grabbed the nearest bag.

Joel's father, Dan, helped Joel carried the suitcases upstairs as Sarah pulled me into the kitchen with one hand while cradling Daniel on her hip with the other.

"Let's have some tea." She buckled Daniel into a high chair and placed a cookie in front of him.

I eyed the treat but kept my protests to myself. She hadn't seen her grandson in months, and I wished we lived closer. Life had been much easier when Nana had taken him once a week.

"How's Boston." Sarah bustled around the kitchen, procuring cups from the cupboard.

"Great. I love the apartment, and this little man keeps me busy." I pasted on a smile even as the guilt swept through me.

"And work?" Her eyebrows rose. "I'd hoped to be hearing about another grandbaby on the way, not about you spending your time in an office. Joel makes plenty of money to support you."

"Daniel's still a baby." I clutched the handle of the cup she set in front of me. "And it's not about money. I love interior design, and it gives me a break. I love Daniel, but I need me time."

"Hmph." She shook her head.

Joel appeared and pointed at the cup in front of me.

"I'd love a cup of that."

I sighed and threw a grateful look his way. Sarah had been winding up for a lecture on the vices of the working mother, and I didn't think I had the patience, considering the circumstances.

"The guest room looks great." He accepted a steaming cup and slid into a seat.

"Thank you, dear." She beamed at him.

Soon he had her chattering about everything but us and our lives. Dan sipped his own cup of tea while entertaining Daniel by pulling funny faces.

I smothered a yawn about the time Daniel began to fuss. "I'm off to bed."

"I'll bring Daniel up." Joel widened his eyes.

"Thanks, honey." I took our cups to the sink and gave dutiful hugs to both Sarah and Dan before preceding Joel up the squeaky staircase.

"I'll change him and put him to bed. You go ahead and use the bathroom." Joel waved me away as I attempted to take Daniel.

By the time I had gathered my things, brushed my teeth, and changed, Joel had come into the bedroom. "Sorry about this." He motioned to the double bed. "I didn't know what to say, and ..."

"It defeats the purpose of the happy couple charade." I slid under the covers and patted the mattress beside me. "Not like we've never shared this room or this bed."

Joel peeled off everything aside from his boxers, crawled in beside me, and turned off the light. He plumped up his pillow, keeping to his side and making no move to touch me.

After a few moments of silence, I wiggled closer and shut my eyes. This whole scenario comforted me, and a tiny flicker of hope blossomed as I drifted to sleep.

My eyes fluttered open, and I laid still, listening to the sounds of life around me. Even through the closed door, I heard Sarah's voice as she talked to Daniel. Moments later, the patter of his feet sounded in the hallway and then silence.

I turned my head and stared into Joel's eyes. "I should get up."

"Stay." He brushed a lock of hair back from my face and trickled his fingertips down my cheek. "You look beautiful."

"Don't." I caught his hand and placed it on the covers over his belly. "The only reason we're together right now is—"

"I get it, Alex. This isn't real. It's us parading our fictional wedded bliss in front of my parents." He pushed upright and swung his legs over the side of the bed. "I'll make sure she's not feeding him sugar for breakfast."

"Joel."

He threw a dark look my way as he yanked on his jeans and a fresh t-shirt. "Don't worry about it. My mistake."

Moments later, the door clicked shut behind him, leaving me staring at the ceiling. His sensitive side had emerged. He'd always been like that—too quick to have his feelings hurt or jump to conclusions.

The thought of making love to him with his mother in the same house made me uncomfortable. Though she'd be thrilled and would convince herself we were busy conceiving a second grandchild.

 That Sarah wanted us to have another baby had never been a secret. She would have loved to have more children of her own, but after Joel, it hadn't happened. Now she projected that need onto her son, but this wasn't the time for us to bring another dependent little person into our lives.

Sighing, I dressed and headed downstairs.

By Saturday I had started to go stir crazy cooped up with the in-laws and a grouchy Joel. When my phone buzzed, and I spotted the message, I planned my escape. "It's Emily." I scanned the text. "She's going shopping with Jenna. Would you be upset if I joined them?"

"Not at all." Sarah smiled. "We don't have much to do today. I'll take Daniel out, and leave Dan and Joel to their guy things."

I tapped out a reply as I hurried up the stairs to change and grab my purse. Not long afterward the doorbell rang, and I bounded downstairs as Sarah answered the door.

"So lovely to see you." Sarah beckoned them inside. "I haven't seen either of you in forever." She hugged each in turn.

"I won't be out too late." I slid on my coat and followed my friends out the door. At the sight of the limo, I grinned. "Nice."

"Aiden insisted we have a driver." Emily smirked. "It's a long drive from Lake Forest, and he worried about the icy roads."

Jenna waved a hand. "Get used to it, honey. Besides, this is perfect. We can relax, and our shopping bags can go into the trunk right away. And we don't have to worry about parking downtown. I'm sure it's insane with the shoppers this weekend."

"There's no argument coming from this direction." Emily smiled as the driver held the door for us. "I will never complain when my husband spoils me."

I watched as the scenery flashed by and we entered downtown. "Where are we going?"

"It's a surprise." Jenna wiggled her brows as the limo pulled up to the curb.

Emily grabbed my hand and pulled me up some stairs in front of a semi-sketchy building.

"Ladies. Welcome."

"Paulo." Emily kissed his cheek.

I took in the owner of that sexy voice, admiring his blondish hair, tight t-shirt, and faded jeans. As I tore my eyes away, my gaze landed on the walls. "Wow." I pointed at the photos. "What are we doing here?"

"Photo sessions." Emily grinned. "Christmas presents."

"You're doing … nudie pictures?"

"Those are not nudie pictures." The delightful piece of eye-candy crossed his arms. "They're boudoir photos. It's art, not porn."

I peeked out of the corner of my eye at the two women beside me who both smothered laughter behind their hands.

"Sorry," I muttered. "Tom and Aiden will love those."

"And Joel." Jenna raised her eyebrows.

"We're hardly at the point in our relationship where I'll parade around half naked in front of a camera for him."

"Then do them for you." Emily grabbed my hand. "Trust me, it'll make you feel amazing."

"You've done them before? For who?"

"No, no." She shook her head. "This is special for Aiden. I've never done pictures before … but"—she glanced at Paulo—"sometimes I wear my sexiest lingerie and my favorite Manolos as a surprise. I throw a coat on and meet him. His reaction is worth it. Nothing's better than the husband who appreciates you just the way you are."

"You wander around Boston with only a coat over …? Nope, never mind. I do *not* want details about your sex life with Aiden."

Jenna giggled.

"Don't tell me you do it too."

"Sure. Tom and I have christened his desk, along with several other surfaces in his office … more than once." Jenna rolled her eyes. "Quit pretending to be a prude, Alex. You're not."

"I'm unprepared for … this." I waved my hands in the air.

"Well, you think about it. I'm ready." Emily turned to Paulo. "Where's the studio?"

CHAPTER 36

Joel

WHILE MY WIFE WENT SHOPPING with the ladies, I spent the afternoon with my dad. My mother laid claim to Daniel and headed out the door soon after Alex to take him to an indoor playground.

An ominous silence settled over us, but my dad beckoned me to follow him to the garage. "Look." He took hold of the edge of the tarp and tugged at it. "My new project."

"Mom know you have this hidden in here?" I skirted around the old Harley, running my fingertips over the fender.

"Ha, she protested, but not much she can do about it." He grinned. "Want to help?"

"Damn right."

"Let's get started. I found some replacement parts. They're over there in the box." He pointed to the work bench.

I retrieved the box, and we set to work removing parts.

"Remember when we restored my Mustang?"

My dad nodded. "Shame you had to sell it."

"Yeah." Selling the sleek fiery red car had broken my heart, but I'd used the money for law school.

"Maybe one day we can restore another one. Bet it feels great to have grease under your nails again."

"That would be amazing, Dad. I wish I had both the time and money, but now with the partnership and having Daniel ..." Some of the best memories of my life had been formed in this garage, working side by side with Dad. He'd been a mechanic most of his life and taught me everything he knew about cars.

"Maybe when he's older, you can teach him."

A smile crept onto my face as I pictured my little boy and all of the things we had yet to do together.

"How's Aiden?" My dad peered at me after we'd worked for several minutes

"Fine." I frowned.

"Good. You two sort out your issues?"

I straightened and met his gaze. "Yeah, we're good."

"I always liked Aiden. He's a good kid, despite what happened." He lined up the bolts and parts as he removed each one. "He seems happy with Emily."

"Who you been talking to?"

"Grace. We've been invited there for dinner on Sunday."

"Mom didn't mention it."

"You know your mother."

"Yeah."

"What's happening with you and Alex?" He kept his eyes focused on his task.

"Nothing?"

"It doesn't seem like nothing. You better straighten it out before you lose her."

I sighed. "We're dealing with it. How do you even know? Grace again?"

He wagged a finger at me. "I might not know much, son, but I can spot an unhappy woman."

"Does Mom know?"

"If she does, she hasn't said anything to me. Fix it. She's a keeper."

Silence fell over us, the only sound the clank of metal against metal as we stripped the bike.

"You know your mother and I have had our moments. We almost split up once or twice."

"What?" I froze in place. "But you always seem so happy together."

"We are, but life isn't easy. She always wanted another baby after you, and well, being unable to have one made her unhappy for the longest time. We wanted for you to have a brother or sister, but some things aren't meant to be." He swept a hand across his forehead, leaving a streak of grease. "We love Alex like she's our own daughter. I hope you two work it out."

"We're in counseling." I hung my head and scuffed my shoe against the cement floor.

"No shame in that, son. Better that than divorce. That would kill your mother."

I nodded, unable to speak. I had feared telling my parents, and expected lectures, but not this quiet and loving support.

⌒⤟

We had only sat at the dinner table when the front door open and closed, followed by footsteps heading upstairs. Five minutes later, she reappeared. "Sorry, I'm late." She placed a kiss on Daniel's hair before sliding into her chair.

"How was shopping? What did you buy?" My mother smiled.

"Lovely. I always enjoy time out with Jenn and Em." She accepted the dish of mashed potatoes and scooped a small helping onto her plate. "Smells delicious, Sarah."

"You'll waste away." Mom frowned at the small portions on my wife's plate. "You're too thin, Alex."

"We had a late lunch." Alex took a bite. "How was Daniel?"

My mother filled Alex in on every detail of their afternoon, while my father ate in silence, throwing glances at Alex, then at me, and back again.

I could almost hear what he was thinking—that in happier days, my wife would have laid a big ole kiss on me. Tonight, she threw nervous glances my way but avoided my gaze.

Once we'd finished, Alex bounced up to clear the table, followed by my mother.

"I'll help Ally. Mom, why don't you bathe Daniel?" I unfastened the safety strap on the highchair.

"Oh, I'd love to." My mom cuddled our boy against her and headed upstairs, followed by my dad.

I heard water running as I packaged leftovers, and Alex loaded the dishwasher.

"Dad figured it out." I broke the heavy silence.

"Yeah, I thought so. Sorry."

"It's not your fault." I moved behind her and wound an arm around her tiny waist. My mom was right. Alex had lost a substantial amount of weight and become far too thin in my view. "What's bothering you?" I rested my cheek against her hair, holding her close.

"Nothing."

"Alex." I turned her toward me, holding her shoulders. "You've been giving me these weird looks all through dinner. What happened with Emily and Jenna?"

"It's nothing to worry about." She peered at me. "I feel like I'm lying to Dan and Sarah, and tomorrow we have to put on this big act. You know we're invited to Grace's mini-castle for dinner, right?"

"It'll be fine." I drew her closer and guided her head to my chest. "Please, can we make this work?" I whispered.

Instead of pulling away as I feared she might, Alex wound her arms around my back. "I'm trying, but I'm scared."

"Of what?"

She buried her face against me but didn't answer.

We stood there for the longest time, holding each other.

I awoke as the first light of dawn filtered into our room. Alex's soft and even breathing told me she slept on.

Last night we'd both been restless, and the atmosphere had been strained. Alex had crawled under the covers and rolled onto her side with her back to me.

"Morning." Dad looked up from his newspaper, his keen eyes scrutinizing me. "You look tired."

With a shrug, I poured a large cup of coffee and sat.

"Ah." He selected a section of the paper and handed it across the table.

We read in companionable silence and sipped from our steaming mugs. As perceptive as always, my dad commented now and again on the news but he didn't ask about me and Alex, allowing me space to ponder.

"Hi." Alex drifted into the kitchen, showered and dressed. "Dan, would you mind if I borrowed the SUV this morning? I thought I'd visit Dad."

"The keys are in the usual place. We have a car picking us up at four for dinner at Grace's."

"I'll drive you." I lifted my gaze. "We could take Daniel to see his Grandpa."

Alex studied me for a moment, then nodded. "Sounds good. Sarah's dressing him now. We should leave right after breakfast."

Two hours later, we arrived at the care facility. I retrieved Daniel from the back while Alex stared at the front doors.

"I wonder if today is a good day, or a bad day." She glanced at me.

I balanced Daniel on my hip, and reached for her hand, entwining our fingers as we proceeded inside.

Alex approached the reception desk. "I'm here to see Mark Carr."

"Jeanine, there's a visitor for Mr. Carr." The woman motioned to one of the nurses.

"Oh, lovely to see you, Alex." Jeanine bustled toward us. "I'll take you to the TV room. He's usually there at this time of the day."

We followed Jeanine, and she pointed toward where Mark sat in his wheelchair.

She touched Alex's arm. "Not a great day, but he'll be happy to see you."

"Thank you." Alex inhaled audibly and crossed the floor. "Hi, Dad."

Mark's head came up, and he stared at his daughter. "Hello, young lady."

A small sniffle escaped her, and I moved closer to rest a supportive hand on her shoulder.

"Look who's here to see you." I set Daniel on his feet in front of Mark and crouched down to his level.

Our son peered upward and gave a gap-toothed grin. "Gampa?" He pointed.

Mark frowned, then his eyes widened, and an answering smile crept across his face. "Is that my Danny boy?" He turned his head toward Alex. "Ally."

"Yes." She nodded and brushed the tears from her face as she wrapped her arms around him. "Happy Thanksgiving, Daddy."

CHAPTER 37

Alexis

SEEING THE ONCE VIBRANT MAN reduced to this broke my heart. My dad had been one of the strongest men ever, but losing my mother had taken its toll on him. That long ago Christmas Eve remained a vivid and horrific memory—the flashing red and blue lights, the solemn officer as he broke the bad news, and how my father had held my hand when I'd insisted on viewing her pale and lifeless body with him.

Only months later, my dad had been diagnosed with Alzheimer's. The disease took hold and stole him from me too soon, leaving me no choice but to find him a secure facility where they could keep him safe.

When Joel had suggested the move to Boston, it had torn me in two. It meant leaving Dad alone in Chicago.

My heart ached as he scooped a small bite of mashed potato into his mouth, then sat with his spoon suspended in the air, as if he'd forgotten what to do with it.

Joel grasped his hand and guided it down to the plate. "More chicken, Mark?"

My dad turned slowly, a furrow appearing between his brows as he looked down at his food. All recognition faded from his eyes. "Who are you?" He stared at Joel, no longer able to comprehend.

"This is Joel, Daddy. He's my husband." I kept my voice gentle and even.

"Oh, right," he said, but I knew he'd disappeared into the depths of his mind, that lonely place we'd never understand.

"Sorry," I mouthed to Joel.

He shook his head and dabbed my father's chin with a napkin.

"Let's take him to the TV room." I pushed out of my chair and clenched my fingers around the handles of his wheelchair.

"I can do that."

"No, I've got him."

Joel picked up Daniel and followed our slow parade down the hallway.

In the TV room, I pointed my dad's chair toward the television and set the brake before bending to kiss my father's sallow cheek. "Bye, Daddy. I'll come see you soon."

On our way out, I spotted Jeanine. "How has he been overall?"

"About the same. He has lucid moments, then he drifts off. I'm so happy to see you again. It's been a while."

"We're in Boston. We relocated for Joel's work, but we're visiting for the weekend. Thank you for taking such good care of him."

"My pleasure." She patted my arm. "I have to get to my patients, but you take care."

We buttoned our coats to brave the cold and the light snow, and we crossed the icy parking lot. I slid into my seat while Joel attended to Daniel.

I leaned my forehead against the cold glass and closed my eyes as we pulled from the lot. Guilt consumed me that I couldn't see my dad more often.

"I'm sorry," Joel said. "That was a rough one."

I straightened and turned my head toward him. "Thanks for being patient with him."

"It's not his fault. This is difficult for you," he said. "Maybe we should move him to a facility in Boston."

"You'd help me move my dad?"

"Yes. You miss him."

"I really do." I studied his profile as he negotiated the snowy roads. "It's sad that only a few of the other residents had visitors while we were there. Dad needs specialized care, but if he were closer, I could see him regularly and take him out once in a while. I hate that he's alone most of the time."

He glanced at me before returning his attention to the road. "Then let's move him to Boston. Ask Aiden for some referrals, and I'll do the tours with you. We'll find somewhere great."

"They're expensive. His pension barely covers where he is now."

"Then we'll supplement the shortfall. Our Boston client list is growing, and Tom is throwing me some big cases. Those, along with the new clients I've brought in, will help. It'll be tight at first, but we'll make it work." Joel pulled into the driveway and turned off the engine. "He's your only family. If having him closer will make you happier, then I'm for it."

I brought my hand up to caress his stubbly cheek. "Someone needs to shave."

"Mmhm. We should get inside." He motioned toward the house. "My mother is watching us."

"She's probably panicking because we're not ready for the big social event." I giggled and peered through the late afternoon gloom as the curtain in the front window twitched and fell back into place. "I love her, but she has to be ready at least an hour before we're set to leave the house."

"She's never heard of fashionably late. If Grace said four, my mother will be there at four on the nose." He grinned at me. "They're sending a car like we can't drive ourselves."

"That's a Hamilton trait, I swear." I sat back. "Did anyone mention the ski trip over Christmas?"

"Aiden invited me."

"He did? I thought Tom ..."

"Aiden and I hung out and watched the game the other night, and he mentioned it. I said I'd talk to you first. It would be fun, but I want to spend the holidays with you and Daniel if you'll allow it."

"Does that mean things are good with you and Aiden?" At his nod, I opened the car door, allowing myself a moment to collect my thoughts. Aiden had forgiven Joel, and invited him for the holiday?

I retrieved Daniel from the back, fresh snow crunching under my boots as I headed for the front door.

"Alex?" Joel hurried along behind me. "Christmas?"

"Skiing sounds amazing. Let's accept the invitation, and we can both share in Daniel's day."

"Thank you." He opened the door and ushered me through.

⌁

My life after the Thanksgiving weekend in Chicago seemed unsettled. Many things remained unresolved, and I refused Joel's overture and request to return to our apartment. We'd moved forward, but a crippling fear clung to me. What if I relented too soon, and we slipped back into our old habits?

Joel hadn't been happy with my decision, but he did accept my suggestion that we take it slow with good grace, and he returned to the partner suite without argument.

He did suggest we team up for Christmas shopping, though, and I agreed without hesitation. Even if it would be awkward, I needed to give a little on my end.

After saying good night to my boss and the other two designers in my office, I gathered my things and headed onto the street. Our sleek black Acura waited at the curb. I slid into the soft leather seat, the warmth enveloping me as Joel pulled into traffic.

"Jenna agreed to keep Daniel as long as needed." He glanced at me.

"Great. I've already bought a few things for Daniel, but nothing for the other kids. We'll need at least two hours."

He nodded but focused on the icy roads as we glided through the heavy Boston traffic.

I adjusted the volume of the stereo, closing my eyes as the soothing music flowed through me. The sense of being watched made me open my eyes and peer toward Joel. "What?" I murmured.

"You're shutting me out." He clenched his hands around the wheel.

"How? With the music?" I straightened and angled my body toward him. "I like the song, and this feels so comfortable and familiar." Extending my arm, I rested my hand on his thigh and rubbed. This seemed to relax him, so I left my hand there and leaned back.

"You crank the music when you're angry and don't want to talk." His voice wavered.

"Is that what you think?"

He maneuvered the car into a parking spot. "It's true." He turned. "You do it when we're fighting to tune me out. Like you did when we came home from the Vineyard."

"Joel." I cupped his face between my palms. "I'm not angry. I promise. Sometimes it's easier than small talk, but things feel good with us. I liked the song. Nothing more."

He gazed into my eyes and smoothed my hair away from my face. For the longest time, we sat there staring at each other, until he leaned in and kissed me. His lips burned against mine, the long, sweet, and slow caress causing the heat to creep upward. My cheeks flushed as I wrapped my arms around him and pressed against him.

"I love you so much," he whispered in a choked voice when we broke apart. Joel buried his face against my neck, his breath coming in heavy gasps. "I'm sorry for overreacting."

I brushed my lips across his temple, and rested my cheek against his hair, not ready to let go. This moment felt so real and true, I didn't want it to end.

He cleared his throat before bowing his head.

I caught the glistening sheen of his eyes and realized how close he'd come to breaking down. So many times recently, *I love you* had rung hollow and insincere, but tonight, it seemed the words had risen from the depths of his soul.

"Ally?" He stared at his hands. "How did we get here? How did we end up so far apart?"

"I don't know," I whispered. "We lost ourselves and wandered off our charted course, but we're finding our way now."

"Maybe." Joel cleared his throat. "I have a confession at the risk of making this worse."

I squeezed my eyes shut to hold back the tears. "Just say it."

"That night at the Vineyard, after sailing"—he dragged in a deep breath—"I went to the pub and Crystal was there. Nothing happened, Ally, I promise, but I wasn't honest with you when you asked about that night. I'm sorry."

A surge of relief ran through me. The knowledge of where he'd been that night had hung over me, but I feared broaching the subject. "Anything else you need to confess?" I kept my face expressionless.

"She phoned me a while back, but I told her I choose you and our son." He reached for my hand as his eyes met mine. "You have every right to be angry, but I hope you can forgive me."

"No more lies, Joel."

He looked down even as his grip on my hand tightened. "Keeping it from you was wrong. I know that, and I won't do it again," he said in a gruff voice and he brushed his cheek with the back of one hand. "We should shop."

As we walked toward the mall, I captured his hand, entwining our fingers and squeezing, my subtle show of support.

Joel hated for anyone to see him cry, he thought of it as a sign of weakness. To me, it conveyed the opposite. The ability to shed tears portrayed strength of character, whether they be joyous or sad or something in between. That he cried for me—for us—and for what we'd lost, made me feel that much closer to him.

Our struggle to reconnect had been rough and wobbly at the start, but it had grown little by little, becoming stronger every day. Tonight we'd leaped forward, and I never wanted to look back.

The final two weeks leading up to Christmas rushed by, giving me little time to regroup before we were landing on the tarmac in Colorado. Butterflies flitted in my stomach. We had two full weeks to enjoy endless runs down the slopes, but it also meant two full weeks in close quarters with Joel.

Tom released the exterior door, and the chill air rushed through the passenger cabin, causing a flurry of activity as everyone gathered belongings and children.

We filled the next hour with bustling activity, everyone helping to stack each of the large SUV's with luggage and strap the multitude of ski and snowboarding equipment onto the roof carriers.

Aiden and Tom attended to the final details regarding the plane for the duration of our stay, while Iona kept the kids warm in the small office.

Then our convoy of three loaded SUV's sped toward our chalet.

I slapped a hand over my mouth to smother a delighted laugh. The massive log house spread before us as our flotilla pulled into the spacious driveway.

"Ohhhhhh." Savannah bounced on her toes, her eyes wide as she viewed our temporary home.

I slid an arm around her. "Incredible, isn't it? Now, go help your dad." A gentle push from me encouraged her to bound toward Aiden, and I turned to help unload our SUV.

Joel released Daniel from his seat and tucked our boy onto his hip. "Why don't you take our little man inside and get him settled? I'll help the guys stow the equipment and bring the bags."

"Thanks." I claimed a squirming Daniel from his arms.

Jenna grinned as I followed her inside. "Joel is extra attentive these days. It's a wonderful thing, Alex, you two look happy."

"It's getting there, but we still have a long way." I glanced over my shoulder to watch the group of men laughing and joking. At least he'd begun making amends with the boys. It made me happy to see them all together, though I wished I could pretend we'd returned to old times. That might never happen.

Though I loved each of the wonderful women surrounding me, an odd longing crept over me. I missed my old friend, Tiffany, even considering what she'd done to Aiden.

Aiden appeared with two bags. "Playpens, if you want to keep Kellan and Adrianna contained while we bring in the luggage?"

"Thanks, sweetie." Emily planted a kiss on his lips.

"Room assignments." Jenna tacked up a floor plan on the wall. "The guys sorted this out, so any complaints can be directed at Tom and Aiden." She grinned.

"Ha, I'm grateful to have a bed." I said.

"We're glad you came. It wouldn't be the same without you." Jenna gave me a brief hug. "The guys are bringing in the bags, so maybe we can start moving them."

I ran a finger over the chart. "They put us in separate rooms."

"You and Joel, you mean?" Emily shrugged. "Share if you like, but since you aren't living together, no one wanted to assume anything."

"No, it's good. We're not ready for that much togetherness." I spotted my bag in the growing stack that filled the front entrance. "I'll go unpack and settle Daniel in his room."

⌒⤛

The morning of December twenty-fourth broke crisp and clear, and the sounds of activity started early. I stretched and rose from bed, crawling into a steamy shower to wash the sleep from my eyes before dressing in layers, ready for another day.

"Morning." Aiden sat at the stone counter, tapping on his computer and sipping at a steaming cup of coffee. He rose and wrapped his arms around me before placing a light kiss on my forehead. "How are you?"

"You know. This is always a tough day." I shrugged. "Where is everyone?"

"Getting ready to ski. You're late to the party."

"You don't look ready."

"My shoulder aches. We've been hitting the runs hard, so I decided to take a day off." He rubbed at his neck.

I stepped up behind him to rub his shoulders, pressing my fingers into the muscles. "You have a huge knot."

"I'm getting a massage today, so that should help." He pushed me toward the kitchen. "Eat, or you'll be left behind."

"You can't be here all day by yourself. I'll stay and keep you company." I poured a large cup of coffee and leaned with my back against the counter.

He waved a hand. "Vanna took pity on her ole dad and said she'd stay in today. She pleaded exhaustion from too much skiing, but I know her game. Go have some fun."

"I'll try." I forced a faint smile before shuffling down the hallway to my bedroom and dropping onto the bed. I draped the back of my hand across my eyes.

"Alex?" The edge of the bed sank as Joel sat beside me. A frown creased his brow. "Not having a good day, huh?"

I shook my head as the tears burned. One escaped and trickled down my cheek.

He brushed it away, and then lay beside me, pulling my head to his chest. "I know you miss her."

"It's silly because she's been gone for years. Still, every Christmas, I wish she were here. She didn't get to meet her grandson."

Joel kissed my temple and tightened his embrace, and I knew he understood. I closed my eyes and listened to the steady beat of his heart.

"Why don't we skip the skiing for today?" he asked. "We could spend the day, just the two of us. I'll tell Tom so they can head out, and then we can go."

⌒≼

Less than an hour later, we were on our way into the village. The sun glinted off the snow-capped peaks and the runs were already filling with skiers.

"Thanks for this. I love everyone, but being there seemed so overwhelming today." I leaned back in the heated leather seat.

"They're a great group of people, but I hear you. Sometimes you need space, even from family."

Joel guided the SUV into an empty spot.

"What should we do?" I glanced around.

"I have something planned for us." He wiggled his brows, a wide grin spreading across his features as he hopped out and opened my door.

Joel wrapped my hand in his and led me down the street, before ushering me through a set of double doors.

"A hotel?" My brows rose in surprise. "What? Our afternoon includes a hotel room?"

"No." He reclaimed my hand and tugged me through yet another set of doors. "It includes this."

"The spa?" My lips twitched. Joel never went to places like this. "What are you planning?"

"You'll see." He approached the front desk and murmured something to the receptionist before returning to sit with me in the plush chairs.

Moments later, a lovely young woman appeared and led us into a private lounge. "Can I interest you in some tea?"

"Please." I nodded and peeked at Joel, who smiled and nodded.

I relaxed into the chair and sipped my tea until another woman arrived. "Follow me."

Joel linked our fingers as we trailed her into a room.

My eyes widened as I took it in. Complete luxury awaited us. Two tables were adorned with soft linens, and fluffy white robes were folded neatly on top. An oversized spa tub dominated one wall, and on the edge rested flutes, an ice bucket with a bottle of champagne, and a plate of truffles. A multitude of flickering candles adorned the ledge around the tub.

I pressed a hand to my lips. "This is amazing."

"Enjoy your bath. I'll be back to check on you in thirty minutes." The smiling attendant closed the door behind her.

Joel took my hand in his. "I figured we could use some relaxation. You like?"

I nodded and swished my fingers through the rose petals floating on top of the water.

Joel unbuttoned his shirt, sliding it off of his shoulders, but stopped short when he noted I hadn't made any move to undress. "I'm sorry, I wasn't thinking clearly. I thought … I don't know what I thought, but I'm not expecting …" He motioned to the jacuzzi tub. "Do you want a separate room?"

Did I? Getting naked and soaking in a tub with Joel opposed the whole slow it down idea. But we'd shared a bed in Chicago all weekend at Thanksgiving and avoided intimacy.

I shook my head and peeled off my own shirt, draping it over the arm of the chair.

Joel undressed and fiddled with the controls, while I discarded the last of my clothes and slid into the depths. The water churned around us, filling the air with a soothing fragrance.

"Mmmm." I sighed as I tipped back my head. "So good."

"Drink?" Joel poured some champagne into the crystal flute and held it out to me.

I eyed him over the rim as he filled his own glass. "I love this."

"I love you." A light ringing sounded as he tapped his flute against mine.

We both sipped the champagne, allowing a comfortable silence to fall over us. After a few moments, I wiggled closer and rested my back against his chest.

"These look yummy." I bit into one of the decadent chocolate treats, letting it melt on my tongue.

Joel lifted my hand and nibbled the remainder from my fingers. "Delicious." He rested his cheek against my hair, skimming his fingertips along my arm before reaching for one of the luscious berries from the bowl.

We traded off, feeding each other from the tray and sipping champagne while mellow music drifted through the air.

I turned my head to smile at him, and he tipped his chin to kiss me, cradling me against him.

I allowed myself to relax and accept this for what it was—a sweet gesture to cheer me up, and an apparent attempt to reconnect on a deeper level.

All too soon, a tap on the door interrupted our solitude.

"Your masseuses will be in soon."

Joel rose from the water and held out his hand to pull me to my feet. He wrapped me in a fluffy white towel and patted me dry.

I stood on my tiptoes to kiss his lips, then crawled under the sheet on the table, twirling the rose from the pillow between my fingertips.

"Ready?" A soft voice sounded from the doorway.

"Yes," Joel said.

The warm oil heated my skin, the aromas and massage releasing the last ounce of tension from my body. I closed my eyes and enjoyed.

It had been forever since my husband had done anything so incredibly sweet and romantic, and I planned to enjoy every second.

⤚⤙

"Ally." Warm breath wafted against my ear as the gentle caress of lips against my skin woke me.

My eyelids fluttered open, and the room came into focus. "Hmmm?" They drifted shut again. My whole body felt so heavy and the blanket over me so cozy, I never wanted to move.

"Time to wake up sleepyhead." Joel stroked my back. "You fell asleep during your massage."

I lifted my head and propped myself on one arm. "Wow." Now that consciousness had returned, I felt incredible.

"Time for a shower." He assisted me upright and pressed an icy glass of liquid into my hand. "Drink."

I sipped the refreshing berry-infused water, savoring the light touch of fruity sweetness while I held the top sheet against my body.

Joel turned on the water in the glass shower stall. "I'll be quick and then you can have it all to yourself." He dropped his robe and stepped in.

My gaze was drawn to him as he tipped back his head and ran his hand through his hair. The water flowed over his body, dripping from his dark full lashes, trickling over that muscular chest and down his tight six-pack as it tapered to his slim hips. My mouth watered as I admired every inch of my man. When was the last time I'd paid attention? He'd been working out again.

I let the sheet fall into a pool at my feet as I took slow, sure steps toward the shower, mesmerized by the sight of him.

He swept a hand over his face, clearing the water from his eyes as he sensed my presence. Those beautiful hazel orbs regarded me, and he cupped my cheek, his touch tender. "Ally?"

My breath caught as I ran a flattened palm up his chest, licking my lips, inviting him to kiss me.

One hand twined into my hair as our lips met, and he pressed me against the tiles. "Baby," he murmured as he planted butterfly kisses on the sensitive skin of my neck.

Fire and passion flared within me, and I clung to him, wanting nothing more than to feel his love.

CHAPTER 38

Joel

I PROFFERED MY CARD TO THE server with a nonchalance I didn't feel. The spa, followed by this light lunch, had been a whim. I'd yearned to lift her veil of sadness and do something special for my wife. It had worked. Her pain had eased, even if only for a short while.

There had been a brief moment when I thought I'd screwed it up. She'd hesitated to undress, and I realized that my gesture might be misconstrued, that my wife might assume I had an ulterior motive. However, the unintended consequences were wonderful.

A glance toward my wife revealed a different woman than had arrived in the village this morning. Her radiant smile lifted my heart, even as my credit card protested at the extravagance of our romantic interlude. But to see Alex's joy made it worth every penny. It meant working extra hard during January to bring in new clients, but this mini-break had worked miracles.

I tucked my wallet into my pocket and took hold of her hand, lifting it to kiss the soft skin of her inner wrist.

She blinked at me with those devastating, brilliant blue eyes and twirled her rose beneath her nose. A smile twitched at the corners of her mouth.

The image of her in the shower streaked through my mind. I licked my lips, almost tasting the sweetness of chocolate and strawberries lingering on her tongue. The memory of her passion and the heat that had risen between us brought a glimmer to my eyes.

A coquettish smile crossed her beautiful face.

"Did you want to explore the shops?" I asked.

"Sounds like fun."

I tucked my arm around her waist and led her outside into the bright afternoon sun.

By the time we returned to the chalet, dusk had descended, and fluffy snowflakes drifted down. As we pulled into the driveway, Alex gasped. The entire place glowed with bright Christmas lights.

We paused to admire the colorful display. The massive tree stood center stage in the window, decorated and fully lit, and the flicker from the fireplace reflecting on the wall.

Alex leaned against me and rested her head against my shoulder as she stared at the chalet. "Gorgeous." She pressed her fingers to her lips.

I rubbed her arm and dropped a kiss on her hair. "Magnificent."

As we stepped into the house, I inhaled, drawing in the wonderful scents. The smell of pine, and the tang of wood smoke, mixed with the savory aroma of dinner made my mouth water.

I held out my hand and my heart skipped a beat when she accepted without hesitation, entwining our fingers as we mounted the stairs.

The main room buzzed with conversation, and a sense of calm descended over me. Alex's soft warm hand remained in mine until our over excited toddler launched himself at us and threw his arms around our legs.

"Up."

I tossed Daniel into the air, eliciting a volley of happy giggles before I released him. "Someone's been busy."

Tom grinned from across the granite counter. "Savannah and Aiden spent their afternoon preparing a feast. Figures you'd arrive in time for après-ski snacks. Join us."

Everyone had gathered in front of the crackling fire to sip drinks and nibble hors d'oeuvres. Ryan presented us with fancy cups of hot chocolate topped with a mound of whipped cream and chocolate drizzle, and Emily slid closer to Aiden on the couch, making space for us to sit.

Alex curled up beside me, and Daniel crawled into my lap, content to suck his thumb and snuggle against my chest. It felt like I had my family back. Utter contentment flowed through me as I sipped my drink and shared from the plate Alex loaded up from the trays on the coffee table, listening to the laughter and camaraderie filling the space around us.

I absorbed it all. Ryan demonstrating a spectacular wipe out with his hands as Kaari squeezed his knee. Tom with Adrianna draped over his shoulder, calming her with loving and gentle pats on her back as Jenna leaned against his other arm. Emily feeding Kellan as her husband slipped the occasional tidbit from his plate into her mouth. Savannah perched on the arm of the sofa beside Aiden, fiddling with her dad's camera, the shutter clicking as she snapped photos.

Aiden glanced at the clock and extracted himself from Emily. "I'd better check on dinner."

Savannah trailed after him as he headed for the kitchen. "I'll help, Dad."

"That's my cue to stoke the fire." Ryan poked at the coals before adding two more logs to the fireplace. He wandered toward the kitchen, trailed by Kaari.

Emily and Jenna disappeared toward the bedrooms with the babies, and Daniel squirmed from my lap, eager to join the fun.

Alex frowned as she watched Aiden and his daughter in the kitchen.

"What?" I murmured.

"That girl looks exactly like her mother." Alex bit her lip. "Sometimes she even acts like Tiffany, which is strange, considering they've spent zero time together."

"Right? But other times she's so like Aiden, you could never mistake that she's his child." I watched as Aiden sampled from the pan Savannah stirred.

Aiden glanced downward and lifted a grinning Daniel to rest on his hip before he tilted his head to listen to his daughter.

"He's amazing with kids." I struggled to keep the disappointment from creeping into my voice. "I swear Daniel likes him more than me." The pain intensified as Aiden perched Daniel on the counter, one arm around our son as he offered him a small taste.

"You know that's not true." The breath seemed to catch in Alex's throat. "Daniel loves you."

The tone in her voice relayed her own disappointment, and my heart sank. "I didn't mean—"

"I thought you were over it. Yes, Daniel loves his uncle. Aiden was there for him when you weren't, Joel."

"Ally."

"No, let me finish." A sad look appeared on her face. One I'd seen too many times to mistake. "You needed reassuring. The DNA test helped, I'm sure. However it happened, you're making time for your son."

Without giving me a chance to respond, she rose and hurried away, disappearing down the hallway.

A hand landed on my shoulder. "Everything okay?" Tom asked.

"Yeah, sure." I didn't have the heart to get into the discussion.

He contemplated me. "Don't worry, Joel. You two have come a long way in a short time. Be patient with her, and it'll all work out."

"How can you be so certain?"

"There are no guarantees, you know that." He shrugged. "But damn, she's worth the wait."

"That she is." I sighed and clenched my hands together. It had been going so well until I opened my stupid mouth.

"Let's eat." Tom motioned to the dining room.

I propelled myself to my feet. Nothing to be gained by hiding in a corner while the rest of the group joked and chatted while gathering around the large, elegantly decked out table.

Alex reappeared moments later, taking the last empty seat, which happened to be beside me. She remained silent and kept her head bowed.

"Are you okay?" I said under my breath.

Her lids fluttered. "Not now." The corners of her mouth turned down.

There would be no rescuing the closeness and intimacy from earlier, at least for now.

I refused to let our issues cast a shadow over the evening for everyone else, so I rose and tapped on my glass. Everyone turned toward me. "This is an amazing feast, thanks to Aiden and Savannah who tore themselves away from the ski hill to prepare it." I lifted my glass. "Tom, Aiden"—I cleared my throat—"thank you for arranging this incredible holiday. Cheers." My throat closed up, cutting off any further words.

The chime of crystal against crystal rang through the room as Aiden met my gaze with the smallest of nods, reminding me of the best part of belonging to this family. Sometimes you didn't need words or a grand speech. They simply understood.

⤎

After an amazing feast of prime rib, the group moved en masse to the deck for coffee and dessert in the well-appointed outdoor living area.

The flames flickered on the outdoor hearth. Even though the snow continued to fall, our oasis grew warm and cozy from the heat cast from the fire and the surrounding patio heaters.

"I can barely move." Ryan set his empty dessert plate onto the side table and patted his belly. "My compliments to the cooks." He tipped his cup toward Aiden and Savannah in turn. "You missed your calling, Aiden, you should've been a chef."

"Nah." Aiden waved a hand. "The stress of working in a kitchen would take the fun out of cooking."

"Because working in an ER is far less stressful than grilling a perfect steak." Emily laughed as she snuggled closer to Aiden, tucking a blanket around them.

"Making a meal for your family is different from working in a restaurant." Tom wrapped an arm around Jenna before leaning in for a kiss.

The banter continued, the topics flowing from one to the next. I reached for Alex's hand, hoping to bridge the gap growing between us.

She pulled from my grasp, angling away from me without even a glance in my direction.

And the dance continued. Some fancy footwork to move me closer, followed by my wife twirling and weaving two steps further away.

I blamed myself. I should've known any mention of our son and DNA in the same sentence would encourage Alex's inner passive-aggressive-angry-chick to emerge.

Conversation floated around me, but I couldn't engage in it, feeling less connected to the group as Alex shut me out and drifted further away emotionally. When the fire died down and everyone began to smother yawns, relief swept through me.

Savannah bestowed hugs on her dad and Emily before saying goodnight and wandering to her room.

Then the tradition of placing presents under the tree began, along with the filling of Christmas stockings.

"Oh, not that one." Emily snatched a flat package from Aiden's hands and hugged it to her chest.

"Have I been naughty?" Aiden curled an arm around her waist as he attempted to reclaim the package. "It has my name on it."

"Noooooo." Emily laughed before leaning in to whisper in his ear. "Goodnight, everyone." She sashayed down the hall, hips swaying as she cast a provocative glance over her shoulder at Aiden, who said goodnight and bounded after her.

Laughter and a squeal from Emily rang down the hallway before their door closed.

Jenna giggled. "Night, all." She disappeared in the direction of her own room.

After a final round of goodnights, I found myself alone with Alex as we distributed the last of our packages.

Her curtain of dark hair fell across her face, obscuring her expression, and she remained silent as she placed the last gift under the tree.

"Alex, what's wrong?" I moved close behind her as she straightened. "We had such a fantastic afternoon, and now ..." I rested a hand on her arm.

She turned, pressing her hands flat against my chest and pushing me away. The gentle but firm move sent the message.

I sank onto the arm of the sofa. "What did I do?"

"You don't know?" She looked at me. "How can you be so clueless?"

"What?" I scrubbed a hand through my hair. "We had a damn near perfect day, but now you can't tolerate my presence. You change faster than the weather, and I can't keep up."

"Shh. Keep it down or everyone will be out here." She held a finger to her lips. "I don't want to say this in front of an audience."

"Say what? All I'm getting is the silent treatment."

"Well, it would have been rude and inappropriate to start something right before dinner after Aiden and Savannah went to so much trouble. I didn't want to ruin Christmas Eve for everyone else."

"No, just for me." I crossed my arms and narrowed my eyes. "So? What is this infraction I've committed?"

"Trust." Alex's blue eyes glistened as she straightened and wrapped her arms around herself. "I almost forgot, but tonight you reminded me. Daniel."

"Daniel?"

She nodded. "I wish you'd accepted the truth and trusted me. It all changed after the testing. That's when you started trying, that's when you came back to me and became a father to him. I needed you to believe in me, Joel. But you didn't, or couldn't. Whatever. It amounts to the same thing."

"And what's that? I never asked for testing. You forced it on me." Sadness filled the depths of my soul. "But it's one more thing you get to hold against me. I give up." I threw my hands in the air. "You're impossible. I've done everything you've asked of me and more, but it's never enough. Nothing will ever satisfy you. I'm out." I stalked to my room and closed the door without looking back.

⤚⤜

After a long, sleepless night I padded into the kitchen, in desperate need of caffeine.

Aiden sat at the counter top, working on his laptop. "Merry Christmas, Joel." He slid from his perch to hug me.

"You're up early."

"I'm waiting for Vanna. I promised we'd make cinnamon rolls for breakfast. It's our tradition now." He sipped his coffee as I poured my own cup. "She used to do it with her mom."

I froze. "With ... Tiffany?"

"Since when has Tiffany done anything even remotely maternal for or with Savannah?" He scowled. "I'm talking about her mom. Jayde Phillips."

I leaned against the counter as he hit a few buttons and closed his laptop.

Her mom. It floored me how Aiden accepted the couple who'd adopted Savannah. "That sounds so strange to me. Even now they're gone, you consider them her parents. How do you deal with it?"

"It's simple." He paused as if gathering his thoughts. "They took my baby girl home from the hospital and kept her safe and happy for the first fifteen years of her life. That is the definition of a mom and dad in my books. Ross and Jayde were her world, all she knew, and I'd never take that away from her."

"Hmm, makes sense." I considered him for a moment. "It's true, blood doesn't define us. You're family to me, even if we don't share DNA."

"We scrap like brothers." He laughed.

"That we do. How are things with Tiffany?"

"We don't talk." He shrugged. "How are things with Alex?"

I bowed my head and concentrated on my cup. "We don't talk either."

"You looked pretty cozy when you got back." He studied me. "What happened?"

"She's sensitive about every word from my mouth." I cleared my throat. "I know we're supposed to be here until the thirtieth, but any chance I can talk you into driving me to the airport later today? If I can get a flight, that is."

"You're leaving?" His eyebrows rose.

"It's too hard being in this house with her. She'll be happier if I go."

"Joel." He rested his hands on my shoulders. "You should stay, at least until tomorrow. Have Christmas with your son."

"And then you'll drive me?"

"If you still want to leave. Maybe things will resolve themselves in the meantime."

I shook my head. "Somehow I doubt it, but you're right, I should stay until tomorrow, for Daniel."

He patted my back and then stepped away as Savannah appeared, her hair tied in a ponytail. "Ready, Dad?"

Chapter 39

Alexis

T HE HOUSE HAD ALREADY COME to life, and the homey scent of bread and cinnamon drifted into my room, making my mouth water. I rubbed my gritty, tired eyes and rolled out of bed, stretching before wandering down the hallway toward the kitchen.

Daniel's high pitched tone carried through the air, and he banged his spoon on his plate. Joel redirected our son's hand, helping Daniel scoop scrambled egg to his mouth. Our boy screwed up his face as his breakfast tipped off the side of his utensil and landed on his plate.

"Here. Let me help." Joel maneuvered a bite into his son's mouth, accompanied by the obligatory airplane noises.

Aiden spotted me and pressed a cup of coffee into my hand. "Merry Christmas, sleepyhead." He steered me toward the table.

A tray of fragrant cinnamon buns caught my eye. "Bless you, Savannah."

"Dad helped." She perched on the edge of her chair, waiting as everyone found their seats.

"Merry Christmas." Tom lifted his glass to salute the table.

The sweet taste of the Mimosa lingered on my tongue, and I sighed in pleasure. These guys never did anything halfway. My happiness faded as I glanced across the table at Joel. He'd refused to look in my direction since I'd arrived for breakfast.

Savannah started stacking plates as soon as everyone had finished eating. "Can we open presents now?"

Aiden wrapped an arm around her shoulders and kissed her temple. "Why? Do you think there's something good under there for you?" He cast a glance at the bonanza of gifts that flowed from under the tree and halfway across the living room.

I caught the cheeky eye-roll Vanna leveled at her dad. A pang rose. That look was pure Tiffany, a vivid reminder of how it used to be and all that we'd lost over the years.

Our large group gathered in the living room and began passing out gifts, starting with Daniel's pile. I kneeled beside him and helped peel the paper off of each, making sure he hugged each of his aunts and uncles before I set him loose to play.

"Savannah." I handed her the gift Joel and I had chosen for her.

"These are amazing." She ran her fingers over the expensive set of artist's pencils we'd paired with several sketch pads. "Thank you." Savannah hugged me without hesitation, followed by a slight pause before she embraced Joel. "These are the best. How did you know?"

I smiled but didn't answer, though, from the expression on Aiden's face, he'd put together why I'd picked that particular brand. Years ago Savannah's mother and I would visit the art store. As a teenager, Tiffany had often fawned over all the things she couldn't afford.

Each gift brought a smile to Savannah's face, but none as much as the last one. She ripped the paper off of one of the remaining boxes, her eyes lighting up. "Dad." Savannah lifted one of the boxes and hugged it to her chest. "It's the one I wanted." She bounced to her feet and hugged Aiden, before turning to embrace Emily. "It's amazing, thank you."

"Open the rest," Emily said.

Savannah's eyes shimmered as she revealed several high-end camera lenses, along with a professional-style case. After she'd given her dad and stepmom a second round of heartfelt hugs and kisses, Tom slipped an envelope into her hands.

"This goes with your fancy new camera equipment."

"You signed me up for a photography course?" Her eyes widened. "Thank you, so much."

Savannah sat cross-legged on the floor and sorted the lenses and fiddled with the adjustments on her new camera as the adults began their gift exchange.

Given how things had turned last night, I wasn't sure Joel would have a gift for me. After he'd stormed off, I'd pulled the album full of photos from under the tree and tucked it into my bag. I couldn't give it to him, considering the circumstances.

Joel placed a box into Daniel's hands. "Take that to Mommy." He observed me from across the room.

"Thank you." I kissed Daniel on the cheek as he held up the gift with a proud smile. I selected Joel's box from under the tree and sent Daniel back to his dad with the gift from both Daniel and me.

My present turned out to be a shiny gold locket, nestled in a blue velvet jeweler's box. Inside, I found a beautiful photo of me, Joel, and Daniel. "When …?"

Joel shrugged. "I enlisted our resident camera junkie." He glanced at Savannah. "She's been taking photos for the last few days, and that one was the best."

"It's gorgeous. Thank you." I fastened it around my neck.

Joel opened his new watch and thanked me from afar, hugging Daniel, and settling him on his knee.

Not one of our friends commented on the awkward dynamics happening between me and Joel, though they'd all noticed. I forced a smile, determined to keep it plastered on my face until the end of the day.

The next morning I awoke to a much quieter household. I glanced at the clock and realized I had slept longer than intended. It was already past nine.

After a hot shower, I wandered through the house, finding Emily curled up in the living room in front of the fireplace with her nose buried in a book.

"Where is everyone?"

She peered up at me. "Skiing, but I didn't sleep well last night. Kellan turned into a grouch. His schedule is off with all the excitement. Iona took the kids out so I could have a break. Once Aiden gets back, I'll coerce him into taking me to the village. I booked a couple's massage for us this afternoon so he'll take it easy on his shoulder for another day."

"Where'd he go?" I sank into the oversized chair across from her.

She frowned. "He drove Joel to the airport."

"Wait. What?" I raised my brows. "Joel … left?"

"You didn't know?"

"Nope." I shook my head. "He didn't say anything. Not that we said much to each other yesterday. He kept himself busy and far away from me. I'll take it up with Aiden when he gets back."

"You will not." Emily leveled her gaze at me. "Everyone's told him to butt out, and he has, but now you plan to give him hell for not telling you? I think not."

"He aided and abetted that little rat in scurrying away."

"That's between you and Joel. It has nothing to do with Aiden."

"Whatever." I rolled my eyes. "I guess it doesn't matter, anyway. Joel's done with me and our marriage if he sneaks off like this."

"And why would he do that, I wonder?"

"We … had a disagreement on Christmas Eve. He made a stupid comment about Daniel. Joel doesn't trust me. The only reason he's attentive to Daniel is now he has the DNA results."

"Seriously?" Emily massaged her temples with her fingertips. "Is that the reason for the silent treatment?"

I bit my lip. "He's angry about the DNA testing. He says I forced him into it."

"Did you?"

"You know I did. He'd been irrational, so I thought we needed to set it to rest. But I wanted him to trust me without it."

"And you put him into an impossible situation. He did the testing for you, but it didn't make you happy or resolve a damn thing. All it did was build more distrust because now you believe the only reason Joel is attempting reconciliation is that you've proven your point about Daniel. Is that about right?"

I narrowed my eyes. "Whose side are you on?"

"This isn't about sides. That man's turning himself inside out to make you happy, and you want him to trust you, but you haven't given him the same consideration. Sometimes you need to have a little faith in your man."

"Yeah, like you had sooooo much faith in Aiden." I glared at her. "Maybe you should take a hint from your husband and mind your own business."

"Oh, sass." Emily slapped her book onto the table as a fiery look crept into her eyes. "Considering how many times you've butted your fat nose into my relationship, you'll listen and like it."

"You should be thanking me. Without my assistance, you'd be shuttling your son back and forth between Boston and Chicago. You couldn't admit you were in love with Aiden, who came this close"—I held my thumb and index finger up to demonstrate—"to dumping your sorry ass. Maybe I should've let him."

"Don't sound so damn smug, Alexis." Emily narrowed her eyes, even as they shimmered. "You're about to meet that fate yourself. You think your man will wait forever while you throw hissy fits and play games? You know better."

I sniffled and swallowed hard as my throat closed up.

"No come back to that one?" She folded her arms across her chest. "I have good reason to dislike Joel after he tried to drown my husband, but now I've seen another side of him. Sure, he's been acting like a complete idiot but even I can see he's crazy about you and his son."

I hung my head and picked at a loose thread on the pillow in my lap. "I'm sorry, Emily. I shouldn't have said that about you and Aiden."

"I'm sorry, too. We're all on edge and exhausted." Emily's tone softened as she rested a hand on my arm. "You can't forgive Joel one day, and then take back your forgiveness the next. I've been there, Alex. It's the hardest thing in the world to forgive and put it behind you, but if you love Joel and want to stay married, you'll have to find a way."

"I'm so angry at him for not trusting me."

"It's destroying you." Emily sighed. "Let it go, Alex. Forgive him or don't. Reconcile, or file for separation and divorce. Your choice. Just quit torturing him and yourself. That only leads in one direction. Do I have to explain it?"

I lifted my chin and wrapped my fingers around the locket Joel had given me for Christmas. My own words were flying back at me. How many times had I demanded Emily sort out her issues with Aiden and forgive him already? I'd begged her to figure out what she wanted and allow the man to love her or let him go. There had never been a single day in recent memory when I doubted how Aiden felt about Emily or her about him, and watching them wrap themselves into those bubbles of fear and denial had been excruciating.

There wasn't a single doubt in my mind that I loved Joel, but had I pushed him away for the last time? Could we get past our fears and insecurities? Would he forgive me for my own mistakes even as I searched for the courage to forgive his? Only time would tell.

CHAPTER 40

Joel

AIDEN PULLED INTO THE DROP off zone at the airport and turned off the engine. "This is none of my business, but I still have to ask. Are you sure you want to leave?"

I twirled the gold ring on my left hand, contemplating my defeat.

"Don't," Aiden said.

"I can't stay. Yesterday …" I shrugged

"No … Don't take off your ring. It's not over."

"What if it is?" I reached for the door handle but paused. "How do I regain the trust? Everything I say blows up in my face, and I'm chasing an illusion of happiness with her."

"What you have with Alex is real. Don't say anything to your parents, Joel."

"I'm supposed to pretend it's normal my wife is celebrating the holidays in Colorado while I'm in Boston? Anyway, my dad figured it out at Thanksgiving."

"Then talk to your dad, but don't give up on her."

I scoffed and shook my head. "You're right, it isn't your business. You can't fix your mistakes through me and Alex. I'm not you, and she isn't Tiffany, so stop with the unsolicited words of wisdom."

"I'm not, I just—"

"Yeah, you are. Your marriage to Tiffany imploded, and then you fucked up with Emily and almost lost her too. So excuse me if I ignore your crappy advice. Get over your shitty divorce and failed life already. I'm out." I flung the door open. "I need my stuff."

Aiden hit the hatch release, and I slammed the door with as much force as I could muster. After grabbing my bag, I stalked into the terminal without another word or backward glance.

I carried the paper bag containing my dinner through the quiet halls into the partner suite. The door clicked shut behind me, cutting me off even further from the outside world. After switching on the television, I reclined against the pillows, letting the noise wash over me as I munched on the fries.

My thoughts wandered as the emotional exhaustion crept over me. I gave up on eating and tossed the bag aside, twirling my wedding ring while I debated my next move. Maybe there wouldn't be one, and I'd be signing divorce papers.

My phone remained silent, but after the stony silence from Alex on Christmas Day and the tirade I'd unleashed on Aiden, what could I expect? *I'd launched an attack and run, devoid of hope that my wife would ever let me come home.*

Every time I allowed myself to hope, some unforeseen event plummeted me back to earth. Now I wished to curl up and let the world pass me by.

The soft tap at the door startled me. At this late hour, and with the holidays, the office should be deserted. I didn't even want company, but after the intruder knocked a second time, I figured I should answer.

I yanked open the door. "Leave me the hell—" I froze, unable to look away as my breath caught in my chest. My heart skipped as those beautiful shimmering blue eyes met mine.

"Sorry. I …" She dropped her chin to her chest and clamped her teeth onto her bottom lip.

"No, it's …" I ogled her.

Her wool coat hung open, revealing a drop-dead-sexy-barely-there black lace bra. My gaze lingered on the luscious creamy breasts threatening to spill over the top. I itched to skim my fingertips across her bare midriff, over the skimpy silk and lace panties, and stroke those smooth shapely legs. The sight of the black stilettos caused a rush through my body as the sound of my heart thudded in my ears.

Her ruby lips parted, and she licked them as she focused on the floor. After a moment, she grasped the edges of her coat and hauled it closed with trembling fingers. "Stupid idea," she muttered. "I'll go."

"Don't leave." I loosened her clenched fingers and opened her coat, grazing her hip as I slid my hand around her lower back. Her scent intoxicated me as I pulled her toward me.

She lifted her chin, and I caught the glitter of tears before she closed her eyes.

I cupped her cheeks, placing a tender kiss on her forehead, holding her, not wanting to wake from this fantastic dream.

Her eyes fluttered open. "I'm sorry." She dragged in a deep breath.

"You're gorgeous." Our lips met. I danced us backward, shoving the door closed as her heavy coat slid from her shoulders and landed in a heap. Words I longed to express caught in my throat so I simply wrapped her in my arms and captured her satiny lips with mine.

With a soft sigh, she wound one arm around my neck and pressed her hot body against mine. The other hand plucked at my t-shirt before it traveled to unbutton my jeans. She tilted her head, allowing me to brush kisses along the sensitive skin on her neck, while we backed toward the bed.

Desire flooded every inch of my body as I lowered her to the mattress, her passionate and demanding kisses egging me on. Our hands were everywhere, and I kneeled on the bed to peel off my shirt as a coquettish smile appeared and she tugged at my jeans. I stood to finish the job, Alex biting her lip as she watched through her half-lowered lids, stretching her lithe form in clear invitation. Her silky smooth legs beckoned me. Starting with her ankle, I trailed my lips against her golden skin, working my way upward, caressing and dropping kisses on every inch of bare flesh.

She twined one hand into my hair as I skimmed my hands and mouth over her hips. Her gentle tug and her soft touch against my bare shoulder made me quiver. Everything faded out of focus until there was only her, the enticing scent of her, the miles of golden skin, those vivid blue eyes and gentle touches as her hands glided down my back.

I savored her heated skin, and took possession of her full lips, passion burning as she opened her mouth, drawing me in. Her nails dug into my back as I buried my hands into her silky hair, and our bodies entwined. This moment felt like a fantasy come to life.

⌒⤚⤙⤚

Alex lay across my chest, her hair tickling my chin as she snuggled closer. A sigh issued from her lips, but still, we hadn't spoken, aside from the whispered words of passion during our lovemaking.

What could I say? I couldn't bear to break the magical spell. We'd been down this road before, and our physical attraction didn't mean we'd solved any of the deep-rooted issues that plagued us.

Instead, I stroked the silky skin of her arm before smoothing her hair away from her face and tipping her chin upward. We gazed at each other for several moments, but she said nothing and only stared at me through sleepy eyes.

"How"—I cleared my throat—"why did you come?"

"You left without saying goodbye," she whispered.

"You flew to Boston and came here dressed like that to tell me … goodbye?"

"Yes … No …" She wiggled away and sat, drawing the sheet up to her chest. "Why did you run away without even telling me you were leaving?"

"I just …" I leaned against the headboard. "Half of the time I'm scared to say anything because I worry it'll upset you. And we have these incredible moments when it seems it'll be okay, but then it's not. Something goes wrong, and we end up back where we started. We're ripping each other apart, and it has to stop."

A tear trickled down her cheek. "This is it? Our final goodbye?" She ran a finger over my wedding band.

I turned to face her and captured both of her hands in mine. "Ally, I want to be with you, so badly, and I love you so much it hurts. Why does love have to cause unbearable pain? Why is this so damn hard?"

"I don't know." She bowed her head, allowing her hair to obscure her face. "I'm sorry. I should have stayed in Colorado." She slipped her hands from my grasp and slid to the edge of the bed.

I caught her arm, holding her in place. "I wish I'd stayed, Ally, but I didn't know how to fix it. Is there any chance we can make this work?"

She peered at me over her shoulder. "Do you want it to work?"

"Damn it. I've tied myself in knots trying to make it up to you, but I don't know what the hell you want from me." After scrubbing the back of my neck, I dropped my head into my hands. "What do you need me to do to prove I love you and to earn your forgiveness? To give me a fighting chance at making it right? Or do I even get another chance?"

Alex sniffled, then angled toward me, clutching the sheet around her. "I wouldn't be here if I didn't want us to try. I didn't know how you'd react to me showing up here," she whispered. "I almost didn't come home."

"My wife showing up in drop-dead sexy lingerie at my door is beyond incredible," I said. "Why would you think that I didn't want us to work?"

"I'm sorry for overreacting about the Daniel comment, but it doesn't change the fact that you sneaked off." She bounced off of the bed with her eyes blazing and the sheet still clutched to her chest.

"It's exhausting trying to figure you out. You've worn me down, and I have no idea how to make you happy." I drew in a ragged breath, then exhaled long and slow, hoping to calm the anger building inside. "No more games, Ally, I can't take another moment of this … whatever we're doing."

Her eyes filled with tears, but I couldn't stand what this relationship had become. Maybe she hated me, as all I'd done in recent memory was hurt her and make her unhappy. Maybe my lack of judgment in leaving spelled the bitter end.

Alex brushed her cheek, and then slid on the dress shirt I'd hung over the back of a chair. Without even looking at me, she gathered her lingerie and her shoes from the floor.

I stood frozen and helpless as she draped her coat over her arm and reclaimed her small bag. Without a word, she crossed the floor, every step taking her closer to the door. Closer to leaving me forever. My eyes burned.

Alex reached for the handle, her head bowed as she swiped at her eyes. She paused, then stepped into the hall, the faint click as the door closed.

What in the hell was I thinking?

"Ally!" I dashed across the room and yanked the door open, catching a glimpse of her coattails as she turned the corner. *How could I let her go?* I bounded down the hallway and stumbled to a halt in front of her as she stabbed at the call button. "Please don't go. I can't be without you. Please forgive me. Please, Ally?"

The elevator swished open, but she remained rooted in place, her chin tucked into her chest. My heart thumped as I dropped to my knees before her, burying my face against her navel and wrapping my arms around her. "Don't leave me. How can I make you stay?"

CHAPTER 41

Alexis

MY HEART TORE IN TWO as Joel clung to me and begged me to stay. These past days had been harder than I could ever have imagined, a dizzying tilt-a-whirl of emotions. I'd bounced from never wanting him back to believing we'd recovered before rebounding to that heart-dropping fear we were past all hope. When he'd allowed me to go, I thought it had been for the last time.

Could I keep on as we had? The questions churned through my mind even as I gripped his shoulders. Push him away, or pull him closer? This would be our defining moment. Forgive him, or end it forever?

A choked sob escaped as I froze in place. We remained in limbo, neither together nor apart. In my heart, I knew we couldn't go on like this, day after day. Time to commit, or pull back and let it fade away. I tilted my head back and blinked away the tears, staring at the ceiling as if the answer would be floating above me.

I gasped for breath and cradled his head before sinking to my own knees and curling my arms around him. With my head buried against his shoulder I melted into his embrace, still unable to utter a single word.

"Please say yes, Ally, " he whispered. "Don't give up on us." His hands rose to cup my face and tip my chin so he could peer into my eyes.

"Let's talk," I mumbled.

He gave a brief nod and helped me to my feet, entwining our fingers as we retraced our steps. Once there, Joel took my coat and draped it over the chair, the lead me to the bed.

I crawled on, crossing my legs and tugging his shirt to cover my bare thighs. My state of undress made me feel vulnerable, but maybe that's what I needed—to bare the part of my soul that wept for us, to show him every fear and doubt and hope he still loved me.

Joel sat in front of me so our knees touched as he reached for my hands. He rubbed the backs with his thumbs. "Ally?"

I sucked in a breath. "I love you, and I don't want it to be over." I bent forward to place a fingertip against his lips. "When you asked me to marry you, I never imagined we'd be here. I thought we'd be together for eternity. But we both know nothing lasts forever, and sometimes love isn't enough."

The corners of his mouth turned down as a furrow appeared in his brow. "Is this one of those famous *we have to talk* scenarios where you dump my ass and tell me you're filing for divorce? That you're taking my son from me?"

"Never. It would be unfair to keep Daniel from you." I closed my eyes, taking several long breaths to quell my anger. "But you're right, we can't continue with this back and forth and running away." I wiggled closer to press a palm to his cheek and gaze deep into those beautiful hazel eyes. "I forgive you," I whispered.

His frown deepened even as his free hand covered mine. "That's it?"

"If we hope to save our marriage, we need to put it behind us. So I forgive you, and I will do my best to allow us a fresh start."

"Five minutes ago, you walked out that door like we were over. Now you forgive me for everything?" He stared at me like I'd lost my mind.

"You didn't let me leave, and that has to mean something. It's time to put our mistakes behind us." I lifted a shoulder. "How else will we continue with us?"

"So now what?"

"How about a trial reconciliation?"

"Meaning … I can come home?" The corners of his mouth twitched.

I bobbed my head, and his smile widened.

"Daniel's in Colorado, so we have four days to ourselves. Do you want to pack a bag and stay at the apartment?"

"Hell, yeah." He bounced to his feet and yanked an overnight case from the small closet. "Wait." His brows rose. "Why is our son in another state?"

"Relax. I didn't dump him at a bus station." I smothered a laugh at the look on his face before reality wiped the grin from mine. "I didn't know how this would play out. Anyway, he'll be spoiled rotten by the aunts and uncles."

His mouth settled in a firm line. "Fair point." He tossed a pair of sweatpants and a sweatshirt into my lap before he returned to his task of stuffing clothing into his bag.

I wiggled into the thick, soft cotton as he disappeared into the bathroom, grateful for the extra coverage against the chilly Boston night. When I'd prepared to surprise him with the lingerie, I hadn't been thinking practicality. I dug into my bag and retrieved the sneakers I'd tucked into my bag to negotiate the icy streets.

Joel reappeared and gave me a look. "That's better. I don't know how you didn't freeze to death walking over here … undressed like that." He stepped closer, adjusting my scarf and helping me into my coat, before putting on his own.

"Seemed like a good idea at the time." I followed him down the hallway.

"No complaints from me." He patted his pockets. "Damn, where are my keys?"

"Here." I held up the set I'd used to get into the offices.

"Ahh, now it all makes sense. Aiden."

"No." I lifted my chin. "Emily. Funny thing, when Aiden got back from dropping you off, he wasn't in the greatest of moods and didn't want to talk about any of it."

Joel avoided my gaze and fiddled with the lock on the office door.

"What did you say to him?" I placed my hand on his, stilling his movements.

"Nothing much," he muttered.

"Uh-huh. Whatever you said, he refused to divulge even the tiniest of clues as to why you left or to give me any advice on what to do about it. Emily helped me with the plane ticket, drove me to the airport, and gave me the office keys."

"Should I just turn around and lock myself back in the suite?" A stormy look rolled across his features. "'Cause here we go again. Another damn useless argument about nothing."

"Don't act like you're two." I dug my nails into my palms. "I'm trying to have a damn conversation with you, and you flip out and get defensive. If we can't have a civil discussion, then yeah, crawl back into your deep dark hole." Keeping my eyes straight ahead, I jabbed the elevator call button.

He slid his arms around me from behind. "I'm sorry. The frustration got the better of me, and I admit I said things to him I regret. I don't mean to take it out on you."

I leaned back against his chest and peered over my shoulder, reaching up to press a palm to his cheek. "What things?"

"I told him to mind his own business." Joel pulled me closer.

"What else?" The guilt written across his face told me he had more to confess.

He gave me a look. "I may have said his advice wasn't worth much, considering his less than stellar history with women."

I cupped his face and forced him to look at me. "Why would you say crap like that to him?"

"He pissed me off, so I retaliated. I'm not proud of it." Raising his hand with palm facing me, he waved it back and forth. "Don't start. I'll apologize."

"Was that so hard?"

"What? Admitting I'd been a stupid ass and taken it out on someone who didn't deserve it?"

The corners of my mouth turned up despite my attempt to remain serious. "Well, yeah. That, and answering a damn question without acting like a Prima Donna."

"Ha-ha." He rolled his eyes. "But maybe you're right. I over-reacted with you and with Aiden."

I studied his face for a moment. There were times this man drove me insane, but I loved him. That fact was inescapable. "Good. Let's go home." With our fingers entwined, we stepped into the elevator.

⤛

The next morning my arm met an empty, but still warm, spot in the bed beside me. I relaxed, enjoying the relative silence. No tiny feet pattering down the hallway, no melee of voices or laughter, no demands. No sounds. Only an enticing, fragrant aroma wafting through the air.

Fresh, hot coffee. My stomach rumbled at the thought of food. The past two days had been such a rollercoaster, I'd barely eaten.

I sat and gazed around the room. It appeared that Joel had tidied up before he'd left me to sleep. His t-shirt hung over the chair, and I pulled it over my head, burying my nose into the fabric to inhale that intoxicating masculine scent before wandering into the bathroom to splash cold water onto my face.

Then I shuffled down the hallway, stopping to watch as a bare-chested Joel flipped pancakes on the griddle and then opened the oven, peeking at a tray of sausages. He hummed under his breath, sipped from his cup, a smile lighting his face when he noted my presence. "You're up." He grinned. "I planned breakfast in bed."

"I rarely sleep late." I moved closer, looping an arm around his waist. "Our boy pries me from bed at six, maybe seven if I'm lucky."

"I noticed." He pressed a kiss to my hair before transferring the golden, blueberry-dotted pancakes onto plates. "I miss him, but having this time for us is amazing."

"I understand. I love him with all my heart, but there are times when his liveliness exhausts me."

Joel wrapped me in a tight embrace. "I'm so sorry I've been absent. I promise it won't happen again. You've carried most of the load, and I see that. When … IF we have another baby, you won't manage it alone."

"Do you want another one?" I peered at him. "It's not something we talked about, and it wouldn't be responsible to do that right now. I don't want to …" The words stuck in my throat, but I saw from his expression he understood. Bringing another baby into this mess of a marriage before we had a chance to resolve our issues seemed wrong.

"No rush," he said, squeezing me before letting go, "but I would love another baby. We talked about a big family, long ago."

"It might not be possible." The journey to have Daniel had been long and heartbreaking, and right now I didn't have the fortitude to slog through another round of the inevitable ups and downs that would come with trying to get pregnant. "It took forever to have Daniel, and then it seemed like you didn't even want a family."

"I've always wanted babies with you, but it's been a tough road. And then once we had Daniel, it felt like he was all that mattered." He sighed. "It's unfair that some people pop out unplanned ones without a second thought."

Another piece dropped into place. The resentment he carried had many layers, but maybe this process had forced him to come to terms with it. I could only hope we'd made progress.

"It sounds petty to say it out loud, but one drunken night at fifteen, and boom, a baby. Another drunken night at a wedding and boom, another kid." He bowed his head. "It's stupid, and I feel like the worst friend ever because I'm happy for him, but …" He scrubbed at his stubble, clearing his throat. "Anyway, we need to focus on you and me. If another baby doesn't happen, then we'll accept it and enjoy what we do have."

"Unplanned doesn't mean unwanted, Joel." I forced my voice into a level and calm tone. "But yes, let's hold off on the baby discussion."

He nodded, and then steered me toward the table. "Sit and eat. What did you want to do today?"

Before taking my place at the table, I retrieved a legal pad and pen from our small built-in desk.

"What's that for?" Joel poured syrup over his pancakes and cut a wedge with the edge of his fork.

Instead of answering, I wrote the words in bold strokes across the top of the page.

"Rules for a happy marriage?" His eyebrows rose.

"Yup. I'll start." I poised my hand over the paper and spoke as I wrote. "We shall never take each other for granted. Your turn."

"We shall have regular date nights." He grinned. "I loved the lingerie."

"Date nights. Yes, that's a good one. We need to make time for each other." With a cheeky smile, I scribbled it down. "And maybe if you're a good boy, there'll be more of that lingerie. Hmm. No running away from arguments. We have to resolve our issues with honest discussions."

We worked back and forth until we'd built a complete list.

Joel scanned it, and then rose to tack it to the front of the fridge. "This was an excellent idea, Ally. Now we have to make sure we live by them."

"Daniel will be back tomorrow." I folded another piece of laundry and tucked it into the drawer. "I've missed him so much."

"So have I, but you have to admit, this time has been incredible." Joel wrapped his arms around me and nuzzled against my neck.

"Yes." I slid a hand across his firm chest and patted with my palm. "Maybe we should move the rest of your things home?"

"Can we?" He cupped my cheeks between his warm hands, the hopeful look on his face lightening my heart.

"Mmhm. But the rules are still in place, and we keep up with counseling, at least for now."

"Deal." Joel nodded.

I stretched to kiss his lips before poking at the bag, still half-full of his clothing. "Let's unpack this."

"Done." He grinned and with a flourish, flipped the bag upside down and shook the contents onto the bed before disappearing into the closet.

"I don't know whether to call you a slob or a drama king." I laughed as I sorted through the pile, freezing at the envelope hidden in his socks. The name and address caught my eyes, as did the unbroken seal. "Joel?"

"Yes, my love?" He peered out of the large walk-in.

"What's this?" I held up the sealed document, waving it slightly.

A frown marred his features as he sat beside me on the edge of the bed. "Oh. I forgot about that."

"You never opened it." I tapped the edge against my palm.

"Am I in trouble again?" His shoulders slumped.

"You've had the proof the whole time." My eyes burned. Now I felt ridiculous for being so crazy on Christmas Eve.

"Ally." His warm hand engulfed mine. "I never wanted or needed it," he said in a gentle voice. "Don't take this the wrong way, but I looked at Daniel and realized it didn't even matter. From the moment I first held him in my arms, he's been my little boy. I adore him."

Tears brimmed my eyes. "I don't know how to even ..." My throat closed up.

"That came out wrong. I've always known deep down that Daniel is my son." He squeezed my hand. "Those comments weren't about me thinking either of you would cheat. The drinking, our disconnection, along with my own stupid resentments and insecurities made me crazy. And I'm sorry. So much of this could have been avoided if I hadn't listened to …" He looked away.

"Crystal."

He nodded.

"She fed you all sorts of crap, didn't she?"

"It's not her fault. Sure, she encouraged it, fueled the fire, as did Gwen, but I should have known better than to get involved with either of them. They're the distant past, you're my future." He emitted a heavy sigh. "Call it an early mid-life crisis, but somewhere along the way, it stopped being fun and there were moments where I wished we could go back and be teenagers again. We had amazing times, and it all ended."

"How about now?"

"Now? I feel like we're on track and can find some balance. The stress of earning my degree, then our wedding, and then we piled the struggle to get pregnant on top of it all." He shrugged. "I'm sorry I didn't handle it better."

I nibbled at my lower lip, contemplating his words. We'd gone from parties on the beach to heavy responsibility in a matter of a few short years. People always told me how hard the first years of marriage could be, but I never understood how difficult until I lived it.

"I did my part in tearing us apart," I whispered. "But it means everything that you trusted in me. Even if it didn't feel like it at the time."

His embrace comforted me as he brought me in closer to his chest and rubbed my back.

"Do I still get to move home?" he asked after some time.

"Yeah, you do." I burrowed in closer, feeling like we had managed another hurdle.

CHAPTER 42

Joel

THE NEXT SEVERAL WEEKS PRESENTED challenges, but every time we ran into an issue, one of us invoked the marriage rules that remained tacked to the front of our fridge. I had to admit, Alex's idea had been brilliant.

Gone were the days where I lingered at the office to avoid heading home. I allowed myself two nights a week to work late, but most nights I rushed out of the door to spend time with Alex and Daniel.

Why had I not worked this hard before on my marriage? Perhaps our struggle had value—persisting through the rough spots allowed our marriage to flourish. I'd learned new things about this wonderful person I'd vowed to cherish forever.

Now a new challenge arose. Our son would soon turn two, and our wedding anniversary approached. How to make this the most memorable celebration ever? We'd been married for eight years, but I'd loved this woman for over sixteen years, and that needed to be acknowledged. Even during our time apart, I had never stopped loving her. A whole story remained to be told. The story of us.

"You're deep in thought." Tom appeared in my doorway. "Need help with the case?" He motioned to the folder on the desk.

"No." I pushed back and stretched. "But I have a favor to ask."

"Another one?" Tom grinned as he sank into the chair.

"Yeah, I'm quite needy these days, but this is for Alex and our anniversary. I'm planning a two-week getaway."

"Hmm. Sounds like a great idea."

"Can I take a couple of weeks in March?"

"Let me know when, line up your workload, and it'll be fine."

"Thank you. I don't deserve it, and you've accommodated me, even with everything that's happened in the past year."

"We're family, Joel." He waved a hand. "This is your marriage, your wife, and your son. Nothing is more important than that. I guarantee if Jenn and I were struggling with our relationship, you all would move mountains for us. Anything you need, it's done."

"Great. Now I have to figure out the finances."

"Speaking of which." Tom slid an envelope across the desk. "Bonus time. We were paid for our big case, and this is your cut. I conferred with our other partner, and we agreed to pay out your share now so you can set your financial house in order."

My brows rose as I slit it open, and scanned the paper. My mouth dried at the number of zeroes on the figure. "No way."

"There will be more like that, so do something awesome for your wife."

"I should repay some of what I owe you and Aiden." I stared at the check in my hands.

"There's plenty of time for that."

"Are you sure Aiden will feel the same?"

"Hell, yeah, he will. I'll clear it with him." A serious expression settled on his face as he leveled his gaze at me. "Neither of us wants you to regret the move to Boston, and it shouldn't cost you everything you hold dear to be here. Do what you need to do. We have your back."

I closed my eyes for a moment and nodded. "Thank you for this. For all of it. I won't let you down, and I will never forget."

The next few weeks were a whirlwind of activity, but toward the end, I crossed the last item off of my list with satisfaction. Everything had come together in spectacular fashion. Now I hoped to carry out my plans without Alex clueing in.

"I don't know if Chicago is the most amazing place for a mini-break." Alex poked my ribs as the taxi wove its way through traffic, speeding away from my parents' house. "We lived here for most of our lives."

"True, but did you see how excited my mom was to have Daniel? She misses us living nearby, and besides, we're together. That's what matters."

"I can't argue with that." She shook her head and grinned. "Wait. We're staying here?" Her eyes widened as she peeked out of the taxi window.

The tall, elegant building towered above us as a bellman opened the taxi door.

"You shouldn't have." She widened her eyes at me. "This place is too expensive," she whispered as our bags were whisked inside.

"Don't worry. I've got it covered." And thanks to Tom, I did. Not only had my two best friends come through with the bonus at a critical moment, Tom had also finagled a sweet deal on the hotel room.

Check-in took moments, and soon we were in a spectacular room with a stunning view. Alex flopped onto the bed and kicked her feet, laughing as she extended her arms. "Like floating on a cloud. This is incredible."

I bounced onto the bed and stretched out beside her. "You like?"

"I more than like. I could get used to this." She rolled onto her side and grasped my chin.

"You know I want to give you everything." I wiggled my brows. "How about we change? We don't want to be late."

"Late for what?"

"You'll see."

~⤨

Two hours later we had both donned aprons and were positioned at our station, chopping and preparing our dish.

Alex grinned at me, her eyes glimmering. "I can't believe you agreed to a cooking lesson." She performed a little happy dance, circling before she scooped out more sticky rice.

"You always wanted to do this, and I never had time." I cringed under her intense stare. "Okay, okay, I never made the time. But here we are."

"Thank you. This is so much fun."

I tapped my cheek, and she stretched on tiptoes to plant a resounding kiss there, before snaking an arm around my waist.

After brushing my lips against her temple, I resumed my own job of creating thin slices of tuna and vegetables. "This isn't so hard. Look at that beautiful sushi roll."

"Magnificent, hon." She patted my arm. "You're a natural."

"And don't you forget it." I wiggled my brows and bumped my hip against hers.

Making the sushi wasn't a difficult task, but this class wasn't about mastering a new skill. Tonight I'd wanted to spend time with my wife and make her happy. To savor the small moments that added up to a complete life together.

A finger poked into my ribs. "Earth to Joel." She lifted her chin and studied me. "All good?"

"Yeah. I'm better than good. Time to eat?"

"The chef is coming around to inspect our finished plates, then yes, we'll enjoy our efforts." Alex stroked my cheek with her fingertips. "I love that you did this," she murmured. "Even though you think it's silly."

Had I been so transparent all of these years? I'd dismissed simple dates as if they were a waste of my valuable time, always pushing for the challenge, the adrenaline rush. That had become a detriment to us as a couple, and I knew it.

My stomach clenched as I thought about my plans for the next day. Did I push Alex too hard? Expect her to embrace the things that thrilled me, but often frightened her? She'd gone along with so many of the things I'd suggested, without insisting on a fair return.

"I don't think that." I laid my palm against her cheek and brushed my thumb over her soft skin. "It's been fun, being here with you, and I'm sorry if I ever made you feel the things you wanted to do were silly or not worthwhile."

"So does that mean we get to do dance lessons next?" Her eyes twinkled as a smile graced her lips.

"Yeah, baby, whatever you want. I'm in."

CHAPTER 43

Alexis

J OEL LEANED IN AND PRESSED his lips to my temple. "I'm going to work out. I'll be back soon."

"Mmhm." I rolled over and buried my head in the pillow enjoying the soft mattress. After a few minutes, I gave up on sleep and crawled out of bed, stumbling into the bathroom for a shower.

Only moments after I'd finished combing my hair, and wrapped up in one of the fluffy white robes, the rap sounded against the door. "Did you forget your key?" I cracked open the door.

"Room service." The sharp-dressed man motioned to the cart. "Mr. Nichols ordered for you."

"Oh. How thoughtful." I stepped back and let him enter.

The attendant flipped a red tablecloth over the small table and set a silver-domed tray in place, flanked by an elegantly folded napkin and cutlery, followed by a carafe and a glass of fresh-squeezed orange juice. A vase with a single deep-red rose provided the final touch.

"Call if there's anything else you need." He smiled.

"Thank you." I reached for my handbag.

"No need. It's been taken care of." He produced a flat cream-colored box with a red bow on top from underneath the cart and handed it to me before performing a short bow and exiting the room.

Curious, I dropped onto the bed and lifted the lid. Inside, an album nestled amongst red tissue paper, with a card on top:

Good morning, my love,
I took the liberty of ordering breakfast. Enjoy, as you will have a busy
day. Your mission, should you choose to accept it (and I hope you
will), is to follow the clues. Please keep each card with you as you will
need them all to find the ultimate destination.
Eat before it gets cold, and be at the front entrance of the hotel at eight
a.m. Dress for comfort, and wear your scarf. It's chilly this morning.
Love, Joel.

Clues? I stroked the soft dark leather with my fingertips before opening the cover of the album. Nothing. Each elegant cream page was empty.

My stomach rumbled, reminding me my breakfast awaited, so I set the card on the table and lifted the silver cover, smiling as I revealed a plate of delicate crepes, topped with strawberries and a light touch of whipped cream. I nibbled at my breakfast. Where should I go first? The note didn't hold actual directions.

On about the tenth reading of his words, the last lines came into clear focus. *Wear your scarf.* I bounced to my feet and hurried across the room to where my dark-blue cashmere scarf sat folded on the desk. And there it was. A card that appeared to be the same size as a four by six photo.

The words danced before my eyes:

My darling Alex,
Remember when we were sixteen and had our first Chicago date? I
will never forget how we shared that amazing afternoon. Visit this
place for your next clue, but don't forget the album.
Much love, Joel

A smile twitched at the corners of my mouth. No way had I forgotten. A glance at my watch told me I had half an hour to meet the car in front of the hotel, so there was no time to waste.

⌒≼

At eight a.m. I arrived at the front doors and peered outside.

"Alex Nichols?" A man in a black suit and chauffeur's cap approached with a smile. "I'm Travis, and I'll be your driver for the day."

"Hi, Travis." My expression must have reflected surprise. For the whole day? I allowed Travis to open the back door of the sleek black town car, and I slid inside, settling into the soft leather seat.

"Where to, madame?" His eyes met mine in the rearview mirror.

"Navy Pier." I brushed my hand over the album tucked into my lap, fiddling with the card I'd laid on top. A beautiful and expensive card I realized, now that I took a moment to inspect it. The heavy card stock looked similar to a fancy wedding invitation, with ornate swirling font gracing the front. It reminded me of the font we'd used when we'd married. Or was it exactly the same one?

I turned the card and stared at the back, trying to make sense of it. The random design covered the back, with hues of jet black and varying shades of gray, with only a small pop of color.

The page corners I'd noticed on the otherwise empty pages came to mind. A faint smile twitched my lips as I opened the album to the first page and inserted the card. A perfect fit.

Trust Joel to notice every detail.

"I'll wait for you here." Travis pulled up in front of Navy Pier.

The grounds were deserted. Not surprising at this time of the day, or the year. Now what? I couldn't stroll into the empty park, could I? I mounted the steps and gazed around.

A slight woman appeared, dressed in one of the park uniforms. "You can go on in." She motioned me forward.

"I can?" My brows rose.

"It's all arranged, Mrs. Nichols."

I'm sure the silliest grin spread across my face as I wandered through, drawn toward the massive Ferris wheel. I craned my neck as it towered above me. This had to be it, a clue had to be here somewhere.

"Would you like to go for a ride?" An attendant appeared behind me.

Apprehension made my palms sweat, but I pushed down the nerves. "Yes, please."

He opened one of the gondolas and I stepped in, getting comfortable as a small shudder ran through the car and I rose upward.

It had been a hot day in September on our first visit as a couple. We'd begun dating at the Vineyard that summer, growing into our new roles as girlfriend and boyfriend after so many years of close friendship.

I closed my eyes, and my stomach did a funny little flip as the car glided downward, and the memories washed over me.

We'd laughed and joked until the car jerked to a stop at the top. The open car swung in the breeze and Joel tucked an arm around me as I dug my fingertips into his thigh. My breathing became choppy. To his credit, he hadn't laughed or teased as I clung to him. Instead, he held me close and reassured me, knowing one of my worst nightmares was being stuck on a ride. Time ticked on, and on, and on, but the car refused to budge from its perch one-hundred and fifty feet above the ground.

"It's okay, baby. We're safe." He cuddled me against him and pressed his lips to my temple. "They'll get us down soon."

My whole body trembled, and he drew me closer. Then he tipped my chin and bestowed the longest and sweetest kiss on me. I'd forgotten to be scared.

By the time they restarted the wheel and we reached the safety of the ground, my knees were knocking together, but whether from terror or the hormones rushing through my system, I didn't know.

I opened my eyes and admired the skyline. With the sun glinting off the water, the view was magnificent, and I wished for Joel to appear and share it with me. I wrapped my arms around myself as the gondola skimmed through the sky, a total departure from that day in the old-style open cars. *Breathe, you're safe.*

That day had changed our relationship. I'd been holding out on him until then, the confusion of teenage emotions along with the enormity of stepping across the friendship line and testing the boundaries of my new-found love overwhelming me.

That night we'd made love for the first time, and our journey as a real couple had begun.

The car glided to a halt at the bottom, and I brushed at my dewy eyes as the attendant opened the door. But it wasn't the attendant who stood before me.

"Ryan?" My eyes widened.

"The one and only." He smiled and offered me a hand.

"Why are you here?"

"We all know about your fear of heights." Ryan winked. "Joel couldn't be here, but he wanted to make sure you were okay if you decided to ride the wheel and to make sure you got this." He produced a vellum envelope with a flourish along with a deep red rose.

Taking care of me, Joel? Even from afar?

"Thank you." I brought the velvety flower up for a long sniff and pressed the card to my chest. "What now?"

"That's for you to decide." He squeezed me in a brotherly hug before he waved and strolled toward the exit.

After he disappeared from my sight, I sat on the nearby bench to open the card:

My sweetness,
I'm sorry I wasn't there but I hope you enjoyed your ride on the Ferris wheel. To reward your bravery, you deserve a treat, along with an extra-hot cappuccino. Your chariot awaits.
Hug & kisses, Joel.

The city streets crawled by as Travis guided the town car through the heavy morning traffic. Nothing new there. Chicago hadn't changed, and I should make wise use of my time. I tipped my head down and inspected the back of the most recent card. Another interesting pattern, much different from the last, but nothing stood out or made sense. With a shrug, I tucked it into the photo corners on the second page of the album.

Fifteen minutes later Travis drew up to the curb and hopped out, rounding the car to open my door before I had a chance to gather my things.

The sight of the cozy coffee shop brought a whole new set of memories rushing to the surface. Joel and I had visited this little shop on many mornings after I'd returned to Chicago from university and during the early years of our marriage.

I pushed through the doors and started toward our favorite booth before I spotted the reserved sign displayed on the table.

"Alex." Lucy, one of the servers who'd worked here for years waved at me. "Your table is ready." She pointed at the reserved booth.

"That's for me?"

"Yup. Sit, sit." Lucy grinned as I removed my coat and scarf and hung them on the wrought iron rack.

No sooner had I slid into the seat, and she presented me with a steaming cappuccino and two golden cornucopia puffed pastries. My mouth watered, and I plucked one from the plate. Though no more than a morsel, each contained a bonanza of rich and creamy lemon mousse.

"Oh, wow." I sighed through a mouthful of delightful tangy mousse. "How I've missed these."

"We haven't seen you in a while. I heard you moved to Boston." Lucy removed the empty plate. "How's that sweet little Daniel?" She tucked the bill folder onto the table.

"Wonderful. He's with his grandmother today, but I will bring him by next time I'm in town."

She nodded and left me as she attended to a young couple who'd entered the cafe.

A giggle escaped my lips as I peered into my cup. It had become a game over the years, and today was no exception. I hated to disturb the intricate teddy bear Lucy had formed in the foam. A picture formed in my mind as I remembered that day from so long ago.

"Not hungry?" Joel pointed at the plate in front of me. "You must be ill." His brows rose when I ordered a peppermint tea instead of my usual cappuccino.

I shook my head as the joy blossomed in my heart. "I'm queasy this morning, and I'm off coffee for a while."

"Oh?" He reached across and pinched off a piece of the cinnamon twist that sat in front of me, untouched. Then his gaze lifted to meet mine, those lovely hazel eyes sparkling as his hand froze partway to his mouth. "Oh. Are you serious? You think you're …?" A grin spread across his face.

"I'm pretty sure. I stopped at the drugstore for a test kit, so when we get home …"

Complete delight had been written on his features, and he couldn't get us home fast enough. The excitement grew as we cuddled on the edge of the tub and watched the little blue plus sign form on the test stick.

This cafe had seen so many joyful moments. We'd sat here with friends, dreamed of our future, drank endless cups of coffee while planning our wedding, and spent hours tossing around ideas for the nursery and debating the best baby names.

This booth had witnessed our relationship through the ups and down, the good times and the bad. That included the heartbreaking day we'd said goodbye as we broke apart for the long university years, and the momentous and life-altering reconciliation when we realized we couldn't live without each other.

Once I'd drained the last drop from my cup, I flipped open the small black folder, expecting a bill, but instead I found another vellum envelope.

A smile crept across my face as I anticipated the playful adventure ahead of me:

> *My beautiful wife,*
> *Now that you have regained your energy, time to put yourself to the test. You have never been fond of heights, but one memorable day, you overcame your fear with grace. Enjoy the journey to the top.*
> *Your loving husband.*

With a small shake of my head, I gathered my things and headed for the door.

"Wait." Lucy grabbed a cup and bag from the counter and extended it toward me. "For Travis."

"Thank you, but how did you know?"

She giggled and lifted one shoulder.

Of course. Joel had thought of this too.

⤛

I adjusted the harness and took a long deep breath before grasping the first handhold. The line tightened, and I steeled my nerves. After a light dusting of chalk on my hands, I had no reason to delay.

Sure, I'd almost conquered my fear of heights, but it had taken every ounce of courage to tackle the intimidating climbing wall. And though we'd come here many times to practice, and my skills and confidence had grown each time, it felt like an eternity since I'd clawed my way to the top of a sheer wall.

"On belay."

"Belay on." Dante's deep voice echoed in my ears. "You can do this, Alex."

"Climbing."

"Climb." Dante said.

After a long slow exhale, I placed my flexible climbing shoe onto the small ledge and pulled myself up. One down. A giggle escaped as I peered upward. Only a hundred more to go.

I stretched my arm, curling my fingers around the next hold—*a jug*— my mind filled in the term as I recognized the familiar and easiest of holds. Balancing on my toes, I brought my leg up and tested my grip before proceeding to the next set of holds.

I squished my fingers tight and wrapped my thumb over the top of one, clinging to the next handhold. I could hear Joel's voice. *Trust yourself, Ally. You've done this a million times. You're ready.*

Deep inside, I knew this to be true. I'd grown in so many ways, and after all that I'd faced, this would be a piece of cake. Right?

Keep telling yourself that, honey. My negative inner voice opined as I extended a hand and pinched my fingers around the oblong hold. "You got this," I muttered under my breath.

My arm twitched, and I fought the urge to look down as I positioned my right foot on top of a hold.

"Never look down, Ally." His admonishment echoed in my ears.

I almost broke the rule to see if he'd arrived to cheer me on from below.

"Don't forget to rope in, Ally. Safety first, always." The words clung to me as I'd glanced over and caught his reassuring gaze.

I'd nodded, and drew on that well of determination that lurked beneath my placid surface.

Contrary to all assumptions, I reveled in a good challenge. I'd struggled to keep up with my rough and tumble friends—most of whom were boys—my entire life, and rarely gave up.

I looped my rope through the metal link and swung my arm up, my body and leg moving together in a fluid motion.

Stretch, cling, test, leverage to the next hold. I fell into an easy rhythm. This mid-level wall would cause a professional climber to scoff, but for a virtual amateur who was sadly out of practice it presented a challenge. Each hold became smaller, each step a calculated and concentrated effort as I inched my way upward.

The many times Joel and I had done this together played in my head, his words of encouragement, his belief that I would persevere and reach the top inspired me to keep moving.

My arms shook, and I stopped, shaking out each one in turn before adjusting my grip and searching for the finish line.

A white flash in my field of vision made me pause. I lifted my chin and squinted, recognizing the now familiar cream vellum. Another envelope, all the way up there?

A snort erupted, and I fought the urge to laugh.

"I dare you." His voice flitted in the air around me as the envelope fluttered above, taunting me.

He'd always challenged me and encouraged me to step outside of my comfort zone, and today was no exception. After another long breath, I pressed my hand against the next hold, clinging to the edge with my fingertips as I used my legs to offset my weight. "Damn you, Joel, you won't beat me," I muttered as I ran my fingers along the ledge to locate the best grip.

At long last, I looped my rope into the final carabiner, and snatched the envelope from its place, giving a victorious cheer and pumping a fist in the air.

"Lower!"

Dante called back and then lowered me to the mats below. "Fabulous climbing, Alex." He grinned and slapped my outstretched hand.

"Thanks, Dante. He didn't make it easy on me." I fanned my face and plucked at my tight top. "Time for a shower."

"You deserve it. If it's any consolation, who do you think put the envelope up there?" He raised his brows and patted my shoulder before offering me a water bottle and a small black overnight case.

I tipped back my head and looked up. Of course, he did. With that thought in mind, I headed to the locker room for that much-needed shower.

—≺—

Forty-five minutes later, I sank into the leather seat, freshly showered, and dressed in the light dress pants and the soft sweater that Joel had provided. Time for my next checkpoint.

The message had been simple:

My bad-ass rock climbing babe,
Great job. I'm proud of you, and I believe in you, always. Now for a
well-deserved break before the next leg of your journey. No salads
today, honey, and the beer's on me.
Your adrenaline junkie.

I rolled my eyes at this corny missive, but the message was clear. He'd teased me during our early dating years on my dinner choices—often a salad—whenever we ate out.

"You'd think you were a damn rabbit. Or that I'd never seen you eat a proper meal." He snickered as he pulled into the parking lot of the pub. *"What is it with girls and their damn refusal to eat in front of a guy? You need protein to build up those muscles if you ever hope to beat me to the top of the wall."*

"What are we doing here?"

"Having a real meal. No salads today, honey."

Over time, this had become "our pub" and I'd never been allowed to order salad. We'd opted for their hearty beef dip with homestyle french fries. Joel had joked about me being his bad-ass babe who was up for anything.

Walking in the door felt like coming home, and I realized I missed Chicago. Maybe over time I'd learn to love Boston, but so much of my life had been here in this big crazy city.

The hostess seated me in one of the booths we'd frequented, and moments later, a familiar server arrived to fill my water glass and place a dark ale in front of me.

"Thank you, Stella." I curled my fingers around the frosty glass. "I suppose Joel ordered for me?"

"Yes." She smothered a laugh. "Is that a problem?"

"Nope. Thanks." I gazed around the room. This popular pub would be packed when the lunch rush hit.

Less than ten minutes later, Stella returned with my lunch, and I tucked into the savory roast beef, dipping it into the dark broth. The exertion of the wall climb had worked up my appetite, and the rich chocolatey ale he'd chosen complimented the meal to perfection.

"Everything satisfactory?" Stella appeared to refill my water glass.

"Delicious, as always."

"Excellent." She slipped a hand into the front pocket of her apron, produced an envelope, and propped it against my glass. "It's all taken care of. There's no rush, and let me know if you need anything." Beaming, she sashayed toward the bar on the other side of the room.

Wiping my fingers on the napkin, I fished out the next clue.

Enchanting Goddess of mine,
Now you've had time to recover, it's time to slow things down. Sit back, relax, and enjoy the scenic route. While you're there, have a glass for me.
Many kisses. J

Travis parked the car in front of the quaint red painted building an hour later. As had become the habit, I exited the car, leaving a cheerful Travis to his own devices. The spring sunshine and earthy smells surrounded me, bringing a smile to my lips.

A small bell dinged as I stepped inside, and a young man appeared as I perused the bottles on the shelves.

"Can I help you find anything?" The young man scanned me with his lovely gray eyes. "Or are you here for a tour and wine tasting?"

"I'm …" I wasn't sure why I was here. But maybe that's what he meant me to do. Take a tour like we had on our visit together. I'd come all the way out here, and today seemed to be about reminiscing over the better times we'd had as a couple. "A tour would be amazing."

He motioned me toward the small group waiting for their tour and took down my name. "Alex. The tour will begin shortly."

One young couple caught my eye. The way they linked their fingers and gazed at each other with such love made me think of how Joel and I used to share that type of bond. Did we look like that the day we visited? With stars in our eyes and the impossible dreams for our future crowding out all sense of reason and reality?

Soon the guide ushered the group outside, and I trailed along listening to the narrative about the wine-making process and admiring the view of the fields. The vines were bare, it being too early in the season for much greenery, but still, a sense of déjà vu washed over me.

Joel offered me a sample of the wine and tapped the rim of my glass, creating a light ringing as we linked arms and sipped. A light rain began to fall, but instead of running for shelter, I tipped back my head and laughed, embracing the sweet droplets as they trickled across my cheeks.

"You're soaked." Joel wound an arm around my waist, pulling me closer.

"I love the rain."

"You're crazy." Lifting my chin, he shook his head but kissed me anyway. "But you look like a goddess."

When I had slipped into the ladies room afterward, my mouth had dropped open in horror at the utter mess I'd become. Goddess, hah. My mascara created dark raccoon rings around my eyes, and my hair hung in damp clumps, but it hadn't mattered in the least. Joel saw past it and made me feel beautiful, even when I was at my worst. It had only been this last year that I'd begun to doubt his feelings, but now …

The group moved toward the main house, and I hurried after them, catching up in time to hear the guide answer questions about the wine tasting.

The small group mingled on the wide veranda as the host served small portions of a selection of the wines along with small slices of baguette and cubes of cheese. The flow of voices swirled around me as I sipped the light and fruity wine.

"Alex." The soft voice made me turn, and I recognized the young man who'd greeted me in the store.

"Yes?"

"This is for you." He handed me a gift box.

"Wow, thank you."

"I hope you'll visit again soon." He moved off to converse with the other guests as they inspected the various bottles and offerings on display.

Finding a quiet spot at the end of the patio, I set the box beside me on the wicker couch and lifted the lid. Inside nestled two engraved glasses, along with a bottle of wine. I plucked the vellum envelope from the top:

My pampered princess,
Time to head back to the city. Your quest is not yet over, but the next
destination will remain a surprise until you arrive.
Love from your prince.

I ran a fingertip over the bottle, noting the intricate label:

Happy 8th Anniversary
Alexis and Joel Nichols

The next spot on my tour ended up being an amazing spa, and I spent the rest of the afternoon being pampered with a massage and a full beauty treatment right down to the hair and makeup.

By the time they were done with me, I felt like the pampered princess as Joel had referred to me in his note. A princess in nondescript sweater and dress pants. I stared at myself, admiring the elegant up-do and incredible makeup. The outfit awaiting me in the change room wouldn't do any of it justice.

The attendant led me to the change rooms and ushered me inside.

"Wait. This isn't mine." I frowned at the garment bag hung on the rack and gift boxes piled on the bench.

"No, it is." The woman smiled and motioned me inside.

The first box made me roll my eyes, but I opened the familiar envelope:

My lovely lady,
I hope you enjoyed your afternoon of pampering. Now back to work.
Don't delay, you have an appointment at our gallery. One of the most
talented artists in the city awaits your visit.
I love you. J.

That could only be one place, and excitement grew within me. I donned each item from the boxes in turn, and by the end, my clothing matched my regal feeling. I emerged from the dressing room in an elegant evening gown.

"You look gorgeous." The attendant held out a wrap. "Let me take those." She gathered the boxes and garment bag and carried them to the front, handing them off to Travis.

Travis settled me into the back of the car and then we were off to our next destination.

Dusk had fallen by the time we reached the studio. The lights from within glowed, but the sign on the door had been turned to Closed.

"Not to worry, he's expecting you." Travis rapped on the door, and moments later, Bailey appeared.

"My dear Alex." He kissed both cheeks and drew me inside. "It's been too long, love."

"How have you been. I'm so excited to be here."

This man had been instrumental in capturing all the special moments in our lives, from our engagement photos, right down to the baby pictures taken after Daniel had been born. He wasn't a typical photographer. Tiffany had introduced him when he'd been a starving artist. He'd earned a reputation for his art and fashion photography and only did baby pictures and weddings for his dearest friends.

"This is exquisite." My gaze fell on one of the paintings.

Bailey performed a little bow before he led me further into the depths of the studio. "Time for a few photos."

"He dressed me up for pictures?" I giggled.

Bailey beamed as he settled me on a sofa and adjusted the lights. Soon he was in full swing, the shutter clicking as he changed angles and then props, positioning me this way and that.

It reminded me of the day we'd done the shoot with Paulo, though that time I'd been wearing far less clothing. That album had been tucked in the back of the closet, hidden from all eyes. As I posed, I made a mental note to add that to the anniversary gift I'd purchased for Joel. Everything had changed since Christmas, and today confirmed that we'd made it through the worst moments.

"Magnificent."

"We're done?" I blinked away the spots and fought the urge to massage my cheeks.

"Yes. I'll print these and send the proofs to you in Boston. Now … this is for you." He reached into his camera bag and offered me a card:

To the most beautiful woman in the world,
I couldn't resist having Bailey take a few photos. But now you have a
final task … to find the ultimate destination. You have all the pieces
of the puzzle.
Yours always and forever, Joel

"The pieces of the puzzle?" My eyebrows went up, and I flipped over the card. More designs. Designs. Puzzle. I reached into my small bag and retrieved the album. Clever. "Is there somewhere I can lay these out?"

Bailey pointed to one of his massive light tables. "Right there, love."

I snapped on the light, extracted each card from its place inside the album, and turned them picture side up. Then I worked at matching the designs and edges. After several efforts, I'd arranged them in what appeared to be the correct order. "There's a gap." I tapped the empty spot. "How did I miss a clue?"

"Perhaps this will help." Bailey moved beside me and handed over another card.

Happy Anniversary, Ally. After all of these years, I only love you more.
Sixteen years and counting.
All my love, J.

I flipped the card, finding a full-color picture. I tucked it into the empty space and pressed my fingers to my lips. "I know this place. I've always wanted to go there." With all the parts in place, it all made sense, no longer a meaningless pile of cards and random designs. This was a room, and the final part was a picture of Joel and me together in another time and place.

The Maldives, in the underwater restaurant, on our honeymoon.

There'd been a photographer in the restaurant, taking pictures of the guests, and this had become one of my favorite memories, captured forever.

Bailey pulled a frame from under the table, and flipped each card, placing them within the frame, and then adding a matte and backing. When he turned it, the picture sat perfectly behind the glass. "Well, my sweet, you shouldn't keep the man waiting."

He helped me with my wrap and kissed each cheek again before handing me the frame. "You come back and visit me soon, love."

"I will, and thank you."

He let me out of the studio onto the street where Travis waited, ready to open the car door.

Chapter 44

*I*PACED BACK AND FORTH AND glanced at my watch before turning and staring down the street again. My palms were clammy, and I brushed them against my suit pants, drawing in a deep breath before patting my pocket again.

My jittery nerves refused to be calmed. What did Ally think about the task I'd placed before her? I'd put so much effort and thought into this night.

We managed eight years of marriage, but this woman had enthralled me for over sixteen years, and I hoped to hold her close for eternity.

At long last, the shiny black car turned the corner, and I straightened as it pulled to the curb.

Travis opened the door for Alex as I stepped forward and held out my hand.

My breath caught in my chest as she emerged from the car. Her upswept dark hair revealed her delicate neck. The deep blue dress set off her golden skin and drew in to emphasize her trim waist and curvaceous hips. "You're stunning." I brought her hand to my lips.

"Thank you. You look pretty handsome yourself." Her vivid blue eyes sparkled as she gazed at me.

I extended the dark red rose and leaned in for a kiss before offering my arm. "Shall we?"

She inclined her head and allowed me to lead her inside.

"Where is everyone?" Alex peered around the room, her eyes widening. "Are they even open?"

"We have the place to ourselves." I pulled out her chair and handed her wrap to the server who'd appeared.

"Wow, Joel." Her eyes grew shiny. "I'm speechless."

After I settled her at the table closest to the four-sided fireplace, our server reappeared and poured our wine.

"So you found all of the clues." I grinned.

"You knew I would. There were so many great memories."

"I hope we create many more. Happy anniversary, Ally."

We tapped glasses and drank.

"I chose the menu. I hope that's okay?"

"It's perfect." She looked around the room and inhaled audibly. "Are those …?" She rose from her seat and crossed the room to the array of pictures displayed on one wall. "It's us."

I rose and looped an arm around her, moving along as she stopped to inspect each picture.

Us on one of our dates as we played on one of the many Chicago beaches. Our smiles as we reconnected upon Alex's return from university. My favorite engagement picture, with her enchanting smile. A picture of our first kiss as a wedded couple, and then another as we shoved cake into each other's mouths. Our honeymoon, and then the first picture of us as a family, my arms around her and Daniel on the day he was born. The magnificent picture of our family at the chalet in Aspen in those happy moments after we'd returned from the spa. I guided her along to an ornate plaque on the wall.

Alex tilted her head and frowned. "What's this?"

"Our marriage rules. I thought they deserved a place of honor above our bed so we never forget. This … us … has been a wake-up call, and I never want to lose you or what we have."

She graced me with a watery smile and dabbed at her eyes. "I don't want to lose you, either." After a long shaky breath, she reached for my hand. "How did you do all of this? It's our story."

"It is." I turned and linked my fingers with hers, bringing both of her hands to rest over my heart. "We've had so many ups and downs this year, and one night I found one of our albums. It reminded me of all the good times we'd had, and I thought maybe …" My throat closed up as I tipped my forehead to rest against hers. "I hoped all those precious little moments of our life together meant as much to you as they do to me. My wish is for us to regain that magic."

"You sweet man." Her soft hands rose, and she pressed her palms against my cheeks. "I love you." Alex stretched and grazed my lips with hers.

My pulse quickened as I wrapped her into an embrace. The whole anguishing and tumultuous year melted away as I held my beautiful wife in my arms, and kissed her in a way she'd never forget.

We stepped from the restaurant hand in hand. The spell had been cast, and my wife had forgiven my many digressions on this journey of life we'd embarked upon.

"Do you have the energy for a walk?" I faced her and linked the fingers of both of our hands.

"I'd love that."

We turned as one, the fingers of one hand still entwined as we strolled. As we had many times when we were dating, we found ourselves at the Buckingham fountain.

"Boston is beautiful, but I miss Chicago sometimes." Alex tipped her chin to watch the water cascade down, the soft glow of lights making it even more enchanting.

"Do you regret moving?"

She remained quiet for several moments. "Not anymore, but there were times when I wondered if we'd stayed in Chicago if things would have gotten so bad. But Boston is the best place for us. After all, most of our family is there."

"And once we move your dad into his new facility, it will be even easier." I curled an arm around her waist.

"Thanks for offering to bring him to Boston. I felt like I'd abandoned him." She leaned into me.

"You didn't, sweetie, he's receiving excellent care. But I understand your desire to have him nearby. And it's good for Daniel to see him."

"Yes." Her head rested against my chest. "Tomorrow it's back to reality. This feels like a fantasy, and I can't bear for it to end."

"It's not the end for us. It's our new beginning." I pulled the last envelope from the inner pocket of my suit jacket. "This is for the love of my life."

"There's more?" She pressed the envelope to her chest and gazed at me in a way that made me believe in miracles. The sparkle in her eyes and the genuine and beautiful smile on her lips made my pulse race. She broke the seal and extracted the folded paper. "What's this?"

"Our second honeymoon." I met her gaze. "Daniel's care is arranged, and we get to lounge on a tropical beach for two weeks. We leave in the morning."

"You didn't have to. I love the idea, but this has been so incredible already."

"We need this, Ally." I pressed my lips to her temple. "When did we last have more than a few hours as a couple, to concentrate on us?"

"It's been forever." She threw her arms around me. "Not so long ago, I wished we could get back to where we were. That will never happen, but that's okay. Where we are now is so much better. It's like we have the best of everything. The most amazing friends and family, a beautiful child, and we have each other."

"The best part of our lives is yet to come." I trickled my fingers over her smooth skin, sending grateful thoughts to the universe that we'd survived the storm. "There are sure to be more ups and down, but together, you and I have something incredible and amazing that's worth fighting for." I grinned. "Speaking of ups and downs, how about another ride on that Ferris wheel before we head back to our hotel?"

She giggled. "That seems like tempting fate after all the heights today."

"Don't you worry, Ally." I wrapped her in my arms and held her close. "I'll never let you fall."

⤞

Enjoy a short excerpt from *Everything Left Unsaid*, Book 4 of *The Hamilton Series*.

CHAPTER 1

Savannah

*S*AVANNAH GAZED THROUGH THE WINDOW, shifting in her seat as the engines roared and their plane touched down. The aircraft slowed, the murmur of voices filling the cabin, along with the bleats of cell phones as the aircraft turned for the short taxi to the Logan International Airport terminal.

She closed her eyes and drew in a deep breath, holding onto the vivid memories of long sunny days at sea. It had required some serious sweet talk, along with major support and encouragement from her Uncle Tom, but Savannah coerced her dad into allowing her adventure. Tom's endorsement had filled her with confidence. *Savannah is a mature young woman, Aiden. She's seventeen. You spent years away from your family, starting at a much younger age, and you managed just fine.*

Not that her dad worried needlessly–he had solid reasons for concern. But, he'd understood her longing to experience life and become self-reliant, and after some discussion, they'd reached a happy compromise.

She'd never regret the three months away from home. As part of a small, but tight-knit sailboat crew, she'd shared the on-board duties in addition to studying Greek history, mythology, marine biology, and earning valuable sailing certifications. All with one of her best friends at her side.

A smile touched Savannah's lips as she studied the handsome young man who'd risen to retrieve their backpacks from the overhead bin.

"I'm sad we're home," Justin said in a deep low voice, a dimple appearing as he rewarded her with a heart-stopping grin. He'd morphed from the cute teenage boy Savannah had dated at fifteen into an attractive fully-grown man. "But it's great your dad is allowing me to stay in Boston for a few days."

"Thanks, sweetie." She accepted her bag. "You do realize it's your reward for taking care of me while we were overseas. If you hadn't come, I swear he would've said no! Like he doesn't trust me to take care of myself!"

Fresh air rushed into the cabin as a crew member opened the outer door. They joined the crowd of eager passengers traipsing through the jet-way.

"It wasn't about trust." Justin frowned. "You've had several rough years, and he didn't want you to be alone, halfway around the world. With the panic att–"

"Don't remind me." She smacked his arm. "Besides, I kept it all under control."

"You did great." Justin nodded, his expression remaining serious. "I've noticed a huge change in how you handle things."

Savannah entwined their fingers, giving his a light squeeze. No doubt his words were sincere. During their three months abroad, she'd nurtured her inner strength, focusing on each new experience, refusing to waste a moment of the unique opportunity she'd been granted. Personal growth, her therapist would call it. For Savannah, it equaled a new perspective and appreciation of everything and everyone in her life.

Justin pulled her aside as they stepped onto the main concourse. "I meant every word, Savannah. And, I respect your dad for taking care of you. When you left Portland to live with a virtual stranger on the opposite side of the country, I worried."

"You didn't need to. Aiden's amazing." She cupped his cheek in her palm, rewarding him a gentle smile and a light kiss. "But, thank you for caring."

"Always. I will never forget our summer together." He linked his fingers with hers. "I bet your dad's waiting. Let's get out of here."

Savannah's smile widened as she tugged Justin toward the baggage claim. She dodged other passengers, while searching the endless sea of faces. "Dad!" She hurried forward, pulling from Justin's grasp.

"Vanna!" Aiden opened his arms, hugging her tight before he lifted her and swung her around. "Have I missed you!" He planted a kiss on her cheek before setting her on her feet. "You look great! How was it?"

"Amazing! The places we visited were incredible, and I have a zillion new pictures." Savannah patted her bag, reassured by the solid feel of the case that protected the high-end camera her dad and stepmother, Emily, had given her last Christmas. She'd put it to good use during the trip. "I missed you so much!" She glanced around, seeking the other two faces she longed to see after her extended absence. A few stolen minutes here and there for a video chat wasn't the same as seeing her family daily. "Where are Emily and Kellan?"

"They wanted to come, but it's a constant challenge to keep up with our little man these days. Neither of us felt like playing hide and seek with a toddler in a crowded airport, so they're waiting at home."

"He's running around now?" Tears sprang to her eyes as she pictured her little brother, who'd only managed a few wobbly steps before she'd left for her trip. "I can't wait to see him!"

"He's missed his big sister." He slid an arm around her waist and guided her to where the younger man waited by the baggage carousel. "Justin. How are you?"

"Great, sir. The trip was incredible. Thank you, for everything." Justin grinned. "I've never flown in seats where you can be comfortable and sleep."

"We couldn't have you banished to economy while Vanna lounged in first class." Vanna's dad gave the boy a warm smile. "And none of that sir stuff! You're making me feel old. It's Aiden."

"Right, Aiden." Justin shook the offered hand.

"Bags are coming down." Aiden pressed another kiss to his daughter's temple. "I'm glad you enjoyed the trip."

"Thank you for sending me, Dad," she said. "I may never have the chance to do that kind of trip again. In a week, I start at Harvard. Can you believe it?"

"Nope. Having a seventeen-year-old daughter still freaks me out." He laughed as he grabbed her bag from the carousel and took her hand in his. "Let's go home."

Vanna settled onto the couch beside Justin, patting his knee as she sighed in relief. "The last of the preparations are done for the barbecue, and the caterers arrived to take over." She rested her head against his shoulder. "I can't believe the summer is over, and you have to go home tomorrow. I'll miss you."

"And I'll miss you, but..." He entwined their fingers. "We knew this couldn't last forever. I start Stanford in less than a week, and you'll be at Harvard, which is crazy!"

"Yeah, my underachieving self got in." She laughed. "I can't believe it, either."

"You're brilliant, and you know it. I'm so proud of you." He gave her one of his crooked, adorable grins.

"There's my girl." Tom appeared. "I heard you were back. How was your trip?"

Vanna bounced to her feet and threw her arms around him. Out of all her honorary aunts and uncles, she'd grown the closest to Tom over the years since she moved in with Aiden. "Wonderful and completely amazing! I'll show you my pictures when we have time. Uncle Tom, this is my friend, Justin, from Portland."

"Right! You joined Vanna for the summer." Tom shook Justin's hand. "And you're off to Stanford soon for undergrad?"

"I am. I would've liked to attend Harvard or Yale, but..." Justin shrugged.

"Stanford is a great school. Our good friend, Ryan, went there and loved it. I've been after Vanna," he gave her an affectionate squeeze, "to apply at Yale once she's finished her undergrad. You could do the same."

"It would be amazing to be near Savannah again." Justin's expression softened. "We've missed her."

A group appeared on the well-appointed rooftop patio.

"That's Piper Nelson, our newest intern." Tom waved and beckoned to a petite young woman with auburn hair. "Piper, come meet Savannah and her friend, Justin. You and Vanna will be working together once school starts, and you may be in some classes together at Harvard."

Piper grinned. "Hi, Savannah."

"I should greet the rest of the guests." Tom patted Vanna's shoulder. "Glad to have you home."

Savannah watched as he strode across the patio, joining her dad who was talking with a woman she didn't recognize.

"It's nice they invited us. I just moved from Montana to attend school," Piper said. "This is some place. I heard it belongs to one of the partners, but I haven't met him yet. Tom hired me."

Savannah nodded, and sipped her drink.

Piper glanced toward the bar where Tom, Aiden, and Joel chatted and poured drinks. "Wonder who that is with Tom and Joel." The girl's eyes skimmed over Aiden, appraising him. "Wish he worked at the office. We could have a hot lawyer trifecta!"

Justin snorted, a laugh erupting.

"What?" Piper stared at him.

"That's Aiden Hamilton." Savannah raised a brow at Piper. "He's the silent partner. He's a doctor, not a lawyer." She bit back the sigh that begged to escape. "And he's my dad."

"No way. He looks barely thirty!" Piper giggled. "You're teasing! How old are you?"

"Eighteen in January." She studied Piper. "My dad's thirty-three."

"You're not kidding?" Piper looked between her and Justin, her cheeks flaming as she peered out of the corner of her eye at Aiden.

"It makes me uncomfortable when girls my age get gushy over him. And he's married."

"Sorry. I didn't know, but I understand. Girls get that way about my stepbrother. He's twenty-three, and my friends think he's super hot. They get weird and flirtatious around him."

"Exactly!" Savannah threw her hands in the air. "I get tons of messed up comments. One time we attended a parent-teacher conference, and the Dean told Aiden she wanted a parent, not a sibling." She giggled. "You should have seen her face when he told her he was my dad. And then, when she realized he was single, she slipped him her phone number! Like I wouldn't notice?"

"Ewwwww!" Piper laughed but then gave her a serious look. "So, this might be nosy, but your mom and dad had you when they were pretty young. Like fifteen? What's your mom like?"

"She's never been part of my life. Emily," Savannah pointed to her stepmother, "has been like a mother to me. She's amazing." She fell silent for a moment, her mind wandering to her other parents. She missed Ross and Jayde, though every day got easier.

"So no wicked stepmother for you! Lucky. Mine's a troll. She looked positively thrilled when I announced I'd be moving all the way across the country to attend Harvard. I'm living in the residences, and I hope to stay in Boston next summer. I never want to live with that woman again!"

Vanna studied the girl. "What about your mom?"

"She died." Piper looked away, brushing at her tears. "Sorry, I'm getting weepy."

"Don't apologize for missing your mom." Vanna shook her head. "How did it happen?"

"Cancer. Our lives were spent in the hospital for about two years. My mom passed five years ago, and Dad married the troll two years later."

"I'm sorry. It's hard to lose someone so special." Tears pricked at Vanna's eyes, and she couldn't hold back her own sniffle.

"Oh, don't cry! I'm sorry. I shouldn't tell sad stories."

"It's okay, but it makes me think of people I've lost." Vanna blotted at her eyes.

Justin wrapped an arm around her shoulders. "How about we get some drinks?"

"Thanks." Savannah smiled at him.

Piper nodded. "Sounds good. People will wonder about us, standing here weeping."

"Do you have any other siblings? Or just your stepbrother?" Justin asked as they moved toward the bar.

"I wish it were only him. I have a stepsister, and she's a nightmare. She's fifteen, and we hated each other on sight." Piper rolled her eyes. "My stepmother is always *Mia this* and *Mia that* like the girl's a damn princess. At least Brandon is cool, and we get along." She smiled. "I hope we have some classes together, Savannah."

"Me too."

You can do this. Savannah gazed at her reflection, taking a long breath and pushing it out slowly, hoping to still the butterflies flitting around her stomach. She pushed her shoulders back and straightened, drawing on the new found confidence in herself, hoping it wouldn't desert her.

Savannah grabbed her snacks and a water bottle from the fridge and patted down her bag one more time, taking a mental inventory. Laptop. *Check.* Charger. *Check.* Ample supply of pens and her notebook. *Check, and check.*

"Morning." Aiden wandered into the kitchen, rubbing a hand through his hair.

"Hey, Dad. You just get home?" She stretched to kiss his cheek. "You look tired."

"We have a whole new batch of medical students to keep tabs on, and the ER was crazy busy last night. And then every kid in Boston came in needing emergency medical care. So much for them enjoying their last day of freedom." He kissed her in return. "You ready for your first day?"

"I'm excited! I still can't believe it." She smiled. "Wish me luck!"

"I can't believe it, either. The last year flew by, and here you are, starting undergrad. And you don't need luck, Vanna, you'll be great."

"*Papi.*" Kellan charged into the room, his tiny feet pounding across the floor as he careened toward his dad. He threw his arms around Aiden's legs before stretching his arms. "Uppeeeeee."

Aiden tossed him into the air, making the boy giggle. "Morning, little man." He planted a kiss on the boy's cheek before tucking Kellan on his hip.

"Manna!" Kellan pointed at Savannah, before stuffing his fingers into his mouth.

"That's right. Vvvanna," Aiden said.

Emily wandered in moments later, her dark hair piled in a messy bun. "Good morning! The gang's all here." She accepted a kiss from her husband before relieving him of his armful of squirming toddler. "Let's have breakfast, Kellan. I bet Daddy needs to sleep."

"Bekfas, *mami*?" He clapped his hands and pointed to the bowl of fruit on the gleaming counter. "Nana."

"Oh, banana, yum!" Savannah grinned. Her baby brother always brought a ray of sun into her day. Her grin widened as Aiden brushed a hand over his son's dark hair, absolute joy reflecting in his eyes. Savannah had wondered many times what it would have been like growing up with him. *Would Aiden have been as great a dad at fifteen as he was at thirty-three?*

"Can I drive you, Vanna?" Aiden scrubbed a hand over his rough stubble.

"Thanks, but you were on shift all night. Go to bed. The subway only takes twenty minutes." She stopped to give Kellan a kiss and waved. "Bye-bye."

"Bye, Manna." Kellan fluttered his chubby hand in her direction.

Emily and Aiden's goodbyes echoed after her. She enjoyed family time, but she didn't want to be late on the first day.

She spotted Piper chatting with a group of other students, who she assumed to be some of their classmates. After the barbecue, they'd compared schedules and found they were in many of the same classes.

"Hi, Savannah. Nervous?"

"A little, but I'm sure it'll be fine." Savannah smiled at Piper. "Did you get your room setup?"

"Yup. We have limited space, so I couldn't bring much." Piper beckoned to the nearby group. "Hey everyone, this is Savannah." Piper pointed around the circle. "This is Rochelle, Jackson, Pete, and Gray."

Savannah waved. "Call me Vanna."

"So, we're planning to form a study group. You interested?" The boy who'd been introduced as Gray swept a hand through his blondish hair, studying her with intense blue eyes framed by long dark lashes.

Savannah's heart flipped as a smile lit up his face. "Sure. Maybe." She noted the wide-eyed look Piper threw her way. "Yes?"

Piper giggled. "She's in, Gray. And trust me, you want her in our group." She nudged Savannah with her elbow.

"Oh?" Rochelle gave Vanna a long cool look. "Why's that?"

Savannah looked her straight in the eye. "I'm planning to work hard."

The girl gave her an assessing look. "We'll see."

"Don't mind her." Jackson casually slung an arm around her shoulder. "You're in."

"Thanks." Savannah tried relax as the handsome young man gave her a light squeeze, while thinking he reminded her of a younger version of Shemar Moore.

"Time for orientation." Pete tapped his watch.

Shouldering her pack, Savannah joined the group as they wound their way through the open courtyards to their orientation.

By the end of the day, she'd met most of her new classmates and had started to feel comfortable on campus.

"We're going for pizza to celebrate our first day." Piper motioned her over to join the group loitering in the common area. "You in?"

"Of course!" As she fell into step beside Piper and Rochelle, her phone buzzed and a text popped up from Justin.

How was it?

As they walked, she typed her reply.

Great! How was your first day?

Incredible. Wish you were here, or I was there.

Vanna grinned as they shot texts back and forth.

Piper eyed her. "What has you so happy?"

"Justin. He started at Stanford today."

"Ohhhhh, right!" Piper smirked. "He's a cutie, that one. How long have you been dating?"

"We're not dating." Savannah shrugged. "Not now, anyway. We used to when I lived in Portland, and we reconnected over the summer, but it's nothing serious. He's in California, and I'm here, so we agreed we'd date other people."

"Reconnected, huh?" Rochelle smothered a laugh. "You have pictures?"

Savannah pulled up a favorite photo from over the summer and held out her phone. "This is Justin."

"He's not a cutie! He's a hottie!" Rochelle snickered. "You're letting that boy go?"

"He's thousands of miles away. I love him, but I'm not in love with him."

"Smart choice." Piper nodded. "Long distance never works, and you get to keep your options open." She tilted her head toward the group of boys who were immersed in discussion and lowered her voice. "Gray's had his eye on you all day."

"He has not!" Heat rose in Savannah's cheeks. "Anyway, it's too soon to be dating someone else."

"Ah, so you did date him!" Rochelle said.

Savannah rolled her eyes but smiled at the teasing of her new friends.

Share the Love

If you enjoyed this story please consider leaving a review at the retailer where you purchased the book, on Goodreads, or even give it a mention on social media. The best compliment an author can receive is positive recognition of their work.

The Hamilton Series

Purchase links for these books may be found at KateSmithAuthor.ca

Everything we Lost

Everything for Love

Everything left Unsaid

Everything we Dream

Everything we Promised

Thank you for reading!

I always love to hear from readers. I can be contacted at http://katesmithauthor.ca

Follow me on social media:

https://www.instagram.com/katesmithauthor/

https://twitter.com/KateSmithAuthor/

https://www.facebook.com/katesmithauthor/